An Ever Fixéd Mark

Jessie Olson

I hope you enjoy reading!
Jessie Olson

Second Edition, 2012

ISBN-13: 978-1460924341

ISBN-10: 1460924347

Chapter One

Lizzie made one last glare at the mirror. Why did she decide to do this? There were so many plausible excuses one could easily conjure to not go. It was, after all, only the fifteenth. Twentieth was of more consequence. Like the tenth. Fifteen is just an in between. Low key… less pressure. Just an opportunity to say hello and have a glass of wine. Or… fifteen.

Still twenty pounds away from the determined goal. Twenty pounds of plateau and stress. At least none of it had come back. But… it wasn't going to make the huge jaw dropping entrance she had oft fantasized about, especially to push through that last mile on humid summer mornings.

They all saw her photos on Facebook anyway. Not like there would be any huge surprise. And people had noticed the loss. Not that those people really mattered. It was just a hello every five years or so. There were a couple who would be there who didn't make it to the tenth… but still… it wasn't like Will was going to be there. Or his wife.

She collapsed into the chair in front of her desk, turning away from the mirror on the back of the bathroom door. There was no use for any further fussing. She regretted her procrastination to get to the hairdresser to mask the grays peaking through her dark hair. She thought the curls she styled made the lack of color in those strands more obvious. It was a nice wave – if only it would last the ride out to the inn. She was satisfied with the touch of mascara and eyeliner. Just enough to highlight her brown eyes, but not too much to look overdone.

She was satisfied enough to look back at the laptop and switch her iTunes to a livelier song. Her head moved with renewed energy as she clicked the mouse back to the invitation to see if there were any last minute additions or deletions.

Sara was still enthusiastically going. Someone to cling to… even if the conversation dried up after the first glass of wine. There were a handful of former classmates, people with whom she was able to make friendly makeshift conversation for how many years? Years when she was actually worried what people thought. Now… after fifteen years of marching to her own distinct beat with a complete disregard for other opinions… why did it matter so much? If all else failed, she could visit her parents. In fact, it would be a perfectly acceptable reason to leave early to give them company on the holiday weekend.

She stopped for coffee before getting on the Pike to make the hour-long journey west from Boston. The barista had a few extra winks and a very broad smile, assuring her that even with the extra 20 she still managed to look nice in her red dress and hoop earrings.

Her caffeine high and confidence for flirting wore off by the time she pulled into the inn's parking lot. Red? Really. Why a color when black was much more flattering and could hide so many more evils? What would she do when Sara cast her disapproving stare over her pregnant belly? At least Sara was 7 months along and not the superlative of beauty for once.

She hesitated before closing the door of the car. Should she bring her purse or put all keys and cash in her coat pocket? She would probably leave her coat and not be able to buy anything at the bar…

"Lizzie Watson?" someone called to her, curtailing any last minute escape.

"Dan Stewart!" she put on her public charm. "How are you?"

"Pretty good," he smiled as he approached with the petite redhead on his arm. "This is my wife, Delany."

"Hi," Lizzie stretched out a hand to Dan and then Delany.

"Hi," Delany offered up a good effort towards friendly. "Did you have a good Thanksgiving?"

"Yeah," Lizzie shrugged as she resigned to the fact she had to close the car door and go inside.

"Lizzie ran a half marathon a few months back," Dan offered.

"And lost a ton of weight," Lizzie said silently to herself, knowing that was the other unspoken half of the sentence. Well, it was public record on Facebook status updates.

"Oh?" Delany looked intrigued. "Are you going to do THE marathon?"

"Not this year," Lizzie shook her head, noticing Delany's calves. "Do you run?"

"I did Boston three years back. And went to New York last year. This year I've cut back because we're trying to get pregnant," Delany smiled as they walked through the doors.

"Do you have any good tips about training?" Lizzie tried not to make her relief too evident. If all else failed, she could find Delany for a conversation.

"Absolutely," the red head nodded as they approached the reception table.

Lizzie collected her seating assignment and shoved it into her purse as she handed her coat to the attendant. She turned around to look for Delany or Dan and bumped into someone else's shoulder. A set of gray green eyes turned around and startled her from her semi-interested state. "Ben?" she spat out as impulse more than friendly greeting.

"Hi Elizabeth," his greeting seemed automated. "Dan."

"Delany, this is Ben Cottingham," Dan pushed Delany forward, allowing Lizzie to step aside from her abrupt greeting.

"Delany," Ben repeated in the same neutral tone and moved toward the coat check.

"Ladies, can I get you a drink while you discuss marathons?" Dan offered, edging towards the ballroom.

"Chardonnay," Delany answered.

"Uh… red – anything South American if they have it," Lizzie stuttered, almost startled that she was accompanying Dan Stewart and his wife into the reunion. She looked back to Ben, who glanced in her direction as he handed over his coat.

"Sara will be here," she nodded before looking back to Delany, whom in spite of nerves and high school politics, she couldn't help but liking.

*****

Lizzie stared at the burgundy liquid in her glass. She doubted one more sip would make the conversation at her table more interesting. But she imagined to finish it and leave to get another glass would invite a look from Sara. Was there really a time in their lives when they spent hours on the phone talking with one another? Lizzie took a sip, leaving two more swallows to tint the edges of the plastic with red. She offered a smile to the table, unable to contribute any suggestions about how to offset the symptoms of morning sickness. She was the only female at the table without that reference point. Maybe she could entertain the Y chromosomes with a discussion of 18th century muskets… but they all seemed the type more interested in Fenway Park and Gillette Stadium.

She waved across the dance floor to Delany, who looked equally disinterested in the conversation with Dan and his old crowd. She contemplated finishing the last two swallows to make a trip to the bar and travel back to ask Delany about sneakers when Sara brought her back to the table. "What about you, Lizzie?"

"I'm sorry. What?"

"Weren't you seeing someone? I thought I remember you mentioning someone last year."

"Oh that? That really… didn't work out."

"I'm sorry to hear that," Sara rested her hand against her proportionate baby bump. "I was hoping that you would have brought him tonight."

"He just got married," Lizzie blushed when she realized her answer was vocal. "It wasn't… it wasn't meant to be." Not that it ever was, Lizzie managed to keep to herself as she swallowed the rest of her glass.

"Sara," Ben Cottingham greeted behind Lizzie.

"Benjamin," Sara smiled with such sweetness, Lizzie knew it was an effort. Lizzie mimicked Sara's saccharine expression to disguise her cynicism. "This is my husband, Ted."

"Ted," Ben nodded. "Congratulations. Your third?"

"Fourth," Sara smiled extra hard, at which point Lizzie twisted her neck to look at Ben.

"Are you still in Connecticut?"

"We just bought a new house in Thompson," Sara slipped her hand into Ted's as the music changed to a slower tempo. Ted took the cue and led Sara out to the dance floor, signaling all the couples at the table to follow suit. Lizzie looked at the vacant chairs and back at her empty wine glass.

"Allow me," Ben offered. Lizzie looked to the dance floor. She could almost smell the cafeteria and see the blue metallic speakers. The flash of memory vanished as a plastic wine glass appeared before her.

She took a sip as Ben sat beside her. "I saw that you ran a marathon," Ben looked at the dancing couples.

"Half," Lizzie took another swallow of wine. "Since then I've been a total slacker."

Ben looked away from the dancers, questions in his green gray eyes. Lizzie didn't remember the freckles across his nose and on his cheeks.

"Okay, not total. But I'm not training… and certainly not… just doing what I need to allow food comas on Turkey Day."

Ben smiled and looked back at the dance floor. "That's good enough, isn't it?"

"Not when I wanted to wear a little black number tonight," Lizzie drank another swallow, almost emptying the small plastic glass. "Amazing how Facebook creates conversation opportunity at reunions."

Ben looked back at her. The eyes that questioned smiled with amusement. "It is a curious phenomenon."

"I have a friend who contemplated a thesis on that. But she opted for something more literary," Lizzie swirled the remaining liquid in her glass. "That said, in spite of the fact you are my friend… what have you been doing for the past 15 years?"

"School. Working. More school. More working."

"Computers?" Lizzie tried to remember the profile page.

"Computer engineering," Ben's green gray eyes looked back again.

"I write letters and plan parties," Lizzie kept looking at her glass.

"I thought you worked for a hospital."

"In fundraising," Lizzie glanced up, almost intrigued that he would have paid attention to her detail as much as she paid attention to his. But that was only because she remembered him from 10th grade study hall and wondered what he amounted to after pining over Sara for three years.

Ben's eyes wandered back to the dance floor. Maybe it wasn't just three years after all. Lizzie finished her wine and let the silence linger in the chairs between them. There was a sudden increase of quiet before the music cranked up the tempo and volume. Lizzie looked at the partners moving into circles and randomness. "Thanks for the wine," she stood and went to Delany's side for jumping and twisting.

She was sweating by the time the tempo changed again and welcomed the opportunity to leave the dance floor and go back to the table for a gulp of water. Ben was still seated amongst two couples who hadn't returned to dancing. He looked even less interested in their words than he was in hers earlier.

"You don't dance?" she felt emboldened by the slight endorphin rush and wine still coursing through her veins.

"I dance," Ben didn't look at her when he spoke, but very shortly after.

His answer silenced the table from their conversation about turkey dinners. "Where are Sara and Ted?"

"Sara was tired," one of the women answered reluctantly. "So they went home," she made a pleading glance at her husband.

"Oh," Lizzie contemplated her empty wine glass versus the keys in her purse as the next song began and continued the slow theme.

"Lizzie, Sara said you had a beau," the other woman Heidi offered an attempt for distraction.

Lizzie coughed on the laughter. "I had a rather severe infatuation last year," Lizzie said pointedly. "I wouldn't say he was my beau."

"Oh," Heidi looked uncertain. "Ben, what about you?"

"I don't have a beau," he smiled and met Lizzie's eyes.

"A girlfriend?" Heidi asked impatiently.

"Not one of those either," he lifted a half empty glass from the table and swirled the liquid.

"Are you still in love with Sara?" Heidi didn't hesitate.

Lizzie watched Ben set the glass back on the table slowly. "If you dance, you must prove it," Lizzie made the determination standing beside him.

*****

Lizzie stepped quickly into the room as Ben held the door open. She looked at the furnishings and decided to set her coat and purse on a chair in front of the desk. Instinctively, Lizzie cast her shoes under the chair. She felt Ben's eyes and turned to face him. "I hate wearing shoes. I didn't want to put them back on when we left," she said hastily to hide her nervousness. She was pretty sure his offer to come up to his room was more than an interest in small talk.

"By all means," he smiled as he took off his jacket. "Make yourself comfortable." Lizzie noticed the contours of his shoulders. He removed his jacket downstairs while they were dancing, but in the crowd and duller light of the ballroom, she really didn't pay attention to how athletic he was. He probably wasn't really that impressed with her half marathon.

"It's a nice room," he went across the suite towards the counter.

"It is," Lizzie agreed awkwardly, starting to regret those extra twenty pounds.

"Do you want something to drink? I think this room includes a bottle of wine," he found the bottle on top of the counter, beside two wine glasses.

"Sure," Lizzie shook her head, resigned to the fact that she wasn't driving any time soon. She managed to dance off most of her earlier drinks and needed something to quiet the unnecessary thoughts in her mind. "That's a nice perk."

"Yeah," he finagled with the corkscrew. "I didn't expect such a nice location. Who knew this area attracted tourists?"

"Leaf peepers and skiers, no doubt."

"Huh?" he looked at her curiously as he pulled out the cork.

"I worked for a couple museums, so I got to know the New England tourist industry pretty well."

"Why did you stop working in museums?" Ben poured one glass.

"It didn't pay enough to make a living. Although, I still work a couple weekends giving tours at an historic house in Cambridge."

"Which house?" he poured the second glass of wine.

"The Fulton House. The history is mostly circa the War of 1812 – the one no one cares about. But it's kind of interesting because the Fultons were loyal to the English and protested the war. It's not as sexy as Lexington and Concord. Or… well, it's mostly about furniture and wallpaper anyway," Lizzie stopped herself, feeling foolish for prattling on about history she figured he didn't care about. "Not many people have heard of it."

"I have," Ben startled her.

"Have you been there?"

He locked eyes with her suddenly. Lizzie felt her cheeks flush as the green in his eyes caught the glare of the lights over the bed. He was looking at her, no doubt wondering what to say to stop her prattling. She caught a deep breath and forced a smile at his serious stare. "A long time ago," he whispered.

"You should come by some Saturday," Lizzie persisted her smile. "I'll give you a tour and tell you all the things we're not supposed to say."

"That sounds intriguing," he offered his own smile as he handed her the glass of wine.

Lizzie flushed again and didn't register the thought to delay her next sentence. "So, seriously, do you still have a thing for Sara?"

"No," he answered pretty quickly as he took up the second glass and sat on the sofa.

Lizzie took a large sip and decided to sit beside him. There was silence for a few seconds, which seemed too long to her. "Did some girl at MIT steal your heart?"

"No," Ben tipped his glass towards him, staring at the red liquid for a few seconds before shifting his gray green eyes back to Lizzie. She remembered a similar glance when he would look up from his homework in the library. She never thought much of his eyes then, hidden under his shaggy reddish bangs. She never thought much of many boys, least of all the ones who liked Sara.

"Someone broke yours recently?" his stare offered an element of sympathy.

Lizzie felt her cheeks burn again, remembering her honest answer to Heidi a few hours prior. "Something like that. I think… I know that I felt much more than he did. Even so, I let myself fancy marriage for a little while. But all it was… really… was a transient flirtation. I have a weakness for musicians."

"Do you play?"

"Ha, no, hardly," Lizzie laughed uncomfortably. "I just know a lot of people who do."

"Do you still talk to Jack?"

"He's my cousin," Lizzie looked at his green eyes.

"That's right," he laughed at himself.

"And he is a good friend. He still has a band. I see them once a month or every other month depending how often I get out to Coldbrook."

"I'm surprised he didn't come tonight."

"He hated high school," Lizzie repeated the answer she heard at Thanksgiving dinner. "I was surprised that you came, actually. You weren't at the tenth."

Ben's lips curled a little as he set his glass on the table beside him. The stare of his green gray eyes unnerved her. Was it admiration? Or lust? Or alcohol? Or Sara treating him so badly? With that thought, Lizzie looked down into the wine in her hand. She took another swallow. "So you're not still pining for Sara?"

"Tonight was the first time I saw her since… well probably about ten years. I didn't see Sara much after graduation. She went off to New York. I went to Cambridge…"

"Then she found Jesus," Lizzie stopped herself with another sip. "I lost touch with Sara, too. We really don't have much in common any more… other than the fact we come from the same small town. She invited me to her wedding, which was weird. All growing up we talked about being one another's bridesmaids. Then when I went, I was a guest… and didn't know anyone… and everyone was so young. I could never have gotten married that young. I'm glad I didn't."

"Was there someone you wanted to marry then?"

Lizzie laughed. "No," she shook her head and took one more sip that warmed and tingled her senses.

"I'm glad," he moved back the hair that cascaded over her shoulder.

Lizzie shook her head, uncertain if that was a compliment. She looked up and met his eyes again, feeling a strong urge to lean toward him… but it was still very strange and odd. The reality of her teenage years wasn't melting too easily into her adult world. Ben took her empty glass and went back to the counter to fill it.

Lizzie bounced her knee nervously, trying to think of what to say. She was unable to relax and appreciate the moment. "How's your brother?"

Ben set down the wine bottle and paused for what seemed a lengthy moment, "Oliver is well." The wine was slowing Lizzie's perception.

"Did he go to his reunion?"

"I don't believe so."

"What is he doing? Is he a lawyer or something? I remember arguing with him on the debate team. He was really good at that sort of thing."

Ben sat back on the sofa and handed the glass back to Lizzie. "He's a professor of biology at a small college in California."

"Wow. You've both done your parents proud. Are they still in the area?" she swallowed more wine to wash down her awkward questions.

"No. They passed away."

"Oh, I'm so sorry," Lizzie was suddenly sobered by her foolish oblivion. "Then… if Oliver is across the country… where do you spend holidays and… family occasions?"

"It was pretty quiet fifteen years ago. I'm used to being on my own."

"Oh. I just assume everyone has a big family like me. Not that I don't know it's different… did you have turkey all by yourself on Thursday?"

"I didn't have turkey."

"Are you a vegetarian?"

"Something like that."

"Oh," Lizzie pouted and allowed herself another sip from her glass.

"I'm not complaining."

"No," Lizzie breathed in uncertainly. She felt as though her conversation was becoming lame. Maybe it was just her concentration fading from multiple glasses of wine. Or maybe it was her incessant need to talk when she was nervous.

She didn't know why she was so nervous. She had become much more comfortable in her body in recent months. Especially when there was wine in her system. It was almost as if she was back in high school… and yet this was Ben Cottingham. Ben. The boy who was a puppy dog to Sara for all those years. She took pity on him. She never feared him. Why did he make her hairs stand on end now?

She looked back and saw his smile and the freckles that went across his cheekbones. He moved her hair back from her shoulder again and took the wine glass from her hands. She didn't notice him set it down, only aware of the kiss that came so silently, suddenly, and hungrily towards her. She lost herself in the movement of his lips, slowly opening her mouth and relaxing into the sensation that spread down her spine. She wrapped her arms around his neck and pulled herself closer into his kiss, leaving it only to catch her breath and go back again. She leaned towards him, pushing him against the sofa and forgetting all the foolish thoughts of her conversation.

In the next breath, he slid his hand up the inside of her dress. He left her lips and kissed along her neck and shoulder as his hand found the top of her stockings. "Elizabeth," he breathed against her neck. She felt her heartbeat speed up with the articulation of her full name. She found his lips and kissed him again reaching behind to unzip her dress. Maybe it was the wine. Maybe it was the fact she saw herself differently that allowed her to see him differently. Maybe it was only one night. But she didn't care. Not in that moment. For that moment, one night was just enough.

*****

Lizzie stared at the ceiling lit by the sun aggressively peaking through the curtains. Her limbs itched with an exhilaration that seemed to contradict the few hours of actual sleep she had, coupled with the multiple glasses of wine she consumed. A smile curved across her chin as she breathed in the memory of the hours before sleeping. She never thought that Benjamin Cottingham, a boy from Coldbrook, would delight her so very much. Her cheeks burned beyond pink as she thought about his touches and kisses and unspoken awareness of what made her feel so… alive.

It didn't bother her that the pillow beside her was empty. There was some relief in the lack of an awkward morning and reality. She didn't know if her conversation would have flowed as readily without so many glasses of wine… or if she wanted to face the uncertainty of the next step. She was perfectly content with his wordless exit and her solitude in the morning. She closed her eyes and let a few more memories resonate throughout her senses. The evening was a success. It went much better than she hoped. She pursed her lips to curve her grin more wickedly as she rolled over and breathed in his scent off the empty pillow. It was the sort of fun that she hadn't thought the evening would lead to. Ben was pretty good company. His conversation was interesting and humored her after Sara's annoying questions. He made the whole evening worthwhile.

Lizzie wondered why she had never really seen him in high school. She knew he was there… always there, following Sara around with those gray green eyes. Did he ever look at Sara with that hunger she felt against her lips? Lizzie was oblivious to such things in high school. Probably. Sara was always the porcelain beauty with her ebony hair and blue eyes. And her perfectly proportionate hourglass. The only boy who never gave her a second glance was Dan Stewart.

Lizzie laughed to herself about that. She took Delany's phone number and the promise to find each other on Facebook to continue their conversation at a later date. Dan even bellowed something about having Lizzie over for dinner after the holidays. How ironic that her best friend from Springs Regional didn't even say goodbye. She wondered if Ben would try to contact her and continue their conversation or start a new one. Lizzie shook her head, deciding she wasn't going to open that door just yet. Her heart wasn't ready to fasten itself on any new affection. The one night was perfect enough.

She took a quick shower and got dressed in the jeans and sweater she packed in her bag. She didn't really remember bringing her bag from the car… but maybe she had. There was so much wine and a delirium of a wickedly good evening filtering out the other details. She paused in front of the mirror as she brushed out her wet hair and saw the healthy flush of her cheeks. She saw the twenty pounds that dissatisfied her before the start of her evening, lingering at her waist and on her hips. Yes, she was glad he wasn't there in the morning light to see those apparent truths.

She twisted her damp hair into a braid and noticed a blemish at the base of her neck. Had she gone the whole evening with the pink spot so glaringly obvious against her pasty skin? Lizzie furrowed her brow at her reflection, noticing a twin blemish by its side. They weren't irritating… except with their obviousness. Two giant blotches on the curve of her neck. She shook her head, forcing her self doubt out of her mind. It obviously didn't matter to Ben.

She grabbed her dress off the floor and packed her other belongings into her bag. She felt compelled to make the room look respectable when she left – even though she knew it would be cleaned not long after she closed the door. Her tidiness compulsion prompted her to put the wine glasses back on the counter by the bottle, still half full. Ben's glass looked as though he hardly took a sip. Lizzie still let herself smile. It hadn't just been the wine.

Chapter Two

Lizzie watched the cursor blink on her computer. She wasn't interested in the minutes she was typing from the development committee meeting or the hours of invitation list pruning that awaited her after lunch. It was a busy Monday, but not very conducive to committed focus. She let her eyes wander towards Richard's office. He was busily discussing a new fundraising project with Dr. Chiang, the chief cardiac surgeon.

Lizzie knew her boss' attention was enraptured by the beautiful doctor and wouldn't notice her distraction from work. She saved the document and switched screens over to the Internet. She checked her email, which included photos of bridesmaid dresses from Nora and Delany's friend request from Facebook. Lizzie logged onto Facebook to accept Delany. She glanced over her profile and pictures from marathons and her wedding to Dan. She was really striking, no surprise she won the heart of SRHS's boy wonder. Lizzie read through her interests and activities and realized after running they might not have much to discuss.

Lizzie returned to the news feed and read through the minutiae of everyone's day. Sara posted a cheesy proclamation of how happy she was to see so many friends at the reunion. She wrote a similar comment on Lizzie's wall… and Ben's. Lizzie clicked on Ben's profile. She couldn't tell if he logged on since leaving her Sunday morning. Lizzie dared the thought he might have checked her online personality… but there was no proof either way. His wall had a few more comments from people she didn't know, much less recent than Sara's vapid ardor. Most comments were idle hellos or thanks for an add. Nothing substantial enough to give a clue about what he did when he wasn't at work or a reunion… or with whom he might be doing them.

She clicked on his handful of photos. Someone tagged him in something from his MIT days. He was a grainy black and white head at the back of a crowd… with a hairstyle that resembled his shaggy high school curls more than the neatly trimmed coif he wore the other night. The other pictures were from a picnic, with various persons. Maybe from his company? Maybe a group of friends? There was one young woman in a couple of the pictures. A pretty blonde with blue eyes and a skinny waist. Of course.

Lizzie clicked on his friends list. She recognized the names of the faces she saw the other night… including Sara. She saw his brother's name and tried to click on his profile. Oliver set privacy options that excluded her from seeing it. The picture showed the older Cottingham didn't look much different than she remembered, with his dark hair and dark eyes. He was straddled across a bicycle, next to a statuesque African American woman also seated on a bike.

Not much. She went back to Ben's photos, appreciating the freckles that went over his nose. She didn't want to like him that much… but she couldn't stop her heart beating more quickly with another glance at his gray green eyes.

She signed out of Facebook and clicked over to Google. She typed in his name. There were a couple publications in vocabulary about computers she couldn't understand. She found his company website, which also required some element of translation. She understood there was a medical link to his computer business. She also knew that he was the founder and CEO. He had an impressive career… and no doubt bank account.

There was a Ben Cottingham in a WWI roster. And a Dr. Benjamin Cottingham came up a few times… but with very few details. Both were much too old to be him. Lizzie couldn't remember if his father was named Benjamin. In fact, she really couldn't remember his father at all.

She typed in Oliver's name. His college appeared, as well as his course listings from the previous spring. She found a syllabus for environmental studies, as well as several papers he had written on the environmental impact of plastics.

"Did you have a good Thanksgiving, Lizzie?" Dr. Chiang passed her desk on the way out of Richard's office.

"I did, thank you," Lizzie offered up that habitual smile. "And yourself?"

"Quiet," Dr. Chiang retrieved her coat from the rack. Lizzie nodded at the small talk, wondering why the doctor suddenly expressed an interest in her holiday. She always knew Dr. Chiang, as she was undoubtedly the most attractive of the department heads. She was also incredibly young. But no one, not even Richard, was bothered by that fact. Her bright blue eyes triggered admiration from everyone with whom she spoke. "Richard said you have a connection to the Fulton Foundation."

Lizzie's cheeks pinkened at the expectation. "Well, I work at the Fulton House on weekends," Lizzie wondered how much of an age difference there was from Dr. Chiang, how much more accomplished she was in her thirties than Lizzie who typed up minutes and gave tours for minimum wage at a museum. Nothing half so impressive as running a cardiac department. "I've met a few of the Fultons when they came to see the house. Gerard Fulton came to speak to the guides one afternoon about his family history. He's probably the only one I can say I know… and even then…

"Would you feel comfortable sending him an invitation to the gala?" Dr. Chiang buttoned her coat and looked at Lizzie with those blue eyes. Lizzie was aware of Richard listening through the door. "We would like to get him interested in the hospital – as a funder for the new cardiac center."

"Of course," Lizzie smiled, even though she thought Gerard Fulton was a spoiled little boy in the body of a 46-year-old, who really had no sense of history beyond the longevity of his family name.

"Great," she smiled back, fueling Lizzie's confidence. "You'll let me know if he responds?"

"I will, Dr. Chiang," she let herself be charmed by the blue eyes.

"Thanks Lizzie," Dr. Chiang lingered a friendly glance before walking out of the office. Lizzie looked back at the computer, no longer interested in Oliver Cottingham or the internet. She felt a sense of purpose and opened the invitation list to add Gerard Fulton.

*****

Lizzie watched the juices ooze out of the tomatoes and across the sizzling pan. She added oregano and garlic before stirring them all up again. "Hey," Meg came into the kitchen and grabbed a glass from the cupboard.

"Hey," Lizzie didn't look away from the pan. "Stranger."

Meg pulled the orange juice out of the refrigerator. "Yeah," Meg filled her glass before returning the carton to its shelf. "Sorry to leave you alone this weekend."

"Jackie got back Sunday," Lizzie stirred her mixture again.

"Even better," Meg took a gulp of her juice.

"Where did you go?"

Meg bit her lip. "Alec's," she sighed out slowly.

"I thought you guys were finished."

"We were," Meg took another drink and set the glass by the sink. "But…"

Lizzie stirred her pan, choosing not to say what came into her mouth. She knew she couldn't criticize Meg for the frailty of her heart or its poor choices.

"I needed a couple books for the thesis," Meg argued. "He offered to loan them to me..."

"So you stayed for three, four days?"

"Lizzie, I forgot how much I like talking to him… and kissing him."

Lizzie watched the juices run together and wondered if her cheeks resembled their color. "So you're back together?"

"Sort of…"

"Are you happy?"

"I don't know," Meg shrugged. "What are you making for dinner?"

"Just sauce for spaghetti," Lizzie looked back at her pan. "There's enough for you – and Jackie, if she wants any."

"How was the reunion?" Meg asked quickly before Lizzie could turn the conversation backwards.

"I saw some old friends. I danced. It was a nice night."

"Did your cousin show?" Meg got the orange juice again.

"No," Lizzie turned the heat down under the pan.

"What about your friend who has lots of babies and is married to the repressed homosexual?"

"Meg!" Lizzie tried to restrain her laughter.

"Was she there?"

"She was," Lizzie bit on her smile. "We didn't talk much though."

"Then who did you talk to?" Meg softened her curiosity, obviously seeing something Lizzie wasn't able to conceal from her expression.

"This guy Ben," Lizzie tucked her hair behind her ear and picked up the wooden spoon to poke once more at her mixture.

"Did you talk to him in high school?"

"Actually, he used follow Sara around all the time."

"Oh."

Lizzie accepted her misinterpretation and concentrated on her dinner. Meg watched as she put the spaghetti into the boiling water and tilted her head. "So what else happened?"

"Um…" Lizzie faded as the smile she couldn't prevent crept onto her face.

"Did you get laid?"

"Meghan," Lizzie laughed at her attempt to scold her friend as the slam of the front door echoed up the stairs and through the dining room into the kitchen. "Jackie is home."

"Who cares? That Ben guy?"

"Yes," Lizzie let Meg see her smirk as Jackie came into the kitchen. "Hi," Lizzie offered.

"Hi," their third roommate muttered as she grabbed a can of soda from the fridge and left the kitchen.

"I'm guessing she doesn't want spaghetti," Meg stuck a finger in the sauce, tasted it, and met Lizzie's eyes. "Do you think you'll see him again?"

"He's nice… but it was just one night," Lizzie cautioned, not wanting to get swept up in Meg's manic concept of romance. "It was great sex, but it's not going to be a relationship."

"You don't think you'll want to get together for more great sex?" Meg lingered by the stove.

"I don't know," Lizzie slowly took the spoon out of the red sauce. "He… I always think of him in terms of Sara. I never had a thing for him myself. I never thought of him that way… really… until right before we went upstairs."

"So it was a good weekend?"

"An excellent weekend."

"Lizzie?" Meg took the strainer from the cupboard. "Don't tell Nora about Alec, okay?"

Lizzie took the strainer from her hands. "Okay."

Chapter Three

Lizzie dusted along the dresser, careful not to upset the few china objects displayed on the lace coverlet. She paused and looked up at the portrait of Harriet Fulton. She wondered if Harriet was ever distracted by a young man. Lizzie couldn't imagine Harriet thought about the things that kept filling her mind. Maybe she did. Over Lazarus Benedict before he became her husband. Or maybe the boy who delivered coal.

Lizzie went over to the window and ran the cloth along the window sill. She looked down at the cold gray parking lot. The outside of the Fulton House seemed a strange contradiction to the scarce 19th century furnishings within. It often seemed that the house was in its own place, its own skewed time. It wasn't quite a step into the past, with fluorescent lights buzzing on some of the ceilings or the motion sensors hanging above the doors. Nor was it completely in the present. Just somewhere in between.

A few guides liked to suggest there were ghosts roaming about the rooms. Lizzie was seldom able to blame the chills she got in the bedrooms on other worldly occurrences. It was just that cold. Then again she often walked into a room and felt her mood change suddenly - as though walking into a memory that was stuck in the air like all the dust dancing in the sunbeams.

Harriet's room, more than any other, made her feel sad. She wondered if it was Harriet's sadness… or another. Or her own. Lizzie accepted the fact she had an active imagination and that the few details of intrigue about the Fultons were not enough to make the talk of furniture and wallpaper interesting … to her at least.

"Lizzie, are you finished in here?" Paula's voice called her back to the focus of the task at hand.

"I just… a few more minutes," Lizzie smiled at her manager.

"Andrew just started a tour," Paula diverted her eyes from a direct glance at Lizzie.

"Oh. Okay," Lizzie persisted her smile. She never knew what to do with Paula. It was difficult to understand whether or not Paula liked Lizzie and her disdain for staying on script with the tours. Lizzie didn't really care about the furniture as much as everyone else. She was fascinated by the Fultons, who actually slept and sat upon the beds and chairs. They were more interesting than the wood and upholstery. That's not really what they were supposed to discuss. Paula had a sense of humor… but Lizzie often thought she was silently cursing her lack of respect. But Paula was too sweet to say anything.

"So if you could do the three o'clock, that would be good," Paula let herself turn her glance back to Lizzie's smile.

"Absolutely," Lizzie moved over to the bed posts and gently wiped along them with the dust cloth. "Paula, do we have any more information about Harriet?"

"What do you mean?"

"We know when she was born, when she got married, when she died. We know whom she married, that she had four babies and lost three of them. What else do we know?"

"You have her portrait," Paula walked to the dresser.

"Do you think she looks happy? Or … like she's thinking of something?" Lizzie stopped herself from leaning against the bed post.

"I think that glassy stare is the paint," Paula laughed. "No, there isn't much information about Harriet. She wasn't as involved in the community as her parents. There aren't many records of her activities. We don't really know much about her."

"Nothing in the archives?"

"I'm afraid not," Paula shook her head. "Why?"

"I was just curious. I guess I was looking too long at her portrait," Lizzie sighed and went towards the headboard.

"Well I don't think you could fit much more info on the tour anyway," Paula shrugged. "Considering you have to talk about the bed and the chair in this room."

"I don't have to talk about the chair."

"Yes, you do, Lizzie. It's a valuable piece."

"Tell that to the mice," Lizzie laughed, but saw that Paula wasn't amused. "Hey – are you going to Andrew's Christmas party next week?"

"I…" Paula glanced over her glasses. "I'm not really into parties."

"Andrew and Davis throw a nice celebration. You should come."

"I'll think about it," Paula looked back at the portrait.

"I'll need a buffer from all of Davis' friends," Lizzie entreated, though not able to articulate the name of the one she hoped wouldn't be there with his wife.

"We should probably head downstairs, before the tour comes through the bedrooms," Paula suggested and met Lizzie's eye with a knowing glance. Paula had been a good sport listening to her crooning about Will and had the graciousness to drop the subject when Lizzie no longer believed the fairy tale.

"Yeah," Lizzie made one last swipe down the bedpost and glanced back at the portrait. She got a brief chill across her shoulders and realized she was standing in the draft from the window. Perhaps it was just the shine of the paint.

*****

Lizzie turned the lock on the gift shop door and went back to the reception desk. Andrew counted the last of his pennies and added it to the tally of the day's take. Lizzie waited in silence for him to figure his math. "Not bad for such a slow day," Andrew shrugged looking up at her.

"We had some Christmas shoppers when you were on your tour," Lizzie explained.

"Ah," Andrew nodded and shut the register. "Well, let's close this joint."

"Paula is still in her office," Lizzie reached for her coat on the hook behind the desk.

"She should be down soon," Andrew wrapped his scarf around his neck. "Do you have a hot date tonight, Lizzie?"

"Hardly," she laughed. "You?"

"Davis and I are going to the movies. That French film that's got all the buzz," Andrew buttoned up his coat. "Are you seriously doing nothing, Lizzie? I can't believe that with all the new attention you seem to be getting."

Lizzie bit on her lip, letting her cheeks flush. "I'm just hanging out with Meg and Nora tonight," she said cautiously.

"What about that doctor?"

Lizzie lifted her shoulders and looked helpless towards an offer of information. "We aren't dating."

"We'll have to find you someone at the party next week."

"Oh God, please don't," Lizzie rolled her eyes.

"You spent all that time and effort to make yourself look this good and yet you still hide yourself away like a nun," Andrew shook his head.

"Not exactly," Lizzie's cheeks burned, thinking of the previous weekend and Ben Cottingham. That certainly wasn't nun-like behavior.

"So there is someone?"

"There isn't some ONE," Lizzie emphasized. "I'm enjoying a few non-committal partnerships."

"Aha, that's more like it," Andrew chuckled as Paula came into the gift shop.

"Everything all set down here?"

"I closed out the register," Andrew nodded. "Lizzie closed the house."

"All right," Paula went behind the desk to look over the paperwork and put a sheet of paper on the desk. "Lizzie, I went through the files. That's a copy of a letter written by Harriet."

"What?" Lizzie edged back towards the desk.

"The only thing we have from her. It's not much… but maybe it could give you a little more insight to her glassy stare," Paula smiled at her.

Lizzie picked up the letter and read it, with Andrew glancing over her shoulder.

"*My dearest Lotty,*

I am sorry that you had to leave and return to New York so suddenly. It was a dear pleasure to have you with us in Cambridge this season. Mother regrets your absence at the dinner table. Your conversation was a lively distraction from Father and Peter's debates.

Please send my regards to Mr. Chester. I hope that he shall return to Boston when his leisure suits him.

Fondly,

Harriet"

"Who is Mr. Chester?" Andrew asked.

"I don't know. Never heard of anyone by that name before," Paula looked at Lizzie.

"An unrequited love?" Lizzie offered.

"No," Paula cautioned. "There isn't anything that you can add to the tour from that, you know."

"Who is Lotty?" Andrew asked the other obvious question.

"I don't know that either," Paula reached for her coat. "I think it's time to head home. What do you think?"

"Lizzie has a hot date with her gal pals," Andrew sniveled. "We don't want to keep her."

"No," Lizzie turned to Andrew. "We don't want to keep Davis waiting. He will hate us all if we make you late for your French film."

*****

Nora and Meg were already drinking martinis in the living room when Lizzie climbed the stairs. She hung up her coat and noticed the swatches Nora spread out on the coffee table. "So these are the colors," Nora explained after they exchanged a quick hello and Meg left to get Lizzie a drink. "What do you think?"

"We each have a different one?" Lizzie picked up one of the red squares.

"Same design, but you all will have a different shade," Nora explained with a look for approval in her amber eyes.

"What is Becca wearing?" Lizzie fingered another square.

"She likes this one," Nora picked up a swatch that was redder than the burgundy color Lizzie had across her palm. "We were thinking a gold waistband or something."

"Fitting for the maid of honor," Lizzie showed her approval with a smile. "I like this one."

"Just like wine," Meg handed her a glass. "I figured you'd go for that one."

"Which design did you pick?" Lizzie sipped from her martini.

"Knee length and strapless. It should be comfortable for June. And Lizzie, you will look fabulous," Nora smiled.

"Well, thank you," Lizzie took the compliment, even as she was still bemused by Andrew's references earlier. "I think the same will be true for Meg and your sister."

"I'm not getting up to go running at six in the morning," Meg rolled her eyes.

"You started running again?"

"Just since Monday," Lizzie answered. "Doing penance for Thanksgiving."

"Good girl," Nora approved. "You'll look better than me in June."

"I doubt it," Lizzie scowled. "No one in the wedding party will outshine the bride."

"Speaking of the wedding party," Nora heaved a sigh. "One of Mark's groomsmen had to drop out."

"Oh no," Meg took another sip.

"Yeah, Patrick is moving to Japan," Nora looked down. "So, he's asked Aaron to take over."

Lizzie darted her eyes to Meg. Years before, when Nora still lived with them, Meg had one of her passionate albeit short-lived affairs with Mark's cousin, Aaron. It didn't end well and added to the tension between Meg and Mark. "Well," Meg breathed out carefully.

"We'll pair him with Lizzie, of course," Nora looked hopefully at Lizzie.

"That's okay," Meg shrugged off her concern. Lizzie realized that she wasn't drinking her first martini of the evening. Nora probably noticed that, too. "Besides, I'm bringing Alec."

Nora looked directly at Lizzie, who smiled awkwardly. "He has been helping Meg with her thesis."

"I'll bet he has," Nora set her jaw. "He sucks the life out of you, Meghan."

Nora picked up the swatches and, in spite of her irritation, still arranged them neatly in her box. Lizzie took a sip from her martini, uncertain if there was a deliberate play on words in Nora's comment. Meg was writing another master's thesis on vampires in literature, something Nora could never comprehend. But she had managed to sum up Alec's effect on Meg quite appropriately with that sentence. Lizzie knew Meg was delaying her reaction because she couldn't argue against the truth.

"Lizzie rekindled an old flame last weekend," Meg made Lizzie's cheek match the color of her favorite swatch.

"What?" Nora shifted to Lizzie. "You aren't obsessing about Will again, are you?"

"NO!" Lizzie choked on her next sip. "I just… I went to my reunion."

"That's right," Nora sighed out. "What happened?"

Lizzie glanced impatiently at Meg but accepted responsibility to divert the conversation. "I just… it was nothing, really."

"She said it was great sex," Meg drank from her glass to stop Lizzie's protest.

"Who was it?" Nora asked.

"Ben Cottingham," Lizzie forced a smile. "He had a crush on my friend Sara for years."

"So you slept with him to prove something?"

"I slept with him because I had a lot of wine."

"Are you friends?"

"On Facebook," Lizzie laughed. "Nora, it was a one time thing. Don't start imagining him as my escort to your wedding."

Nora closed the lid on her box of swatches. "Don't you think it's time, Lizzie?"

"Time for what?"

"To find someone… who isn't just a one time thing."

Lizzie looked at Meg for help, irritated that she opened up that can of worms to avoid her own reprimand from Nora. "I never wanted that, Nora," Lizzie sighed out.

"You did with Will."

"Not really," Lizzie set her glass down and walked over to the mantelpiece to get away from the direct line of Nora's eyes.

"But you used to say…"

"I said a lot of crap about Will. I never really believed it, not deep down. I mean… I always knew I was never what he wanted," Lizzie looked at her fingers, feeling uncomfortable with a conversation about a guy she hadn't seen in over a year.

"Is that why you're not calling this guy?" Meg asked suddenly.

"What?" Lizzie turned quickly.

"Are you afraid of a Will encore?" Meg continued softly.

"I just said I never really wanted… I don't want a relationship right now, okay?" Lizzie breathed out hastily.

"Oh, Lizzie. They aren't all like Will," Nora sighed.

"I don't know that the ones like Ben are any better. He didn't say goodbye," Lizzie snarled.

Meg and Nora looked away from her. Lizzie told herself that part of the morning after hadn't bothered her. It hadn't… until she spoke it to her friends and realized there was a part of her that did feel slighted. Because it was Ben Cottingham. Because she saw the look in his eye for Sara with which she used to follow Will. Because she bothered to feel sorry for him… and he didn't even say goodbye.

"Are we getting pizza?" Lizzie broke the silence. "Or Chinese food?"

"Chinese food, are you kidding?" Meg said. "Alec hates that stuff."

Nora rolled her eyes at Lizzie, providing the comfort that Meg was not off the hook.

Lizzie could not sleep. It was already 3:30 by the time Nora left. The sleepy buzz of martinis wore off while she awaited Nora's sobriety. Within a half hour she changed and readied herself for the sleep that would not come. Too many thoughts trickled into her brain. She wished Meg hadn't brought Ben up in front of Nora, prompting a discussion of details she resisted acknowledging even to herself. Nora politely avoided the subject, even as the evening hours started to wane into morning. She was easily distracted by wedding details and did not return to the subject of Lizzie's flings.

Ben wasn't the only transient lover she had. She had a surge of confidence in her sexuality as she approached the last two months before the marathon. That was aided significantly by Eric, a surgical intern, whom she met in the cafeteria after a lunchtime run. He asked to join her next run, which led to a drink, and then to his apartment. She gave him her phone number, which he didn't hesitate to use in the following weeks.

Lizzie liked Eric. Maybe because that's really all it was with him. Sometimes running… but usually just a drink and then his apartment. No awkward mornings. No hope for anything else. He was attractive. He was young – younger than her, but definitely more accomplished. He was on the career path, no doubt hoping to be a chief surgeon someday. But she couldn't imagine herself having a conversation with him every day, much less every day for twenty years. She didn't expect anything from him and didn't always answer his calls.

She couldn't understand why Ben Cottingham hit a nerve. And why… a week later… she let herself admit it. She didn't like him in high school. She liked Adam Jackson… and that was like Will… a silly crush she never believed could be a reality in spite of her public wishes it would be. She didn't like Ben. She didn't bother to think of him. Not that it would have made any difference if he was following Sara around all the time. And wasn't he still just following Sara by choosing her?

Lizzie shut her eyes in annoyance. High school was long ago – almost four times the number of years she actually spent in it. And that many years since she sat across from Ben Cottingham in the library… when she was a very different person herself. How could she not let the idea that he changed enter her mind?

He may no longer like Sara… but he didn't like her enough to stay until the morning.

Lizzie tossed onto her side, annoyed that the thoughts were keeping her awake. She didn't want to do this to herself again. She was too old for ill-fated affections. She managed to survive the majority of her 33 years without a serious relationship. She once blamed her appearance for that singularity. But she knew it was a choice to remove herself from the dating game. She still had no real desire to enter it. She certainly had no desire to let her heart fall for someone who didn't want her for more than flirting.

Lizzie forced those thoughts from her head, even as her exhaustion lacked the strength to fight their doggedness. She tried to think of something else entirely and went back to her day at the Fulton House. She liked working there. Even though she only managed to guide three people through the house at the end of the day. It was still an opportunity to bring strangers through a place she loved. She couldn't explain her affection for the two hundred year old home. She really didn't care about the wallpaper and furniture. She was fascinated by Margaret and John Fulton and their political activism. Although… didn't that letter from Harriet imply that

Margaret thought politics less interesting? Or maybe that was Harriet trying to be clever. Lizzie shut her eyes and laughed thinking of Paula's disapproval for her speculation. It was difficult to not speculate about Harriet. There was so little to know of her… just to imagine what she was thinking when she sat for that portrait or stared out her window…

Lizzie felt very very tired. She knew she was obligated to finish her tour. She wanted to lie down, but knew Paula would be upset if she decided to take a nap on one of the beds. Not that Lizzie would want to sleep on one of those beds. The mice liked to scurry across the linens. Lizzie saw a mouse as she continued talking about Mr. and Mrs. Fulton in the dining room. Mrs. Fulton liked to give dinner parties. She was very fond of her friends and grateful to those who supported the belief that the United States should not be at war with England.

Mrs. Fulton's favorite dish was roasted pork with potatoes and carrots. Lizzie looked at the dining room table and was startled to find all the dishes were dirty and in need of clearing. She didn't want Paula to come in and tell her she hadn't cleaned the room properly. Lizzie collected the plates and brought them into the kitchen. She noticed the fire was dying and went to add another log. She pushed it into the coals and watched the flame lick around it. She sensed someone in the room and wondered if it might be Harriet's Mr. Chester. She turned quickly and saw Ben. He smiled at her and crossed the room. She put down the iron and let him pull her into his arms for a long passionate kiss.

Chapter Four

Lizzie scraped the remaining guacamole into the container, catching a splatter she licked off her finger. She attached the lid and collected the other containers to put in the refrigerator as Andrew entered the kitchen with two martini glasses and a shaker.

"Why are you hiding in my kitchen?" he scowled, setting the glasses down to fill them.

"I like the kitchen."

"There's a party in the living room," he gave her a glass.

She looked at the pile of dirty dishes by the sink and sighed. "Yes, go enjoy it. I'll clean up so you can be with your friends."

"They are your friends, too, Lizzie," he held the glass until she took it.

"I have a thing about dirty dishes. You know I do. I even dream about them."

"Oh really?" he laughed over his green drink.

"I dreamt I was washing them at the Fulton House," she smirked and took a sip. "Mmm, a triumph."

"The pear vodka."

"Goes nicely with the cheese," she saw the abandoned goat cheese spread and decided one more cracker wasn't going to hurt her.

"I liked that mushroom thing you brought."

"We can add it to our list," Lizzie set down her glass to bring the empty guacamole dish to the sink and run water over it.

"Christmas parties are a good niche for catering," Andrew savored his next swallow. "You must know some doctors' wives that could hire us."

"Andrew, we aren't… if we ever have a business…" Lizzie sighed hopelessly and went back to her drink. She didn't know any doctors with wives. The only doctor she really knew was Dr. Chiang. She wasn't likely to hire her to cook for a Christmas cocktail party. Not that it was a real possibility. They only really talked about it after parties. The idea went out with the trash the following morning.

"So what did you think of Paula's date?" Andrew proved her thought true with the rapid switch of subject.

"She was nice," Lizzie fingered the stem of her glass. "Quiet."

"She'll be good for Paula."

"I think this was their second date, Andrew," Lizzie rolled her eyes and took another piece of cheese.

"You know Bob," Andrew tilted his head towards the living room where Davis and the remainder of the guests were sitting. "He's available."

"I'm not looking."

"He's available tonight."

"I have someone I can call for that," Lizzie went to the drawer she knew held the foil and saran wrap.

"Why don't you want to get serious with the surgeon?" Andrew annoyed her. She glared at him as she lifted the foil out to cover up the cheese platter. He was too drunk to justify anger.

"He's boring," Lizzie shrugged.

"Most of the straight ones are, lovely."

"Not all of them," Lizzie bit her lip hoping his swallow of martini would blur his hearing.

"Oh?"

Lizzie shut her eyes quickly to regain composure. She focused on the platter and quickly covered it. "Just, um, he's not the only one right now," Lizzie hastened to put the platter in the fridge. She was relieved when Davis entered the room.

"Are you having a little party in here?" he took the martini shaker to fill his glass. "Or are you making Lizzie play housekeeper again?"

"I can't get her away from the dishes," Andrew laughed.

"Lizzie, come on, we can do the dishes in the morning," Davis took her hand.

"It is morning."

"Exactly. You don't have to worry. He isn't going to show up this late," Davis looked at her directly.

"That's not…" she gave up and took her glass. Going back and talking to Davis' friends … and Will's … was a lot easier than having to explain to Andrew that she was thinking about another man who didn't care much for her. She took a quick swallow of Andrew's vodka drenched martini. "Let's go have some holiday cheer."

*****

"Did you have a good Christmas?" the nurse, Polly, asked as she hooked the bag on the stand.

Lizzie shifted her head slightly to avoid seeing her blood leave her arm. "It was crazy, but pretty good. Yours?"

"A lot of food," Polly smiled. "Are you still running, Lizzie?"

"Yeah. I've been pretty disciplined since Thanksgiving," she leaned her head back.

"Good for you. Good for your blood. I'll be back in five minutes," Polly glanced at the bag and moved to the next donor.

She shut her eyes for a few minutes, once again contemplating the option the hospital gave for the afternoon off after donating blood. The days got busier as the gala approached. She completed all her required tasks for the day, but there were still plenty of details that could be completed before five. She opened her eyes and met the glance of Dr. Chiang standing in a discussion with Polly. Lizzie remembered she had to tell the cardiac chief that Gerard Fulton was coming to the gala, but didn't have the energy to speak with her blood draining from her arm. The doctor offered a friendly smile and turned back to Polly before leaving the room.

Polly came back to check on the blood bag. "Dr. Chiang is very pretty," Lizzie avoided looking at the needle Polly took from her arm.

"She is lovely," Polly agreed. "She has many admirers."

Lizzie was surprised the blood could still rise to her cheeks. "She's Chinese?"

"Mm hmm," Polly put the gauze inside her elbow and propped it up over her shoulder. "Do you want some cookies?"

"I think I'll rest a bit and then get lunch in the café."

"Sounds good. Thanks for coming, Lizzie. We always appreciate it," Polly smiled again, validating her decision to come to the blood bank. She felt badly she skipped December, but was determined to make it back in March, when the required eight week wait was over.

*****

Lizzie lifted a tray and glanced over the shoulders of the staff in front of her to see what options were available. She saw her favorite salad was already gone. She wasn't interested in the overcooked pasta or soupy chili. She bit her lip, wondering if Polly's cookies might have been a better option after all.

"Hey," a warm breath whispered in her ear.

"Hi," she broadened a grin before turning to Eric's dark eyes. Maybe she would take the option to not return to the office. She set her tray down and picked up a packaged turkey sandwich. "Are you just starting your shift or nearing the end of it?"

"In the middle," Eric grabbed a sandwich without a tray. "But I've got time for lunch."

"Do you have a surgery today?"

"With Kate Chiang," Eric beamed.

"That's great," Lizzie wondered if that had anything to do with her presence in the blood bank.

"What have you got going on this weekend?" Eric stepped ahead of Lizzie and paid for her sandwich. It was sweet… but… different from his usual attention.

"I have to go to a funeral tomorrow," Lizzie found a table with four empty chairs.

"Oh geez, I'm so sorry," he sat across from her.

"A friend of mine from high school lost her father this week," Lizzie pulled apart the plastic carton of her sandwich. "I didn't know him very well. But she was a good friend… and I spent a lot of time at their house when I was younger."

"How did he die?"

"Heart attack," Lizzie let herself reveal the empathetic sorrow she felt at the news of Sara's dad. No matter how many years since they were best friends or the differences that came between them in those years, Lizzie still felt the grief of losing Joseph Miller.

"Does that mean you have to drive all the way out there?"

"Out there?" she laughed and found the levity of conversation again. "It's just over an hour. Not much more than driving to New Hampshire."

"I don't go to New Hampshire either," he shook his head, with a knowing grin. She suspected his questions had more to do with her availability in the Cambridge area than Coldbrook or New Hampshire. She could easily be back by the evening… except she hoped someone else might be at the funeral. He did like Sara for all those years. If he was a decent guy, Ben would demonstrate his sympathy for his former crush. Lizzie knew it was awful that she was excited to go to a funeral because she wanted to see him. And yet… it was a chance to see him and prove if he had a shred of decency.

She took a bite of her sandwich and met his knowing grin. He was so attractive. She appreciated his runner's frame even more when he was wearing scrubs. She liked the fact he was letting his black hair grow out from its weekly cropping. His dark skin was so smooth and so lovely… why did she want to hesitate an invitation with Eric just on the off chance she would see… and it wasn't even appropriate to think something would come from an encounter at a funeral.

"Well, it is supposed to be cold this weekend. But if you are up for a run…"

"Hello, Eric," Dr. Chiang came behind Lizzie. "Have you had a chance to review for this afternoon?"

"Yes, Dr. Chiang," Eric shifted his eyes and softened his confidence in deference to his superior. Lizzie saw his awe with her beauty and felt slightly jealous.

"Hello Lizzie," the doctor greeted, prompting Lizzie to turn around. "Richard tells me that Gerard Fulton is attending."

"Yes," Lizzie nodded quietly.

"Well, whatever charm you possess to lure him here, we shall have to use to get him to fund my new center," Dr. Chiang grinned.

"I'll do what I can," she looked back at her sandwich, aware of Eric's observation.

"Eric, stop by my office after lunch," Dr. Chiang touched Lizzie's shoulder briefly. "Lizzie."

"Who's Gerard Fulton?" Eric asked after Lizzie ate some of her sandwich.

"He's a man with a lot of money," Lizzie pulled the bread off the second half and debated if she wanted that much turkey.

"You know him?"

"Hardly," Lizzie shook her head. "I just work at a museum about his family."

"Why is there a museum about his family?"

"Because they have a lot of money. And they've had a lot of money for centuries," Lizzie didn't bother to explain the politics or the artistic accomplishments of the Fultons. She doubted that Eric really cared about such things.

"Do you think he'll give us money?"

"Who knows?"

"Then maybe Chiang will hire me permanently," Eric grinned and looked at his watch. "So, Lizzie, if you want to go out for a run on Sunday, you know how to find me."

"I do," she bit her lip and watched him head towards Dr. Chiang's office. She hoped there would be a reason she wouldn't have to make that call.

Chapter Five

Lizzie sat in a pew with her cousin. It was a long time since she sat inside St. Mary's. Probably not since another funeral… or wedding. She was once a devout Catholic… but not since she left Coldbrook and went to college. She scanned the crowd for Ben before the mass started, but was able to push him out of her mind when she resolved he wouldn't be there. That the important part of the morning was to support Sara and her family.

"Hey, so how was Christmas?" Jack whispered as the crowd moved slowly towards the back of the church to share condolences with Sara's family.

"It was…" Lizzie looked up and saw Ben further down the line. "It was fun. It would have been more fun if you and Jen were there. How was Jen's family?"

"Less rowdy."

"I bet you missed us," Lizzie tried not to make her observation of Ben obvious.

"Of course I did. I missed the food. What did you make this year?"

"Something healthy. I missed the guitar playing at the end of the night," Lizzie laughed. "Hey – when is the next gig, Jack?"

"We have some shows coming up in the spring. I hope you'll come to one or two."

"I've been known to do such things on occasion," Lizzie felt someone's eyes on her. She turned from Jack and met Ben's gray green eyes. He paused for a second and looked away.

"Hey – is that Ben Cottingham?"

Lizzie hoped the blush wasn't too obvious in her cheeks. Fortunately, it was cold and the indoor heat had already made her a little ruddy. "It was."

"Do you think he still has a thing for Sara?"

"Who knows?"

"Was he at the reunion?"

"Yes."

"I'm surprised. I mean… I always thought he would be the sort to leave this town and never look back."

"Why do you say that?"

"I don't know. He was smart. I bet he made a small fortune."

"He went to MIT. And he has his own computer company."

"Really?" Jack looked curiously.

"At least that's what he says on Facebook."

"Oh yeah…" Jack nodded.

"Sara," Lizzie said abruptly, realizing the line had already reached the greeting family. "I am so sorry."

"It was such a surprise," Sara clung to her embrace. "He was so alive at Christmas."

Lizzie stepped back and offered a friendly smile. "I will always have happy memories of him," she kissed Sara's cheek and looked to Jack.

"Jack," Sara leaned into his embrace.

"Jen sends her sympathies," Jack explained his wife's absence as Lizzie moved through the line of Sara's siblings and mother. It was always weird trying to say the right thing, when nothing was ever right to say… especially when she was really impatient to go outside and see if Ben was still there.

She opened the door of the church and saw him standing on the bottom step. "Hi Lizzie," he said in a tone that dashed her hope to the pit of her stomach. It wasn't just sobriety that reflected the occasion. It was the sobriety that proved the reason he hadn't called her back. The reason he didn't say goodbye the morning after.

"Hi Ben," she forced a small smile.

"Good to see you," he didn't meet her eyes as Jack followed through the door.

"Ben!" Jack nodded his greeting. "So there's no cemetery because he's cremated, right?"

"Yeah," Lizzie nodded, still looking at Ben. She recognized the contours of his muscle, even under his winter coat. He had strong shoulders.

"Are we going back to the house? Lizzie, what about you?"

"Yeah, for a little bit," Lizzie didn't move her eyes from Ben to look at Jack.

"I've got to head back to Boston. Good to see you," he repeated and disappeared into the mass of cars. Lizzie heaved a great sigh, glad the sad occasion didn't make her disappointment look obvious.

*****

"I thought you worked on Saturdays," Jack finished his plate from the buffet of casseroles and sandwiches.

"I took the day off," Lizzie glanced over the crowd of heads in the living room, hoping to catch Sara's eye.

"Don't you get sick of giving the same tour every week?"

"I only do it twice a month," Lizzie looked back at Jack. "I like it. I work with one of my best friends… and the house is kind of creepy at this time of year."

"Ever see any ghosts?"

"I wouldn't call them ghosts," Lizzie softened her voice, uncertain if the topic of ghosts was appropriate at a funeral reception. "Just some odd energy… if you believe that sort of thing."

"Are you sure you aren't drinking on the job, Lizzie?"

"I'm pretty sure," Lizzie shook her head at him. "Most of the time anyway."

"One of these days I'll come check it out. Jen wants to see it. She likes old houses."

"Well, you live in one," Lizzie took a bite from her plate as a book on the shelf by her side caught her eye. "Oh my goodness! Is that our yearbook?"

"I have a copy of that somewhere," Jack said with half interest as Lizzie pulled it off the shelf. She flipped through the first pages coated with signatures and sentimental messages and stopped at the aerial class photo.

"It's difficult to tell who anyone is from that perspective."

"It's about getting everyone in the photo, Jack," Lizzie looked for herself at the bottom of the crowd. Jack was behind her, wearing his infamous leather jacket. Sara was on top of Ben's shoulders. Lizzie couldn't have sat on anyone's shoulders. It was long before marathon days.

Jack turned the pages with more interest than his initial response to her discovery. He stopped at a candid of a science lab. "Wow, Lizzie you look good. I mean now. I know this is probably going to be tacky – because I'm your cousin… and a bit of an idiot. But, geez, I think half these girls would kill to improve so much since high school the way you did."

"Thanks, I guess," Lizzie was used to the awkward uncertain compliments.

"But I did think you were pretty then, too."

Lizzie couldn't restrain the laugh. "It's okay, cuz. I understand what you are trying to say."

"And there's Sara and Ben," Jack looked at the opposite page. "He left pretty fast today. Surprised he didn't stop in for a little ambrosia."

"He's kind of a health freak."

"Was that on his Facebook, too?"

Lizzie looked up at Jack. "No, something he said at the reunion."

"I saw him checking you out, Lizzie. I think you scared him away."

"Stop," Lizzie looked down at the photo of him with Sara. She recognized the same muscular contours she discovered that night. How was she so oblivious 15 years ago?

"I forgot I left that here," Sara's voice caused Lizzie to look back up. "I brought it with me during the reunion so I could look people up if I met someone I couldn't remember."

Lizzie offered a moderate smile. "How are you doing?"

"I just want to have this baby," Sara took the seat that Jack offered. "I don't feel like I can grieve until I give birth." Sara took the book out of Lizzie's relaxed palms. "Oh my God! Look at the hair in this picture. Why did we ever think spiral perms were a good idea? Ben looks the same. Well his hair isn't as long. But he still looks 25. Ben didn't come back, did he?"

"No, he said he had to go back to Boston," Jack offered.

"It was nice of him to come," Sara sighed and looked some more at the yearbook. "Oh, look at you, Jack. Whatever happened to your leather jacket?"

"I still have it," he smiled proudly.

"No way," Sara gleamed. "Does Jen let you wear it?"

"I'm not that skinny, Sara," he shook his head. "Not anymore."

"You wore that thing to the prom," Sara laughed and skipped ahead a couple pages. "Did you see those pictures? See, look, there you are in your leather jacket."

Jack took the book back and looked at the picture. "You look stylin in your mermaid dress, Sara," he retorted. "What did you wear, Lizzie?"

"I didn't go to the prom," she shook her head.

"She protested, remember?" Sara rolled her eyes.

"I just didn't have someone special to take me," Lizzie sighed. She actually didn't miss having that memory. Especially when she spent half of her working day planning parties like the prom to raise money for health care.

"Really? I could have sworn you were in my limo," Jack gave the book back to Sara.

"No, that was Melissa Benson," Sara said softly.

"Oh," Jack nodded and then remembered. "Oh yeah…"

"She went as Kyle Granger's date, don't you remember?"

"Why was I in a limo with Kyle Granger?"

"I don't know," Sara shrugged. "Probably because the Bensons were your neighbors."

"Oh… yeah. He was dating Melissa … but she was a year older than us, wasn't she?"

"Yeah," Lizzie sighed, wondering if she should bring up Melissa's fate at a funeral. It didn't seem appropriate, when Melissa never had one.

"They never found a body," Sara said what Lizzie wouldn't. "I can't imagine facing that as a parent."

"Or as a teenager," Lizzie muttered. She remembered a conversation she overheard when someone described Melissa as a thinner version of Elizabeth Watson. Lizzie wasn't ever sure if that was what the person actually said, but it did creep her out sixteen years ago.

"She was in my astronomy class," Jack took a cracker from Lizzie's plate. "You were, too, Lizzie. Do you remember her?"

"She was the best in that class," Lizzie answered absently. "Sort of a teacher's pet."

"So were you," Jack tried to smile.

"Hey," Sara sat up quickly. "She's kicking."

Lizzie turned to look at Sara with a genuine smile. Sara grabbed Lizzie's hand and placed it on her stomach. Lizzie felt the foot press against her palm. "Wow," she beamed.

"I've decided to name her Josie – short for Josephine. After Dad," Sara sighed.

"He'd like that," Lizzie remembered why they were there in that room, in Sara's company. She removed the yearbook from Sara's lap and put it aside, deciding the visits to Springs nostalgia were no longer necessary.

*****

"Thanks, Lizzie," Jen smiled as she came back into the living room.

"We read two books," Lizzie picked up the beer she left on the side table when she brought three year old Isabel up to bed.

"I bet she wanted two more," Jen grinned.

Lizzie sat uneasily on the edge of the sofa as Jen shifted back to the conversation between Jack and his band mates. Lizzie was glad she accepted their offer for dinner, but felt awkward in the group of Jack's friends. Especially when the drummer, Mike, kept looking at her. She knew it was because she went with him to his car one night after a gig. Now he had a girlfriend.

"Hey Lizzie, didn't a friend of yours play at a place in Central Square?" Jack brought her focus back to the conversation.

"Yeah," she muttered not sure how Will still qualified as her friend.

"Maybe his band could play with ours."

"You're not really going to start doing gigs in Cambridge," Jen shook her head with a glance at the bass player's wife.

"Why not?"

"Because it's a lot of work and a lot more time you won't be here," Jen explained lightly, but Lizzie knew her intention was not very light-hearted. Lizzie took the final swallow of beer and decided to leave the room to get another.

Instead of returning to her uncomfortable seat, she went through the dining room onto the back deck. The January air was cool, but clean. There was a half foot of snow blanketing their backyard, chopped up with children's footprints. The air was quiet, the eerie calm of Coldbrook that always startled her at first, but eventually calmed her.

"Hey," Mike slid the door shut.

"Hey," Lizzie was conscious of her smile. She wasn't going to try to be inviting. Not that he wasn't attractive. He was. She always thought so. Even in high school. But she was wary of musicians. And… she had to remind herself… he had a girlfriend.

"Couples," he leaned on the railing beside her.

"I'm sure Amy would agree with Jen," Lizzie put the name out to remind him.

"She's not here," there was a knowing look as he took a sip of beer.

Lizzie turned away to look at the snowy backyard. "Hey, didn't you used to hang out with Oliver Cottingham?" Lizzie asked suddenly as the memory entered her mind.

"Kinda," Mike shrugged with disinterest. "Why?"

"His brother was at the funeral today."

"Yeah, he was part of your little group. I remember that. It was because of Ben that I found out about Jack's band," Mike turned his lean around, bringing himself closer to Lizzie's side. She appreciated the warmth, but not the intimacy.

"Do you keep in touch with him?"

"With Oliver?" he laughed over another swallow. "Naw, he moved to California or something. We just hung out on occasion. Once the band started, we didn't have much in common. It's nice Ben showed up. He had a thing for your friend, didn't he?"

"Yeah," Lizzie's heart sank. Why was she having a conversation about the Cottinghams? Not like Mike the drummer would know anything about Ben now. Or why he had to leave to go back to Boston. Or why he would actually want to talk to Lizzie after their night together.

Mike wanted to talk to her. Maybe not talk. She felt his hand touch her lower back. He wasn't put off by the awkwardness of seeing her again after a hasty fuck in the back seat of his Mazda. She didn't want to think about Ben anymore. She didn't want to think about stupid guitar players who married someone else. She peered through the glass doors into the dark dining room. The living room wasn't visible from that angle. She looked back at Mike and decided to forget about Amy. Screw it. She let him kiss her and slide his hand over her breast. She grabbed his hand and pulled him towards the back wall of the house. She kept kissing him as she reached for the button of his jeans. He reached under her skirt and pulled her tights towards her knees.

She drank the rest of her beer after he went back in the house. She took in the cold air, knowing its reaction against her skin would qualify the blood in her cheeks. She shut her eyes and let the sting of guilt creep in as her pulse returned to normal. She preferred the guilt hovering in her brain over the disappointment that Ben walked away and didn't want to see her.

Chapter Six

Lizzie saw Alec's car parked on the street in front of the house. She decided to leave her bag in the stair hall and settle on the couch without going upstairs. It was well after noon, but she knew that might not matter with Meg and her on and off again boyfriend. She was tired and all too happy to lose the heels she put back on her feet before leaving the South End. She arranged the pillows to support her neck comfortably and found something on the television from which she could easily fade away as her lack of sleep enveloped her.

She was too tired to relax into her subconscious. She numbly watched the romantic comedy on the television while her mind toyed with the idea of sitting up to organize the books Meg left on the coffee table. Her eyes were heavy, making the images on the television blur. She vaguely understood the storyline… college friends who separated over the years and then found each other as well as the unspoken attraction that hadn't disappeared in the years of separation… or something like that. She let her eyes close and saw a warm orange settle into view. She felt herself falling backwards, but then opened her eyes to finish watching the movie. It turned out the guy had a thing for her best friend all along. Not the girl. Lizzie didn't really like the movie all that much. She wanted the story to be different and decided to stop watching the television. She got off the couch and went into the dining room, where her friends were standing around a table full of food. They were laughing and talking. Davis turned around and pulled Lizzie into the circle. She saw Ben immediately across the table. He smiled at her. She didn't want to look at him, annoyed by his cold reception at the funeral. He offered her a glass of wine and said, "I'm sorry." The other people in the room seemed to fade away. He took her hand and led her out of the room into the hallway. Only it wasn't her hallway. It was a big old house… was she at work? Was a tour about to come through? They couldn't be found talking. Lizzie pulled his hand out of the hallway into the living room, where a different movie was on the television. Meg was sitting on the couch with Alec asking Lizzie to get out of the way. She was watching vampire films for research. Lizzie sat herself in the chair and started watching, remembering that she was once in a vampire film and played a girl who was killed by a vampire. She remembered that Ben was there with her, but when she looked up…

Lizzie felt a sudden jolt to her body and woke harshly to a rock song blaring on a car commercial. "Hey sleepyhead," Meg set a glass of water on the coffee table.

"Hey," Lizzie sat herself up groggily. Darkness settled into the room. "What time is it?"

"Five-thirty," Meg picked a couple books off the table. "When did you get home?"

"Noon," Lizzie took up the glass that Meg left on the table.

"You're still in your dress," Meg smirked.

"Yeah… well…" Lizzie didn't have the alacrity to offer a snappy reply. "Where's Alec?'

"He went home an hour ago," Meg sat in the black chair by the fireplace.

"Oh," Lizzie set down her glass.

"So the gala was a success?"

"It was," Lizzie paused, knowing the detail for which Meg was waiting. "There was a good turnout."

"Any surgical interns?"

"He didn't come to the gala," Lizzie took a sip of her water. "But he picked me up after I shut down the reception table."

"You've been seeing him a lot lately."

"I'm not in a relationship with Eric," Lizzie said very purposefully.

"So … you don't like him?"

"He's attractive… I like him. I like being with him… for a little while, at least."

"Just a little while?"

"I don't think he's boyfriend material, Meg."

"Yeah… but he likes you."

Lizzie didn't want to say what was really on her mind. That she was still obsessing about her former high school classmate, who didn't have any interest in talking to her whatsoever and only visited her dreams. She couldn't admit that … even to Meg. Because even to Meg, it seemed foolish and deluded. And a little too close to her preoccupation with Will.

It was easier to explain that she had no interest in Eric beyond a couple nights a week than any element of truth relative to her heart.

"I'm not going to stop seeing him… I guess…" Lizzie was starting to wonder if Eric was taking things more seriously than she was. She had seen him more in the month since her fifteen minutes on the back deck with Mike. It kept her out of trouble and occupied her thoughts. But she didn't want it to be real.

"Maybe you've got the right idea, Lizzie. No attachment. Just love the ones you know will never love you back. That way you don't tease yourself with hope for something you won't get in return," Meg picked up one of her books and pursed her lips.

"Alec?"

"Mm," she nodded, still focused on the book.

"Why are you with him again?

"Because when it's good, he makes me… I feel at ease with him. We can talk about anything and everything. I feel comfortable in my skin when I am with him. He makes my skin feel real good…" Meg smiled to herself. "But when I'm not in his company, the spell wears off and he's…"

"Meg," Lizzie didn't know what to say. She wasn't qualified to give any relationship advice. Especially when her moral barometer was closer to Alec's than decency.

"I bet Eric made you feel good last night – even if it wasn't about your heart," Meg still stared at her book.

"He did," Lizzie admitted quietly.

"Yeah," Meg hesitated and set the book back on the table. "You know it's Valentine's Day today."

"I suppose it is," Lizzie groaned and leaned back against the pillows.

"I forgot about that," Meg sighed. Apparently, Alec had forgotten, too.

*****

Lizzie had a Saturday off from the Fulton House and chose to make use of the milder March weather with a lengthy run. She decided to train for another race. A local 10K. It wasn't a marathon, but something with which to occupy her time… and thoughts. Thoughts that tempted her after helping Nora address wedding invitations. Tempted her to remember feelings to which she didn't want to pay attention – wanting someone to take to Nora's wedding, that someone would look at her with as much appreciation for her company as her transfigured body, and the yearning to have someone beside her when she woke up in the morning. She didn't want to think about those things… especially when there were signs that Eric was interested in something more than a drink and his apartment.

She figured she would try a new route to challenge her muscles and provide enough distance to gauge her time for the 10K. She took the train across the river so she could run the Cambridge side of the Charles. She walked to the end of the Longfellow Bridge and started her run towards Harvard Square, losing her concentration to the beat of her music.

The song ended and changed to an 80's song. It reminded her of the reunion and took her out of her focus on the next benchmark. Why? Oh why… couldn't she let it go? It had been two months since she saw him at the funeral. He wasn't interested in talking to her. Why was she so interested in talking to him? Why? What was there to Ben Cottingham beyond some thrilling gymnastics after dancing to 80's songs for one night in November? What was it about him that made him latch into her memory and ache for realization?

He was attractive… but not in an obvious way. His russet hair and freckles weren't more impressive than… well than Eric's dark curls and chiseled jaw. Eric was a runner. Ben had strong shoulders. Eric was a doctor. Ben was an entrepreneur with technical genius. Maybe he lacked the skill with people that he had with machines… but Lizzie thought his conversation was compelling to keep her talking. For a couple hours, with the lubrication of much wine. Eric liked… what did he like? Other than her? He didn't go to museums or have interest in history. He didn't know that any part of Massachusetts existed outside of 128. Eric knew her and was interested in her. Ben only had an interest after Sara turned him away. But no matter the point of observation, both were attentive to her physically… and neither were part of her emotionally. Only one might want to change that. But it was the other with whom she wanted to explore it.

Why didn't she want Eric? Why the hell did she want Ben?

She was just being stupid. Eric was a real opportunity. And Ben… well… she couldn't really write him off as a failure. She failed to talk to him, too. Didn't she? Not that it would have mattered… not that it would have mattered if she ever spoke up to Will. He never wanted her. Ben didn't want her. But Lizzie was different when Will was in the picture. Now she was … running up and down the Charles. She still wasn't at her ideal weight, but she was pretty close. She looked good in a red dress and a black dress… and out of those dresses.

Lizzie felt the surge of endorphins as she saw a crowd of runners approach from the opposite direction. She leapt off the paved path and started running along the damp grass. She increased her speed and let the high empty her brain of all that stress. She was ready to run all the way back to Newton.

She landed her foot and slid on a patch of mud. Before she realized what was happening, she fell on the ground, with her right foot going in the opposite direction from the rest of her leg. She looked up quickly, tears filling her eyes. She felt stupid. So stupid. How many people saw her land on her ass? She looked and saw that everyone was walking, running, or cycling in an opposite direction from a view of her. She saw the cars pass on Memorial Drive and caught one driver looking at her.

The pain shot up her calf. She needed to get herself up. There was a bench a few feet away. She managed to pull herself up with her arms and good leg and limp over to the bench. She took out her earphones and shut her eyes, hoping that it would stop her from babbling like a baby. Why hadn't she brought her phone? She was at least a mile from the train. Probably two at this point. She could hail a taxi… if one passed by on the street. She didn't think she could stand that long. She didn't bring any cash. Just her Charlie card.

Her ankle really really hurt. It was probably just a sprain. She hoped. She tried to lift it to get a better look, but started to cry again as it smarted more. She set it down and took in a deep breath as a pair of walkers went by. She hated to be helpless. To look helpless. To not be able to take care of herself. She could do it. She just didn't know how…

"Elizabeth," a voice came behind her and numbed her completely.

"Ben."

"Are you okay?"

She was pretty sure her cheeks were already rosy from the exercise, but now they were flaming. "I…" she tried to think of a way to argue that she would be fine, but the tears were still wet on her cheeks. "I think I sprained my ankle."

He sat in front of her and lifted up her muddy shoe. How did he know which one to look at? He unlaced her sneaker and removed her sock. She felt his warm fingers against the throbbing joint. "I don't think it's broken," he looked up at her, revealing his gray green eyes she found so charming and unforgettable. "You would be howling right now if it were."

"Good," Lizzie said succinctly. "What are you doing here?"

"I live a few blocks down the road," he stood up slowly, still holding her sock and muddy sneaker.

"Oh," Lizzie felt suddenly very embarrassed, taking her sock and putting it into the sneaker. Would he think she decided to stalk him? "I thought I'd go for a run along the river."

"Yes," he was looking at the river. "Did you drive here?"

"No, I took the train," Lizzie looked down and decided to forsake her pride. "Can you – could you get me back to the train station?"

"I'll give you a ride home," he looked at her and smiled. "Unless you want to go to the emergency room?"

Lizzie shook her head. With her luck, she would end up having Eric examine her. Maybe this was her karma for avoiding her running partner. "You're sure it's not broken?"

"I'm sure," Ben smiled. "Do you mind sitting here while I get the car?"

"Yeah, of course," Lizzie bit her lip to stop the ridiculous tears she felt like letting out. She wasn't sure if it was the pain, the embarrassment, or the torture of being in his company.

She watched him walk away and disappear somewhere across Memorial Drive. She was happy to see him and excited that he wasn't just going to disappear. He was helping her… coming to her rescue… like some dopey fairy tale. Lizzie got annoyed with her thinking and grounded herself. Maybe it was a fortunate coincidence. Maybe it was an opportunity… an opportunity for her to say something to him.

She watched the runners go by and avoid the muddy patch into which she so blindly slipped. Her ankle still hurt. She tried not to think of it as she rehearsed ways of entreating Ben to seeing her again. Expressing her gratitude for his assistance and offering to buy him a drink – or dinner. Or… what did he like to do anyway?

"Hey," his voice called her back to the present. "Let me give you a hand."

Lizzie didn't speak and allowed Ben to pull her off the bench. He draped her left arm around him and guided her to his Prius, parked illegally on Memorial Drive. Luckily it was a Saturday and not rush hour. Even so, there were a lot of angry drivers irritated by his position. Ben didn't seem to mind and took his time easing her into the passenger seat. Soon enough he was beside her and starting the ignition.

"Where to?" he met her eyes briefly before getting back into the traffic.

"Newton. You can just cross the river and get on the Pike. Get off at the hotel exit… and that will get you pretty close to my apartment."

"That sounds easy enough."

"Thanks," Lizzie wasn't able to segue into her invitation.

"Not at all," Ben shook his head. "I wasn't going to leave you to hobble back to the T."

"I'm lucky you happened to walk by."

Ben took in a short breath. "Pretty lucky."

Lizzie didn't understand why he hesitated like that. Did he regret being her savior? She felt her confidence sink deep into her stomach.

"So are you training for another marathon?" he asked casually, as if it were an automated response to picking up women with sprained ankles.

"I'm running a 10K at the end of next month. Hopefully this will heal by then," Lizzie sighed as they crossed the Charles

"It takes four to six weeks to heal completely. You can get a brace and work back gradually," he said matter of factly and turned his head. "When's the race?"

"Six weeks."

"I'm sure you'll do okay. You've got strong muscle."

Lizzie bit her lip. Was that a compliment or a casual observation? "I work at a hospital," Lizzie laughed at herself. "I know a doctor or two."

"I know… just take it easy for the rest of the weekend," he cleared his throat. "Have you heard from Sara lately? How's she doing?"

Lizzie let out a sigh and with it her hopes for dinner. "She seems okay," Lizzie answered, not that she was an authority on how Sara was doing. Pretty much anyone who was a Facebook friend could deduce what she could tell Ben. "She had her baby."

"Oh?" Ben clearly didn't pay attention to Facebook.

"Jack and I talked about going to Connecticut to visit her," Lizzie continued. "But we haven't really gotten around to it."

"How's Jack? Have you been to see his band play recently?" he continued as though the questions were predetermined and the answers didn't really matter.

"Jack's all right. I haven't gone to see the band lately," she didn't want to think about the band… or the drummer. She looked away to the sign indicating the necessary exit.

"Send him my regards," Ben nodded as they took the exit. "You'll have to guide me from here."

Lizzie was glad to give up the conversation for navigation of the half miles and turns to her house. She didn't see Meg's car and figured Jackie wasn't apt to come down and help her up the stairs. Lizzie picked up her sneaker and looked at Ben. What would it hurt to ask him? Just to say thank you?

He looked straight ahead, through the windshield. His thoughts seemed to be somewhere beyond Jefferson Park or the fact that she was sitting beside him. Was he thinking back to his question about Sara? Or a regret that he ignited a conversation with a one night stand he preferred to let alone and ignore? Lizzie was sure she had his expression on herself when she left Jack's house that January night.

"Elizabeth," he began and let a deadening silence rest between them. "I…"

"Thank you so much for driving me home. I'm sorry if I got mud on your seat," Lizzie said quickly and opened the door to get herself out. Before she knew it, he was beside her to help her out of the seat.

"You need to keep the pressure off your ankle," he lifted her into his arms. He took the key from her hand and carried her up the stairs. He settled her softly back on her good foot, slowly unwinding his arms from her side. She was very close to him. Almost touching her torso against his. She could feel his breath against her exposed neck. She wanted to kiss him. She didn't want to kiss him. She couldn't do that to herself and let him walk away. He would walk away. She saw that in his vacant gaze out the windshield. She wanted to kiss him very very badly. She felt herself slowly lean a little closer as the door to the bathroom opened at the end of the hall.

Lizzie stepped back and remembered the pain of her ankle. Jackie came into view and quickly surveyed the situation. "Hi Jackie," Lizzie recovered herself. "This is my friend, Ben."

Jackie narrowed her dark eyes with semi interest. "What happened to you?"

"I slipped when I went running and hurt my ankle."

"Oh," Jackie's unpleasantness softened into sympathy. "Let me get you some ice."

"You should get off that foot, Elizabeth," Ben urged as Jackie left for the kitchen. His eyes looked at her... was it sadness or pity that reflected against their green tint?

"Yeah," she locked his gaze for a few seconds, feeling another urge to leap at him for a kiss as Jackie returned with a bag of frozen vegetables.

"We don't have peas," she laughed. "But I think broccoli will work. We forgot to fill the ice trays."

"Broccoli will work," Ben winked and went down the stairs.

"Thanks, Ben," Lizzie said softly and let Jackie guide her to the sofa.

Chapter Seven

Lizzie looked at the Facebook updates and switched back to her word document. She had been alternating screens every five minutes for two weeks now. There was never anything indicating the presence of Ben on the social networking site. Nothing to reveal what he was doing since he left her at the top of her stairs. Nothing in her inbox to ask if she felt better. It was a foolish habit and just made the day drag even more.

She started typing a status update about her boredom but was distracted when the door to the office opened, ushering in Richard, Dr. Chiang, and their lunch partner. "Lizzie, you know Gerard Fulton," Richard approached Lizzie's desk after taking Gerard's coat.

"You're the girl from the house," Gerard paused to recognize her with his waspy blue eyes. It wasn't a look of admiration.

Lizzie forced her smile. "Yes I work there on alternate Saturdays," Lizzie held out her hand kindly.

"We are lucky to have Lizzie on staff," Richard said as his phone rang. "She has told us many interesting facts about your ancestors."

Lizzie smiled at Gerard and Dr. Chiang as Richard politely excused himself to take his call. She wondered if the Fulton heir was as charmed by Dr. Chiang as everyone else when a pager buzzed the surgeon's coat pocket. Lizzie directed her to another desk and phone to use, leaving Lizzie alone with Gerard Fulton. She tried not to linger too long in awkward silence, knowing how important Gerard's money was to the hospital. "Have you visited Brattle Street recently, Mr. Fulton?" she asked politely.

"Not since the end of the summer, I'm afraid," he actually seemed to perk up at the opportunity to discuss the house.

"I was there last Saturday. I always like the early spring in that house. The light seems to best highlight some details in March and April – before all the leaves block out the sun," Lizzie smiled, but was uncertain when he offered nothing to fill the next silence. "Do you know who Lotty might be?"

"Lotty?"

"A few months back, my manager showed me a letter that Harriet had written to someone named Lotty," Lizzie was inspired by her preoccupation with the Fulton daughter.

"That was probably Charlotte," Gerard stated the fact proudly. "The wife of Horace, John's son from his first marriage."

"Oh," Lizzie felt satisfaction for both intriguing him in conversation and answering a minor mystery. It was something she could include on the tour. She had it straight from the mouth of a Fulton.

"She was English," Gerard continued. "I can't remember the history of her family. Horace started to invest in a ship building company south of Boston, but he died before making his own fortune."

"I didn't know that," Lizzie responded. She actually didn't want to know that.

"I didn't know there was such a letter," Gerard said abruptly.

"Yes, it is in the museum archives."

"Hm," Gerard muttered. "Harriet married Lazarus Benedict. He was from the North Shore."

"We don't know very much about Harriet," Lizzie commented hopefully.

"It is a pity about that chair," Gerard looked at her.

"The chair?"

"In Harriet's room. It gets far too much exposure from the sun. It is a fine piece. You must do something about preserving it."

"Yes," Lizzie smiled empathetically.

"Tell Jonathan he should get some better shades for that room," Gerard advised as Dr. Chiang returned to the conversation.

"I will," Lizzie assented, even though she seldom had reason to speak with the curator never mind the authority to tell him how to maintain the property.

"Gerard, I apologize for that," Dr. Chiang interrupted.

"That's all right. Leslie is very kind."

"Yes, Lizzie is very helpful," Dr. Chiang smiled once more before leading him into Richard's office.

Lizzie laughed to herself and returned to her computer as Richard closed the door. She sat back at her computer, with no added tasks from her idling before. She clicked over to Google and typed in Charlotte

Fulton. She saw a genealogy page that confirmed she was married to Horace Fulton, son of John and his first wife, Caroline. There was a link to an art collection, tracing the original purchase back to a Charlotte Fulton in 1858. Lizzie wasn't sure if it was the same Charlotte Fulton. Perhaps. But… not much else. She clicked on the image option – just in case there was some random portrait out there. There were a lot of modern photos of Charlottes and Fultons… but no Charlotte Fulton. On the next page, she found a silent movie star in a mysterious black and white photo. Lizzie clicked on that picture and found a profile. That Charlotte Fulton appeared in a number of films in the 20's of which Lizzie had never heard. Well… she had some more information, but nothing interesting or in depth enough for a good story on her tour. All she could say, really, was that Harriet wrote A letter ONCE to her sister in law. Not really that exciting.

Lizzie remembered there was another name in the letter. Mr. Chester. She typed in Charlotte Fulton Chester in the search icon. Another genealogy page showed up. There were too many words and too many names for Lizzie to understand how they all connected to one another. She scrolled down to find Charlotte Fulton or Chester. Her eyes froze on the sight of Benjamin Chester. Her heart skipped as her cheeks flushed immediately. So much for distracting herself from those thoughts.

She clicked out of Google and back to Facebook. A red notification popped up to say she was tagged in a few photos someone finally put from the reunion. She was in three of them. There was one with Sara. One with Dan and Delany Stewart. And one with Ben. She lingered on that image and let herself be mesmerized by the happiness of the gray green eyes. She liked how she looked in that picture. The multiple glasses of wine didn't show. She looked… happy. Like he did. They looked like… a couple.

She habitually clicked to see who else was logged on. She saw Ben's name. Was he looking at the picture of them together and thinking… what might he be thinking? Lizzie went back to the picture and selected the link to his profile from his tag. It looked as though he caught up with his negligence of Facebook within the past ten minutes. He was friends with ten new people… including Delany Stewart. There wasn't much else. Nothing to show what he was thinking. She looked over to his profile and saw the same succinct explanations for his place of employment and education. He hadn't revealed his interests, activities, music, or films. She went back to the picture of them together and saw he removed the tag identifying himself.

Lizzie's heart sank. It was so silly and so relatively minor. But… why didn't he want the Facebook world to see him partnered with her? Did they look too much like a couple? Did he not want anyone in particular to see that and get the wrong impression? A girlfriend he already had? Or… God forbid… a wife?

She shut her eyes and took in a deep breath as the door to Richard's office opened. Dr. Chiang hastened back to the desk to make another phone call. Richard escorted Gerard to his coat and thanked him for his time. Gerard Fulton nodded to Lizzie, muttering something else about the chair in Harriet's room. All the words blended together, but she managed to force a smile and keep her eyes dry enough to not make the wretchedness she felt more obvious.

"He was impressed with you, Lizzie," Richard's words were clear as he came over to her desk, landing a small piece of paper in front of her.

Lizzie looked down at the check for fifty thousand dollars. She managed to place herself back to the hospital for a few seconds and met Richard's eyes. "That was generous of him."

"And it's just the first installment," Richard winked. "Make sure you follow up about that chair business if you can. Mt. Elm will appreciate it."

"Yeah," Lizzie said mechanically.

"If you want to type up the thank you letter, you can leave early this afternoon," Richard offered.

"Thanks," Lizzie smiled and made herself close the Internet browser and go back into Word.

"A success," Dr. Chiang took Richard's hand before he returned to his office and shut the door. Lizzie looked away from her computer to Dr. Chiang lingering by the desk. "Do you like working at the Fulton House?"

Lizzie was startled by the sudden question and didn't know how to quiet her thoughts to register an honest answer. Just a polite, simple, "Yes."

"Maybe I'll take a tour someday. I've heard so much about it."

Lizzie resisted the disbelief from registering on her face. Lizzie knew she had reason to flatter Gerard Fulton about his family's history… but why offer Lizzie the insincere comment about hearing so much about a museum people only discovered by accident or through tourist guides? Lizzie took in a deep breath, annoyed with her peevish lack of patience. She shouldn't jeopardize her professional relationships because she was insulted by Ben Cottingham. "I'd be happy to give you a tour sometime."

"Enjoy your afternoon off," Dr. Chiang left the office.

Lizzie watched the door close and reached for her phone. She found Eric's number and pressed send.

*****

Lizzie gazed through the large windows at the view of the Charles. She always thought the image of Boston from across the river was breathtaking, even at three in the morning when her breath had already been vigorously spent. She wondered if they should have closed the blinds… not that anyone was looking across the river to see what was happening on the fifteenth floor.

She wanted to leave, even though she felt badly that Eric splurged on a hotel room when they could have easily gone back to either apartment. It was a nice variation to their routine, but not enough to quiet her mind enough to allow sleep. Not enough comfort to make her want to stay beside him.

He was sleeping. The room was silent except for the faded echo of a car horn. The view was… the evening was worth it to have that view of the city in the darkness of pre-dawn. She couldn't feel the stiffness of her ankle anymore. It wasn't a bad evening. It wasn't an awkward morning. It just wasn't… it wasn't… it wasn't what she wanted. It wasn't Ben.

She stared at the silver waters reflecting the street lamps and lights of the boats along the river. She watched the boats, some in shadow. Some were lit by a lantern. She saw the ferry move across the river. Then she saw him, standing at the edge of the water. His feet were in the marshes. She walked towards him, knowing she would get her feet wet. She saw the russet hair and waited for him to turn around and look at her with the green eyes. She reached out to touch his shoulder and when he turned around he laughed. Nobody laughed at her jokes. Not even Jack. Jack leaned forward over his lunch tray and rolled his eyes at her lame punch line. Sara smiled politely, but she could tell she wanted to roll her eyes at Ben. Lizzie was annoyed. Annoyed that Sara could determine what was funny at their table. Then why was Ben laughing at her joke? He was always nice to her. Nice so she would convince Sara to give him a second look. Convince her to let him take her to the prom. Then he would give her a corsage of lilies. Lilies. Lilies were Lizzie's flower. Not Sara's.

Lizzie opened her eyes. The sun reflected off the blue river straight into her pupils. She rolled away from the window and let the images of her dream collect before falling away from her memory. Was it a memory? Sitting across from Ben in the cafeteria as he laughed at a joke Sara didn't think was funny. To impress her so that she would convince Sara to go to the prom with him. Or was she just wishing he was he trying to impress her?

She tried to hold onto the images of her dream as she turned onto her back and saw Eric's smiling eyes. "Good morning."

"Morning," she wished the sound of her voice didn't break the spell of her dream.

"I have a surgery this morning," he grinned.

"Okay," she shut her eyes to try to bring back the Springs' cafeteria.

"I'm off tonight. How about dinner?'

She opened her lids to the attention of his dark eyes. It was a genuine invitation. Not a spontaneous drink. Not the impulse to stay at a hotel. Or maybe the hotel was part of it? Had he been waiting to ask this question for a while and planned out the detail? "Eric, I..."

He sat up and took her hand so she would do the same. "What if we take a couple steps back and just go on a date?"

"I don't..."

"We can still... we can still end up in the same place. I just thought maybe we could make this a little more serious."

"No," she was surprised the answer came so bluntly from her lips. She was too tired to control herself.

"I like being with you, Lizzie," she watched him curl his dark hand around her pale fingers.

"I don't want to date," she couldn't buffer herself.

"But don't you want to… I mean you're 33. Don't you want a family?"

She retracted her hand. "That's not what this was about, Eric."

"It could be."

"I'm not good enough for you," she shut her eyes. "I'm a bad… I would be a bad girlfriend."

"Not if you let yourself … let's just try it."

"I'm sorry Eric. I'm sorry if I led you on. I… I…" she stopped the temptation to be completely honest with a look at his eyes. He really liked her. For a few seconds she let herself imagine the possibility. She could be one of the doctors' wives for whom Andrew wanted to cater. "I'm flattered. But I don't… I think we should stop seeing one another."

"Oh."

"I really should get to work," Lizzie left the bed clumsily and went quickly to the bathroom.

She took a shower and didn't fuss too much when putting her clothes back on. She wasn't eager to impress anyone with her appearance at the hospital. It was going to just be a day she had to get through. She left the bathroom and saw Eric sitting in a chair by the window, looking at the Charles River. He turned to her, the invitation still hopeful in his eyes.

"I'm sorry," Lizzie grabbed her bag and coat. "I'm really sorry, Eric," she said a final time and walked out the door.

Chapter Eight

Lizzie looked at her watch in between sips of water. She resisted the letdown as she emptied the bottle and tossed it in the recycle bin. She walked a few yards and turned back to where she was waiting.

"Lizzie!" Meg shouted through the crowd of spectators and runners.

Lizzie shut her eyes and breathed out relief. "Hey."

"Congratulations!" Meg hugged her, forcing Lizzie to put pressure on her exhausted ankle.

"Did you just get here?" Lizzie tried not to let the pain make her voice too sour.

"Kinda. Well, it took me forever to find a parking spot. And even then, it's a couple blocks from here," Meg offered sheepishly as she handed Lizzie another water bottle and her bag. "I should have left the house earlier."

"It's all right," Lizzie prepared to start the walk back towards the car.

"You made better time than you thought?" Meg tried to deflect the culpability.

"Ten minute miles," Lizzie breathed out. "Not bad considering my ankle."

"Your ankle is okay?" Meg frowned.

"It's all right. It will be fine when we get back to the car."

"Why don't you go sit over on that bench? I can bring the car around. It just might take a few minutes to get around the road that's still blocked off for the finish line."

Lizzie nodded, willing to be a wimp and indulge her ankle. She ignored the instinct to limp. Her legs pulled through six ten minute miles. Not bad. There would be friends and dinner to make her forget the resurgence of swelling. She rubbed the sweat off her forehead, breathing in deep. She lifted her glance towards the bench and saw the gray green eyes looking at her. She quickly changed her direction towards him and felt the stiffness of her ankle melt away with the eagerness of her steps. He looked the same, his freckles still obvious under his eyes. “Ben, what a surprise,” Lizzie concentrated on a determination to be kind.

“I saw your Facebook status and thought I would witness you overcome your injury,” he smiled graciously.

“Oh,” Lizzie was startled by his answer, not sure if it was because he paid attention to her update, or because he was checking on her ankle six weeks later.

“You did it. Even with a slight malfunction,” he smiled, making her forget everything that upset her in the months since the reunion.

“It’s still not perfect,” she concentrated her pressure on her right foot so her pain wouldn’t give her away. “But better.”

“Well, congrats,” he touched her arm. “I imagine you… well done, Elizabeth.”

“Um, listen, we’re heading back to my place for spaghetti and drinks. Just a small group of friends. You wanna come? It should be fun. My friend Davis is always entertaining,” Lizzie offered. “I still owe you for giving me a ride home.”

“You don’t owe me. I was glad to help you,” he paused and shifted to a smile. It wasn’t a real smile. “Thanks for the invitation. I would like… but I don’t think I will be able to.”

“Oh,” she felt the pain creep back into her memory.

“Maybe some other time,” he nodded as Lizzie’s bag started ringing. Ben looked at the satchel dangling from the clutches of her hand. She couldn’t ignore it. She looked for the phone and saw Andrew’s name come up. Ben nodded as he touched her shoulder again and walked away.

Lizzie let out a sigh and flipped open her phone. “Hi,” her eyes followed Ben until he faded amongst the crowd of runners and spectators and water bottles.

“Lizzie,” Andrew’s voice was foreboding of disappointment. “You’re done?”

“I’m waiting for Meg to bring the car,” she sighed, looking towards the bench that was now occupied.

“Congratulations,” he lacked enthusiasm.

“What’s up?”

“Davis is sick,” Andrew sighed. “He hasn’t been able to eat all day. I would leave him but he … well, you know how he gets.”

"No worries. I don't think I'm good company right now anyway," Lizzie took the patience out of her answer.

"What happened, lovely?"

"Just my ankle flaring up," she looked towards the road, hoping Meg would appear soon.

"Maybe tomorrow?"

"Plans with Nora."

"Well, some time this week. I will cook you a fabulous dinner."

"Yeah, sure," Lizzie said quickly seeing Meg's red Focus. "Meg's here. Talk to you later."

"Call me tonight if you need to bitch."

"Tell Davis I hope he feels better," Lizzie closed her phone and walked to meet Meg's car.

"I would have pulled up closer," Meg said as Lizzie put on her seatbelt.

"Andrew just called to cancel," Lizzie explained before Meg could question her sour mood and infer any other cause.

"That's too bad."

"So I guess it's just us," Lizzie leaned her head back and closed her lids. All she could see was the gray green eyes.

"Alec called."

"Mm?"

"He wants to go to a movie."

"Well, we can eat early."

"The movie is at five-thirty. So… well, seeing that we're having dinner with Nora tomorrow…"

"I'll just go home and take a shower."

"Sorry Lizzie," Meg sighed. Lizzie didn't answer. She just kept her eyes closed to dry the tears before they had a chance to escape.

*****

Lizzie didn't know if the quiet of the apartment was a blessing or a curse. She wasn't doing much to take the pressure off her ankle. She lingered an extra ten minutes under the steam of her shower. Then she cooked her small bowl of spaghetti. She went for sauce in a jar and frozen meatballs. Not the fancier version she planned with Andrew… but it refueled her weary limbs. She cleaned up the kitchen and was contemplating one of Meg's DVDs when the doorbell rang.

She felt the swollen joint as she walked down the steps and had to pause before reaching for the door. She forgot the irritation and almost lost her breath completely when she saw Ben on the other side of the door with a bottle of wine. "I hope it's not too late to change my mind," he smiled.

"Well," somehow she laughed. "Actually my friends were sick. And Meg went out with her boyfriend. So… there's no dinner."

She breathed out, hoping he didn't think she made up the dinner story to lure him back to her apartment. But he came to her apartment. He remembered where she lived. He changed his mind. "We can still have wine," he offered, not lifting his gray green eyes. Lizzie realized she was in jeans and a t-shirt. Her hair was still wet from her shower. She was barefoot and didn't… well, she was more attractive than the last two times he saw her – sweaty and muddy after a run.

"Come on up," she turned around and went back up the stairs.

Lizzie let herself pause in the doorway with the two wine glasses and bottle to take in the reality of the moment. He stood by the mantelpiece of their inactive fireplace. He was in her living room. He accepted her invitation. He came to see her at the end of her race. He came because he thought she wanted that. She felt giddy and unreal… and suddenly very foolish and guilty for letting herself doubt.

He sensed her presence and turned to her frozen stance. He took the glasses from her hand and paused. "Is everything all right? How's the ankle?"

"It's been better," she smiled and set the Malbec on the coffee table. Lizzie sat in front of the table and silently filled the two glasses. She offered him one and took a large sip from her own.

"Where is your roommate?" he disturbed the silence without taking a sip from his glass.

"I have two roommates," Lizzie explained. "Jackie – the one you met – is visiting her sister this weekend. My other roommate, Meg, is the one who went to the movies with her boyfriend."

"It's a nice apartment," he looked around the room and settled on the couch beside her. Lizzie was glad she cleaned in anticipation of guests.

She managed to hide away all of Meg's vampire novels and washed all the dirty wine glasses.

"Yeah," Lizzie nodded. "There's a lot of space for three people. I like the fact we have two floors. I really like the spiral staircase."

"That is a nice touch," Ben agreed. "It's always been the three of you?"

"Well, originally it was Meg, myself, and our friend Nora. We all worked together at an historic village during college and decided to get an apartment together."

"One of your other museums?"

"Yeah. We used to dress up in period costume and give tours in character. We had a lot of laughs together and learned how to deal with stress. I think it was a pretty easy transition to living together. I'm lucky to have such good friends."

"You are," Ben set his glass down. "Do you all still work in museums?"

"I'm the only one. Meg is perpetually in grad school, teaching undergrads and writing another thesis. Nora became a middle school teacher. She's the most grownup of us. She actually got a fiancé and moved out."

"So Jackie moved in."

"Yup." she saw his gaze and then dropped her eyes to her wine.

"Did you study history in college?" Ben broke another awkward silence.

"I did," Lizzie took another sip.

"You read a lot in high school."

"I still do," she lifted her eyes to him, curious at the observation. "It keeps life interesting when my job is so dull."

"You think your job is dull?"

"Dreadful."

He lingered his gaze on her eyes for a second and shifted towards the coffee table where she rested her feet. "Your ankle is swollen," he observed. "Do you have an Ace bandage?"

"I do," she muttered into a sip of wine. "On the shelf over the bathroom sink."

She drank the rest of her glass and a sip of another before he came back with the Ace bandage she abandoned a week ago. He sat back at her side and turned her legs so they rested in his lap. She watched him silently as he slowly pressed his fingers into the bottom of her foot, concentrating his thumb inside her arch. She felt the wine warm her skin and breathed deeply as he progressed down to her heel.

"How did you end up at Mt. Elm?"

"Money," she shrugged and took another sip as he started to wrap the Ace bandage around her relaxed ankle. "I worked on fundraisers at all the museums. It wasn't a lot of skill to switch the concept to hospitals."

"But it's boring."

"Hellishly boring."

"Why don't you do something else?"

"I've thought about…" she watched him circle the bandage around her foot. "I don't… I don't think I'm all that qualified."

He fastened the bandage and lifted his eyes to her. "Qualified for what?"

Lizzie looked at her wineglass. She didn't know how to answer that. It was a relatively simple question. It was an answer she would have easily found had Andrew not bailed and stayed home. If Andrew hadn't stayed home with Davis, she wouldn't be sitting with her legs across Ben's lap on her second glass of wine. "I…" she muttered, looking at her hands. Suddenly his hands were unclasping the glass and taking it away from her to put on the table. He moved his hands to her chin and pulled her against his lips for a lengthy kiss.

He pulled back from her and slid her feet back onto the floor. He moved a dangling strand away from her eyes and held onto the side of her face. "I keep thinking about you, Elizabeth," he whispered. Lizzie kissed him again, unable to think how to answer the echo of her own feeling. She pressed herself against him, forcing him towards the sofa. She lifted herself onto his lap and pulled back from the kiss to look at him and his green gray eyes.

She started to unbutton his shirt and leaned back towards him, kissing his mouth, across his cheek, down to his neck. She felt him breathe in and out against her own neck. "I tried not," he breathed. "I tried not to do this."

Lizzie didn't understand what he was saying. She figured it was the wine or just the elation of the moment clouding her head too quickly. She lifted her face and kissed his mouth again. "I'm glad you changed your mind," she met his stare and stopped undoing his buttons. She smoothed along his temples. "Do you really…" she couldn't stop her eyes from welling. "Am I really what you've wanted all this time?"

He took hold of her face gently and kissed her again. She barely noticed his hands leave her cheeks and slip under her thighs as he lifted her and carried her up the spiral staircase.

*****

Lizzie heard the doorbell ring as she stepped out the shower. She threw on a towel and ran down the stairs, her wet hair dripping on her shoulders. Nora laughed as she opened the door. "I always forget traffic is better on Sunday afternoons," she offered.

"Meg is still at Alec's," Lizzie took one of the dresses and walked with Nora up the stairs.

"Is she on her way?" Nora asked as they got to the top of the staircase.

"I just came back from a run," Lizzie tightened her towel after hanging the dress up on the coat rack.

"Another run? The day after your race? I take it the ankle is back to normal," Nora took the sheeting off of Lizzie's dress. "Don't bother getting dressed. Go put this on."

Lizzie went back to the bathroom and put up her wet hair in a clip before trying on the dress. The burgundy material fitted her frame flawlessly. She rushed back out to the hallway to show Nora. "It's perfect," she beamed.

"It is," Nora grinned as she unclipped Lizzie's wet hair to see it on her shoulders. "No, I think we should see your shoulders."

"Are you wearing yours up or down?" Lizzie let herself wander over to the mirror in the hallway. She once avoided it at all costs.

"Up," Nora put the clip back in her hair. "How did it go yesterday?"

"I made good time," Lizzie turned away from the mirror.

"And you decided to go for a run today."

"Ben came to see me."

"Ben? High school Ben?" Nora smiled. She was impressed by the story of his chivalry on Memorial Drive.

"Yes," Lizzie smoothed along the skirt.

"Did you know he was coming?"

"I didn't know he was there until I was waiting for Meg to bring the car."

"And?"

"He ended up coming over last night," Lizzie couldn't prevent the smile that eked across her chin as she heard the door at the bottom of the stairs.

"Are you going to see him again?" Nora asked, unmoved by the sound at the door.

"I hope so," Lizzie smiled and ignored the lump of doubt that prompted her to run on her bandaged ankle. Ben was gone when she woke up. She didn't know how she should feel about that when he made her so happy by coming to her apartment. When he said that he couldn't stop thinking about her…

"Oh my God, Lizzie!" Meg got to the top of the staircase. "You look amazing!"

"Thanks," Lizzie let the praise warm her memory and fade out the sickening sense of uncertainty.

"There is no way my dress is going to look that good on me," Meg dropped her bag and went to her dress on the coat rack.

"I think you might be surprised, Meg," Nora offered. "Margie did an amazing job with the dresses. You should see Becca's."

Meg took her dress off the hook and disappeared down the hall into the bathroom. Lizzie turned back to her reflection once more. She let Ben slip back into her mind and hoped that he might be able to see her in that dress. "You know, Nora," Lizzie sighed at her reflection. "I think I really like him."

"Ben?"

"Yeah," Lizzie shut her eyes accepting the fact she just made it real. She hoped that by wishing it she didn't just curse it by making it too much like her last wish for a man for whom she let herself feel.

"He would be a fool to walk away from you."

"A fool," Lizzie repeated to her reflection in near silence.

"Hey, I think you got a bug bite," Nora said suddenly.

"What?" Lizzie turned away from the mirror.

"At the base of your neck," Nora touched a spot that Lizzie couldn't see in the mirror or her periphery. "You don't feel it?"

"No."

"Actually, you've got two of them."

"Is it really obvious?"

"No," Nora laughed. "That's a funny place for a bug bite."

"Something probably found me while I was running."

"Maybe it's the Chicken Pox."

"I had those when I was seven," Lizzie looked at the mirror trying to see what she knew she couldn't.

Meg came down the hallway, beaming at the fit of her own maroon dress. "Margie is a genius."

Nora smiled. "I am going to have beautiful photographs!" she exclaimed.

Lizzie caught the contagious elation of her friends and let it fuel her hope that there would be much more to smile about in June.

Chapter Nine

He disappeared. Well, it seemed like it. She knew he was probably somewhere in Cambridge living his life as usual, going to his office and back to wherever he lived in Central Square. But there was no word from him, no confirmation of the fact that he really was thinking about her. That he wanted to talk to her again. No email. Nothing on Facebook. Not even a phone call. Not that she had given him her number. But it couldn't be that difficult to find it if he wanted to contact her.

Lizzie spent a week talking herself in and out of all sorts of possibilities. She idled over Facebook and Google looking at whatever the name Ben Cottingham yielded. Nothing proved anything. She saw no evidence that he was married. He wasn't gay. She knew that for sure. She didn't know why he left without goodbye. Or why he hadn't bothered to make any contact since. Was he going to wait another six weeks and show up spontaneously with a bottle of wine to check on her ankle? Was she going to wait another six weeks for him?

She wanted to see him. She didn't want to send a message across Facebook and not be able to see the expression when he saw her name in his inbox. She wanted to catch him in the moment and see if he was glad to see her. Or if he had an impulse to run away. She couldn't just keep hoping for another sudden appearance. She wasn't running any races in the near future. She thought briefly about finding one and posting it on Facebook to lure him with another update. She didn't want to resort to deceit… not yet. She knew he lived somewhere close to the Charles River. She could at least run there and hope that whatever led him to walk a few blocks from his house on a Saturday afternoon would lead him to cross her path again. Maybe. It was a stretch, but it would be good exercise… for her ankle.

She directed herself towards the JFK Bridge. With each step, she let her mind go back and replay the night in her apartment over and over. He said he couldn't stop thinking about her. Then he said he tried not to… to what? To see her? To obsess about her? To bring a bottle of wine to her apartment? To seduce her? To stay away? What did he mean? If he wanted to stay away, why did he show up after saying he couldn't come to dinner? Why didn't he stay away?

Why didn't he contact her? He knew how to find her. He knew where she lived. He knew she was on Facebook. Was he still trying to talk himself out of whatever it was that he was trying not to do? Maybe it was Sara. Maybe he didn't want to go back down that road to Springs. Who could blame him? He had a successful business in Boston. He didn't need to look back.

She turned around at the Harvard Bridge and headed back towards the train. Maybe she wouldn't see him. She would have to email him. She wasn't going to allow another week to pass without giving herself the opportunity to ask him these questions that she asked over and over. Never mind her own question. If it was a real possibility, would she stay? Or would she find a reason to run away?

She passed the Mass Ave. Bridge when she saw him. She didn't see his face, but she knew it was him. He was walking away from her, at a pretty brisk pace. She increased her run to a sprint and then slowed when she was a few feet from him. As if sensing her, he turned suddenly and gave her the reaction she hoped to see. He smiled.

"Hey Ben," she took out her earphones.

"Elizabeth," he responded. "I see your ankle is doing very well."

"It is," she felt the runner's high release her grin without any effort.

She saw the breeze ruffle his short hair. He closed his eyes for a brief second as if collecting a thought. He stepped back from her and looked down the river. "I'm glad to see you," he finally looked back at her.

"Me too," she was confused by his look and increased distance. The oxygen drain from her head often impaired her perception. She felt the endorphin rush fuel her confidence. "Maybe we could get dinner some time?"

Ben looked down the river a second time. "Lizzie," he startled her with her nickname.

She felt the coolness enter her brain. There was something holding him back. Damn it. She didn't care. "I feel badly that you showed up and there was no dinner last week. I also appreciate your attention to my ankle.

Whatever you did made it feel much better. You don't know how much that meant to me," she smiled.

He looked at her intently. She sensed the urge she felt at the top of the stairs when he brought her home. She wanted to go towards him and pull him into her kiss. She was about to take a step when he lifted his hand and ran his fingers through his hair. He moved his face back towards the water, but she could tell he was still looking at her. She knew he desired her. She knew that much was true. If that was all… if she was to him just what Eric was to her… maybe… maybe that would be okay.

"I saw that you are going to see Jack's band next weekend," he turned back to face her.

"What?" Lizzie was surprised by the fact he knew that. Facebook. "Oh yeah. Yeah, on Friday."

"I'd like to see the band. And go with you," he smiled. "I'll drive."

"To Worcester?"

"I'd enjoy your company," he returned his smile to the one she saw at the beginning of the conversation.

"Okay," Lizzie nodded. "Pick me up at… seven? That should get us there by 8. Jack's band goes on at 10. The opening band is pretty decent, too."

"Sounds good," the strain returned to his face. "Listen, I have to get to an appointment. I'll see you on Friday."

"Yeah," Lizzie nodded and put her earphones in to stop herself from lunging at him. She picked up her feet and ran back to the train. She was elated and confused. She didn't understand his restraint. There was honesty in his reaction. She knew in spite of whatever he was hiding, he was happy to see her.

*****

Lizzie decided on jeans and a sleeveless shirt. She told herself she wouldn't care so much, but she changed her outfit several times and would have continued to be indecisive if the doorbell didn't ring. She let Meg answer it, knowing she was eager to meet the guy who made Lizzie blush.

Lizzie didn't tell Meg or Nora about Ben's mysterious behavior, but figured the observation of one of them might help with some perspective.

"Hi Ben," Lizzie came into the living room.

"Hi," Ben turned around and grinned at her. Lizzie saw Meg's nod of approval over his shoulder and rested her gaze on Ben's friendly eyes.

"You've met Meg," Lizzie felt her whole body lighten.

"She was just telling me about her thesis," Ben made a strange smile. Lizzie couldn't tell if it was amusement, approval, or the attempt to curb himself from laughing outright. Lizzie noticed all the books spread on the table and realized how the topic probably came up.

"He actually recommended a couple books I have never heard of," Meg explained her enthusiasm.

"That's impressive," Lizzie warmed at the fact that he was in her living room, talking with her best friend, and still looking at her with admiration. "I didn't know you were a fan of gothic literature."

"I've had time to read a few genres."

"Really?" Lizzie was surprised to hear a man who built and managed his own company spent time reading literature.

"Yes," Ben came to her side and touched her elbow. "We should probably get going. Meg, it was wonderful to meet you."

"The same," Meg looked at Lizzie one more time before they went down the stairs.

Lizzie let him open the car door for her. Normally she hated that gesture. It was too old fashioned. With Ben it seemed charming, not patronizing. She watched him sit beside her. He looked tired. His skin was paler, making the freckles more pronounced under his eyes. He turned those eyes to her as he fastened his seat belt. The gray seemed to overtake the green. He looked… nervous. Lizzie knew she should say something, anything to start the conversation and stifle the oppressive silence that had overtaken the car. "Weather's nice, huh?"

"It is a nice night."

"The moon is supposed to be full, I think," Lizzie felt like a dork. Was she trying to sound too desperate for a story out of a romance novel?

"It's the perfect temperature. Not too warm, not too cold," he started the ignition.

"The way May is supposed to be."

“I don’t expect anything of May weather. It’s always different. Sometimes hot. It’s even snowed.”

Lizzie tried to remember a May when it snowed. “Well, I brought a sweater just in case,” she was impatient with herself for her lame conversation.

“So, you’ve been to a lot of Jack’s gigs?”

“Yeah. I don’t know if you remember the band he tried to start in high school. Most of those guys moved away after college. Just Mike…” Lizzie paused, wondering if Ben remembered Mike from his friendship with Oliver. She didn’t want to remind him or remind herself of the conversation on the back deck of Jen and Jack’s house. Or the wordless fifteen minutes after. She wasn’t sure how much of her history she should reveal at this point, if ever. “Mike’s the drummer. Anyway, after Jack and Jen had Zach, they got serious and recruited some other musicians. They’ve been together for about ten years. I think they are pretty decent, even if I’m family. “

“It’s good to see he is still devoted to it. I remember his love of guitar back in high school.”

“Yeah. Jen really supports him. Have you met his wife?”

“No.”

“They got married real young,” Lizzie knew she was talking a lot, but couldn’t think how else to fill the silence. “They thought she was pregnant. She was. She lost it, but they were engaged and decided to elope anyway. Two years later, they had Zach. They have a daughter, Izzie, who is three.”

“Sounds like a happy family.”

“You know, I think they are soul mates. They were probably married in their last life, too.”

“You believe in that stuff? Reincarnation?”

“I think so. I mean… I really don’t KNOW. I don’t necessarily know that any of it is THE answer. But, yeah, it’s nice to think we come back here eventually. I would like to see another century. See what new gadgets teenagers have two hundred years from now,” Lizzie laughed at herself.

“But you wouldn’t be you?”

"I don't know how it works, Ben. You probably think it's all... silly."

"I like what you said about not knowing THE answer."

"So you're not an atheist?"

"Did you think I was an atheist?"

"I guess I did. Are you?"

"No."

"Hm," Lizzie looked to the cars they passed on the Pike.

"You were pretty religious in high school," Ben commented.

"I was a good little Catholic girl from a small town," Lizzie kept looking at the blurred cars. "I am definitely not that now."

"You live in a suburb."

"I'm no longer Catholic... and I'm definitely not good."

"You're good."

"I don't think we'd be in this car right now if either one of us thought I was good."

Ben pursed his lips together and tightened his grip on the steering wheel. Lizzie knew she hit some sort of nerve. She couldn't tell if it was his sin or hers that caused his immediate tensing. He took a deep breath and relaxed his arms. "Do you really think that makes you a bad person?"

"Well..." Lizzie faded her voice. If he did have a wife or girlfriend, obviously what they did together did make her a bad person. She still wasn't ready to ask him that question. "Sometimes it does."

"To do something that makes you feel good?"

"It's not the physical act," Lizzie argued. She couldn't believe the conversation about weather shifted to sex before they got beyond 495. "But the motivation."

"The motivation?" he glanced at her.

"I slept with Mike – Jack's drummer." Lizzie spoke before stopping her whim for honesty. "He has a girlfriend. I knew that. But I went ahead and slept with him because he wanted me. Because it felt good knowing he would choose me when he had someone else. Because for so much of my life I didn't feel wanted. I don't love Mike. I didn't do it out of love. I did it to make myself feel good for five minutes. It was stupid. It was cruel. And it was not good."

Ben took in a breath. He clearly didn't know what to say. He was stuck in the car with her, on the Mass Turnpike, with very little option to turn around and drive her back home. "That doesn't make you a bad person, Elizabeth."

"Yes, it does," Lizzie looked down. She was doing a great job towards retaining his interest and sympathy. "That isn't my only indiscretion. There have been a lot of indiscretions…" Lizzie faded off and found a question forming in her mind. Maybe she would ask it to cut to the chase and end it before her hopes got the better of her. "You know that I'm promiscuous. Is that why you are here?"

"What?" Ben shook his head as he switched lanes.

"Are you just taking me out tonight so you can get laid?"

"Well, I'm not going to deny that I have hopes for the end of this evening. I enjoy being with you, Elizabeth. In your bed. And sitting in this car right now. I …" he faded his conversation off to another gaze. "I think you are beautiful and funny and smart. I think you are good. We all make mistakes. We all do things to hurt other people – most often because we feel hurt. I certainly can't point my finger at you. I don't think less of you for what you've done. I don't think any less of your ultimate goodness. You spend every day helping to raise money for a hospital. You are a devoted friend. You show appreciation to those who help you... and you obviously care enough to let it bother you enough to confess it to me."

Lizzie looked at Ben, who kept his gaze at the left lane of the highway. She felt the anger and apprehension she had about his character dissolve. "You really think I'm good?"

"Yes, I do."

"Even when half of the time we've spent together has been in a bedroom?" Lizzie couldn't believe she said it.

"You are good in the bedroom," he turned his attention away from the road long enough to smile. Lizzie met his smile and breathed in deeply and confidently. He looked back to the road, still grinning mischievously.

She let silence slip into the car between the next two exits. It wasn't that uncomfortable silence of uncertainty. It was a mutual comfort with one another's company. Like she had known him for a long time and such silences were perfectly acceptable parts of the routine. She had known him for a long while, much longer than she knew Nora and Meg. And yet there was still so much mystery.

"I don't remember you being an athlete," she broke the silence after fifteen minutes. Her thoughts didn't venture far from his last comment.

"In high school? I wasn't," he laughed.

"But… you look like an athlete. Even in the yearbook pictures, you have the same… well I didn't really notice it then. But…"

"You were looking at our yearbook?"

"A few months back – at Sara's… she had an awful spiral perm. I was really unattractive," Lizzie wanted to eat her words again, wondering if she hit a sore spot with mention of Sara.

"You weren't unattractive," he answered without a pause at Sara's name.

"Your hair was longer… but not much else," Lizzie looked at him without fear. "But I don't remember you being athletic."

"I told you, I wasn't."

"Then where does the muscle come from? Heavy duty mouse clicking?"

"We did a lot of work around the house back then. I guess that's…" he let his eyes look at her and then back to the road. "Now I go to the gym."

"That's not fair. I work so hard to …"

"Females have to work harder."

"I know a few men who would hate you, too."

"They probably have a better appreciation for beer than I do," Ben started switching lanes towards the exit. "You don't hate me?"

"I've thought about it," Lizzie said lightly, albeit very honestly.

"You like running though," he showed a little confusion.

"I do. It took me a while, but once I discovered that runner's high, it got a whole lot easier to drag myself out of bed every morning."

"Endorphins," Ben smiled a different grin.

"You're not an athlete and you grin over endorphins?"

"I wouldn't know what to do with a baseball if it was flying straight toward me."

"Your brother was on the baseball team, wasn't he?"

"Oliver?"

"Yeah, I thought I remember that… or maybe that was someone else's brother."

"I don't think Oliver played sports either."

"Too busy working around the house?"

"I guess so. I don't remember," he turned off the ramp onto the main road.

"It's just after the next light," Lizzie offered. "Not a bad place. Pretty decent crowds – and far enough from the colleges so it isn't a bunch of frat boys."

Ben followed her directions and parked the car in front of the restaurant. Lizzie decided to put her sweater on when she got out of the car. She felt an arm around her waist turn her. Ben pulled her close and kissed her suddenly and passionately. Lizzie had to pull herself back to get some air. "We have to go in," she looked away from his eyes so he wouldn't continue and tempt her to go back into the car. He slipped his arm around her back and led her into the restaurant.

*****

"So what gives, Lizzie? Are you dating Ben?" Jack muttered the moment Ben got up to buy the next round.

"I don't know," Lizzie saw Ben's gaze as he waited for the bartender. "I don't know what's happening."

"He's cute," Jen smiled. "Jack said he's an engineer or something."

"Computers," Lizzie forced herself to look at Jen.

"Isn't he the one that followed Sara around all the time?" Jen asked. "I always imagined some nerdy, scrawny kid with broken glasses."

"He wasn't scrawny. And I think I wore the broken glasses," Lizzie laughed. "Besides, everyone liked Sara. Even this one."

Jack finished his glass of whiskey. "I was 14 and hormonal."

"It's okay, Jack," Jen laughed. "I liked Drew Armstrong. He was a beautiful boy, but cocky as shit. Turned out he was gay."

"I've often wondered if Sara was a repressed lesbian," Lizzie said flippantly. "It might explain all the Jesus love."

"Don't give him any ideas, Lizzie. You know he's imagining very bad things right now," Jen laughed.

"It might give you something to look forward to," Jack pinched his wife's side.

"Isn't your break over?" Jen sniveled and then kissed him on the lips. Lizzie glanced back up at Ben's constant gaze. She felt her own smile creep across her cheeks.

"I'm going to hit the loo before you start," Lizzie excused herself, but Jen decided to follow her.

"He is really nice, Lizzie," Jen stood over the sink in the bathroom, dodging the crowded line behind them. "It's obvious he is really into you."

"You think?"

"Yeah… you don't?"

"I… we've had a couple great nights. Then weeks go by without… anything."

"I imagine he's a little scared. If he was in love with your best friend as a teenager that might bring some stuff up."

"Great," Lizzie peered into the reflection of the mirror. "I don't want… I don't want to be his choice because he's been carrying a torch for Sara all these years."

"I don't think that's the case," Jen looked at her own reflection. "Didn't you like someone in high school?"

"Yeah… but I never really thought I had a chance. You know, Jen. I have a self-defeating attitude towards men. I don't ever pick the ones who like me back as much as I like them."

"I think he likes you back, Lizzie," Jen sighed. "Maybe you are the one who is still hung up on Sara."

"I didn't say she was a lesbian because I had a crush on her."

"No… but you were in her shadow. Her pretty, perfect shadow. That's a tough shadow to leave. Even after running for two years."

"I've been in a lot of those shadows."

"Did you ever think that maybe he liked you?" Jen turned away from the mirror. "Maybe the Sara thing was just an excuse to be around you."

"Not likely," Lizzie could still see the reflection of her frumpier self in the mirror.

"Would you have given him the time of day if he did?" Jen had a direct approach much like Nora's.

"You know what's funny? I used to be in a club with his brother," Lizzie remembered the thought as she spoke it. "We had a lot of fun together. Oliver made me laugh. I thought for a little while that he liked me. But he was two years ahead of us… and he had a girlfriend. I decided it was just my imagination."

"Maybe Oliver paid attention to you because he knew his brother was secretly pining for you," Jen winked as the bass vibrated through the bathroom door.

"Secretly pining?" Lizzie laughed as they edged towards the door. "For Sara's less attractive friend?"

"You know Lizzie, you didn't just suddenly become beautiful," Jen paused before opening the door. "You lost weight, but you have always had beauty. It's just when you got thinner, you decided to believe it."

Lizzie looked at Jen but lacked the wit to retaliate. She pulled open the door and went back out to where Ben was waiting for her.

*****

Lizzie looked down at Ben as her heart rhythm slowed. She breathed in deeply and dropped her chest onto his. She kissed him passionately once more and slid down against the mattress, not removing her glance from the green gray eyes that followed her movement. Her heart was still accelerated and her every nerve enlivened. She felt her limbs itch with the energy to run several miles, but she had no desire to leave the spot where she lay opposite him, staring into those gray green eyes.

He moved a hair that fell from her temple across her nose. The touch of his fingers against her face thrilled her smile to a broader width. She didn't know when the last time was that she felt so content, so elated, so glad to be in a moment. She wanted to hold onto it… but not by herself. She felt the hope and adrenalin of risk rise to her throat. She kissed him again and narrowed her eyes as she pulled away. "Ben."

He rested his palm against her scalp and slowly caressed down the length of her hair. "Elizabeth," the breath of his voice was still close to her lips.

She rolled onto her back to leave the temptation of another kiss and excuse to abandon what she was daring herself to say. "What I said about being good before," she looked up at the stripes of her blinds silhouetted by the street light. "I was telling the truth. I have been a pretty heartless whore the past several months."

"Elizabeth," he said her name again as he draped an affectionate arm across her breasts and rested his chin inside the curve of her shoulder.

"I…" she felt his kiss against her neck. It made her nerves tingle, as though each one were an electric charge. She instinctively arched her head, making it easier for his seduction. He eased his arm back so one palm landed on her exposed breast. Lizzie leaned into him but moved her motivation back into her head. "Ben," she whispered. He moved away from her neck and lifted his eyes that burned with an intensity she never saw before. He kissed her lips briefly until she closed her mouth and stopped reacting. She lifted her hands and held them against his temples.

"I don't think you are a whore," his concentrated stare said with determination.

"I know," she smoothed along his hair and cupped her hands at the base of his skull. "I know what I did and why I made the choices I made. I was running away from something. From myself. When I'm with you, I'm not running away. I feel like I am running to something I want. I want to be here. I want to be myself here."

Lizzie took in a deep breath and felt the weight of his hand as her chest rose and fell. She dropped her hands from the back of his head and let him relax back onto his elbow. He moved his hand from her breast and gently traced down the length of her torso with his finger. He stopped at her pelvic bone and retraced his finger back between her breasts, all the way along her neck to the base of her chin. He paused, turning his fiery eyes back to her neck. Then he fell back against the pillow and let silence fill the room.

Lizzie heard a car pass on the street below. She didn't want to be distracted by the outside world. It was as if the spell were breaking. The longer the pause after her confession, the less warmth she felt inside and out. She didn't want to lose that warmth. She didn't want to lose that chance to be with someone now that she had finally decided to be honest. "I want you to stay, Ben," she made one last attempt. "Stay with me through the morning."

He shifted his position again and leaned over to kiss her. "I want to stay," he looked at her. "I want to be the one you run to. I want you, more than you know."

Lizzie let her next breath plunge all the way to where he dragged his finger. As her chest rose, his palm found her breast again, followed soon after by his mouth. She let the conversation fade as he revitalized the sensation of her nerves and skin. She allowed the hope to enter her mind that he would be there through the morning. That he wanted her more than she knew.

When she woke up the next morning, he was gone.

Chapter Ten

She resisted the crushing sorrow that started to work its way into her mind and strangle the hope that sweetly lulled her to sleep. It was a challenge to distract her thoughts. Meg hadn't returned from where she disappeared for the evening. Jackie was already out of the house by the time Lizzie brought herself down to the kitchen. Not that Jackie was the company she sought… but any conversation… even an aggravation was better than the empty pillow that haunted her.

She didn't understand. Why did he say he would stay? She was already lying naked next to him. He could have stayed silent and had the two more hours of sex she gave him readily before falling asleep. She wouldn't have refused him, even if her heart was disappointed. It wouldn't have been half so disappointing as the waking.

Lizzie tried to eat some toast, but lost her appetite before swallowing her first bite. She drank some juice before dressing herself for a run. She ran for eight miles, twice her average. Eight miles to lose her mind to the music of her headphones and the determination to each benchmark. Eight miles to avoid going back home to her empty home to figure out what to do next.

The run exhausted her. It was after dawn when she closed her eyes on Ben. It was only two hours later when she opened them and found him gone. She took her water bottle and sat herself on the couch, where she sat mindlessly in front of the television for six straight hours.

She heard the key in the lock, but didn't bother to prop herself up when she heard footsteps on the stairs. "So, how did it go?" Meg poked her head around the door frame.

Lizzie leaned her head away from the television. She saw the tall frame of Alec shadowing behind Meg and decided a simple answer was best. "It went."

"We have pizza," Meg indicated her confusion. "Do you want any?"

"I'm not hungry," Lizzie muttered, even though her stomach ached and she still felt the drain from her run.

Lizzie didn't say anything as Meg and Alec brought their pizza and beer into the living room. She didn't protest when they put in a DVD. She didn't offer up the couch, forcing them to sit close together on the loveseat. She could have gone upstairs and avoided them. But for some strange reason, she decided to stay there and observe Meg and her boyfriend.

Lizzie had known Alec for three years, but she was still startled at the obvious age difference between him and her friend. It almost made her uncomfortable to see Alec touch Meg with affection. She knew they had sex. She knew that Meg enjoyed the sex. But Alec – mostly because of the aging of his smoking habit – looked old enough to be her father. It didn't stop the sight of them together from stinging. To see them whisper and laugh together or find some reference Meg could use for her thesis was more than a little irritating.

At some point during the second movie, Lizzie fell asleep. She woke in the darkened living room. Someone slammed the front door and was walking up the stairs. Lizzie smelled Jackie's perfume as she looked in to see who was on the couch. Lizzie breathed in slowly, pretending to be asleep. She waited for a quiet half hour until Jackie left the bathroom and closed the door to her bedroom.

Lizzie pried herself off the sofa, her joints stiff from not properly stretching and lying on the couch for so many hours. She went to the kitchen and refilled her water bottle, quickly swallowing it before filling it again. She found a few remaining pieces of Meg's pizza in the refrigerator. She stood by the window, picking off the anchovies and doing her best to not swallow it in one bite.

There was a full moon. Her silly small talk wasn't completely off base. Full moons made people do foolish things. Like confess feelings. Or lie about them. Lizzie forced her eyes shut. She didn't want to hurt like that. Not again. No. This was a lot worse. It was worse because this time she actually believed that it might be.

She heard something drop on the ceiling. Meg and Alec apparently stayed at the apartment… and weren't asleep. They probably weren't going to sleep any time soon. That made the idea of going upstairs even less appealing.

Lizzie went back to the couch and altered her position from her thirteen hour sloth. She turned on the television to shield her ears from any reminders of upstairs. She mindlessly surfed through all the channels, finally settling on a documentary about the American Revolution. She drifted in and out of concentration, mixing up the details of the show with her tour at the Fulton house and Meg's latest thesis description and the echo of Ben's empty promises. Her semi-conscious wandered to Harriet's chair and fell against the cushions as someone bit into her neck. She opened her eyes and saw Ben watching from the doorway.

In the quiet of early dawn, she returned to her room and the bed she left untouched since the day before. She ripped up the sheets and removed the smell of him from her pillows and then went back to sleep.

She checked her email after waking in the afternoon. She knew there wouldn't be anything from Ben, but looked anyway. She logged onto Facebook just to make sure no feed indicated where he went. She knew her phone was somewhere… in a pocket… or her purse. She could check to see if anyone called on Saturday, but the effort to sift through the pile of clothes on her floor was too depressing. She tried to read a book but just drifted back to a vacant stare towards her window. The constant inactivity slowed her mind, allowing the time to pass with surreal speed. There was nothing accomplished as her weekend drew to a close. Merely, she managed to stop thinking.

The phone startled her ears at four o'clock. She followed the sound to the jeans still on the floor from Friday night. It was probably Nora, searching for her own distraction from stress to hear about Lizzie's outing with Ben. WHY had she told her friends? Why hadn't she learned that all the men she wanted never wanted her… and to tell anyone differently was just a fanciful story?

She flipped the phone without bothering to confirm Nora's identity. "Hello?" she greeted with moderate pleasantness.

"Hi, Elizabeth. This is Ben."

Lizzie sat slowly on the edge of her bed. "Hi Ben," she let her voice return to her actual mood.

"I'm… I regret that… I really enjoyed seeing you on Friday."

Lizzie felt a calm chill in her mind take over. 'You did," she inflected no emotion in her voice.

"I would like to see you again," his explanation was kind but equally distant. "I think I should explain some things."

"Explain what?" Lizzie released meanness into her words.

"Are you available tonight?"

Lizzie paused, letting a few moments slip into silence while she contrived possible excuses. She could call Nora, or see if Meg and Alec wanted more pizza, or even invite Eric over for a one night reunion. Anything would be better than seeing him again so soon. "I have to work tomorrow."

"It doesn't have to be a late night," he hesitated. "I just want to talk to you."

Lizzie wrestled between disappointment and insult. "I can meet you for coffee."

"Okay. Where?"

"Um…" Lizzie felt her brain clear and reconsidered. "I really shouldn't have caffeine that late. Why don't you come back here and I'll think of somewhere else to go."

"Elizabeth, I…"

"What?"

"I can be there by 6."

"See you."

Lizzie closed her phone and paused in her seat. He was going to tell her whatever it was he was avoiding. Or he was going to try to avoid it again and lure her … to… she had to keep her head. She was in too deep now. He could really hurt her.

She was pleased to see both Meg and Jackie disappeared again. She took a quick shower, but didn't put much effort or thought into getting dressed. She threw on the jeans from the floor and a t-shirt with paint stains. He wasn't worth any more of her time that weekend. But it left her with idle time. She finished cleaning up her bedroom and remade the bed. She tidied up the sofa, the cushions and blankets still a mess from her campout in front of the television.

At 6 o'clock exactly, the doorbell rang.

Lizzie led him up the stairs silently. They paused in the hall. "Let me get my jacket. We can get ice cream," she made the decision on her feet.

"Can we stay here?" he put his keys on the table by the radiator.

Lizzie breathed in deeply, knowing she should insist on more neutral territory. "Sure," she didn't make an attempt at pleasure with her answer. She led him across the hall into the dining room, the most formal of all the rooms in their house. She pulled out a chair and looked at him as he took the one opposite. "Can I offer you some coffee – or tea?"

"I'm all right. Do you want to get yourself something?"

Lizzie looked at the bar and determined she would save that until he was gone and her heart was broken. She waited for him to settle in the chair and sat rigidly to face him.

"I can tell you are not happy with me," he looked down.

"I don't understand…" Lizzie breathed out her anger and her sorrow.

"Of course you don't."

"Are you married?"

"No."

"But there is someone."

"Not someone else," he met her eyes. The gray green was filled with that burning she saw in the darkness of her room. "There is you."

"So you like me?" Lizzie couldn't stop herself from asking such a desperate question.

"I like you very much," he revealed a pained smile.

"Then what's wrong?"

He continued to look at her, letting several minutes pass into silence. Lizzie felt uncomfortable under his watchful gaze, but was frozen in the expression of her last sentence. She heard the clock tick in the kitchen and felt the light of the evening sun slip slowly behind the trees outside the window.

"You are a very intelligent, perceptive individual," Ben finally broke the quiet of the dining room.

Lizzie released an annoyed sigh. That was neither an explanation nor a compliment. She turned in her chair away from him, feeling the urge to leave the room and the frustrating conversation. "What is that supposed to mean?"

"You see the world and maintain a certain amount of skepticism and doubt."

"About you, yes."

"About what I am finding incredibly difficult to even start to tell you."

Lizzie turned back to face him. He was struggling. "You are going to tell me something about how you like me, but don't think we should be together."

"It could be," he nodded. Lizzie glared at him, tossing aside any swell of sympathy she felt at his grief. "The other night you said you were looking at my yearbook photos and thought I looked the same as I do now."

"Except for the hair."

"Except for the hair," Ben repeated. "I haven't changed since high school," he paused and took in a deep breath. "I haven't changed for two and a half centuries."

"WHAT?" Lizzie shouted, more in anger than anything else.

Ben reached across the table and took hold of her hands to stop her from leaving her seat. "I know this is quite incredible, Elizabeth," he hesitated again. "I don't look older because I haven't aged for over two hundred years."

"What? Are you a vampire or something?" she clenched her fists under his grasp.

Ben caught her eyes and looked at her with more gravity than she had ever seen in him. "Yes."

Lizzie squared her jaw. Was this some sort of demented joke he contrived with Meg? "That stuff isn't real," she wanted to move her arms, but felt fear creep into her stomach. A fear to do anything to make him angry. What if he really believed it? What if he was psychotic enough to try to open up her veins and kill her?

"It's very real."

"But you… you… you are Ben Cottingham. You went to Springs Regional High School. Vampires don't go to Springs Regional. Or live in Coldbrook."

He laughed, lightening the severity of his look. "You think I should live in Bavaria?"

"I don't… I think you are full of shit," she hardened her eyes, still unable to move her arms.

"You're scared," Ben sighed sadly. He relaxed his grip on her arms and slowly unclenched her hands to clasp them in his own.

"I'm scared because you are delusional. No wonder you were attracted to Sara. You both live in fantasy worlds," Lizzie still couldn't move.

"Elizabeth…"

She decided to not say the next thing that came in her mouth. She bit into her lip, not sure what she could say. What would anger him. What would anger her. What was or was not completely crazy. Her mind swelled with confusion and could no longer fight the tears that filled her eyes.

"Elizabeth," he repeated.

"Why?" she wept. "Why are you telling me this?"

"Because I feel if I am going to include you in my life, you need to know this about me."

"You don't feel like it's something you should keep to yourself?"

"Not from you."

"I don't understand."

"It wouldn't take you long to notice that I don't eat anything. Or drink anything."

"But all that wine… and at the bar you had beer." Lizzie hissed. He was always getting her drunk.

"Did you ever really see me drink?"

"No," Lizzie assented weakly thinking of the unfinished bottles. Her fingers fell limp in his grip. "Do you want to suck my blood?"

"Yes," he shut his eyes and bent down his chin.

Lizzie retreated her arms quickly and folded them across her chest. "I think you should go."

"Is that what you want?" he lifted his eyes back to her, but they still burned.

Lizzie felt the tremble of her lip rattle all through her bones. She was terrified of what he could do to her. But there was something deep within her that was terrified if he left, she would never see him again. "I don't know what I want," she hugged herself to calm the trembling.

"I won't hurt you," his voice was calm.

"But you want to kill me," she articulated the reality she couldn't grasp.

"No," he shook his head and tried to reach out his hand, but retrieved it on a second thought. "Not at all."

"You just said," Lizzie shut her eyes, unable to repeat his confession. "You said you wanted to."

Ben sat back in his chair and looked as though he was choosing his words very carefully. "You've taught yourself to not eat when you aren't hungry, haven't you?"

"Most of the time," she couldn't look at him.

"You've taught yourself portion control?"

"More or less," she was still crying. How dare he hit that nerve in the middle of this conversation.

"It's the same way for vampires."

"This is insane," Lizzie stood up from her chair. She looked at the bar and thought about getting a drink. She also measured how close the bottles were if she needed to defend herself.

"It isn't insane, Elizabeth," Ben's voice was still calm. "Think about everything you taught yourself about diet. A person needs a certain amount of nutrients and calories to function well."

"And many people overeat."

"And become ill," Ben continued. "It's the same way for me. If I drink too much blood, then it doesn't do me much good. If I drink a regular schedule, then I won't overeat."

"Do you keep a regular schedule?"

"Until this week," Ben hesitated. "You might say I was too distracted."

Lizzie looked at his eyes. He was hungry. "How much is a serving?"

"A pint."

"That's what I give at the hospital," Lizzie muttered.

"Exactly. Nature isn't illogical. If I keep a steady feeding pattern, I never need take more than a pint… which is precisely how much the human body can lose without any consequence."

"What if you don't feed regularly?"

"Then there are tragic costs for the source," Ben said quietly.

"Source? You mean people? Or do you drink from animals?"

"Animals work in a desperate situation. It isn't healthy. One tends to mimic qualities of the source. Vampires who feed on animals tend to be more like animals."

"And you become more human by feeding on humans?"

"Simply… yes."

Lizzie allowed herself a lengthy look at him. He was the same Ben. With the freckles under his eyes and the strong shoulders. He didn't look like a monster. She didn't even see if he had sharp teeth. She kissed him and had been inside his mouth… but never felt the cut of fangs. She saw so much of his body, his perfect ageless body. Was he – could he – really be immortal? Lizzie was in disbelief. But to disbelieve this would mean disbelieving everything else he told her. Was she that desperate to have this man love her? That she was willing to buy into his fantasy just to feel the thing she wanted to feel?

"When was the last time you ate?"

"Last Saturday."

"How often do you need to eat?"

"Once a week."

"What happened yesterday?"

"I lost my appetite."

Lizzie thought of the pair of blemishes she saw in the mirror just below her neck. And the other mysterious bug bites. "Did you bite me?"

"There is a sort of venom in our fangs that is like anesthesia. It just… numbs… the person… so they don't feel pain. I wanted you to sleep so I could leave quietly," he confessed awkwardly.

"But you didn't…"

"I didn't take anything. Just a touch to prolong your sleep."

"Why did you leave?" the question brought Lizzie back to the reality before this strange conversation started.

"Because…" Ben breathed out slowly. "Because I wanted very badly to take your blood. All three times, Elizabeth. I never knew if I would be able to resist in the morning."

"But you could resist at night?"

"Because you had alcohol."

"So?"

"Alcohol weakens the blood and bitters the flavor."

"So my intoxication stopped you from …" Lizzie struggled with the completion of the sentence. "All that red wine put you off?"

"From drinking your blood. Not from you," he said with determination.

"You made sure that I had wine," Lizzie looked at him.

"I didn't know I was going to tell you this, Elizabeth," he paused. "I haven't tried to see you with the intention of making you a source. So I needed to take precaution… because there was always that desire. I never take without consent of the source."

Lizzie uncrossed her arms and allowed them to fall to her side. "How many sources do you have?'

"That's complicated."

"I'm pretty good at figuring things out."

"Yes," he looked amused and worried at the same time. "You are."

"So how many?"

"I go to a clinic."

"Oh," Lizzie thought of a hundred new questions, but didn't have the energy to start asking them. A part of her was willing to accept this bizarre and strange new way of seeing things, of seeing Ben. She let herself look at him again and saw his gray green eyes. Those hadn't changed. They were still hungry. They still looked at her with the same look that glanced across the library table at Springs High School.

"Do you want me to go?" he asked as Lizzie remained frozen by her inability to select a question.

"No," she shook her head. She felt as though she was in a dream she was writing as she was dreaming. Maybe she spent too many hours on the couch. Maybe Meg had put something on that pizza. And yet it was starting to feel as if she knew this all along… as if she had just been waiting for him to say something so they could move on to the next step.

"You have fangs?" Lizzie blurted out. Tangible proof to his identity could confirm once and for all whether or not she was in some grief laden psychosis.

"My teeth are a necessary tool for feeding," he answered. "I can't just … I don't think I should take that risk right now."

"Because you would try to feed?" Lizzie met his gray green eyes.

"I might."

"Do you want to?" Lizzie let that question articulate before she had a chance to talk herself out of it. She saw his breath quicken the rise and fall of his chest. He was looking at her. She didn't know where on her body he was focused. She wondered if he had some extrasensory ability to see the blood rapidly coursing through her veins and was allowing himself to imagine something he had been fighting so fiercely.

Lizzie laid her left wrist across the table. "Maybe I'm as crazy as you are, Ben. I don't know that I am sane… or even awake. But more than anything… right now… I want to believe this thing you are telling me. I want to believe you," she stretched so her fingertips almost touched the fabric of his shirt.

He curled her fingers into her palm and slid her arm back towards her torso. "This isn't why I told you."

"You're hungry," Lizzie pushed his hand back and turned her wrist up on the table.

He sat back in his chair and put distance between them.

"Are you afraid?" she looked directly at him.

"Yes."

"Why? Will you kill me?"

"No. It's..." he flickered his eyes up, looking confused and pained. He drew in a breath and revealed a smile of deeper admiration. "You are brave."

"And stupid," she lifted up her left arm. "I want a Twinkie when you're done."

He laughed and took hold of her wrist. He stroked the inside of her arm gently. His fingers were neither warm nor cold, but left an electric sensation along her skin. He pulled her hand towards his mouth and kissed her palm with delicate eagerness. He kissed the base of her palm, then her wrist. He rested his lips there for a few moments. Lizzie resisted the urge to clench her fist shut and forced her fingers to relax. She saw him pull back his lips and expose his fangs before they plunged into her skin. She shut her eyes quickly, expecting to feel pain. She immediately opened them to see if it really happened. She felt something move down her arm, but no pain at all.

She wasn't sure how long he bent over her wrist. She heard the clock ticking in the kitchen, and saw the last ribbons of sunlight stream through the large windows. She felt her heart beating fast like in the last leg of her runs. She was terrified and yet calmly aware that it was real. It wasn't a ridiculous story he made up as an excuse. He was really a… vampire. He was really drinking her blood.

He lifted his eyes and gently rested her hand back on the table. His lips were closed. She couldn't see if there was anything dripping from his teeth… his fangs. She looked at her wrist and saw two red marks the same distance apart as the mysterious bug bites. She touched the marks with her right fingers. "It doesn't hurt."

Ben was breathing slowly and watching her. He wasn't ready to speak. He looked as though he just came back from a ten mile run. "I'm not even bleeding," she lifted her arm closer for inspection. "How…" she looked to Ben's satisfied stare.

"The chemical in our fangs cauterizes the wound," he said slowly.

"Magic?"

"No more magic than amino acids or chromosomes. The body is an amazing machine."

"But you aren't human."

"I'm a different genus of human."

"Homo… vampyre?"

"Yes."

Lizzie perked up her ears as she heard the front door. Neither she nor Ben spoke as someone climbed the stairs to the foyer. Jackie looked through the doorway. "Hi Lizzie."

Lizzie tucked her arms in her lap. "Jackie, you remember Ben?"

"The guy who carried you home," Jackie smirked and then turned back into the hallway. Lizzie looked at Ben silently until she heard the door close at the top of the stairs.

"I can go get you a Twinkie."

"I don't eat Twinkies. "

"Are you okay?" Ben asked softly.

"I honestly don't know," she looked at her wrist again. "I… am glad you aren't married."

Ben took hold of her hand. The burning look was gone from his eyes. His cheeks had more color and his skin looked smoother. Did she really do that to him? "I won't ever hurt you," he said softly.

She wanted to believe that, but there was still a small part of her that was scared. A much larger part of her was mesmerized by this new Ben. He was still the old Ben, the guy who carried her home. She didn't want him to go away. If this was another one of her strange dreams, she didn't want to wake up. Not alone. "Will you stay here tonight? Will you stay until the morning?" she asked. "Can you?"

"Can I?"

"Will you burn up in the sun?"

"Um, no," Ben laughed. "You've seen me in daylight, Elizabeth."

"Right," Lizzie nodded, feeling a little lightheaded.

"I will stay," he squeezed her hand. It was warm and sent a sensation up the length of her arm.

Lizzie smiled across the table. At Ben. A vampire.

Chapter Eleven

Lizzie opened her eyes facing the clock. The green six formed in her groggy perception. She closed her eyes, feeling weighted down from her habit to get out of bed. It was too warm and soft and comfortable where she lay. She opened her eyes again and smiled, realizing there was an arm draped around her waist.

She kept her eyes open, staring at the clock but not paying attention to the time. She didn't want to move, still warm and comfortable inside the half embrace of Ben behind her. She never felt that comfort before. She never wanted to feel it and never let herself trust it to make it real. The reality was still settling into her mind. A reality that was so easy to disbelieve. It could all be a dream. She was waking up on Saturday and the two days of lonely misery were just part of the nightmare. But she could see the red marks on her left wrist.

She couldn't remember if there was a moment when she suddenly decided she wasn't Catholic any more. It sort of wore away slowly after she went to college. She slept in on Sunday mornings and didn't feel guilt for skipping mass. She studied history and read about the Crusades and all the horrible things the church did to preserve their reality… and eventually decided that reality was not hers. It didn't change so abruptly.

This new reality was sudden and swift and altered the color of everything. She didn't mourn the loss of her previous perception. She didn't curse herself for naiveté or begrudge her ignorance. She didn't fear more of the unknown. She simply started to accept this was the way the world really was… and that it meant that she could curl up under Ben's arm.

There was still a part of her that questioned her eagerness to so easily accept what he was. She was a little crazy for offering up her wrist like that… and yet… it was harmless. It showed how ridiculous the myths and legends were. She was more tired than anything when they left the dining room. Too tired to do much more than throw her jeans back on the floor and fall against her pillow. She didn't even remember Ben falling with her. He was still there in the morning light. He was true to his word. He stayed.

She felt him stir and allowed herself to turn around to face him. She liked the way the morning sun fell across his freckles. She liked the smile that broadened across his cheeks even more. She felt so many sentences start to form on her tongue, but couldn't resolve how to begin. She leaned to kiss him and felt the exhilaration of his touch she was too exhausted to allow the night before. He slid one of his hands under her paint-stained t-shirt, alarming her spine with the warmth of his fingers. She pulled herself back, remembering it was Monday and the fact she had to get to the shower before Jackie and Meg.

"I actually have to go to work today," she laughed as he tried to kiss her again.

"No you don't," he lifted up her t-shirt and started kissing her exposed skin.

"I do," she argued. "I don't own my own company. I need to get paid."

"You can call in," he lifted her shirt completely over her head.

"I have a lot of time," Lizzie looked at the ceiling trying to make an honest decision.

Ben touched a few fingers across her forehead. "I think you should call in. I think you aren't feeling well and should take a few days off."

"A few days?"

"Let's go somewhere. We can take a drive anywhere you want to go," he kissed her forehead where his fingers had just warmed her.

Lizzie was silent. She was both elated and apprehensive of his suggestion.

"If you are worried about what your boss might say, I can give you a doctor's note."

"You can?"

"I was a doctor once," he started kissing her neck.

Lizzie pushed him away and sat herself up. She retrieved her t-shirt and put it back over her head. "When were you a doctor?" Lizzie felt all the excitement drain from her as another part of this new reality began to take shape.

"It was the profession I had the longest. I graduated from medical school in 1922… and was a doctor until the early 80's," he tried to kiss her neck again.

Lizzie turned her head away from his. It was a difficult thought to process - that while she was playing Barbie, he was an adult with a career. "How many professions have you had?'

Ben took in a deep breath and decided to sit up as well. "I'd say six or seven."

Lizzie expected a much larger number. Truth was, she hadn't stayed in any job for more than five years. She was pretty close to his tally and she was only 33. "You've lived many lives," she spoke her thought out loud.

"Yes," he said simply. It was simpler than she hoped.

"How does that work?"

"Let me take you away somewhere. Call in. Then we can go and talk about all these things."

"Why do you have to take me some place else to do that?"

"Isn't that what couples do? Go and spend time away so they can learn more about one another?"

"Some just have dinner or a cup of coffee."

"Do you think you can ask me all your questions at Starbucks? Or a restaurant where there will be a waitress interrupting every ten minutes?" he looked at Lizzie. She couldn't argue against him. "Even here, you have two roommates who could walk in on us."

Lizzie thought of Meg and wondered what she would think of this. Her vampire fantasies would require some serious redefinition if she overheard Lizzie asking Ben about his last two centuries. Then again, Meg would be there if anything happened…

"I'm not going to take you into the woods and eat you, Elizabeth," he touched her arm softly. She felt a charge excite her arm.

"Not until Saturday anyway."

"Nope. Not for another 55 days. Just like the Red Cross, I have to wait two months for your red blood cells to reform," he explained, tempting Lizzie with so many more questions. She didn't know how she could possibly work with so many thoughts in her head. She didn't think any number of Google searches would satisfy the questions. She couldn't see herself having these discussions with Ben on Facebook chat.

"Where will we go?"

"That's up to you."

"You will answer all my questions?"

"As best as I can," he paused. "I can't promise that I know and understand everything."

She hesitated and looked at the gray green eyes. "Okay," Lizzie reached beside the clock and picked up her cell phone.

*****

Lizzie hadn't made a decision three hours later when she packed a bag and was seated beside Ben in his car. She felt the silent hum of his Prius and didn't say anything as he decided to go west on the Pike. He went through the tollbooth and turned to face her. "You tell me where to get off," he smiled.

"Why couldn't we just go to your place? You don't have roommates?"

"I don't," he focused on the merge into traffic. "I thought we could go somewhere more neutral. Not to mention someplace more interesting than my condo."

"I want to see where you live."

"You will," he said as if there was no question about that. He paused and looked at her. "If that's what you really want, I'll take you there."

"No," Lizzie shook her head. "You live in Central Square. That's not very far from Mt. Elm. With my luck, I'd see Richard and he would know I'm playing hooky."

"Where do you want to go?"

"Let's just drive," Lizzie leaned her head back and watched him turn his focus back to the highway. Had he really not aged for two hundred years? How could that be possible? She thought of the amount of gray that interspersed with her brown hair. His hair was still the rusty brown it had been eighteen years ago when she first met him. Apparently he was the same age then as he was sitting next to her. Physically. Emotionally and intellectually… he was old enough to be… even creepier than Alec was with Meg. Then again… it wasn't creepy. Lizzie thought of all the historical periods she studied in college and tried to imagine herself living. Ben must have witnessed so many amazing moments and lived through several changes in humanity.

The questions filled her mind rapidly. So many things she wanted to know, but didn't know how to begin asking. She let the quiet hum of the engine fill the space until she saw a sign for Rte. 91, when she decided to tell him to go to Vermont. She resolved not to ask any questions until they reached a destination and made small talk about work and the gossip from Coldbrook.

"So why did you end up with the drummer?" Ben asked suddenly after they left the gas station in Brattleboro.

"Um," Lizzie looked at his expression to see if there was any hint of jealousy. She didn't expect the mention of Coldbrook to remind him of their conversation on Friday. Lizzie couldn't remember if Ben was paying attention to Mike that night. She was too busy worrying if he was going to stay through until morning. "The first time it was just alcohol. The second time it was because alcohol couldn't distract me." She felt his eyes shift away from the road and look at her. "I was trying to not think about you."

"It happened more than once?"

"He wasn't with Amy the first time… I don't think he was. Anyway, it doesn't matter. I won't do it again. I don't want to."

"You said there was someone you wanted to marry."

"I was at a point in my life when I believed I should get married and have kids like everyone else. There was this guy – Will. He was a musician who made me delirious with his mere presence. I thought we were soul mates."

"What happened?"

"Hardly anything. Will and I had some fantastic conversations and a few tense moments, but that was as far as it got."

"Did he know you felt that way?" Ben made Lizzie squirm. It sounded like something Nora would ask.

"No. I didn't think much of myself then. I knew he was attracted to another girl who came to the parties. They always are… but then he ended up falling for someone outside of our circle entirely and married her.

I think they are having a kid now. It doesn't matter… I mean it does. It had to end that way because I WAS devastated and so angry with myself for not being someone he could love that I put my whole heart and soul into running and relearning how to eat," Lizzie breathed out. "The strange thing is I realized I didn't like the person I was when I had that crazy infatuation."

"Do you like the person you were when you were with Mike?"

Lizzie felt her cheeks burn. "Not really," Lizzie looked down at her jeans, noticing a coffee stain on her thigh. "That wasn't the right thing to do."

"No," Ben said quietly.

"There was some satisfaction in doing the wrong thing. Maybe it made me feel better about not having what I wanted. Because I didn't deserve it," Lizzie stared out the window and caught sight of a road sign. "Let's go to Quechee."

"The Quechee Gorge?"

"Have you been there?"

"A long time ago," he said mindlessly. Lizzie sighed at the green trees outside the window. "Elizabeth…"

She turned her head back to look at him. "What?"

He met her eyes briefly. "You deserve to have what you want," he looked back to the road, but touched her hand. "I have met so many people, Elizabeth. Many women. Generations of pretty women, intelligent women, sexy women, brave women. You are one that I can't keep myself away from."

Lizzie breathed in slowly and blinked her eyes a few times to fight the moisture she wasn't quick enough to resist. "I… thank you," Lizzie muttered awkwardly, uncertain what else to say.

"You are…" he faded as he put his focus back to the highway. "It means a great deal to me that you are here."

"It… it means a lot to me, too," she paused. "The whole Will thing sucked. I hated myself for being so stupid. But I think that had to happen to get me here."

Ben smiled at the road. "Let's go to Quechee."

Chapter Twelve

Lizzie remembered the trail she walked a few years before with Meg. It led them down into the gorge along a road covered with pine needles and signs warning of floods from the river. "We used to take a lot of road trips. Some were planned out… some were spontaneous," Lizzie looked about and wondered if she really recognized the trail or if it just looked like some other pine needle covered path she once hiked.

"You had a sense of adventure."

"Meg has had a few… volatile relationships," Lizzie shrugged. "Our travels about New England were a way of distracting her from fits of screaming and crying."

"But you got to see a lot of different places?"

"Yes," Lizzie smiled at him, wondering how many places he lived in never mind traveled to. "I always remember this place."

"Why?"

"The majesty, the awe… the secret. Hardly anyone I know has ever heard of Quechee," Lizzie walked a few paces ahead of him. "When did you come here?"

"With a few friends… I think it was before I went back to France," Ben stopped walking and looked about as if that would prompt a more specific memory.

"You lived there?" Lizzie dared herself to start.

"I was at Verdun," Ben resumed his pace at her side.

Lizzie got a chill. "That was more than 90 years ago," she said more for her own benefit than his. They walked a few minutes in silence. Lizzie could hear the currents of the Connecticut River and the birds above their heads. "Ben, how long have you been … well, you know?"

"Since 1779."

Lizzie stopped walking. The birds still continued to chirp over her head and the rush of the water echoed nearby. "You are older than the country."

Ben laughed. "I suppose I am technically. I never thought of it that way."

"You were here to see it happen."

"What?"

"The United States change from colonies to… states," she felt her history geek cloud her ability for interesting conversation.

"I didn't see it happen," Ben shook his head and leaned against a tree. "I was a farmer. I didn't go to Philadelphia and see those men write a bunch of sentences to sever ties with the king."

"Did you want… did you support the Revolution?"

"I got swept up in the fever. I fought even though I had no idea what I was fighting for," Ben narrowed his eyes. "It was very long ago, Elizabeth. I don't remember the details."

"Oh," Lizzie looked down, unable to hide her disappointment.

"I don't feel I resemble that person very much anymore," Ben stopped leaning against the tree and reached for her hand. "I've lived through so many things that have matured me and made me less… well, there are things in my youth of which I am not proud and let myself forget."

"Fair enough," Lizzie couldn't argue, even though she told him about Mike.

Ben squeezed her hand and started walking the trail again. Lizzie hesitated and followed his pace. "Were you a soldier at Verdun?" Lizzie backtracked to something that didn't make him so tight-lipped.

"I was drafted, believe it or not," he let his amusement escape the green of his eyes. "I wouldn't have had to go. I was a medical student and had enough money to buy my way out. But it seemed the right thing to do in 1916."

Lizzie thought of a history paper she wrote on the lack of foresight of World War I. She stopped as another thought entered her mind. "A battlefield is full of blood."

"Elizabeth, I don't spend all my days thinking about food."

"I do. I really have to think hard about not eating chocolate cake sometimes."

"Sometimes. Is that what you are thinking about right this second? Would you rather have a piece of chocolate cake than walk with me?"

"No. But if I was surrounded by it all the time…"

"If anything would make me lose my stomach for drinking blood, it would be war. In fact, it was going to war that made me realize finally that what I am is not a monster. There is a blood thirst on the battlefield that is very different from my need to survive."

Lizzie softened her eyes. She knew from her father that there was no way for her to comprehend the horrors of war. No matter how many movies she saw or books she read, she could never fully know how terrible the death of battle was. She knew from her father those images did not fade away. Lizzie looked at Ben and wondered if a near century eroded the visions of mustard gas and machine guns. "Did you … use your ability against the enemy?"

"It isn't a weapon," he said with all severity. "I put a man out of his misery once…" Ben's eyes wandered towards the sound of the rushing water.

"I'm sorry," Lizzie broke the silence. "It isn't fair for me to make you remember awful things."

Ben fixed his eyes back on her. She didn't understand to what memory his mind shifted as he looked at her, but she could tell that it wasn't any more comforting than the echoes of Verdun. "It isn't fair for me to make you feel guilty for asking," Ben returned quietly.

"What did you do after Verdun?"

"I went back to Princeton and earned my medical degree," he smiled.

"When did you graduate?"

"From medical school?" Lizzie nodded to his question. "1922."

"How many times have you gone to college?" Lizzie started walking again.

"Three."

"Princeton, MIT, and…"

"Harvard. It was my first degree."

"Of course," Lizzie laughed. "You must know many things."

"The world changes and there is always more to learn. Plus, it helps one change professions."

"Right," Lizzie paused. "You didn't like being a doctor?"

"I liked it very much." Ben saw a bench and led her over to it. "I was doing something very important."

"Then why did you change?"

"I wanted to," he looked at her and let out a deep sigh. "I was a doctor for nearly sixty years. Most men retire after so long."

"So you retired by going to high school?"

"Pretty much," he laughed.

"Why go to high school? Why go back to high school when you can clearly pass yourself off as a young man? Why put yourself through all that emotional agony?"

"It gave me a history to get into college."

"Yes… but that doesn't make sense."

"I never went to high school before Springs. I didn't know that it was miserable… or why it was so wonderful that people have reunions every five years."

Lizzie laughed to herself. "I guess … but why be such a … well, you could have easily been a jock or someone popular. You can't be that inept at sports."

"I'm not," Ben sat slowly on the bench. "Participating wouldn't have been a good idea. All those endorphins running rampant would have been a difficult challenge."

"Endorphins?" Lizzie sat next to him.

"That runner's high you get courses through your blood stream. It's intoxicating."

"You don't like a high blood alcohol level… but you like endorphins?"

"Mm hm," he nodded, not looking at her.

"Well, I guess I was safe company then. I couldn't run and I certainly wasn't getting any other sort of endorphin rush in high school."

"I liked your company," Ben pushed some of her loose strands behind her ear.

Lizzie wasn't affected by his tenderness. "But if you were going back to high school… why did you choose Springs? In the middle of nowhere? Why not choose a better school system, with more educational opportunity? With a more diverse student body to seem less… obviously different? Why did you pick Springs?"

"Going to high school helped immerse me in culture and learn current vernacular. It wasn't just about the classes I was taking. I needed to fit into a younger generation. I chose Springs because I liked Coldbrook," he kissed the top of her forehead.

"What about Oliver?" Lizzie asked abruptly and looked up to his eyes.

Ben dropped his hands at his sides and sighed. "He is like me."

"He's a vampire?"

"Yes."

"Your parents?"

"Did you ever meet our parents?"

"No."

"That's because we didn't have parents."

"Are you really brothers?" Lizzie suddenly realized Ben's red tinted hair and greenish eyes didn't match Oliver's darker colors.

"We were both changed by the same vampire," he said slowly.

"Where is he?"

"She is dead."

"You said you were immortal."

"No, I did not."

"But you… can't die."

"I never said that," Ben shook his head. "I assure you I can die."

Lizzie's mind filled with another hundred questions. It was difficult to decide which was more important to understand. "How did she die?"

Ben looked at her, hardening his gaze. "Her heart stopped working," he said coldly, confusing Lizzie and discouraging her from continuing the pursuit of that subject.

Lizzie paused and let the sound of the water fill the air for a few minutes as she let her mind stop buzzing. She wanted to stop, breathe, and simply appreciate the fact she was with Ben. It was overwhelming … and yet, as she saw his eyes shift back to her… amazing. "Is Oliver really older than you?"

"Younger," Ben's voice was warmer, but not as light as her question.

"I really was an idiot in high school," Lizzie laughed at herself. "I had no idea."

"There is a lot of self-absorption in high school," he lightened.

"But what of the teachers? The principal?"

"They have enough to worry about with teenagers without suspecting there are vampires. Besides, Oliver and I kept a pretty low profile."

"Mm," Lizzie mused, thinking of her more outrageous classmates. Dan Stewart was definitely a bigger handful than a geeky closeted vampire. "So, really… after all those years of being alive, you liked my company of so many other choices at Springs?"

"I did," Ben put his arm around her.

"And Sara, of course," Lizzie tensed her shoulders with the memory.

Ben lifted his hand and turned her chin to make her face him. "I never had a thing for Sara," he met her eyes.

"Never?" Lizzie felt her head spinning with a truth more dissembling of her reality than any of the other things Ben had told her in the past two days.

"Never," Ben caught her next breath in a passionate kiss, silencing her questions to the sounds of the birds and the Connecticut River rushing in the distance.

*****

Lizzie shut off the television as Ben walked into the room with two paper bags. He set them on the small table. "I got you some dinner," he removed a Styrofoam carton.

Lizzie smiled uneasily. "Thanks."

He pulled out the chair and waited for her to take the seat. She sat and lifted her hands up awkwardly as he slid her closer to the table. "You can't wait a week until you eat again."

"I can't believe got me a hamburger," Lizzie lifted the lid of the container.

"You don't like hamburgers?" he sat down in the chair opposite.

"No, I love them. I just… I didn't run today."

"You just hiked through the gorge and back. You need iron. Red meat is a good source of iron."

"I know," Lizzie lifted it to her mouth and set it back down. "I feel weird eating while you just… sit there."

"I'm used to it."

"Yes, well… I am very self conscious about eating more than other people."

"Elizabeth, this is something you will need to get used to. Besides, you watched me eat the other night."

"That was… different," Lizzie pulled apart the layers of the burger. She found the pickles and pulled them off of the roll. "Have you ever had a hamburger?"

"No," he shook his head in amusement.

"So you missed out on the whole McDonald's thing?"

"I bought some of their stock," he continued his amusement.

"There's something very odd about a vampire making money on what people eat," Lizzie shook her head as she put the burger back together and took a bite. It was lukewarm, but tasty. She realized how hungry she was. She only ate a few protein bars since leaving Newton. She took another slow bite and was aware of him watching her. "You said there was a clinic."

He softened his gaze with a short smile. "I did say that."

Lizzie set down her burger and reached for her half empty water bottle. She took a drink, watching his eyes to see if there would be any more answers during her silence. She set it on the table and decided to prod him before taking another bite. "How does that work?"

"The clinic?" Ben asked as though she could just as easily be discussing her hamburger. "There are a number of sources who come in and provide blood. It's a lot like the Red Cross. There is even juice and cookies for them."

"Do you bite them?" Lizzie felt a burn of jealousy more than anything else. Was it something over which she should be jealous?

"Sometimes there is that option. It is frequently a transfusion."

"With needles?"

"That's how it works," he shrugged as if it were obvious. "Is it not a good burger?"

"No," Lizzie shook her head and forced herself to take another bite. "Are the sources… do they do it for… pleasure?"

"I imagine some do," Ben looked at her plate, prompting another bite before he spoke again. "They all are compensated. I suspect a fair number do it for the extra cash."

"How can there be enough people who know about this and… yet vampires are so unreal?"

"Most sources find out about the clinic because they had a connection with a vampire. Some come as referrals. Everyone is discreet."

"You must pay them well."

"Very well."

"How did you find out about this… clinic?" she took another bite so he would answer her swiftly.

"I helped create it," he answered very nonchalantly. "It was based on a model in Europe that I discovered in France. "

"Clinics for vampires."

"Think about it. It's an opportunity for us to screen the blood and regulate intake. It's a very good service."

"So is that why you became a doctor?"

"No, I had a practice for about fifteen years. Then when my youth became obvious, I decided to do something for vampires as well as their sources."

"What do you screen blood for?" Lizzie didn't think she could force herself to eat any more of her hamburger.

"Drugs. Alcohol. Cholesterol. Metals. Diseases. The healthier the blood, the less likely a vampire is to go out and drink irresponsibly."

"What happens if you drink blood with AIDS?"

"It makes us weaker. Same with diabetes. It takes a while to flush it out. AIDS sometimes stays for years."

"People die from it," Lizzie was almost irritated with his matter of fact tone.

"I know."

"Is there anything in our blood that can kill you?"

"Not directly," Ben looked at his hands. "Lead has the most severe consequences."

"Lead?"

"Yes," he hesitated. Lizzie could see he was editing the information before he began to speak. "A lot of the superstition and myths about vampires come from our reactions to lead poisoning."

"Really?"

"The mutation of our DNA has weakened our defenses to lead. In addition to human reactions of pain and insomnia, we are at high risk for developing intense porphyria. This leads to a sensitivity to light and severe mania."

"Lead was in so many things. It's still in so many things. Lead paint was everywhere."

"Yes it was," Ben nodded. "A number of vampires were infected as a consequence."

"Did they die?"

"Most of them," he nodded. "Some became monstrous and were killed as a result. Some were able to purge the lead from their system. If they drink quality blood now, the symptoms do not recur."

Lizzie looked at her cold burger and pushed the plate away from her. Ben was vulnerable… even if it seemed obscure. She wondered if vampires considered lead paint a pandemic. "Is there a way of knowing quality blood without going to the clinic?"

"Our sense of taste is distinctive," Ben dropped his eyes to her unfinished dinner. "Everyone is different. If someone has had a bad reaction to something, they are more likely to know the taste of a metal or a disease or lipids."

"If you taste something bad, do you stop drinking?"

"I do. I can't speak for all of us."

"What could you taste in my blood?"

"You are on birth control."

"You can taste that?"

"Estrogen."

"Does it taste good?"

"It's insignificant. It isn't necessary for you now," he said quietly.

Lizzie wasn't surprised at that implication, but felt enough of a sting at the thought she decided not to linger upon it. "What's the best kind of blood?"

"From someone with a healthy heart. The blood is full of oxygen."

"And endorphins?"

"Endorphins are… well perhaps a little like caffeine is for you."

"Wakes you up?"

"Sort of. It feels really, really good."

"So is that why vampires and sex go so well together?" Lizzie looked at him blatantly.

"It can be pleasurable for both if the timing is right," Ben answered her stare.

"Do you ever have sex with your sources at the clinic?"

"Not at the clinic. There are other less regulated operations that are … well pretty much a brothel. But they can't guarantee clean blood."

"What did you do at the clinic for fifty years?"

"I managed operations and helped to establish others throughout the country based on the same model. I also worked in the lab and tested a lot of blood. Partly, to evaluate sources. Partly as research."

"Research?"

"On diseases of the blood. In humans and vampire humans."

"Identifying or curing?"

"A little bit of both. I tried to cure the reaction to lead. Unfortunately, I only came up with a chelation agent, that works the toxic metals through your urinary track. Vampires don't use their digestive systems, so it doesn't do much good for vampires."

"Oh," Lizzie found the information more confusing than helpful at this point. "Do you miss working at the clinic?"

"I still consult every once in a while," he rested his gray green eyes on her again. "I left the clinic in good hands."

"Where is it?"

"Near Central Square," he answered more readily than Lizzie expected. "I was on my way home the day I saw you sprain your ankle."

"Oh," Lizzie smiled, thinking of that afternoon and the tense moment at the top of her stairs.

"I was on my way to the clinic the second time I saw you running along the river," he continued. "You were very tempting that day."

"I was running," Lizzie saw the pieces come together. "You wanted my endorphins."

"I did."

"Ben," she looked down at her abandoned plate. "Did you like my blood?"

"Very much."

"Even without the endorphins?"

"You were scared," he smirked. "Fear excites the nerves, too, you know."

"I was scared," Lizzie wouldn't look at him.

"I know…" Ben started but stopped when Lizzie looked up to meet his eyes. He reached across the table and took her hand as he had that night. He turned over her wrist and looked at the marks that were still red. "I also think you were extraordinarily brave. I only saw that fearlessness once before." He paused and stroked her wrist, igniting the electric sensations she knew came only from his touch. "I found that more alluring than any amount of endorphins in your blood."

Lizzie caught the smile that gazed at her. She forced her mind to quiet all the new questions that came into her mind. It seemed every answer ignited ten more questions. She was weary of asking. She relished the smile and the touch of his fingers against the inside of her arm. And the fact he found her alluring.

*****

Lizzie closed the door quietly. She pulled off her sneakers and happily sighed with a glance at him asleep on the bed. His face was so still. His breaths were barely noticeable even with just the fragment of sheet covering his bare chest. She bent down and rolled up her spine for one last stretch and returned her gaze to his open eyes.

"Were you really sleeping?"

"Did you go running?"

"I went along the river. The dewy morning was breathtaking," she reached for her water bottle.

He smiled at her and slowly sat up. "Will you come back to sit with me?"

"I'm all sweaty and gross. Plus you'll want my endorphins."

He restructured his smile and shifted his look towards her. "You don't sleep much, do you?"

"Not these days," she smiled. "I'm going to take a shower."

Lizzie looked into the steam covered mirror. She was satisfied with her reflection. She never gave pause to the fact that she met her goal in the fury of months that passed since meeting Ben. Running became more an excuse to forget him and less a determination to drop the last stubborn pounds that lingered on her body. They were gone, as was the worry he wouldn't call her again.

She hung up the towel and collected her dirty clothes and went back into the room. Ben was dressed and watching the morning news. "How many days are we going to stay here?"

"How sick do you think I am, Dr. Cottingham?"

"At least through the week."

"I have to get back by Friday. Meg and I are helping Nora with more wedding preparations," Lizzie paused at his lack of response. "Weddings must seem ridiculous when you've lived through so many different ideas of marriage. When you know that forever isn't… well, really… could you ever see yourself staying with one person forever?"

"I couldn't, unless it was another vampire."

"But even then… wouldn't you… well you wanted to try a new career. Wouldn't you want to have a new mate after so many years… centuries?" Lizzie went to her bag.

"Are you afraid I am going to get tired of you, Elizabeth?"

"Well… yes. No. I don't ... of course you will," she pulled her jeans out her bag. "Damn it. I always say stupid things like that. I didn't mean… I just don't see myself as someone who could be compelling for 50 years. Besides, I'm getting old. You will always be… how old will you always be?"

"Twenty-five."

"Well," Lizzie sighed. "There it is. I'm already getting white hairs."

"You aren't old, Elizabeth. You just ran through a gorge."

"Running isn't going to make me twenty-five again."

"I look twenty-five. I am not… I've seen too many things to have any sense of naiveté."

"But you've got this perpetually youthful body. Why would you want to be with someone who is older?" Lizzie sat on the edge of the bed.

Ben came behind and circled his arms around her waist. "Don't worry about growing old, Elizabeth. You don't know how much I envy that."

"Do you ever wish you could go back? That you were… mortal and could grow old?"

"I've been a vampire long enough to know it is foolish to wish such things."

"I don't know if I would want to outlive everyone I love."

There was a sad glimmer in his eyes. "That is challenging. It gets … people are taking better care of themselves now. They live longer."

"We still die."

Ben breathed out unhappily. "I can't say it gets easier to witness. But I've learned that it shouldn't stop me from appreciating when I find someone who makes the present interesting, nor does it stop me from wanting to spend as much time as possible with them while they are with me."

Lizzie felt a huge sorrow overwhelm her. She turned to see if he had any of that sorrow in his eyes or any expression on his face. She didn't find the emotion and couldn't curb her next thought from articulating. "But humans are still your source, first and foremost?"

"No, Elizabeth," he unwrapped his arms. "No."

"Have you…" she shut her eyes, able to catch the question in her mouth.

"Go ahead," he looked angry.

"Never mind."

"Ask it."

"It's not important," she got up from the bed, uncertain if she felt comfortable in the presence of his anger.

"It is important. You want to know. You need to know. Ask me." Lizzie went back to her bag for her hairbrush. She turned to the mirror and began brushing her wet strands. "Ask it."

Lizzie breathed in and finished her hair. She set the brush down and turned to face him. He was waiting. "How many people have you killed?"

"Five."

Lizzie shut her eyes and looked back to the dresser for an elastic. "Five," she repeated, putting the elastic around her fingers but losing momentum as she saw the bite marks on her wrist.

"Yes."

"Only five?" Lizzie asked. "In two hundred and thirty years? I would think you would have been hungrier than that."

"To go that far… it isn't healthy."

"Indeed," she breathed out.

"One was…" he stopped. Lizzie turned around to face his downcast eyes. He fumbled with his hands. "I take the blame for one I allowed to happen… but didn't stop."

"I want to go home," Lizzie felt sick.

"I will tell you everything, Elizabeth. I won't…"

"I don't want to know," she cried. "I don't want to know about that part of you… not yet."

"We can go back to Newton," he sighed.

"I don't want to… I want to… not care. But I don't know how to not care."

"It's what I am."

"Have they been recent? Even after you became a doctor and did all that blood research?"

"No. The last one was in 1918."

"You said you put someone out of his misery."

"I did."

"What about the battlefield? Did you feed on corpses?"

"I can't feed on corpses. But it was a war… there were a number of willing … I didn't kill anyone by feeding in the war. I was a soldier. That was a much more brutal way of killing."

"With no purpose," Lizzie looked blankly in front of her. "I don't know what is real anymore. Or what is right."

"Do you think it isn't right to be here with me?"

"You didn't… you stayed away. You ran away. There must have been a reason," Lizzie still looked ahead blankly. She couldn't look at him, even as she knew she should to see his reaction.

"I was scared."

"Scared you would kill me? Or scared that I would think you were a psychopath and never want to see you again?"

"I was scared for you…" he answered slowly. "And scared that I would never see you again."

Lizzie looked up and met his pained eyes. She felt a surge of sympathy warm within her. "I don't want to go home just yet."

"Okay."

Lizzie pulled her hair back and wrapped her watch around her left wrist. "Why me, Ben?"

"I told you, Elizabeth. I like you very much."

"But … all this for some mousy girl you met at Springs High School and spent one night with fifteen years later? I don't understand."

Ben stood up and went to pull his keys from his coat pocket. "I think you need some breakfast. You just went running and still haven't eaten a decent meal since we got here."

Lizzie met his eyes again. She felt her stomach growl with the recognition of the truth of his words. "Are you going to answer my question?"

"Why I chose you? I don't think that explanation is any different for me than it is for you," he shrugged. "Why are you here with me even though you know what you know? Maybe it's just because we like one another's company?"

"Maybe," she agreed to end the conversation followed him out the door.

*****

Lizzie didn't know how to talk to him as they sat in the dining room eating breakfast. She ate breakfast. He sat with a cup of coffee from which he never drank. He talked about the activities of the past three days – walking in the gorge, driving across the state border into Lebanon and Dartmouth, and all the pine trees. Lizzie filled her plate at the buffet so she didn't have to talk and wasn't even sure if she was completely listening to him. She tried to empty her thoughts of their conversation in the room. The reality of the situation was starting to wear off the warm glow of infatuation.

Was that what it was? She found herself asking that question. She hated sappy emotion. She hated to be all girly and swoony. The last time she was such an idiotic fool. And… really… that stupid love thing was always so messy. But this… this wasn't just messy. Was she really debating sappy emotion with herself when there was a very real fact of danger hovering in her mind like a bad cloud?

"Elizabeth?" he asked in a tone that made her wonder how many times he repeated her name.

"Mm?" she swallowed another bite of eggs.

"If we aren't driving back to Boston, what are we going to do today?"

"I don't care," she took another mouthful. She saw the annoyance creep across his face.

"You don't want to go home?"

Lizzie looked around the dining room. It was empty but for one other couple at the opposite end. "What about your brother?"

"I told you."

"Yes, he's like you," Lizzie was careful with her words, even in the empty dining room. "But how?"

Ben took in a deep breath. "He was changed almost forty years later."

"Why did he go to Springs? Did he want to change careers, too? He went back to high school so he could go to college and stay there?"

"Oliver had a different reason for going to Springs."

"You don't like talking about Oliver," Lizzie observed. "Did you have a falling out?"

"We have gone separate ways for a while," Ben tried to offer a smile.

"But he… well, he's someone who knows what you are," Lizzie said sadly. "It must be lonely without him. It must be lonely for him."

"Actually, he is married and perfectly happy."

"To a… non-vampire human?"

"To a vampire," Ben laughed. "They have been together for just over ten years… which was the last time I spoke with him."

"But you are friends with him on Facebook," Lizzie remarked.

"We can see what one another is doing and not have to speak to each other," Ben still seemed uncomfortable.

"Does he know about me?"

"No," Ben said emphatically.

Lizzie watched him grip his coffee mug. His fingers clung tightly around the ceramic handle. Lizzie scanned her memories of Oliver to recall any acrimony between them at SRHS. She could only remember him being there for a year. In that year, her memory was mostly of the debate club. "You don't want him to know?"

"It's not really any of his business," Ben loosened his grasp of the mug and tried to lighten his voice. "We've gone our separate ways."

Lizzie suddenly thought about Sara and how that friendship turned to disinterest and latent bitterness. She could understand Ben, even if he didn't articulate what or who came between them. Besides, Oliver was in California and unlikely to cross her path again. "Have you told anyone about me?"

"Like who?"

"I don't know," Lizzie bit her lip, her annoyance with Ben shifting to annoyance with herself for acting so stupidly girly. "Your friends at the clinic?"

"I don't think they would … I keep to myself, Elizabeth. I don't have the circle of friends that you do."

"Aren't you lonely?"

"I have my work."

"I have work, but that doesn't… it isn't enough," Lizzie frowned. "Then again, I'm just a secretary essentially. I'm not inventing cures for lead poisoning or computers that do things I can't explain in English."

Ben laughed and reached for her hand. "Elizabeth, in the six months since I saw you at the reunion, I realized that keeping to myself isn't enough. That's why I decided to do this. That's why I came to tell you my truth. That's why we are here now. I don't want to be on my own when there is an option to be with you."

She swallowed, overwhelmed and uncertain what to say. She didn't want to ruin it with a clumsy response or ignore it with the chill of silence. "I…" she squeezed his hand and breathed out. "Ben, of all the things you've explained in the past few days, that is the most important thing you've said. We can stay here for the rest of the week or go back to Boston. Wherever we are, I want to spend the time with you."

She saw his green gray eyes lock on her. She felt a sudden chill across her shoulders, like the ghostly drafts she felt in the rooms of the Fulton House. It ebbed away quickly as the look of the green eyes warmed her. They were familiar, as if she knew that stare from before and had been waiting for it to return. As if she were meant to be sitting there across from those green eyes all along.

Chapter Thirteen

Lizzie sat beside Ben on the couch. She put her bottle on the table in front of her, making sure it was very close to Ben's. She was aware of Meg and Nora looking in their direction whenever a lull in the conversation lasted more than a beat. She supposed it was a novelty. Lizzie never had a date to anything, not even informal gatherings among friends. And now, for once, she wasn't the odd extra single.

Ben was telling Mark about his business. Mark worked in pharmaceuticals and found interest in Ben's medical computers, something Lizzie still didn't quite comprehend. She probably now understood more about the science of vampires than the science of the machine in front of which she sat each day for hours. She was glad that Ben had something to talk about with Mark, who didn't mix so well with Alec.

Meg brought him to the evening of drinks Nora suggested. Lizzie knew Nora wasn't thrilled to have the philandering professor in her living room, but was able to keep her reservations quiet in light of the fact there was a new member of their company. Meg stayed by Alec's side, as if protecting him from Nora and Mark. Ben didn't seem much interested in striking up a conversation with him either. Lizzie didn't know if that was because she had told him about Meg's manic infatuation or if it was because he was the professor guiding Meg's thesis on vampires.

"Have you ever been there, Ben?" Lizzie turned her focus back to Mark and his question to Ben about County Kerry.

"No," he shook his head. "I've only been to Dublin, I'm afraid."

"The whole country is amazing," Alec startled everyone by entering the conversation. "You should go back. Rent a cottage anywhere along the Ring of Kerry. Get a car and explore the county."

"Maybe I will," Ben slipped his hand into Lizzie's palm.

"Good answer, Ben," Meg nodded. "Otherwise we would be here for hours while Alec tried to sell you on Ireland over any other vacation on the planet."

"There's no other place like it," Alec took a sip of his Guinness.

"Yes, I know your poetic soul yearns to go back," Meg smirked. "I think you must have lived there before."

"I spent two years teaching at Trinity," Alec looked at Meg.

"I mean in a former life," Meg answered.

"I think Mark played for the Red Sox in his last life," Nora spread some cheese on a cracker. "And he can't seem to let go of Fenway Park."

Mark laughed. "Sure, Nora," he took a swig of his beer. "What did you do in your last life, Ben?"

"He was a doctor," Lizzie said absently and caught the sudden glances of everyone, including Ben. "That's what I think. He understands a lot about physiology."

"Oh really?" Nora laughed on her cracker.

Lizzie felt the blood rise to her cheeks, realizing the hole she just stepped into. Ben caught the laugh and looked at Lizzie, kissing her gently on the cheek.

"I bet Nora was a matriarch of some Victorian family," Meg sobered Nora's laughter.

"What were you Meg?" Nora retorted

"Oh I was a spinster, who died of a broken heart."

"And Lizzie?" Mark asked.

"I bet she broke the hearts," Nora winked.

Ben let go of her hand and picked up Lizzie's bottle. She watched him pretend to take a sip. She could tell he wasn't really swallowing anything. "I didn't break anything," Lizzie looked back at Meg and accepted the bottle from Ben to take a drink.

"Not that any of that is real," Mark took a handful of crackers and sat back in his chair.

"What? Reincarnation?" Lizzie found herself attentive.

"Well, yeah… I mean, once you die, you die," Mark plunged a cracker into the cheese spread.

"That's a depressing thought," Meg pouted.

"You don't think it's depressing to think that you could come back here and have no idea you were alive a hundred years before?"

"I don't think we have no idea. What about déjà vu? What about things that draw our attentions for no obvious reason? I really do think Alec has some connection to Ireland," Meg argued.

"Yeah, his last name is McCaffrey," Mark muttered.

Lizzie thought of her conversation with Ben on the way to Jack's gig. She looked at him to see his reaction. What would Mark say if she told him that Ben was perpetually undying?

"Or what about Lizzie? That house she works at on the weekends? Even she admits that there is something about that house that she can't explain."

Lizzie looked away from Ben, annoyed that Meg was using her in an argument with Mark, which was more about her disinterest in Mark than about any belief about death. "Meg, I don't think I was one of the Fultons."

"No... but don't you think you were there when it was a house and not just a museum?"

"It's been a museum for over a hundred years."

"Precisely."

"Meg, we all believe what we want to believe," Nora jumped up and headed towards the kitchen. "Can I get anyone something else to drink? Ben?"

"No thank you, Nora," Ben smiled and looked at Lizzie.

"I think we are all drawn to things that had something to do with when we were here before," Meg maintained her position.

"So, what... does that mean you liked vampires, Meg?" Mark sneered. "Maybe you were killed by one in your last life."

Lizzie felt Ben's arm go over her shoulder. Lizzie watched Alec's reaction to Mark. Lizzie didn't think he was the type to throw down a gauntlet and protect his wounded girlfriend. Not that she could imagine Alec succeeding in any challenge against Mark. She knew Ben was calm and collected. She imagined this petty squabble was like a bunch of teenagers to him. She liked his protective arm and wondered why Alec didn't offer one to Meg.

Nora reappeared quickly with another plate of food. Lizzie smiled up at her and decided to spread some of the tapenade on the sliced bread. "Thank you, Nora," she leaned back against Ben's arm waiting to hold onto her. "You know I like the idea of reincarnation," Lizzie offered when no one spoke after she finished chewing. "I like the possibility of getting a chance to put things right."

"How can you put them right if you don't remember?" Nora sighed, annoyed that the conversation was continuing.

"Well… maybe it's just the idea that it's possible that counts. It's hope for us before we leave this planet. Hope that no matter how much we mess up, we can fix it," Lizzie reached for another piece of bread. "Even if it never gets the chance to be fixed. Just the hope that it can be… isn't that worth something?"

No one answered. "Well… if nothing else, it makes for great speculative conversation when I introduce my boyfriend to my crazy friends."

Mark laughed and put his arm around Nora. "True, Lizzie. Very true."

Meg breathed out and managed a smile. "I think we can all agree about that," she accepted the piece of bread Lizzie just covered.

"That you are all crazy?" Ben chided. "Absolutely."

*****

Lizzie dropped her purse and jacket on a brown leather chair in the living room. She took in the details of his apartment slowly. It was the top floor of a three decker, probably a hundred years old. Lizzie noticed the modern furniture mingled with the historic moldings. It was tidy, well furnished, and comfortable. It wasn't what she expected… and yet… not unusual at all.

"That was fun," Ben led her into a dining room.

"You have a dining room."

"So do you," Ben returned. "And even with three people who eat food in your house, you never use it."

"You really… it was okay?"

"Elizabeth, I like your friends," he kissed her sweetly and went towards an antique buffet set up as a bar. She watched him pour a glass of wine and hand it to her. "Between the two of us, you only drank half a bottle of beer tonight."

"I like how you get me drunk every night."

"Not drunk. Just… a precaution."

"Are you hungry?" Lizzie touched her wrist.

"Just enjoy it," he smiled.

Lizzie smiled shortly and looked at her glass. She followed him back into the living room and accepted his invitation to sit beside him on his sofa. She took a sip of her wine and let it warm her. "I'm sorry if the acrimony between Meg and Mark was unbearable. They often… they aren't friendly."

"Why is that?" Ben touched her hair as she leaned against his shoulder.

"It's just the way it is with boyfriends of best friends."

"You get along with him."

"I get along with most people. I can see that Mark really truly loves Nora. Meg just … well, she thinks he's boring. She would rather we all ran off with…" Lizzie stopped herself from what would have easily been an amusing thing to say. She heard Ben chuckle under his breath. "She thinks a little danger is sexy."

"Alec …"

"They've got nothing on you," Lizzie looked ahead and took a sip of her wine.

"No," Ben took in a breath as he continued to smooth his fingers along her hair. "I think I've met Alec before."

"What?" Lizzie almost spit out her wine.

"I'm not sure if he recognized me."

"From where?" Lizzie pulled herself away from Ben and set down her glass on the coffee table.

"I'm pretty certain he used to be a donor at the clinic," Ben said cautiously, but without concern.

Lizzie looked away, finding a sudden fixation on the pattern of browns and reds in his carpet. "So that means he knows… he knows," Lizzie looked up at Ben.

"It's a strong possibility," Ben smiled shortly.

"But he's… he smokes and sleeps with so many… women and men. He can't have the best blood," Lizzie took up her wine glass again. Her intolerance for Alec sank even deeper.

"I don't think he still goes there," Ben touched her hand. "I just thought you should know."

"In case he tells Meg?"

"It is her favorite subject," Ben's smile was more polite than encouraging. Even so, Lizzie couldn't stop a little bit of hope from entering her mind. It was a week since she came back from their getaway to Vermont, but she already felt the limitations of her conversations about Ben. Even when there were drinks at Nora and Mark's. Ben could integrate well enough with her friends, pretend to drink his beer and eat cheese and crackers. But Lizzie was still left without anyone to talk to about the weirdness of it all… or the possibility of fear.

Lizzie shook her head and leaned back against his side. She didn't want to think of Meg or Alec while she was in the already familiar comfort of his side in his apartment. "How long have you lived here?"

"I rented the apartment when I first worked at the hospital," Ben restored his arm around her shoulder. "Then I bought the whole building in the 60's. The rental income was useful when I went to Springs. After graduating from MIT, I restored all the units and sold them as condos. I figured my company was enough responsibility and no longer had interest in being a landlord."

Lizzie looked down at her wine glass. She still expected him to say he bought the place five years ago… not fifty. She breathed in slowly and then looked at him suddenly. "What hospital did you work at?" she lifted her eyes to see his reaction.

He pursed his lips on the smile. "Mt. Elm."

"That's… where I work," she faded on the obvious words of her sentence.

"Yes."

Lizzie took the last sip from her glass and replaced it on the coffee table. She rested against his arm and gazed at the entertainment center and shelves across from her. She couldn't identify the DVDs or books on the shelves. "It is one of the older hospitals in the city," Lizzie said to herself, thinking of some of the more antiquated buildings on the campus.

"It is."

"Ben, is there such a thing as reincarnation?" she didn't look at him with her serious tone.

"What?"

"You've been around a while. Maybe you've seen someone come back."

He breathed in deeply. "I don't know much more than you about what happens after a person dies, Elizabeth. I just know I don't die as easily."

"But you have been on this planet much longer. That gives you more opportunity to observe things... to understand that things can't be as neat and tidy as Mark would like to believe," Lizzie sat up and turned to look at him.

"I think some people come back," Ben readjusted his posture. He looked at Lizzie intently. "I'm pretty certain I've met a soul in different lifetimes."

Lizzie met his stare and then twisted herself back against his shoulder. "Oh," she couldn't bring herself to ask the next question.

"But I don't know... I don't know that is what happens to everyone."

"Well, of course not," Lizzie took his hand and intertwined their fingers. "Could you come back? If your heart was destroyed, would you come back as a vampire?"

She felt his breath go deep into his stomach. "If someone destroys my heart, Elizabeth, I am done with this world."

"What happens?"

"I don't know."

"Do you go to hell?"

"I thought you didn't believe in hell."

"I didn't believe in vampires either," Lizzie let go of his hand and looked at him. "I didn't mean that in a ... mean way, Ben. If there is a hell, I'm probably going there, too."

"I think we've both already experienced our own versions of hell," he looked away from her, his thoughts following his gaze.

"Karma?"

"I guess you could call it that," Ben returned his focus to her and took her hand in his again.

"I think..." Lizzie sighed, welcoming the fingers in between her own. "I think this is my good karma."

Ben smiled. "Me too."

*****

Lizzie awoke expecting to see the green numbers of her clock. Her mind slowly awakened, realizing she wasn't in her bed or her room. She was under Ben's arm in his apartment. She let her mind retreat back to sleepiness with the conclusion there wasn't enough sunlight to require getting out of bed for another Saturday at the Fulton House.

She drifted back to sleep as she imagined taking Ben on her tour. She wondered if he remembered using objects like they had in the museum… if it would be at all interesting or nostalgic for him to see them. Maybe he could explain all the fuss about the chair in Harriet's room. That way she could tell Richard to tell Gerard Fulton to stop worrying…

Lizzie stood in the passageway from the stairwell to the great room. She kept in the shadows watching all the people mingle and drink their cocktails. She watched Gerard Fulton whisper to Jonathan, the curator. Paula and Richard stood close to them, both aware of Lizzie in the passageway but more attentive to the discussion of upholstery. Lizzie wondered if she should enter the room and clean up the empty glasses cast on the side tables, but thought her jeans and sweater were too informal for the party, making it obvious that she didn't belong in the crowd.

She looked away from the conversations and focused her attention on the string quartet at the back of the room. The notes of Vivaldi quieted her mind and took her from the room and her aching feet. She leaned her head against the wall and felt the heat of someone behind her. She turned slowly and met Ben's friendly gaze.

Lizzie rolled over as she opened her eyes from her dream. Ben was gone. A moment of panic filled her thoughts, but then talked herself back to reality remembering she was in his apartment. She found his shirt on the floor and buttoned it as she crossed the hall to look for him. She heard the click of a keyboard and followed it into his office. He looked up from his screen as she walked in. She saw the burning look in those eyes. He was hungry.

"Morning," he softened the glimmer in his eyes.

"Morning," she sat on a leather couch opposite his desk, not able to completely quiet the question of how hungry he was.

"I made you some coffee in the kitchen," he rose from his chair.

"You make coffee?"

"It's a good skill to have as a businessman."

"You must have a secretary," Lizzie tried to imagine Richard making his own coffee.

"There's milk in the fridge," Ben said lightly and watched her leave the room.

Lizzie went to the kitchen, opening three cupboards before finding the mugs and glasses. She was surprised to see so many dishes and silverware. It was clean, almost brand new. She wondered how many guests he had for whom he kept up the pretense… or fed if they knew… if he fed from them. Lizzie shook that thought from her mind as she stirred the milk into her coffee. It was good coffee.

She took her mug and went back to her seat on the leather couch. Ben typed another few minutes before returning his gaze to her. "What time do you have to be at the museum?"

"Ten," Lizzie rested the mug on her knees. "What time is it?"

"Eight," he smiled again. "I can give you a ride if you don't feel like taking the train."

"Thanks," Lizzie took another sip and grinned to herself as she thought of her dream. "I could give you a tour."

Ben took in a light-hearted breath. "I can't today," he paused as if contemplating a change in his plans. "I have to finish up this project before noon. Then I have to get to the clinic."

"Right," Lizzie summoned the neutrality to mask her disappointment. "If it's too much to give me a ride, I can take the train."

"It isn't too much," he shook his head.

"Next time," Lizzie shrugged as she lifted her mug to her lips and let her eyes wander to the details of the room. She noticed the old volumes on the bookshelves and thought the Fulton House might not be so interesting to him anyway.

"You're going back to Nora's tonight?"

"Yeah, I'm helping her with the favors."

Lizzie saw the amusement in Ben's his sweet gray green eyes. "Will Meg be there?'

"She's supposed to be… but after last night probably not," Lizzie walked over to the books that caught her eye. She pulled a volume of Keats and looked at the title page. "This is a first edition."

"I got it in England," Ben left the desk and moved to her side.

"You like poetry?"

"I like Keats," he pulled another volume.

Lizzie took the book from his hand. "Shakespeare's sonnets," she admired the binding and the pages. "This is three hundred years old. I really shouldn't be touching this without gloves."

"Why not?" Ben shrugged. "It really makes no difference what it's printed on. Isn't it the words that matter the most?"

"But there is a craftsmanship…" Lizzie stopped herself and looked at Ben. "It is in good condition."

"Yes."

"Have you read all these books?" she looked at the companion plays to the collection of sonnets in her hand. "Even with all your medical and computer studies?"

"I confess I haven't read them recently," Ben watched her pull out another book and look inside. "A few I reread because they were important to someone I like to remember."

Lizzie closed the copy of *Candide* and shifted her focus quickly enough to catch a glimpse of sadness in his expression. "These are valuable to you for a reason beyond bindings and printing dates," Lizzie sheepishly returned the book to its place.

"Yes," Ben looked at the book she replaced and looked back to her. "You can touch all these books without gloves, Elizabeth. I like to think you will enjoy them."

She wanted to ask him a dozen more questions. She wanted to know who the someone was and why he still wanted to remember her… if it was a her. Was it the vampire who changed him? Was it another human... from another century? She shifted her eyes back to his, the first of her inquiries poised on her tongue. She saw the burning look of his hunger. "I should probably get ready," she said quickly, deciding to move away from him and her curiosity.

Ben heaved a deep sigh and nodded. "I'll be here if you need anything," he offered as he returned to his desk. Lizzie felt his eyes follow her out of the room.

Chapter Fourteen

Lizzie leaned her head against the window and watched the blur of the white lines passing beneath the car. She listened vaguely to Nora and Meg discuss who was expected at the rehearsal dinner and staying at the hotel through the weekend. She ran through her own checklist of things she promised Nora she would take care of at the hotel. Lizzie didn't much agree with Nora's sentiment that multiple hospital galas made Lizzie an event planning expert, but she was happy to do whatever she could to alleviate the stress of the bride.

"Is Ben coming up tonight or tomorrow?" Meg took a sip from her iced coffee.

Lizzie lifted her head away from the window. "Tonight," Lizzie answered. "He probably won't make dinner. But he should be in time for dessert."

"It's too bad he couldn't change that meeting," Nora sighed. Lizzie showed a weak smile even though neither turned from the front seat to see her expression. Ben offered a different schedule, but Lizzie thought it would be less rude for him to not eat sorbet than the steak dinner Nora's father planned. Besides, Lizzie knew his meeting was important. He moved his clinic appointment to Friday so he could be in Gloucester all day Saturday into Sunday.

She appreciated the excuse for his absence, but there was a part of her that disliked his clinic visits. She knew they were necessary. She knew it guaranteed her own safety and health. She knew… all these quantifiable details… but the clinic was still unknown to her. It was a part of him that would be easier to know and understand than the vague details of his transformation or his falling out with Oliver. And yet it was still a mystery. The sources… were unknown. Except, apparently, at one time Alec McCaffrey.

"I'm surprised Ben didn't change the meeting so he could see you. It's been what? Almost a whole week since you've seen him?" Meg turned around as she took another sip from her straw.

Lizzie repeated her strained smile. Alec evidently said nothing to Meg about Ben's secret. Lizzie couldn't imagine Meg would have her attitude if she knew Ben could add a whole new dimension to her thesis. Lizzie also suspected that Alec smoked enough pot to affect his memory and may well have forgotten Ben altogether. "I saw him on Sunday."

"After practically living at his place for two weeks," Meg turned back to face the front of the car.

"Like you're one to talk," Nora picked up her iced drink.

"He lives close to Mt. Elm. It's easier when I have to work," Lizzie leaned against the window again. She wanted to avoid the argument with Meg, who was at the apartment even less than Lizzie. It was apparently not okay for Lizzie to be gone on the one or two nights she returned to Jefferson Park.

"Poor Jackie is all by herself," Meg returned in a tone that Lizzie couldn't tell was mean or funny.

"I think Jackie is all right," Lizzie answered. "Will Alec be there for dinner?"

"Hopefully by five, if traffic doesn't suck too much."

"Has he finished proofing your thesis?" Nora set her cup back in the cup holder.

"Not yet," Meg looked out her window. "But he's liked what he's read so far."

"I still want to read it," Lizzie always wanted to support her friend, but now she had an additional motive.

"Next time I see you at the apartment, I'll give you a copy," Meg darted a glance towards Lizzie.

"Okay," Lizzie decided to let that one slide and get back to the subject of the day.

"Can you get my Chapstick?" Meg held her hand between the front seats. Lizzie reached for Meg's bag. She pulled out a book and felt through the cluttered contents until she found the Chapstick. Lizzie turned over the book and recognized one of Meg's favorite novels. The cover had an illustration of a handsome man with pale, pale skin – white to the point it was nearly blue. He had dark hair and dark eyes and wore a long black cape that swept in the wind around the waist of a voluptuous blonde. His fangs bared as the glint in the eyes focused on the blonde's neck.

Lizzie felt a shudder as she placed the book back in Meg's bag. It was kind of ridiculous. Ben didn't go around in a black cape staring at her neck. He did… sometimes look… but not… like that. He wasn't a monster. Of that she had become most definitely certain. And Lizzie wasn't a young blonde virgin either.

*****

Ben laughed as Lizzie kicked her heels under the chair by the desk. "If you hate them so much why do you wear them?" he closed the door to their room.

"They look good," Lizzie felt an urge to grab him and go immediately… he came to her side and pulled her into his arms before she could finish her thought. He kissed her lips and moved his hands to the zipper at the back of her dress.

She let him slide the straps off her shoulders and moved towards his belt when the phone rang. She pulled away from his excitement and went to her bag. She managed to answer Becca's questions about Nora's jewelry in spite of Ben's continued touches and kisses. She closed the phone and turned back to face him.

"I missed you."

"I missed you, too," Lizzie kissed him until Becca called back looking for Nora's stockings.

Ben took off his jacket and moved into the room. He opened the bar and found Lizzie a glass of wine. "Why don't we wait a little bit?" he offered. "In case you get any more calls tonight."

Lizzie readjusted her straps and zipper then took the wine. "I thought you went to the clinic," she looked at the glass.

"I did," he undid his tie. "But you need to relax."

Lizzie sat herself on the couch. She could smell the salt air through the open window of their room. "Becca is a good sister. She lives too far away to be on top of all of Nora's details."

"I like Becca very much," Ben sat beside her. "Because she is staying the night with the bride. Which means… when she is done calling you every five minutes, I have you to myself."

Lizzie laughed over her first sip of wine. She hardly swallowed when the phone rang again. Nora's mother asked about the flower delivery for the groomsmen. Lizzie took another sip after closing her phone. She looked at the color beneath Ben's freckles and then turned her chin away as he lifted a finger to her cheek. "Who was your source today?"

Ben dropped his hand in his lap. "There is a protocol of anonymity."

"Would I know this person?"

"It's doubtful," Ben answered. "Her name is Belinda. She's a grad student."

"You know her name?"

"Yes."

"Do you speak to her?"

"Very briefly."

"Have you met her before?"

"A couple months ago."

"So she is always your source?"

"It's a good match, so yes."

Lizzie touched the rim of her wine glass. "Do you know the names of all your sources?"

"I try to," Ben touched her hair gently. "There is only one whose clothes I try to take off."

Lizzie looked up at his eyes. "But before... before we... did you try to take their clothes off?"

"Officially, I should say no. But I won't lie, Elizabeth. I dated some of my sources before."

"Did you sleep with them?"

"Yes."

"Did you love them?"

"No."

"Did they love you?"

"Probably not."

"How do you know?"

"No one has told me... but..." he faded, looking at her sadly. "I suppose that doesn't mean I know."

Lizzie set the wine glass aside and turned towards Ben. "Has there been anyone... have you ever been married?"

"Not since before."

"Before what?"

"I became vampire," he explained quietly.

"Oh," Lizzie heaved a great sigh. "Did you love her?"

"Marriage was different then," Ben looked down. "I married because I thought she could help me with my farm. We had two children. Then I went to war. I came home and found she and the babies died of small pox while I was gone. It wasn't until that point I realized I loved her."

"Oh God," Lizzie felt a huge amount of emotion. She spoke of Harriet Fulton losing her children on her tour all the time, but never felt any amount of sympathy. Ben didn't seem sad, but distant… as though his mind had gone to a faraway place.

"It is sad," he nodded coolly.

Lizzie let the silence enter the room. She looked at her phone, half expecting it to ring and disturb the conversation. "What is it like going to a wedding like this… when yours must have been so different?"

"I've been to a lot of weddings. The difference doesn't shock me," he smiled.

"It's so much more ridiculous."

"In some ways. There is a lot less fire and brimstone," he smirked. "It is nice to see people who love one another get married because they want to."

"Even though half of them get divorced?"

"Is that what you think will happen to Nora and Mark?"

"No," Lizzie shook her head. "I hope not. I think they've waited for the right person and the right moment in their lives. Tomorrow isn't just about the wedding. They truly want to spend their lives together."

"So you aren't a complete cynic?"

"No," Lizzie looked up at his watchful eyes. "If you are such a romantic, Ben, why haven't you married again?'

"I almost married," he looked towards that distant memory again.

"For love?" Lizzie emboldened herself as the phone rang again.

Ben nodded as she picked it up off the table. She breathed out, contemplating not answering it. She turned back against the sofa and flipped open her phone. "Hello?"

"Hey Lizzie, sorry to bother you again," Becca said sheepishly.

"That's okay," Lizzie turned her periphery to look at Ben's pensive expression.

"Nora is a little worried about Meg."

"Why?"

"Alec still hasn't arrived."

"Oh," Lizzie felt a sudden drain.

"Could you go and check on her? I think it would make Nora feel much better if she knew Meg wasn't alone right now," Becca pleaded.

Lizzie heaved a great sigh. "Yeah, I'll go check on her."

"Thanks," Becca said before hanging up.

Lizzie pursed her lips. "I have to check on Meg. Professor McCaffrey is still MIA," Lizzie groaned.

Ben touched her hair gently and pulled her in for a kiss. "Will you be back?"

"Who knows?" Lizzie found her heels under the chair. Ben breathed out his muted irritation. Lizzie wondered if it was their aborted conversation or the possibility Lizzie wouldn't be back to finish what they started earlier. "I'm sorry."

Ben stood up and reached behind to pull up the rest of her zipper. "You are a good friend."

"But apparently not a good girlfriend," she smirked at him.

He touched her shoulders and pulled her around to kiss her again. She was tempted to stay… just for another hour… but he pulled away and enveloped her in an embrace. "Oliver is the same way."

Lizzie pulled back to look at him. "How so?"

He shifted his eyes away briefly and then looked at her. She wondered if he meant to say that thought aloud. "She falls pretty easily for people, doesn't she?" Lizzie nodded to his question. "Manic?"

"Yeah," Lizzie agreed almost silently, fingering her phone.

Ben cleared his throat and turned her towards the door. "Go see Meg. Be her good friend. Tomorrow night, I'll be good to you." Lizzie eyed him before opening the door, her fingers ready to press send back to Becca's number. He smiled at her quickly and held the door as she left the room.

*****

Lizzie let herself into the room quietly. She set her shoes down as she sat on the couch. Ben was already asleep. She liked to watch him sleep. She knew he slept longer after feeding. His breaths were deeper and the color under his skin made him look less like the book cover she found in Meg's bag. His t-shirt exposed the contours of his muscular shoulders. His strong shoulders. Strong arms. She felt safe in his arms. In spite of that constant lurking fear, she felt safe against the warmth of his body, a warmth that became familiar and comfortable in the past six weeks.

She thought about waking him. She wanted to know what he was about to tell her, about Oliver and his manic emotions. Was it anything like Meg's drunken depression that flipped the second Alec texted to say he was parking his car four hours after dinner ended? Did he fall and forgive as readily as Meg did? And why… why did it bother Ben?

Did Ben fall so easily? Did he love her? Did she love him? Did she know from that first night together? She knew him before. She knew him… the wave of exhaustion leaked out with a yawn. She knew him in high school. She didn't feel anything for him then. What changed? Was it her? Was it simply that she started to believe someone could love her?

There was something else. There was something that her mind was too tired to remember. Was it their unfinished conversation? The fact he almost married someone else? No… she wanted to know about that. But there was something she needed to think through before she could think about her feelings. She didn't know what it was… something about Springs or Coldbrook or… it was something she knew she had to remember… but it wasn't important now. Now she was happy. Happy to be sitting in the dark watching him sleep.

*****

Lizzie let out a sleepy breath. She could see where the water separated from the sky. The sun hinted its arrival with tiny specks of gold on the creeping waves. She relished the comfort Ben's arms loosely enveloped about her waist. She liked the feel of the sand drying on her legs. She laughed briefly. "I'm watching the sun rise with a vampire."

"There is no place I'd rather be," he said softly.

"I hope Nora and Mark are this happy," Lizzie admired the sky's lightening shade of lavender.

"They looked happy. It was a happy day. Even Meghan was in good spirits."

"Yes," Lizzie was relieved to see that Alec's late night arrival brought Meg back to her better mood. Lizzie unfolded his hands to intertwine his fingers with hers. The marks on her left wrist faded to two subtle pink dots. "Do you remember your wedding?"

She felt his fingers loosen their grip around hers. Lizzie felt ashamed. She always avoided being obsessive about weddings and marriage. She wasn't one of those females who only thought of men in terms of an engagement ring. She didn't want that from him. But, as the business of Nora's wedding slipped away with the waves, the unfinished conversation from the night before ebbed back into her mind.

"Elizabeth," he began quietly.

"I'm sorry. That was an inappropriate question," Lizzie let go of his hands and sat up. She looked at him quickly and saw the struggle for words in his eyes. She looked back at the horizon and began removing the pins from her flattened curls. She rested her palms on the sand and listened to the waves recede from the shore. She was tired and upset with herself. She blinked her eyes to prevent them from betraying herself too much.

Ben sat up slowly and pulled her hair behind her shoulders. "Elizabeth," he whispered softly, making the ocean breeze chill her even more. Lizzie didn't respond but clutched some sand in her palms. "I want you to know who I was before. But that young man is not … he is dead, Lizzie. He was impulsive and reckless and much more selfish."

"You said you loved her. You were sad when she died," Lizzie relaxed her hold of the sand.

Ben smoothed down the hair he held in his hands. "I imagine it is a comfort to you to know that I have had women in my life who were more to me than a source."

Lizzie looked at him hastily. She hated that cold word. "That's not what I meant by asking," she looked away, annoyed with herself for ruining her happy moment. She couldn't stop the impulse of her next question. "How many women were… more than just a source?"

"I stayed with the one who changed me for some time. It wasn't love. She was exciting and introduced me to my new way of life. She took me to Europe. I enjoyed her company. She liked mine… until she found another distraction. But we were friends and business partners. She taught me a great deal about being what I am … and about women."

"Do you miss her?" Lizzie swallowed nervously.

"I do. Although when she died we weren't friendly," Ben looked down at the sand.

"Did Oliver come between you?"

Ben looked up in surprise. "Why would you ask that?"

"I don't know. I just assumed because you said she changed him after you… and you get so strange when you talk about him."

"A variety of things came between us," Ben looked towards the horizon that was slowly edging to yellow. Lizzie noticed his fingers curled tightly against his palm. "She enjoyed the power too much. She didn't value… she did not have a pleasant end, I'm sad to say. I think she deserved it."

"Oh."

Ben let out a slow breath. He relaxed his fingers and turned back to Lizzie. He saw the unrelenting curiosity in her eyes. "Like you Elizabeth, I find it difficult to let myself love someone."

Lizzie felt a chill over her bare shoulders. She never expressed that feeling to him. But anyone paying attention to her would understand that. She didn't fight her eyes and let the tears confirm his honesty.

"That doesn't mean that I never did or never will again," he interrupted Lizzie from her melancholy. She lifted her palm from the sand and wiped her cheek with the back of her hand.

"You said that you almost married," she swallowed, unable to look at him completely, "for love."

"Before I went to Princeton, there was a woman. Her name was Maria."

"Did you leave her to go to medical school?"

"She left me."

"How long was she with you?"

"Twenty-five years."

"That's… these days that's a long time."

"It was a long time then."

"The 1890's?" Lizzie did the math in her head. "Was she a vampire?"

"No," Lizzie saw him swallow hard.

She imagined a fair haired woman in a dark blue dress with ruffles and a tiny corseted waist. She felt a twinge of jealousy, more than the mention of the one who changed him. "Did she know you were a vampire?"

"Not at first," he turned his gray green eyes to her suddenly, as if looking for his own answer in her reaction. "She worked in Oliver's mill. She was his secretary."

"Oliver's mill?"

"He owned a wool mill in Raleigh, along the Connecticut River."

"Did you own a mill?"

"I was dabbling in some local government, but Oliver decided to leave Raleigh. I took over the management, making Maria my secretary."

"She fell for her boss?"

"We were under a great deal of stress when Oliver left. She was a good friend and comfort to me when I … well had to pick up his mess."

"Oliver wasn't a good business manager?"

"Oliver has a different set of priorities."

Lizzie looked at her fingers in the sand. "You were grateful to Maria for helping you."

"It was more than gratitude. She surprised me. I never expected to feel that way after…" Ben glanced briefly at her and then back towards the ocean. "Maria was so very different. She was a good worker. She had an eye for detail and worked many long hours to make certain my office ran smoothly. She was discreet."

"She knew what you were?"

"Maria's family was from Italy. She was a Catholic. Innocent … but clever enough to know that I was not… that there was something unusual about Oliver and me. She confronted me about it. I was already in love with her and couldn't make myself lie. I told her. Like I told you."

"Did she offer you her veins?" Lizzie struggled to keep the snarl out of her voice.

"She ran away," Ben cleared his throat. "I never found out what she did in those two years. I imagine she was nursing her father, who was very ill. When he died she came back. She didn't have anyone else. There was no one left to judge her for being with me."

"She loved you."

"In spite of herself," Ben said almost inaudibly. "I was too in love with her to see her sorrow."

Lizzie felt another twinge of jealousy as the sound of the waves took the place of his conversation. "Why didn't you marry her? Wasn't marriage more important then?"

"She wouldn't marry me. I asked her. We left Raleigh. I bought a house in upstate New York. We lived like man and wife. She used my name. Everyone in town thought we were married. We couldn't have children. Sometimes I think she didn't want to get married so she could leave."

"When did she leave?"

"She was happy at first. We were both happy. I invested in the local store and made a modest living. She kept the house and was active in the community. After a few years, she became depressed. She stopped eating. She stayed in her room for days. She wouldn't talk to me. She was miserable because I wasn't growing old while she was. She was jealous of young women who came to the store. Then I found out about Coldbrook. Do you know about the springs they used to have?"

"No," Lizzie was startled by the shift of conversation.

"There were springs where the state forest is now. They said the springs had healing powers. People came from all over the country to stay in two big hotels. I brought Maria there for a couple summers. She liked those waters. She was happy again. We talked about buying a house in Coldbrook so she could be there all year round. But the idea of living in Coldbrook didn't make her any happier. She drowned herself on her 47th birthday."

"Ben, I'm so sorry," Lizzie gasped at the ending to his story she did not expect.

"That's when I decided to become a doctor. I couldn't help her. But I wanted to help… I wanted to stop being the cause of so much woe and injury," he shut his eyes and opened them to look at the brilliant sky over the ocean.

Lizzie straightened out her knees and decided she needed to stand. She felt the stiffness of her joints from sitting on the sand for over an hour. Ben was at her side and took her in his arms, resting his chin on her shoulders.

"Ben, can I ask you an awful question?" she knew exhaustion eliminated her sense of tact.

"Yes, Elizabeth."

"Did you take her blood?"

He stepped back from the embrace. "She didn't want to know about that part of me. She knew I fed, but pretended for a long time that I wasn't a vampire. She would cook me dinner. I played along to make her happy. After the first summer at the springs, she asked me to do it. I only did it once. She was anemic from not eating. I think it made her more depressed. I think she did it because she was jealous and afraid that I was going to leave her."

"Did you want to leave her?"

"No. Not even when she stayed in her room for days and days."

"You really loved her."

"I did. I do."

Lizzie made a short smile of empathy. She bent down to brush the dried sand off her knees. She didn't know what to say. She was fascinated to know about him, about his life one hundred years ago. It was almost as though it was a different person who lived that life. How could the Ben who was her classmate at Springs be a mill owner in Raleigh during the 1890's? He knew about parts of Coldbrook that were long buried under seventy year old trees. And yet the sadness in his eyes made it real and present. She felt her own grief to know there was such unhappiness in his life. She caught herself gawking at him as she let these thoughts go through her mind. She shook her head quickly and looked about for her abandoned shoes.

Ben found the shoes and winked playfully. "Do you want to go back to the room? Or do you want to get breakfast?"

"I am tired…" Lizzie realized she had been in her dress for almost twenty hours. "Ben?"

"Mm hmm?"

"Thank you for telling me," she touched his shoulder lightly. "It does … I am sorry that she was so unhappy. But I am glad that you... loved her."

Ben put his arm around her shoulder and started walking back to the hotel. He paused and turned her into him quickly. "I love you, Elizabeth."

"Ben," she felt panic freeze her limbs and feared her knees would succumb to her exhaustion.

He took hold of her and kissed her passionately. Before she had a second to notice, he lifted her into his arms and was carrying her back to the hotel. Lizzie couldn't find the words to express the swirl of emotion inside of her. She let the quiet of the dawn speak it for her.

Chapter Fifteen

Lizzie unwrapped her cottage cheese and stirred it as she settled back into her chair. She had broken her rule about eating at her desk lately. She didn't want to risk running into any nurses from the donor bank. She hadn't given in four months. She gave Polly a lame excuse that she was low on her iron. It was a lie. She was taking Ben's advice about vitamins and supplements. She wanted her blood to be healthy and better than anything he could get at the clinic. It prompted her to get up and run before the summer sun warmed the earth too much. It made her anxious for the next Saturday when her eight weeks would be up.

She wondered briefly if it was wrong to want it so badly. The first time she was hardly aware of what she offered him. She was confused and tired and desperate to believe that he wasn't some delusional freak. Maybe she was still confused and unaware of a danger to which she should pay attention. But Ben was… he said he loved her. She couldn't imagine he would let her do anything that was a danger to herself.

She logged into Facebook to check the status of her friends. There was nothing from Ben, whom Lizzie realized, really didn't care for the social networking scene. Nora signed in from Scotland to say she was enjoying the hikes and pubs with her new husband. Sara uploaded the latest pictures of six month old Josie. Meg vented a new tirade against editing.

Lizzie couldn't come up with something clever or interesting to add for her own status. She didn't really care anyway, knowing Ben wasn't going to be reading it. Meg and Nora both knew she was on cloud nine. She didn't really need the other 109 people on her list to know that. She debated changing her status from single… but decided she didn't want to prompt the comments Davis and Andrew would leave on her wall.

Lizzie logged off as she scooped out the last of her cottage cheese. She fingered the slices of apple and switched her screen over to Google. She stared at the cursor for a few seconds before deciding to type "vampire clinic."

She rolled her eyes at herself for being so ridiculous. She saw links for role-playing and fan sites for novels and movies. Nothing remotely legitimate. She added Ben's name to the search words. All it managed to do was pull up the sites with members by the name of Ben. She clicked on one that teased her with the words "blood donor.'" But the screen just showed a bunch of pale faced Goth girls with stage blood dripping out of the corner of their mouths.

Lizzie jumped as the door to the office opened. She quickly switched her screen, lest Richard should see the half naked women on her screen. "Good afternoon Lizzie," her boss closed the door. "It's hot out there."

"Is it?" Lizzie looked up from her computer screen.

"I hope you aren't running in this weather."

"I got up at five this morning. Soupy air, but I kind of like it," Lizzie smiled at her boss. "It's quiet in the morning, before the rest of the world starts going."

"That's devotion," Richard sighed. "Good for you."

"Good for my heart," Lizzie took up a piece of her apple to show she was eating lunch and not interested in talking. Richard took the hint and went back to his office.

Lizzie returned to Google and changed vampire clinic to blood clinic, keeping Ben's full name in the line. There were still a number of gothic fan sites, but halfway down the page there was a site with the words "to ensure safety, health, and well-being." Followed by Dr. Benjamin Cottingham.

Lizzie clicked on the site and found herself helpless at a login. There wasn't an option to create a login, just a generic email to which one could write and request information about hematological health. Lizzie entertained the thought of creating an alias and email, but quickly talked herself out of it. It was dishonest. And whoever screened her alias probably knew Ben.

She went back to Google once again and typed "wool mill Raleigh MA."

The first few options were links to tourist sites. She scrolled through a couple genealogies of people from Raleigh and a few newspaper articles about strikes. She went back to the top and clicked on the tourist site. There was a handful of color photographs of brick buildings along a river framed with the golden leaves of autumn. It could be any mill in

Massachusetts, really. They were modern photos. The mill was no longer active, but appeared to have some recently abandoned businesses.

She scrolled down the page and saw a black and white photo dated from 1891. There were a few women with long skirts and serious expressions, but none with blond hair. Why was she convinced Maria had blond hair? Raleigh had a lot of Eastern European immigrants. Wouldn't it make more sense if she was one of those dark haired women? Lizzie doubted any of them was the owner's secretary.

She clicked back to the search page and selected one of the strike articles. The words blurred in her mind, not really appealing to her curiosity… until her eye caught the phrase "negotiated with owner, Oliver Thomas."

The name echoed in her brain as though someone just said it aloud to her. Ben and Oliver's surname was Cottingham. It sounded so familiar. Was there someone connected to the Fulton house by that name? Oliver Thomas. Lizzie couldn't find it in her memory.

She went back and searched for Oliver Thomas Raleigh Woolen Mill.

Again, there were a number of irrelevant results, including a link to a theater for an upcoming production of the musical, *Oliver!* She clicked through several pages until she found an article from the Raleigh Historical Society. Lizzie scanned through the article, which was basically a general survey of Raleigh history. Nothing seemed to justify its inclusion on search results. Then halfway through, she found a few sentences that grabbed her attention.

"The Thomas Bros. Woolen Mills operated from 1885 until 1905. The founder and original owner, Oliver Thomas, opened the mill to manufacture textiles and yarns. His brother and co-investor, Benjamin Thomas, took over management of the mill in 1890. Raw materials were supplied from local farms throughout the Connecticut River Valley all the way up to Canada. Thomas Bros. Woolen Mills employed many immigrants, primarily young women, who settled in Raleigh and surrounding towns. The mill was highly successful, due principally to a contract with the government to provide blankets to military hospitals. In spite of the success of the factory, Benjamin Thomas chose to sell the business to Pennsylvania businessman Edward Stapen.

"The mill brought a moderate amount of fame to Raleigh in the fall of 1889. Fourteen year-old Eloise Hutchins was employed at the factory. After a factory picnic on June 5th, she did not return home. Her body was found several months later not far from the mill. There were several accusations and suspects for her murder. Two years later, family friend, Luigi Parinoli, hanged himself and left a confession for the murder.

"Lizzie, can you run a report on the Capital Campaign to date?" Richard reappeared at her desk.

Lizzie slowly lifted up her eyes, not quite digesting all of what she had read. "For this fiscal year or years prior?" she hoped her questions hid the flush that had risen to her cheeks.

"Both. Can you run them in separate reports?"

"Sure," Lizzie nodded and looked back to her computer. She waited for the door to Richard's office to close. She read the two paragraphs three more times. Benjamin Thomas. He changed his name. That wasn't startling. Not… too startling. Not so startling as the murder of a young girl so close to the time that Oliver decided to leave the mill. Lizzie closed her eyes and did her best to push the information out of her brain as she pulled the data for her reports.

*****

Lizzie led her group up the stairs and into the master bedroom. She smiled graciously as she waited for the stragglers to enter the room and quiet their comments about how small the beds seemed. She shook her head as two middle-aged women from Texas explained to each other that everyone was shorter because they didn't eat enough meat. Lizzie thought about challenging them, but decided to tell how John Fulton married Margaret, two years after losing his first wife to consumption. She described the abbreviated details of their wedding in Boston and the names of their children. Only Harriet and Peter grew to adults. She pointed out the bed that really wasn't that much smaller than her own, as well as the intricate hooked rug beneath their feet.

She paused barely long enough to allow her visitors breath to process a question. She went back across the hallway into Harriet's room. As the two Texan women straggled across, she looked at the young woman's glassy stare and then at the faded upholstery of the infamous chair.

She still didn't understand what made that chair so impressive. It was three hundred years old. Well, closer to two hundred and fifty. It looked three hundred. The fabric was faded. Gerard Fulton had a legitimate point. The sun was brutal against the dark brocade. The walnut frame dried out and lost its sheen. The stuffing of the cushion was beyond uncomfortable. She supposed even the mice found no delight resting there. It was French. She knew that, but was unimpressed. The material wasn't likely original. She couldn't imagine the glassy eyed Harriet sitting in that chair. Maybe her sister-in-law Charlotte sat there and listened to Harriet swoon over Mr. Chester as she got dressed or ready for bed.

She suddenly remembered a dream. Something about a vampire biting her in that chair. When did she dream that? Did she know what Ben was? Or was that Meg's influence? She shook the thought out of her mind as she focused on her Texan tourists and began her discussion of Harriet's short-lived history. She felt a cool draft fall against her shoulders as she left the chair behind and took her small party into the guest bedroom. Was it a breeze pushing through the leaky windows? Or had something... Lizzie shut her eyes, trying to wrestle between reason and her distracted mind. It was a hot July afternoon. Maybe the pocket of cool air startled her because of the warmth throughout the house.

She discussed the dresser and the few objects displayed on top of it. She listed some of the famous visitors to the Fulton House. She concluded her tour by bringing them down the servant stairs and back into the gift shop. The image of the vampire biting her floated back into her mind. The chill had nothing to do with ghosts or cool air. She was anticipating her date with Ben later that evening when the dream would be real.

"How'd it go?" Paula asked.

"Pretty good," Lizzie reached for her water bottle and offered a pleasant smile. One of the Texan women approached with a pile of postcards, which Lizzie put in a bag as Paula rang them up. Within ten minutes the shop was empty.

"So when are you going to bring Ben here so we can meet him?" Andrew appeared from behind one of the bookshelves. Lizzie was sure her cheeks burned with the memory of the thoughts she indulged while giving her tour.

"I don't think he's interested in taking a tour."

"Why not?" Paula left the desk to straighten the books on antique French furnishings.

"He's more of a scientist," Lizzie shrugged and took the seat behind the desk.

"Yeah, but I want to meet him," Andrew persisted.

"We should go out some time," Lizzie suggested. "Ask Davis when he's available."

"He's available next Friday," Andrew concluded. "I'll cook dinner."

"Ben works late on Fridays," Lizzie stopped herself from accepting. "What if we did cocktails and nibbles?"

"We'll do a late dinner. Paula, are you in?"

"I don't think so."

"Your loss. What does he eat?"

"Actually, he has food allergies."

"What?" Andrew's eyes lit up. It was a challenge, not an impediment. "Does he eat meat?"

"Kind of," Lizzie saw Paula look up.

"I'll think of something brilliant," Andrew beamed, obviously not concerned. "And a fabulous cocktail."

"Of course," Lizzie smiled.

"Maybe you can inspire yourself by dusting the kitchen," Paula smirked suddenly. "You were supposed to do that an hour ago."

"Of course, lovely," Andrew sneered and disappeared down the corridor.

Lizzie let the quiet fall between herself and Paula. Lizzie looked away and noticed an open newsletter of the American Museum Association. A small grayscale photograph caught her attention. It was… Oliver. She picked up the newsletter and read how Oliver Cottingham, known as Professor Ol to his students, had finished a summer workshop with a California science museum about the repercussions of campsites in reserve lands. A group of students and museum staffers spent several weeks in a local state forest evaluating carbons released into the air by RVs and cars brought into the park. They also measured the number of non-degradable objects left behind by campers and the effect on the water. The study was profiled by local news stations and furthered the partnership between the science museum and the college. Professor Ol and his group were already busy planning to expand the project to research the environmental impact of other tourist sites.

"Hey… Paula, weren't you at a museum in Pioneer Valley before this?" Lizzie disturbed the quiet as her mind wrestled between the article she just read and the searches on Google.

"Yeah, I worked at a local historical society while I was in college."

"Did you ever hear about a wool mill in Raleigh?"

"There were a lot of mills on the Connecticut River."

"Yeah, but there was a murder of a girl at this one. Oliver Thomas was the owner. Does that ring any bells?"

Paul looked at her and squinted as though it would prompt her memory. "That sounds vaguely familiar. The victim was young, right? And they blamed it on an Italian. Very Sacco and Vanzetti."

"So the Italian didn't do it?"

"I don't remember the details. I think a friend of mine did a paper on the prejudices against immigrants in the area. He works at a museum in New York right now. I can shoot him an email and ask him if you'd like."

"Yeah," Lizzie offered her smile again. "Someone I know might be related to the owner."

"Huh," Paula gazed at her.

"If your friend has any pictures, that would be a nice present for my friend."

"I'll email him today."

"Thanks," Lizzie folded the newsletter shut. She lifted her eyes when the bell sounded the door opening. "Hey!" she exclaimed happily as Jen and Jack walked in.

"Hi Lizzie!" Jen greeted her with a hug.

"What are you guys doing here?"

"We came to see a friend perform in Porter Square tonight. Jen made me come early so we could take one of your tours," Jack explained.

"We were hoping we could convince you to join us for dinner when you are done?" Jen asked. "That is if you don't have plans?"

Lizzie paused, torn between her dinner and Ben's. "I am supposed to meet up with Ben," Lizzie caught the look of satisfaction from both of them. "He might not be able to join us for dinner, but maybe he can come hear some music."

"Don't let us ruin your plans," Jen argued.

"No," Lizzie shook her head. "Ben will be glad to hear you are in town."

"Great," Jack looked at his wife. "Let's do it."

*****

"Lizzie gave us a great tour," Jen smiled. "I'm surprised you haven't gone on one yet, Ben."

"It is a terrible faux pas, I admit," Ben looked at Lizzie.

"I think he would make me self conscious," Lizzie avoided his eyes.

"Yes, but you are passionate about the history of that place and the people who lived there," Jen argued. "I think you would enjoy sharing it with this guy."

"Yeah, even I found it interesting," Jack grinned.

"And that is a remarkable thing," Jen laughed. "It's okay, Lizzie. It took Jack two months to recognize the fact I painted the bathroom. The one that we use every day."

"I'm not thinking about walls when I do," Jack scowled at his wife.

"I really liked that fireplace in the master bedroom," Jen ignored her husband. "I wish I could do something like that in our house."

"We don't have a chimney in our bedroom," Jack argued.

"No, but I could tile the one in the living room. Do you think that would be possible, Lizzie?" Jen asked seriously.

"It's possible," Lizzie shot a bemused glance at Ben as she took the last sip from her glass. She was amused when people asked her decorating tips. She was able to talk about one house's wallpaper and furniture. It didn't necessarily make her an expert on how to make any other house look the same way.

"Another round?" Ben stood with his bottle. She could tell he would bring it to the bar and pretend to exchange it for another. "Jack, another Guinness?"

"Yeah."

"I'll have one, too," Jen echoed.

"I'll have another seltzer," she offered her empty glass, seeing the burn in his eyes that made her impatient for the band to start.

"Lizzie, are you pregnant?" Jack asked abruptly.

"What?" Lizzie couldn't restrain the volume of her voice. She saw Ben look suddenly from the bar.

"You haven't had anything to drink all night," Jack disregarded Jen's disapproving glare.

"I…" Lizzie was able to contain herself from expressing the humor of his question. All the reasons that made a yes to that suspicion impossible. "I'm planning a long run tomorrow. It's better if I don't drink."

"It's going to be 95 degrees tomorrow," Jack rolled his eyes.

"Exactly why she shouldn't be drinking, Jack," Jen elbowed his side.

"Right," Jack glanced over to the bar where Ben was waiting. "Things are working out with Cottingham?"

"Yes," Lizzie beamed. "Yes, they are."

"Good for you, Lizzie," Jen grinned.

"Yeah, that's great," Jack took the last sip from his pint glass. "Has he met Aunt Joan and Uncle Steve yet?"

"Not… as my boyfriend. They know him from high school," Lizzie looked down, not ready to think too long and hard about that step of a relationship. Her parents.

"They will like him, Lizzie. How could they not?" Jen asked as Ben returned to the table with drinks, including his recycled beer bottle. Lizzie smiled at Jen, masking her discomfort. She didn't know how to tell her parents that she finally had a boyfriend. And that he was a vampire.

"Jack, when is your next gig?" Ben settled back into his seat.

"We just agreed to play for a BBQ in September. It's a fundraiser, so you'll come for sure won't you Lizzie?"

"What's the cause?" Lizzie noticed the band finally take the stage.

"It's a scholarship for… Melissa… my parents' neighbors. You remember… that girl in the class ahead of us? She disappeared right before her graduation?"

"Melissa Benson," Lizzie felt the joy of her evening suddenly sober.

"Her parents are hosting a barbeque in Coldbrook in September. It would have been her 35th birthday," Jen explained.

"Sounds like a noble cause," Lizzie glanced at Ben. He looked away from Jen and met her gaze with friendly eyes.

"Jack isn't noble, Lizzie. He just wants the free beer they get for payment," Jen smirked, as the band started their first song at top volume. Jack pulled Jen under his arm and turned to the musicians. Lizzie watched Ben, trying to observe if he would let down his guard for a second and show a delayed reaction to Melissa Benson. He didn't show anything. Not one little expression.

*****

Lizzie held Ben's hand from the bar back to his apartment. Her ears slowly unclogged themselves, but left her with little desire to speak. It was a good concert and a good evening spent with family. She was glad for the spontaneous visit they made to the Fulton House. And yet, in spite of those happy – good – details, she felt drained.

Her desire for the completion of the evening left her. She no longer let her mind drift back to her dream or supposing how Ben would bite her. She resisted a temptation to let Jack buy her a beer at the end of the night. She lost her desire, but knew from the burning look in Ben's eyes that he had not.

She let go of his hand as he unlocked the door and walked silently up the two flights to his apartment. He stayed silent as she set down her purse in the living room and left to get a glass of water. She came back and saw his silhouette against the window. He was looking down into the street and turned very slowly to face her. Lizzie didn't feel the impulse to return his smile. She set down her water glass and stayed motionless. "Which of you killed Melissa?"

Ben's expression cooled suddenly. "I told you, Elizabeth. I haven't killed anyone in many years."

"So it was Oliver?"

"Have you been thinking about this all night?" Ben slowly left the window.

"I tried not to."

Ben reached towards her and pulled her into his arms. "I'm sorry."

"Did he kill her?" Lizzie didn't reciprocate his embrace.

Ben straightened his spine and looked over her shoulder. "I don't know."

Lizzie pulled herself away to look at his face. "So you think he could have?"

"I think it's a strong possibility," he looked directly at her.

"What other possibility could there be?"

"I hope that he didn't do it."

"That doesn't mean anything."

"There was no body, Elizabeth," Ben shrugged. "I know as much as the police know about this case."

"Except that your brother is a vampire."

"So am I."

"Yes, but you know that you didn't do it," Lizzie was unable to stare any longer at the burning expression of his eyes. "You don't seem that confident about what Oliver did not do."

"I'm sorry that this has upset you."

"Me? What about her family? They didn't even have a body to bury," Lizzie cried. "She was only… seventeen."

"I know," Ben walked back to the window, the juxtaposition of the street light darkening him in the shadow again.

"That poor family," Lizzie felt the exhaustion of a long day wash over her. She sat on the couch and rested her head against the cushions. She looked up at the ceiling, seeing the shadows of headlights move across the room. "Would you let that happen to me, Ben?"

"No," Ben said immediately. "Why would you even think that?"

Lizzie let herself look at him and saw the anger in his jaw. "If something happened to me, how would you tell my family?"

"Nothing is going to happen to you, Elizabeth," his voice was harsh. "I won't let it."

Lizzie felt a chill pass across her shoulders. There was something terrifying in his voice that Lizzie thought she should fear. There was something very honest and exposed, more than his declaration on the beach after Nora's wedding. The strength of his anger was proof of his vulnerability. It was the reaction she hoped to see earlier. Only it wasn't over Melissa Benson. It was about her.

"I won't ever hurt you," he declared with the same raw emotion. "I won't let anyone else hurt you."

"Do you think someone is going to hurt me?" she felt the thrill of her fear. "Do you think Oliver could hurt me?"

Ben paused without looking away. He breathed in slowly, "No." He walked to the couch and sat beside her. Lizzie felt an immediate comfort with his closeness, even as she still felt a haunting sensation frighten her senses. Ben's arm pulled her close to him. He gently kissed the top of her head as she leaned against his shoulder.

"Andrew wants us to come to dinner on Friday," Lizzie decided to let the subject fade into the silence.

"Oh?" Ben's lighter tone indicated his relief.

"He and Davis want to cook us a meal," Lizzie explained. "I told him you had food allergies."

Ben laughed. "What allergy?"

"I didn't say… but do you want to go? Or shall I make up some excuse?"

"I want to go," he moved the hair away from her cheek. Lizzie felt the cool air of the AC blow against her exposed skin.

"They are my harshest critics."

"You respect their opinions," Ben paused after he moved all her hair behind her shoulder. Lizzie felt his fingers gently trace the curve of her neck. She felt his chest rise and fall with a deep breath.

"They are always completely honest," the quieted thrill electrified her body again. "But neither judges me for my past wrongs… or present ones."

"Elizabeth," Ben spoke on his next exhale. His fingers rested on her pulse, which accelerated with the last syllable of her name. She guided his hand away from her as she sat straight against the sofa. She didn't need to look at his eyes to know the intensity of longing. Instead, Lizzie looked at the floor, blurring the image of the carpet as fear and desire agitated her body too much to make decision. Ben retrieved his arm and slowly left the couch. The removal of his warmth pushed her to the impulse to go after him. She took his shoulders and turned him in to kiss her. He kissed her with an intensity she hadn't felt from his lips since the night of the reunion.

She felt light headed as he stepped back to let her breathe. She paused a second and kissed him again, almost falling backwards when he renewed his intensity. He caught her lack of balance and lifted her off her feet, carrying her down the hall into the bedroom. He removed her dress before pushing her gently down on the bed. She took in slow deep breaths to calm her heartbeat as he undressed. She locked with his eyes as he lowered back down over her and pushed himself between her legs. She forgot everything that troubled her in the living room as the sensation escalated. She inhaled deeply and lifted back her head, exposing the curve of her neck. His eyes left hers as she arched her entire body into his. His breath warmed the inside of her shoulder before the feeling of a small cut into her skin. She was aware of the blood rush to her head and then the pulse through the artery of her neck.

She closed her eyes, letting the sensation wash over her, as if cool blood were running through warm veins. Under the lids of her eyes, everything seemed to glow as if lit by candlelight. Every nerve felt awake and aware of the slightest touch. She felt his body grow in warmth against her own, as her blood started to pump through his heart and into his veins, enlivening his nerves to excitement.

The warm electricity ebbed from her mind, fluttering her eyes open when he lifted his gaze back to her. The green glowed against the dim light from the street as the color faded the freckles across his cheeks. Lizzie breathed out slowly, letting her chest rise and fall against his. His heart echoed against her, in a more rapid rhythm than hers could ever survive.

She reached her arms to pull him back into her kiss. It was still aggressive and she felt the sting of a scratch inside her lower lip. Lizzie continued to kiss him until she needed to breathe. She looked up to his glowing green eyes. His lips curled into a satisfied smile. "Are you okay?" he whispered softly.

Lizzie nodded slowly, afraid her voice would be too loud for that moment. He kissed her lightly on the forehead and smoothed the disheveled strands from her face. "Are you tired?"

"No," Lizzie managed to whisper just long enough for him to kiss her again.

"There is no place I would rather be right now," he kissed her lips and then looked at the side of her neck. He touched the spot where she felt the brief cut of his teeth. She couldn't see it but imagined the red marks she had on her wrist. He bent his head down to kiss that spot gently, leaving a warm sensation with his lips. She could still feel his heartbeat racing her blood through his body, empowering his actions. He moved away from her neck down towards her breasts and slowly down along her torso.

"Ben," she touched the rusty brown hair that was just beginning to curl. He looked up at her, leaving another impression of warmth between her breasts where his lips had just been. "I …" she breathed out and looked away from the brilliant green eyes. "I want to be here, too." He smiled broadly again and bent his head back over her torso, slowly moving his lips down to her pelvis.

*****

Even with the AC, Lizzie sensed the warmth of the July afternoon streaming across her as she lay besides a sleeping Ben. She felt tired but not enough to sleep. She lingered a half hour with her eyes closed, but the dryness of her throat irritated her out of bed. Ben hardly moved as she left his side. She went to the kitchen to moisten her throat and abate the pang of hunger resonating in her stomach.

She removed the meat from the pan and replaced it with the chopped peppers and onions. The sizzling sound and sweet aroma of their juices filled the kitchen. She wondered if Ben could smell them down the hallway or if, like the taste of food, the appealing scent faded into inconsequential. She was used to cooking for herself. So many years she made meals without having to worry about anyone else. Sometimes Meg would sample a helping or two. There were always dinner parties. But she figured that one day there would be a family of some sort she would feed and impress with her skill. She was going to have to let that go.

She filled one of the pristine plates with her stir fry and took it into the living room to eat by the television. Nothing appealed to her so she shut it off and sat in a chair by the window. She could tell from her glance outside that it was a hot afternoon. The people walking down the street were dressed in the least amount of clothing without being offensive… although some probably were in the eyes of Davis. She laughed to herself and looked back to the room, noticing for the first time a Victorian table beneath a gilded mirror behind the couch. It was an interesting juxtaposition to the modern leather furniture and carefully organized media in the room. The legs were elaborately carved and had intricate detail beneath the table top. Centered on top of the table was a ceramic vase filled with white roses.

Lizzie finished her plate almost too quickly to satisfy her hungry stomach. She put the empty dish aside and went over to the table to look at it more carefully. It was probably too late to be something the Fultons might have owned, which was normally the extent to which Lizzie bothered to care about antique furniture.

Her eye caught her reflection in the mirror above it. Her hair was still untidy despite her hasty attempt at a ponytail. Then she saw the bright red marks inside her left shoulder. She touched her skin, not irritating the wounds with pain or reopening them. They couldn't be mistaken for bug bites and wouldn't be hidden under anything without a collar. She let herself smile again as she thought of her blood flowing through Ben's veins and how it made his heart beat. She gave him life. She bit her lip on the smile as she thought of the endorphin rush and satisfied grin that remained even as he slept.

She looked away from the reflection back at the table. The ceramic vase was rather plain, but very likely from the same period as the table. The white roses inside them were exquisite. She never noticed that he had fresh flowers in the apartment, never mind such lovely roses. They weren't the $5.99 variety Lizzie bought herself at the supermarket. They were perfect and pure and bloomed into a brilliant layer of white petals. She lifted one out of the vase and inhaled a breath.

She felt a sudden swirl of exhaustion spin her brain. She lifted her eyes back to the mirror and shook her head to regain the balance of her senses. She had a sudden thought of rain soaking through her clothes, but it vanished quickly as she saw Ben's reflection behind her.

She put the rose back in the vase and turned to him with a broad smile. He looked half awake, but breathed in a happy expression to respond to hers. "Are you feeling all right?" he stifled a yawn.

"I feel wonderful," she didn't hesitate the honesty. "I was just hungry."

"Did you want to get something to eat?" he looked at the table behind her, almost too briefly Lizzie thought she was tricking her mind.

"I made some lunch. Do you want…" she stopped herself from the instinct to offer him some.

"That's good. I honestly never know if I have the right instruments in a kitchen."

"It's not bad for someone who has nothing to do with food," Lizzie restrained herself from commenting on his knives.

"I had some help buying those things."

"Oh?"

"Yeah," he shook his head. "I'm pretty clueless. You like cooking?"

"I do," she decided to end the awkward separation of the couch between them by sitting on it. "Andrew and I have a friendly competition with our cooking. We always try to outdo one another at our respective parties. We are also one another's biggest fans… which was very difficult when I was trying not to eat."

Ben sat beside her and rested his arm over her shoulder. "So when I go to dinner I should say his cooking is great, but not as great as yours?"

"It doesn't matter," Lizzie rested her head against him. "You know we always talk about starting a catering business."

"Why don't you?"

"It's a lot of work. Not to mention a lot of money. I have no money. Andrew has a good job and can't take time away from it… so we just host parties and cook for our friends for free."

"Well, feel free to invite him over here to cook with you any time you like," Ben fingered the edge of her collar. "In fact, I hope you will. I have to go away for a few weeks in the beginning of August."

"What?" Lizzie pulled herself up straight.

"There is a new clinic opening up outside of Chicago. I agreed to consult on the organization of the donor screening lab and registry."

"Oh," Lizzie tried not to be too obvious with her letdown. Her birthday was in the beginning of August. She couldn't remember if she ever told him that… if birthdays even mattered to someone who had been through 255 of them.

"I made the offer before we were seeing one another and completely forgot about it until she called me last week. I will miss you," he touched her cheek.

"I will miss you," Lizzie decided to get her dirty dish to bring back to the kitchen.

"You can stay here while I'm gone," Ben stood up behind her.

"I might," she turned to get the plate from the chair.

"Elizabeth," he called her attention back and focused his green eyes in the way that made her feel so calm and right. "Last night was very special."

Lizzie felt the smile form on her lips and melt away the peevish irritation about her birthday. "It was special for me too."

He cupped his hand along her chin, pulling her towards him. The green eyes locked upon her intensely. "I love you." Lizzie kissed him, still unable to form the response. He pulled back and smoothed along her hair. "Did you…" his eyes seemed to gain concentration and looked for something in her. Was he trying to see what she felt but couldn't say? "What did you…"

"I felt it, too," she breathed close to him and touched his lips gently. "I wish I didn't have to wait two months to do it again."

Ben dropped his eyes, softening the intensity of his gaze. "We have to. For your safety."

"I know," Lizzie agreed even though she didn't really understand it. He stepped back and lifted his eyes again, but the moment was broken. "I should wash my dishes."

"Yes," he nodded, even though Lizzie knew he didn't understand how important that was.

"Ben, I..." she lingered wondering if the leap of her articulation would bring that moment back.

"Mm?"

"Thank you for letting me stay here while you are gone."

He looked at her and shifted his eyes to the white roses again so briefly. "You are always welcome, Lizzie." She grabbed the plate and took it to the kitchen, not sure why his pronouncement of Lizzie unnerved her so much.

Chapter Sixteen

Lizzie dropped a five in the tip box before going to the bar to wait for her iced latte. Starbucks was bustling on Monday morning. She appreciated the speed with which they delivered her portion of caffeine, allowing her spare time to sit in a vacated plush chair and eat her turkey bacon sandwich.

She knew she was groggy from the humidity and the lazy hours of her Sunday. But there was no mistaking the gray haired gentleman in the opposite corner beside a tiny waisted brunette. Lizzie bit her lip to restrain from going over to where he sat with his hand on the lap of the frivolous twenty-something. She took in a sobering breath and tried to concentrate on the newspaper left by her chair.

"Lizzie Watson," Professor McCaffrey called her back from the newspaper.

"Alec," Lizzie made her smile overt and her articulation loud.

"You've been visiting your boyfriend this weekend?" he smiled with no shame over the girl clinging to his elbow.

"I work at Mt. Elm," Lizzie muttered, not wanting to admit she was anywhere close to Ben's apartment, in case Alec should remember another location in Central Square with which to affiliate him.

"Yes, you do," Alec looked at her with no indication to the brunette.

"I'm Lizzie," she offered out her hand.

"This is Claire," Alec still looked at Lizzie when the young woman didn't offer a hand in return.

She felt the gaze of his eyes and made sure her hair was still draped over her shoulder. She wished she went home to get a better outfit. "Do you have a class?" Lizzie couldn't think of anything better to say, unsure how to confront him.

"I'm not teaching this summer," Alec didn't change his intensity.

"Then you must have lots of time to help Meg with her thesis," Lizzie hissed, relieved she said it but terrified for his response.

"Meg's a bright girl," Alec answered. "She's doing quite well on her own."

"Does that mean you…" Lizzie looked at Claire's vicious bored expression. "Do you know Meg, Claire?"

The brunette rolled her eyes at Lizzie and then turned a pleading stare towards Alec. "Can you get me a refill?" Alec handed Claire his reusable mug without looking at her.

"You haven't told Meghan about your boyfriend," Alec whispered when Claire joined the line.

"What's there to tell?" Lizzie shrugged, determined not to show how she really wanted to react.

"I always thought there was more to you than a frumpy little secretary."

Lizzie hardened her eyes. "What is that supposed to mean?"

"It means that you should give me a call when he loses his taste for you," Alec said calmly. Lizzie clenched her jaw, unable to scream in the midst of the hectic morning coffee crowd. She knew the brunette hadn't stopped turning her head from the line.

"Meg doesn't know about this?" she let herself spit out when Claire reached the cashier.

"About Claire?" he laughed.

"About Ben," Lizzie spoke between her teeth.

"Meghan likes the fantasy too much," Alec lowered his voice in a way that made her skin crawl. "She couldn't handle the real thing."

"Is Claire the only one?" Lizzie glared at him.

"No," Alec said lightly. "Like I said, when you and he are done, call me. "

Lizzie didn't turn her eyes to watch him meet Claire and walk out the door. She felt an urge to call Ben, but thought inciting his anger wouldn't be a wise reaction to Alec's swarminess. He was too old and powerless to be a real threat. Not to Lizzie. About Meg's heart she wasn't so sure.

*****

"I like that one of you and Meg best," Nora leaned her chin on Lizzie's shoulder.

"Yeah, I like it, too. I want a copy of this one," Lizzie took it off the top of the pile of pictures in her hands and handed it over to Meg.

"I have to agree. Those dresses do look pretty fabulous," Meg laughed.

"That's a nice one of Ben, Lizzie," Nora continued to look over her shoulder.

"Mmm," Lizzie agreed as Meg took it.

"He always looks so pale," Meg scowled. "But he is handsome."

Lizzie studied Meg's expression as she looked at the photograph. Meg was in slightly better spirits, but still on the cranky side of her romantic mania. She didn't seem able to say anything kind without layering it with a jab first. She told Ben she was going to go home to Jefferson Park, but decided if Meg continued she was going to his apartment instead.

As if sensing Lizzie's dissatisfaction, Meg lifted her eyes and softened. "You're very lucky, Lizzie."

Lizzie's irritation melted away as quickly as it came, making her feel foolish for begrudging her long time friend who wasn't as lucky. She felt badly that she avoided Meg since encountering Alec in Starbucks. She knew the good friend would have gone home to Jefferson Park and said something about his blatant, unapologetic infidelity. But Lizzie was scared to even mention Professor McCaffrey. Scared to ignite Meg's moodiness and even more scared that any mention of him would lend itself to another conversation about Ben. It wasn't until she knew Nora would be there as a buffer that she felt comfortable to be in Meg's company again.

"I am very lucky," Lizzie wondered if she should say anything further. Not that she could say a lot of the things she found endearing about him. That he was once a doctor or that he invented a medicine or that he decided it was more important to be with her than stay alone as he had been for nearly a century. There were so many things to say. "He said he loved me."

Nora pulled away from Lizzie's side and sat up with a broad grin. "And what did you tell him?"

"I…" Lizzie stopped from confessing that she let him drink her blood.

"You didn't," Meg reverted to cranky and tossed the picture of Ben on the coffee table. "What the fuck, Lizzie? He's a good guy. He's good to you."

"It…" she tripped again, unable to tell them about Oliver and Melissa Benson or Eloise Hutchins. Not that Oliver really had anything to do with how she felt about Ben. She was making up excuses for a fear that had nothing to do with vampires. And yet… there was still something she felt she should know before she would let herself love him completely. She didn't know what, but it seemed to be lurking around the corner.

"Lizzie isn't as impulsive as you, Meg," Nora touched her hand. "Ben isn't Alec."

Lizzie straightened her spine, wishing that Nora hadn't gone there. She held her breath anticipating the explosion from Meg. Instead, Meg took in a gasp and left the room. Lizzie looked at Nora. "Why did you bring him up?'

"Because I am tired of being nice about the professor. She should feel this so she will leave him for once and for all," Nora shook her head. "I know she's in pain, but it will be better for her if he is gone from her life. Did you hear how he shredded her thesis? That bastard was just jealous because she is the better writer."

"He shredded her thesis?"

"She didn't tell you? He held onto it too long for her to submit it on time for her deadline. When he gave it back he undermined every one of her opinions. So now she's not even touching it, thinking it's not good enough."

"When did she tell you this?"

"Last week," Nora took a sip of wine, allowing Lizzie to realize she saw Alec more recently with Claire on his arm. "I don't think she's seen him since he gave it back to her… but…" Nora lifted her glance as Meg came back into the room, not bothering to hide her red eyes. She had a few tissues in her hand and blew her nose loudly.

Nora left Lizzie's side and sat beside Meg. "Why don't you just leave him?"

"I want to… I am always so helpless and go back to him, just when I think I am over him," Meg let the tears stream again. "It's like I am attached to Alec and will forever be predetermined to love him."

"You will always love him," Nora shrugged. "It doesn't mean you always have to go back to him. You need to get over your fantasies of destiny and past lives, Meghan. If he brings you harm and is this destructive against your feelings, you should not be with him. I can't imagine any law of fate mandating that you have to be with a bastard who hurts you. Otherwise you cut yourself off from any other fate of happiness or living."

Meg looked at Nora and smiled in spite of her tears. "How did you get to be so wise?"

"It isn't wisdom to tell your friend she doesn't have to be in a relationship with a jerk," Nora rolled her eyes.

"Well Lizzie found Ben after her Will fiasco," Meg sighed.

"There's hope for us all," Lizzie made herself laugh, deciding that every one of her worries about Ben wasn't important when he so plainly cared about her, in a way Alec McCaffrey couldn't care for anyone.

"Too bad Ben doesn't have a brother," Meg smiled in Lizzie's direction.

"He does. He's married," Lizzie thought of Ben's absent minded comparison of Meg to Oliver.

"Too bad," Meg picked up a wine glass.

"Does this mean you are going to leave him?" Nora asked.

"I think I already did," Meg looked down.

"What about your thesis?" Nora was brave enough to ask the questions Lizzie was afraid to articulate.

"It was a load of crap," Meg rolled her eyes. "No, really, it was. I think I'm done with vampires for now."

Lizzie straightened her collar, making sure the inside of her left neck wasn't exposed. She wasn't eager to argue the legitimacy of Meg's theories or encourage her to pursue the subject any further. She remembered Alec's comment about her not being able to deal with the reality. Maybe it would be best if Meg let the thesis and Alec McCaffrey go.

"So what does Mr. Wonderful have planned for your birthday?' Meg picked up the pile of photographs again and handed one to Lizzie.

Lizzie looked at the picture of Nora and her sister. "I don't know," Lizzie shook her head with an attempt at cool. "Probably something simple. Birthdays aren't a big deal to him." She didn't really know that. She just decided it couldn't be a big deal to him. It wasn't important when everything else about him was incredibly wonderful.

Meg looked briefly at Nora and bit her lip. "He's probably got something up his sleeve," Nora laughed.

"Maybe," Lizzie looked at the next picture of her standing with Ben. He was happy at her side. More importantly, she was happy. She didn't have to make any effort to smile for that photo. That was all she needed to know.

Chapter Seventeen

Lizzie wrapped her fingers around the coffee mug. The AC in Ben's office was too cold. She logged in and took a sip of her drink as the desktop finished loading. The quiet of his office was unsettling. Even as the room was familiar to her, it was still strange to be in his chair, in front of his desk on a Sunday morning when he wasn't in the next room.

She clicked on the server and logged into her newsfeed. Jack posted the notice about his fundraiser. Nora tagged her in several wedding pictures, most of which Lizzie saw in Nora's living room a week ago. She smiled at the one she liked so much of her and Ben. She contemplated making it her profile picture when a red flag popped up on the screen.

Lizzie clicked her mouse again saw a friend request from Oliver Cottingham. Lizzie felt her spine straighten and turn cold. She didn't know if it was another burst of AC or the fact she read that name while sitting in Ben's office. She clicked the name and was allowed access to his page. She saw a different photo than the one she studied months ago. He was well dressed and young and outdoors. But pale, not like someone who was in that warm sun all the time. Further down the page, there were wall comments from friends and colleagues. He was listed as professor of environmental studies. Married. Nothing indicating his secret. Nothing indicating he was Benjamin's brother. Lizzie hastily accepted the request and felt her nerves tingle. Ben would see that. He didn't always go on Facebook, but Nora just tagged him in several photos. He would be isolated in his hotel in Chicago. He might go on to send her a message, knowing her love for skulking.

Lizzie looked away from the screen, as if that made her less responsible for impulse. She looked about the room, noticing details she ignored when Ben was there. She admired the antiquated books, certain she could identify Keats and Voltaire. There was nothing but books on the shelves. No tchotchkes. There were no photographs. There was a painting on the wall opposite the desk. Something modern with red and black and not really resembling any sort of image, just an impression of shadows and color.

She saw the computer screen, and the picture of Oliver. She hastily went to her page and deleted the detail that Lizzie Watson is friends with Oliver Cottingham. Maybe Ben wouldn't see it. She didn't know why it mattered so much, why the panic set in so swiftly. Did she really think Ben capable of such wrath? Over Facebook? She breathed out slowly and stared back at the strange red and black painting. Ben had two and a half centuries of perspective that made the trivialities of social network politics pretty ridiculous.

Lizzie picked up her mug and drank, but the AC made her coffee tepid. As she set it down, she noticed the desk drawers on either side of her. Without thinking about talking herself out of it, she opened them. The two larger drawers were full of papers. Personal finance, tax files, investment folders. She didn't know what she was hoping to find, but nothing like that. She opened the smaller drawer to her left and found pens, a stapler, and other desk supplies. The smaller drawer on the right had a small leather book. It was a neglected calendar. A newspaper article fell out as she opened the pages. It was a clipping from a local paper about her 10K. She saw her name listed next to her time. Lizzie smiled with the memory of his appearance at the end of the race and her apartment after. She placed the calendar with the clipping inside it back in the drawer.

She brushed her hand against some disheveled photos. Lizzie pulled out the pile, grinning over a handful of images from their trip to Quechee. Most were of Lizzie, which made sense if he was taking the pictures. Underneath were pictures of a setting she recognized. Coldbrook. The pictures were older. She didn't know the house. Was that his house, the one he lived in with Oliver? A big old farmhouse. She couldn't remember what street he lived on … but she recognized the center of town in another photo. A parade or a fair or something. There was the library and the post office. She thought she recognized some faces, but she usually recognized most people or at least their relatives.

She carefully straightened the pile and replaced them in the drawer. There wasn't much else but some odd scraps of paper and receipts. She closed the drawer and looked back to another red flag on Facebook. She clicked the message indicating Oliver left a comment on her wall. She clicked on the page and read quickly. "Hi Lizzie! Looks like life has been good to you. Drop a line if you ever make it out to Cali."

Lizzie felt a lump in her throat. No mention of Ben. He could easily have seen Nora's pictures of them together. He would know they were together. Would that make Ben angry? Did it matter? Lizzie didn't tell everyone she knew that she was with Ben. But if they went on Facebook and saw the pictures of them together, it really wouldn't bother her that much…

She didn't understand the acrimony between them and decided it was best not to think about it. She let her mind drift back to other unopened drawers in his apartment. Did any of them have anything in them that would reveal… what did she think she would find? Her eyes wandered through the doorway to the dining room. There was a buffet full of drawers, but no need to keep china. Lizzie left the desk and her coffee chilling under the AC.

She went to the buffet and opened a drawer where she found silverware. It was tarnished and untouched, but a beautiful set that would make the Fulton House conservationists drool. The cabinet opened to exquisite bone china. Dishes, bowls, and even serving platters. She went to the furthest drawer and found a pile of silk napkins. They were embroidered with purple flowers. Lizzie lifted up the napkins and felt something scratch her finger. She put her finger to her mouth and with her other hand retrieved the frame buried in the material.

It was a black and white photograph of a blond woman in Victorian dress. A dark, ruffled dress. The shape of her corset was evident in her unexpressive pose. Her blond hair was up but stylishly curled. She was very slender, almost too thin. Ben said she didn't eat. She looked as though the corset was the only thing forcing her posture – as though without it she might collapse into a formless mass. She looked sad and hid the honesty of her eyes from the camera. It was just as she imagined Maria.

Lizzie took the photo to the brown leather chair in the living room. She stared at the details. She was very pretty. Fair. Her eyes were light – either blue or light gray green like… like Ben's. Sad. Lizzie could tell the determination to look at the camera was a mask to something else. Maybe Lizzie decided that because she knew what happened to Maria.

Lizzie shut her eyes. She was upset with herself for making such harsh assessments. Why was Lizzie so bitter towards Maria? That poor soul… Maria lived in a different time. It couldn't have been easy for her to love Ben. A vampire. A killer. A man she couldn't marry. A man who didn't age. A man who wasn't a man…

Lizzie rested the photo on the arm of the chair. Her gaze wandered out the window at the brilliant morning sun. She let out a sigh, letting herself admit her own questions that settled in her brain. She wasn't going to be like Maria. She wasn't Maria. Maria didn't run a half marathon. She looked too prim and proper to appreciate the benefits of Ben's youthful physique. Lizzie knew Ben loved Maria. She saw it in his eyes when he spoke of her. She saw it in the fact he kept her china, silver, and linens in a dining room he didn't use. She knew Ben was capable of that emotion. She wondered if in her depression Maria ever did.

Lizzie heard her phone ring. In a panic, she put the picture back in the drawer of the buffet… as if Ben was calling he would see her looking at that picture. She arranged the napkins hastily and got to her phone as the beep sounded to alert a missed call. She held her breath and pressed the button to identify the caller. She breathed out a sigh of relief at Meg's name, glad it wasn't Ben.

Lizzie went back to the office and computer. She moved the mouse to wake the screen saver. She clicked the bottom of her Facebook home page and breathed relief when she didn't see Ben's name online. Not that he would be online. He was busy working. Of all things, he wouldn't log onto Facebook.

She skipped back to the news feed and wasn't much interested in the changes since she left the computer fifteen minutes before. There was nothing at all from Oliver. Nothing to show whether she should fear him or fluff off her worries as ridiculous. She felt slightly foolish about trying to hide her contact with him. She went back to her wall and reread his friendly message. It was friendly, but what would Ben say? What would Oliver think if she deleted it? Did it matter? Honestly. She was two weeks away from turning 34. She wasn't in high school where she needed to worry about what someone might or might not think. She shook the idea out of her head and logged off of the computer.

*****

"I'm surprised you don't have big plans for tonight," Paula smiled sheepishly over her pint.

"My friends are taking me out tomorrow," Lizzie rationalized the lie of omission she told Nora and Meg. She didn't want their pity or reproving glances. She furthered the pretense by determining to spend the night at his empty apartment. The idea of Maria's objects still unnerved her so she delayed going home by inviting Paula out for a pint. "Ben is back on Monday. So I'll be busy enough. Besides I had a fabulous birthday cake from the Fulton House staff today. That is worth a million restaurant dinners."

"Andrew must appreciate your compliments," Paula set her glass down after deciding against another sip. "I'm surprised he didn't want to come out for drinks."

"He and Davis had plans. But this is nice," Lizzie felt foolish with her lame compliment.

"It was a busy day. I'm glad I am not going home to drink on my own."

"I'm surprised YOU don't have big plans tonight."

"It isn't my birthday."

"Things didn't work out with Nicole, huh?" Lizzie sipped from her beer.

"I think after we finished comparing notes on our favorite historical periods, we didn't have much to talk about in the present," Paula looked at Lizzie.

"Yeah," she nodded her head in her own absent thoughts of Ben. "Well, I'm sure there is someone more interesting about to come in your life."

Lizzie bit her lip to stop from rolling her eyes at herself. She always hated it when someone said that to her… after Will. She did end up with Ben… who was unlike…

"My friend answered your Raleigh mill questions," Paula offered. "He sent a couple articles and scanned some photos, too. Nothing too exciting. He didn't find any pictures of the owner you mentioned… Oliver. But he found a picture of his brother. I guess he was part owner of the mill. He said there was some speculation about Oliver's involvement with the murder. Apparently he had a thing for his pretty young mill workers."

"That sounds interesting," Lizzie swallowed another mouthful from her glass to shield the honesty of her reaction. She forced a moderate smile as Paula handed her a manila envelope. She was impatient to see the picture of Ben and to read the proof of the connection to Oliver… if it really was any sort of proof.

"I didn't look through all of it. It seems like some information was swept under the carpet. You said your friend was related to the mill owner, right? Or was it the girl?"

"The owner," Lizzie said shortly as she pulled out the papers. It was difficult to focus and read in the light of the bar. She paused at the series of photographs. There was one with a number of workers and Ben was in the middle, in a long black coat and bowler hat. Lizzie looked up at Paula watching her. "He looks a lot like him," Lizzie felt the lie form on her lips instantly. Paula would have seen the pictures and had a sharp enough mind to notice the resemblance to Ben… if she ever had the opportunity to meet Ben. "My boyfriend. I guess they are related. They even have the same name."

"Huh. Then he's related to both owners," Paula let out a breath and glanced towards the bar. Lizzie welcomed her distraction and tried to look closer at the picture. He had the same strong shoulders and serious expression. She wondered if he was thinking about Maria when that picture was taken. Lizzie set down the paper and watched Paula's focus on the bar. She wondered if there was someone in particular, or if she was just that uncomfortable being with Lizzie.

"Too bad nothing that mysterious or scandalous ever happened at the Fulton House," Lizzie called her attention back to the table. "No murders of poor innocent girls."

"Huh? Oh yeah, I don't think so," Paula looked at Lizzie, her restraint relaxed by her beer. "I don't know. I can't imagine John Fulton killing one of the house maids."

"Or Margaret."

"Definitely not Margaret," Paula perked up as the waitress came to collect Lizzie's empty glass. Lizzie nodded to her gesture about a refill and watched Paula dodge her eyes.

"She's cute."

"Yeah, but not…" Paula drank some more of her glass. "I also photocopied something I found in the archives last week."

"What?" Lizzie sorted through the papers again.

"It's just a tiny paragraph about Horace Fulton's wedding to Charlotte," Paula explained. "Thanks to your detective work with Gerard Fulton, I was able to find this article from the Boston Examiner."

"In 1815," Lizzie briefly scanned the article describing the wedding celebration held at 127 Brattle Street on April 22nd. The groom was the son of John and Caroline Fulton. The bride was the daughter of Ephraim and Jane Chester of New York. Several notables were in attendance to wish the couple well. Lizzie got the gist of those details and decided to revisit it and the other papers when she was alone in Ben's apartment. She knew there was a bottle of wine to keep her company with Maria's ghost.

"Didn't Harriet write about a Mr. Chester in that letter?" Lizzie took a sip of her fresh beer.

"Yes, she did," Paula looked back towards the bar, making Lizzie realize she was glancing at a clock. "I assume that was Charlotte's brother."

"Oh," Lizzie breathed out slowly. The fact Paula openly made an assumption about Fulton history and the constant glances at the clock showed that Paula didn't intend to stay at the bar much longer. "Well, it's all pretty interesting. Thanks for the info, Paula."

"Sure," Paula nodded as Lizzie drank more of her beer quickly.

"And thanks for coming out with me," Lizzie smiled. "But I should probably head out."

Paula looked at the half full pint glass, but wasn't able to mask her relief. "Yeah," Paula nodded. "Happy birthday, Lizzie."

*****

Lizzie took the mail out of Ben's box and balanced it with the bags and leftover cake in her hands. She juggled the objects as she turned the keys in the lock and shut the door. She managed to cart everything down the hallway into the kitchen, where she saw Ben staring out the window over the back yard.

He turned to her and smiled. "Happy birthday, Elizabeth."

"Ben," she stood still with her hands full in the doorway of the kitchen. She felt her breath leave her body as Ben left the window and went directly to her. Lizzie dropped everything and grabbed hold of him as he leaned in to kiss her. She felt the ache of longing to be in his arms that resonated in the quiet moments of every day of the past two weeks. She didn't let herself think how much she wanted him there on that day until he was there, kissing her and holding her in his arms. She pressed her body towards his as he completed his embrace. "You're home," Lizzie whispered when she pulled herself out of the kiss.

"You have to get dressed," Ben kissed her again. "I am taking you out to dinner."

"What?" Lizzie asked breathlessly.

"For your birthday," he cupped her chin in his palm.

"I don't want to have dinner," she kissed him and jumped up to wrap her legs around him. Ben caught her and balanced her all the way to his bedroom. Then he let her go and made her stand up at a distance from him.

"I am supposed to bring you to your favorite restaurant."

"What do you mean supposed to?" Lizzie felt the one and a half beers swim in her head as the oxygen slowly returned her thoughts to speed.

"Meg arranged a little something… but I didn't tell you," Ben managed a confident smile in spite of his struggle. She saw the burning in his eyes and knew he hadn't made it home in time to visit the clinic.

"Meg?" Lizzie wished she hadn't had those beers.

"I'm only telling you so you won't… tempt me to stay home," Ben presented a bag branded with a name of some designer she vaguely knew from conversations with Andrew.

"This is from your harshest critics," he winked. "The box inside is from me."

"But you weren't coming home until…" Lizzie pulled out a red dress and a velvet box.

"I wouldn't miss your birthday, Elizabeth," he watched as she opened to see two ruby studs.

"They are beautiful."

"You got home later than I expected."

"I had drinks with Paula," Lizzie looked back at him, overwhelmed and still slightly buzzed. "How long have you been planning this?"

"I haven't been planning this," he smiled. "It's all Meg. For about a month now. My only part was getting the band. I have a connection."

"Jack?"

Ben grinned broadly. Lizzie threw herself at him again, not giving him much opportunity to resist her grateful kiss. He started to lift her shirt over her head and finally stepped back. "Now get dressed," he showed his struggle through his gleam.

Chapter Eighteen

Lizzie wasn't surprised to find Ben absent from her side when she finally opened her eyes at noon. He hadn't fed and was more restless – in spite of the fact the party didn't leave the restaurant until midnight and then continued at Andrew and Davis' apartment. She imagined quite a few people stayed after she and Ben made an exit some time around three. She didn't remember shutting her eyes until after six, completely missing her normal run time.

Lizzie hastily put on a tank top and walked into the kitchen, where Ben sat reading at the peninsula. She thought it would be appropriate for him to have a cup of coffee and then focused her brain back to clarity, remembering he didn't drink coffee. She sat on the stool opposite and rested her chin in her hand to gaze at him happily. She didn't think it would be difficult to coax him back to the bedroom when she was just wearing her tank top and boy shorts. She wondered if he was hungry enough to forgive her lower red blood cell count.

Ben met her eyes, but didn't return the smile. Lizzie looked down and saw the pile of mail he was reading. On top of the bills and junk mail he sorted, Lizzie recognized the papers Paula gave her at the pub. Lizzie straightened her smile and recoiled her posture away from him.

"Elizabeth, I understand," he said softly, but couldn't completely disguise his sadness.

"What do you understand?" she asked quickly, not sure if it was motivated by self defense or shame.

"You want to know things."

"These are from work," Lizzie sheepishly pulled the papers away from him. It wasn't a complete lie. There was an article about Horace Fulton's wedding.

"Elizabeth," Ben spoke in a tone Lizzie knew was of consequence. She looked up and met his eye, which did not offer the consolation of levity.

"I need coffee," she got off her stool.

Ben quickly presented her with a steaming mug. "Elizabeth."

"I…." she took the mug from his hands and went back to the stool.

"I'm not angry with you."

Lizzie set her cup down and looked at the papers, then Ben. "There's a picture of you."

"Not much different. I'm glad hats aren't a necessity as they once were."

Lizzie stifled the urge to laugh. She knew there was something much more grave coming. "Ben…" she stopped herself, feeling the need to say something but unable to say anything… really.

"Oliver killed Eloise."

Lizzie couldn't look at him, but felt his stare watching for her reaction. She breathed in deeply and took a sip from her coffee. It was still black and too strong for her preference. She didn't want to leave her stool to get the milk in the refrigerator. The silence settled between them, disturbed only by the hum of the appliances. Lizzie glanced again at the papers, but they blurred in her focus. "I know," she muttered, even though she didn't realize her intention to say those words.

"How?" Ben sat across from her again.

Lizzie lifted her eyes suddenly and saw the intensity of Ben's stare. "I don't know."

"Elizabeth," he touched her hand, saying her name for the third time.

She curled her fingers into her palm under his touch. She knew she should feel ashamed, but his sympathy startled her more than the anger she feared would. She did not settle her eyes away from him, nor did she respond to his call of her name.

"I want you to know," Ben wrapped his fingers into her clenched palm. "I just… don't want to overwhelm you. I don't know how to begin."

"Oliver…" Lizzie muttered, wondering if she should say he contacted her.

"I feel responsible for him, Elizabeth," Ben sighed. "He tries to do the right thing. But he hasn't had as much… his sense of discipline is different than mine."

"There is a sort of sibling rivalry between you?"

"I guess you could say that," Ben let go of her hand. "But… Elizabeth, what do you know about Eloise Hutchins?"

"She worked in your mill."

"Is that all?"

"She was young," Lizzie felt her mind cloud and the words jumble together in her brain.

"She was… is that really all you can think of?"

"She had red hair," Lizzie didn't know where that detail came from.

Ben leaned back and smiled, but stopped it as if it was painful. "There isn't a photograph of her in those papers."

"Maybe I'm wrong," Lizzie rested her fingers around the handle of her coffee mug. She wanted to tell him she guessed the color of Maria's hair, but didn't think that was an appropriate argument. She looked at the black coffee, tempted to drink in spite of its bitterness. She didn't know what to say next, but was more afraid of the silence that hung heavy in the air. "Are you going to tell me what happened?"

Ben looked at her, as if expecting her to answer her own question. He slowly pulled one of the pages out from the pile. It was the article about the wedding. "Why is this here?"

Lizzie clenched her jaw. She didn't want him to avoid the truth any more. "Paula copied it for me," Lizzie hissed. "We were trying to figure out who Charlotte was. But that has nothing to do with Eloise Hutchins."

"It has a lot to do with Eloise Hutchins."

Lizzie took the piece of paper back from him and reread the article, not deriving any clearer detail in her fury than she did after a pint in a noisy bar the night before. She couldn't imagine what a fourteen year old mill worker in 1889 had to do with a Cambridge wedding in 1815. She scanned her memory of the Fultons' history to determine if they had any dealings in western Massachusetts. Her head clouded more and more, aching with each additional thought.

Ben breathed out slowly. "You asked me if I believe in reincarnation."

"Are you telling me that Eloise Hutchins was Charlotte Fulton?"

"No," Ben said quickly, almost angrily.

"Horace Fulton?" Lizzie tried to laugh, but fell short.

"She lived with the Fultons," Ben looked directly at her.

"Oh," Lizzie felt her whole body grow cold. She drank her coffee all the way to the bottom of her mug. She was still cold. She rubbed her bare arms and avoided Ben. He got her another cup of coffee. Lizzie decided to maintain the silence and get the milk. She kept quiet as she slowly blended her coffee and drank half of the mug again.

"How do you know these things?"

"There isn't an easy way to explain it. I honestly don't know if I can put it into words, Elizabeth."

"Were you at the Fulton House?" Lizzie asked suddenly, not feeling warmer in any part of her body in spite of the scalding on her tongue from her coffee.

"Briefly," Ben didn't blink.

"Why?" Lizzie gasped.

"Because Charlotte Fulton was a vampire. She was the vampire who changed me."

Lizzie felt suddenly very awake. She realized everything had changed and everything she observed and heard after this was her new reality. She felt it more than the night Ben sat in her dining room and revealed he was a vampire. That was a relief. This revelation didn't provide any relief or excitement. It made everything slow down and inescapable.

The calm entered her gaze and made her voice very articulate. "Who was Eloise?"

"The Fultons' house maid," Ben said slowly.

"What was her name?"

"Lily."

Lizzie shuddered again, wishing she dressed in more than a tank top. "What does she have to do with Charlotte?"

"Horace Fulton was the primary heir of the Fulton fortune. Charlotte wanted that fortune. So she married him."

"Did Horace Fulton know she was a vampire?"

"No one knew Charlotte was a vampire. She had a youthful appearance and played the part of innocent very well…" Ben faded. "Horace Fulton was a self-righteous man, who would never be publicly associated with someone who didn't uphold his virtues. Privately, he had no virtue and had more interest in the young housemaid than the secrets of his wife. "

Lizzie looked down, trying to remember anything she could about Horace Fulton. There wasn't a room in the house in which they were required to talk about him. Only… at some point the tour pointed out that Peter Fulton was the only child of John to produce heirs that survived into the twenty-first century. "Horace Fulton didn't live very long," Lizzie muttered the only detail that her memory produced.

"No."

"Did Charlotte have something to do with his death?"

Ben's eyes searched for something in her question. "She killed him."

"What happened to Lily?" the name fell out of her mouth heavily.

"Charlotte liked Lily. They were friends."

"Did she know… did she know what Charlotte was?"

"Lily was one of her sources."

"Just her source?"

"No," Ben looked away from her. "They were lovers."

"Did Charlotte kill Lily?"

"No."

Lizzie glanced at the article, seeing the names and words blend together on the paper. The year of the wedding stood out suddenly, prompting the memory of the other few details. "Was Oliver around when all this happened?"

"He was still human," Ben returned his glance to Lizzie's intent eyes. "He and Lily were childhood friends. He wanted to marry her, but there was some complication with his family. He fought in the war and came back after Lily met Charlotte…" he faded, eyeing her again. "Lily … she and Oliver renewed their affair until Charlotte found out."

"Then she turned him into a vampire out of spite?"

Ben's focus drifted to a place other than the kitchen. "Spite."

"What happened to Lily?" the name still left her lips like a stone.

"Oliver always loved her. That didn't change when he became a vampire," Ben looked towards the window over the sink. "He didn't know his new strength. He didn't know what he could do to her when he tried to take her blood."

"He took too much."

Ben looked away from the window and met her eyes. "Too fast. It wasn't wickedness. It was… accident. He loved her. He just loved her … too much."

"So Lily was the reason he became a vampire… and she was the first person he killed," Lizzie felt her calm start to agitate.

"The guilt never left him. He never forgave Charlotte. But he stayed with her for several years."

"Where were you? Were you still Charlotte's lover?"

"I was in Europe for most of that time. I was taking care of Charlotte's property in France. I was there for Charlotte's wedding and … when Oliver became a vampire," he met Lizzie's eyes again, not trying to shield his shame. "When Oliver… he didn't have much use for me until he parted ways with Charlotte. After the Civil War he needed financial independence and asked my help to open a mill."

"Where Eloise Hutchins came to work for him."

"I never met her," Ben looked at Lizzie. "I never even saw a photograph of her. I doubt there was ever one taken. She was an orphan and worked in the mill to support the aunt and uncle who took care of her. But you can read that in your papers."

"Did she have red hair?"

"Yes, Elizabeth," Ben breathed in slowly. "Yes she did. But that… that isn't in anything you could have read about her."

"How do you know it?"

"Because I had to help dispose of the body."

"Oh my God," Lizzie felt a sudden swim in her stomach. She stood up immediately and made it to the sink before she vomited. She kept her head over the sink. Ben came behind her and ran the water to splash the back of her neck and clean out the sink. He massaged the back of her skull and slid his hand gently down to her mid back.

"We can stop."

"No, we can't," Lizzie stood herself up and leaned against the counter to stabilize the dizzy feeling behind her forehead. "If you never met Eloise, how do you know she was Lily?"

"Oliver recognized her. I believed him."

"So Oliver killed her again?"

"Yes."

"Why? Because he still didn't know the strength of his own power?"

"Because he can't control himself when his emotions… he never stopped loving Lily or hating her."

"Hating?"

"For bringing Charlotte into his life."

"How do you know saying Eloise was Lily wasn't some lame excuse for murdering an innocent girl?" Lizzie avoided his eyes.

Ben took hold of her chin and forced her focus back to him. "Because the next time he saw Lily, I did too."

Lizzie shook her chin out of his grasp and started to walk away from the counter, but her knees wouldn't support her. Ben was at her side in time to stop her fall. He guided her back to the stool and went back to the sink to get a glass of water.

"You haven't eaten," he said as she drank her water.

"Neither have you," Lizzie saw the burning in his eyes. "You want to, don't you?"

"Elizabeth…" Ben took the empty glass from her hand and put it aside.

"It's me, isn't it?"

"Do you think it's you?"

Lizzie paused for a second then went into the bedroom. She hastily put on a shirt and some shorts, not even checking to make sure they were the right side out. She grabbed her purse and stopped in front of the mirror. She looked tired and disheveled. She didn't want to leave. She wanted to know more. She didn't want to know any of it. She couldn't go home. She couldn't return to anything she knew before.

She threw her purse back on the bed. She went to the bar and poured herself a shot of whisky. She swallowed it hastily, breathed in quickly, and then promptly drank another. She turned and saw Ben watching her in the doorway.

"How do you know I'm Lily? Did you ever meet her?"

"Yes, she..."

"Is that why you came to Springs?"

"No, Elizabeth. I told you why I went to high school."

"Is that why Oliver went? Or did he know where I was?" Lizzie still had the shot glass circled in her fingers.

"We came to Coldbrook because I wanted to move there with Maria. I bought a house that she wanted to live in. I didn't want to go there alone. I asked Oliver to come with me… because I thought he needed a fresh start."

"A fresh start? From? Killing more mill workers?"

"He killed Charlotte."

The shot glass slipped from her fingers and crashed to the floor. Lizzie bent to pick it up and sliced her palm on one of the shards. She looked up at Ben and saw him swallow hard. "I'll pick it up, Lizzie. Go wash your hand."

Lizzie glared at him and opened up her bloody palm. The whisky made her head spin. She didn't want to move. She didn't want to give him the relief. "If I'm Lily, why didn't Oliver ever… why did he keep his distance?"

"Because he was determined to improve himself," Ben looked away from her and her exposed hand.

"But you were there… fawning over my best friend…"

"To protect you," Ben met her eyes. "I put myself in your class and your company more so I could see if Oliver was ever tempted."

"But he wasn't?"

"He was."

"But I was… I wasn't as attractive then. My blood wasn't as attractive," Lizzie said to herself, more than to Ben.

"I think that stopped him from trying to take your blood, but not from …"

Lizzie reached for a chair and sat before her legs gave way again. "So all those years of self loathing was actually a past life self preservation?" she laughed madly, losing her sense of appropriate conversation. "And Oliver resisted temptation and went off to San Francisco to marry a vampire?"

Ben almost smiled. "He did."

"What about Melissa Benson?" Lizzie felt her mind clear suddenly. "He did that, didn't he?"

Ben held her gaze and went to the broken pieces of glass on the floor. He looked at the one with her blood a few minutes longer. He took the pieces out of the room and came back with a wet paper towel and a broom. "You really should wash that hand."

"Tell me about Melissa."

"I told you I don't know."

"Did you have to dispose of that body, too?"

"No. I don't know what happened. I don't know," he stared at the tiny remnants of glass.

"She looked like me," Lizzie felt her eyes grow heavy.

"Yes, she did," Ben swept the small pieces off the floor.

Lizzie touched her palm with the paper towel Ben left on the table. She realized the blood dripped onto her legs and the floor beneath her. She stood up quickly and went into the kitchen to wash it under cold water until the bleeding stopped. She wrapped gauze around it and took an aspirin. She let herself cry, not from the pain but the wish that someone else could have wrapped the gauze for her.

Ben was in the living room, leaning on the window seat, staring at the empty vase beneath the mirror. "I need to go home," Lizzie had her purse in her hand.

"Elizabeth," he didn't turn to look at her.

"I need to think," she said very calmly.

"Yes."

"Ben, why are you with me?" she let herself ask it. "Is it revenge against Oliver? Or… is it guilt?"

"Guilt?" he turned to her.

"Because you let those other… girls… die. Are you just with me to make sure it doesn't happen again?"

Ben quickly embraced her. "I don't want it to happen again, Elizabeth. It would have been better if I hadn't…" he breathed in slowly and out again. "If I hadn't gone to that reunion"

"Why did you?" Lizzie kept her arms at her side, unable to return his embrace.

Ben pulled away and touched her chin. "I wanted to see you. I knew where Oliver was. I found out you were at Mt. Elm. I thought that meant…"

"Meant what?" Lizzie's head clouded even more.

"I wanted to see you," he pressed his lips to hers.

Lizzie relaxed into the kiss and then resisted. "I need to go."

Ben stepped back and let go of her. He released a sigh and nodded his head. Lizzie clutched her purse and walked out the door.

Chapter Nineteen

"What happened?" Nora exclaimed as she and Meg hurried towards Lizzie in the ER waiting room.

"I broke a glass at Ben's," Lizzie explained, her energy drained from sitting alone with her thoughts.

"Where was Ben?" Meg frowned.

"He wasn't home," Lizzie said the lie she already formed in her mind. She wasn't going to explain she was afraid to show him the soaking gauze and have him take her to the ER after she ran out of his apartment. "He had an emergency at his office."

"Oh Lizzie," Nora hugged her. "Do you want us to bring you back to his place?"

"No, we're supposed to have dinner, aren't we?" Lizzie pulled the energy for a smile. "Or were those plans just part of the ruse?"

"Uh uh," Nora shook her head. "Meg threw the party. Dinner is from me. Besides, you look like you could use a drink."

"Yeah," Lizzie tried another smile but lost her enthusiasm. "Thanks for coming to get me, guys."

"Did you call Ben?" Nora asked. "Does he know what happened?"

"Yeah," Lizzie nodded.

"He was a big help with the party," Meg held open the door. "I swear that guy would do anything for you."

Lizzie swallowed hard and merely nodded as she followed to Nora's car. She was glad for Meg's happy spirits and the lack of sleep that made her chatty. Lizzie paid enough attention to offer a few phrases, but found her concentration still trying to clear a path through all the information she received earlier that afternoon. It all seemed to go around in the same cyclone that filled her mind as she waited to see the doctor and got her stitches.

To let the thoughts settle and take shape would be accepting everything that Ben told her. That the Fultons' maid was a lover of the vampire who made Ben a vampire. That Lily was Oliver's lover. That Lily was the reason Oliver became vampire. That Lily made Oliver a killer. That she, Elizabeth Watson, was Lily. And Eloise. Was she doomed to have their fate?

Ben said Oliver was determined to improve himself. It seemed believable. Lizzie remembered the article about his environmental research. He didn't seem like a monster. He evolved, as Ben evolved. Ben said that he couldn't control his emotions as well… that he was like Meg. Emotionally manic.

Lizzie always knew Meg had the ability to rein herself in. She just didn't. She relished the immaturity of her extremism, knowing it got her attention and sympathy. Eventually, it was Meg herself who grew weary of the highs and lows and settled into calm… until the next round of polarity and the next obsession with Alec McCaffrey. Ben seemed confident in the fact that Oliver moved on without succumbing to whatever pulled him back to Lily. Except for Melissa Benson.

"Are you okay, Lizzie?" Nora asked as she looked over the menu.

"I'm just tired. And hungry," Lizzie sighed out.

"Eat up before the wine gets here," Meg slid the basket of rolls towards Lizzie. "Does your hand hurt?"

"Yeah, kind of," Lizzie broke a piece of a roll to dip in the olive oil.

"Here," Nora slid an envelope over to Lizzie. "Maybe this will make you feel better."

Lizzie tore it open with her good hand and slid out a card. She opened it, allowing a folded brochure to fall in front of her water glass. Lizzie picked it off the table and looked at the photos of an historic inn. "It's from Mark and me, for you and Ben," Nora smiled. "I knew you had such a good time in Quechee. You love old places. It's in New Hampshire. I think it was built around the same time as the Fulton House. "

"So you can entertain Ben with your comments about moldings and wallpaper," Meg laughed.

"Thanks, Nora," Lizzie managed another false smile. "That's very thoughtful."

"I thought you would like it," Nora said happily as her phone rang. She saw her husband's name and excused herself from the table.

"You guys have been so generous with this birthday," Lizzie looked at Meg. "All that work for the party… that's time you could have spent on … other things. I really, really appreciate it."

"What other things?" Meg said with honest joy. "Nora's just over the moon that you've got Ben. But I… I felt like I was pretty shitty to you this year. I wanted to do something to show that you really are important to me and I am so glad to have you around. Plus, it was one helluva party."

"It was," Lizzie felt a genuine expression of happiness escape her lips.

"34 never gets any credit," Meg shrugged. "I think it should be a big birthday for everyone. Especially when they've had the year you've had. Running all those races – a half marathon! Finding your soul mate."

Lizzie looked towards the lobby where Nora was talking on the phone. "Do you still believe in that… even after Alec?"

"Soul mates?"

"Yeah."

"Of course. I just try to convince myself that Alec is in no way, shape, or form my soul mate."

"So… what does that mean?" Lizzie took a sip of water. "That you were with someone in another life?"

"Maybe," Meg grinned. "Why?"

"But if… well say Alec was your soul mate, wouldn't you want to go into the next life and not see him again?"

Meg breathed out, letting the sadness reveal itself. "If Alec is… my soul mate, I'd like to think in the next life he could improve himself."

Crap. Lizzie shouldn't have opened that Pandora 's Box. "But what if he just keeps repeating his bad behavior over and over?"

"Then he isn't good enough to be mine forever," Meg looked up as the waitress brought over the wine and poured three glasses. "Alec McCaffrey isn't good enough. And he isn't good enough to still be a subject of our conversations."

Lizzie took a sip of her wine and darted her eyes once more to the lobby. Nora was still on the phone. "Do you really believe that it's possible?"

"I don't know," Meg shook her head honestly and lifted her wine glass. "Like Nora always tells me, it's easy to use fate as an excuse to not make an effort. But, there is a comfort when you lose someone to think that you will meet them again."

"Yeah," Lizzie nodded as she saw Nora head back to the table.

"Mark says hi," Nora slid back into her side of the booth.

"Everything okay?" Lizzie looked to see if her expression indicated any stress. Nora didn't hide emotion as well as Lizzie did.

"Everything is wonderful," she beamed, still the glowing newlywed. Lizzie focused her eyes so they wouldn't tear up. She was still as happy as she was on her wedding day. The happiness Lizzie found that day was a distant dream, clouded with all her thoughts about Lily.

"Thanks for the present," Lizzie looked at the envelope, wondering how she could bring herself to visit an historic inn with Ben now.

"You're welcome," Nora acknowledged the waitress who returned with their salads. Then she lifted her glass. "Happy birthday, Lizzie."

Meg clinked against Nora's glass and then Lizzie's. "Happy birthday. May this be your best year yet."

Lizzie made herself smile and immediately took a bite of salad. If she opened her mouth to any more words, she knew she would cry.

*****

Lizzie knocked on the door to the gift shop, certain she saw movement through the curtained window. "Lizzie?" Paula opened the door.

"Hi Paula," she entered the vacant gift shop. Even though she often sat there without any customers, it had a different feel on a day the museum wasn't open. "I think I left my phone here. Did anyone find it yesterday?"

"No," Paula looked at her. "I didn't see it at the reception desk."

"I remember taking it out to look at the time on my last tour. Do you mind if I go upstairs and see if I left it there? I looked all over the place and haven't been able to find it anywhere else."

"Do you think you left it at the restaurant?" Paula asked, making Lizzie scan her memory for any time during her party when she might have used her phone.

"Nope," she smiled, almost annoyed with herself that she could lie so easily. "I even checked the pub where we had drinks. I think this is my last hope."

"I haven't done a walk thru today," Paula explained. "If you want to look, go ahead."

"I shouldn't be very long," Lizzie emphasized the flirtatious as she started walking down the corridor towards the great room. She followed the steps of her tour, but decided the second floor was her destination. She didn't really know what she was looking for, or thinking she might see… or feel.

She stopped in the guest room and lifted up the shades. If Charlotte was a visitor, that was the room in which she would have spent her time… with her lover. Lizzie looked at the posted bed and its lumpy straw mattress. The coverlet was yellowed and worn thin. From what? No one used that bed in at least a hundred years. How could the fabrics be so worn? Lizzie knew the answer had to do with dust and insects and air quality. It probably wasn't even the same coverlet that Charlotte would have seen. Lizzie looked about, seeing more dust in the expanded sunlight. She let herself touch the post at the foot of the bed. She closed her eyes and breathed in slowly, wondering if something… something might enter her mind. Did Charlotte really seduce Lily? Was there really a Lily? Lizzie slowly sat on the mattress, forgetting her disdain for the antiquated stuffing. She imagined a woman getting dressed… but she knew the pulling of corset strings was her imagination. It wasn't a memory.

Lizzie heard movement from one of the offices on the third floor… in the old servant quarters. Maybe she could contrive a visit to Paula's office. It wouldn't be too difficult. There was nothing about the converted space that resembled where someone like Lily might have slept. She left the bed and walked across the room. The dresser had a few hair pins and worthless pieces of jewelry the curators thought made a display to suggest a woman might walk in to get ready for dinner. In a glance that lasted more than two minutes, the pieces looked old and abandoned on top of the ratty lace that covered the mahogany. She went to the dresser and pulled open the drawers she knew were empty. The top drawer was swollen with humidity and required extra effort to close. Lizzie added an extra push and looked up to make sure she hadn't disturbed the mirror hanging above it.

The mirror was old and had a murky reflection. She could see the circles under her brown eyes and even the last hint of pink dots inside the curve of her neck. Did Lily look in this mirror and lament the teeth marks on her skin? What did she look like? How could Lizzie know? No detail like hair color surfaced in her memory. There would be no photograph in 1815 and no portrait of a servant. Would Ben tell her? He said he recognized Lily in her. Was that because she looked like her? Did she have long dark hair and brown eyes? Were her cheeks rosy against pale white skin? So many people fell for Lily… she must have been prettier than Lizzie. How could Lizzie have been her?

She left the mirror and went towards the window. She looked down at the grassy lawn, abutting the small parking lot. Once there was a garden full of Margaret Fulton's favorite flowers, with hedges to hide the house from the street bustling with horses and carriages. But that too wasn't a memory. She read that in an article by the garden curator in the monthly newsletter two summers ago. The room, like its view of the outside, was just a shadow of something that she studied for several years.

"Did you find it?" Paula disturbed Lizzie from the window.

"Oh no," Lizzie returned to her pretense. "I hope I didn't lose it."

"I could try calling you. Maybe we'll hear it ring."

"No, I think this was a desperate attempt," Lizzie said in vague enough truth.

"So did your boyfriend like the information about his ancestors?"

Lizzie swallowed and paused before trying to speak without emotion. "I haven't… it was a busy weekend."

"Your friends threw a nice party," Paula smiled. "Did you take today off from the hospital?"

"Yeah, I took the whole week off to spend time with …" Lizzie faded. "Especially seeing that I worked on my birthday."

"I would have given you the day off, Lizzie."

"And miss that cake? No way," Lizzie wondered what Ben did with the cake she dropped on the floor with all the papers about his past. Her past.

"I'm sorry you didn't find your phone."

"It's not a big deal," Lizzie shook her head. "Paula, we don't know about any of the servants, do we?"

"The Fultons' housekeeper, Annie. There was a cook," Paula didn't mask her surprise at Lizzie's abrupt topic switch.

"But the maids… or a butler, perhaps?" Lizzie added carefully.

"No."

"Hm."

"Why do you ask?"

"I don't know. I was just thinking about how much dust there is here… and who had to clean it."

"Sorry Lizzie," Paula shrugged.

"Maybe they didn't want us to know who they were," Lizzie sighed. "Maybe they were content being invisible."

Lizzie left the Fulton House without any more tranquility than when she went there. She didn't know what she expected to see… or hear… or know. She knew that Charlotte was real. That Harriet was fond enough to write her a letter. She could prove that she married Horace Fulton. Her maiden name was Chester… or maybe not. Maybe she changed her name like Ben and Oliver changed surnames when they opened the mill. If Ben was right. If she was a vampire. Why would he lie? Why would he tell her that when she had absolutely no clue of the connection between him and Charlotte? Why would Ben make up a story about Oliver being so madly in love with Lily that he killed her twice? He had more reason to not tell her. Lizzie wondered if he never saw those papers if he would have told her.

He never liked to talk about Oliver. Was that the reason? Was it the danger? But with the danger came another truth. Oliver was in love with Lily. Did he love Eloise, a fourteen year old orphan? Lizzie once thought that Oliver gave her extra attention… was it really because she was someone else nearly two centuries before? Then it wasn't Lizzie. Lizzie wasn't a servant in the Fulton House… and yet… she was. She dusted and cleaned the furniture. She led guests through the house and talked about the owners as if they were revered gentry. She was the closest thing to a servant that one could be in the 21st century.

But if she was meant to relive Lily's life… why was she with Ben? And not Oliver?

*****

She shut off the ignition and took a glance in the rearview mirror. She appreciated the lightness and red tint of her new bob. It was a ridiculous impulse, especially when she glimpsed at the receipt she signed. But she needed to do something, anything to make herself not what she was. She breathed in and looked away from the reflection, feeling the heaviness of her soul weigh her down again. She worked so hard to change herself over the past two years. She ran 13 miles after barely being able to run 1 mile. She lost weight. She lost the part of herself that hated how she looked. Why did she suddenly feel the necessity to change it again? Even if she was Lily, cutting and dyeing her hair wasn't going to make that part of her go away. It wasn't the same as losing 75 pounds. Lily and her tragedy would not go away with diet and exercise.

She collected the other bags from her mindless retail extravagance. It managed to pass the afternoon and enough of the evening that she could hear the crickets as she left the car. She turned onto the walk and saw him on the front steps. Her heart leapt to her throat with the relief that he was there. But the anger in her still lingered.

"What are you doing here?"

"You cut your hair."

"Yes," she couldn't think of the million things she wanted to say to him. The questions she wanted to ask. The accusations she wanted to scream. All she could do was wilt.

"Elizabeth…" he stood up from the steps and touched her arm. "I wanted… here, this is for you."

Lizzie set down her bags to take the small package. She knew it was a book. She knew before uncovering it that it was an old book. She turned the embossed cover to a title page in small font indicating a collection of Shakespeare's sonnets. "Ben," she breathed in a sob. She looked up and couldn't stop her eyes from releasing the tears she tried to hold back.

He looked at her as if expecting her to say something. What? She felt more flustered and cried harder as her inability to articulate a clear thought overwhelmed her. Did he expect her to remember? Did he want her to forget? Why was he giving her a book?

"I meant to give it to you yesterday," he pulled her into an embrace. "I wanted to take you out for brunch and… Elizabeth…" he tightened his arms around her as she cried even more.

"I don't want to talk. I'm tired," she said when her eyes finally exhausted the tears.

He stepped back and smoothed away the short strands of hair that stuck to her wet cheeks. She wouldn't look at his eyes. She knew there was something there. A challenge to make her think, which she didn't want to do. She shut her eyes and went up the steps towards the door. She held the screen door open behind her as he picked up the bags she left on the walk.

*****

Lizzie stared at her clock. She didn't want to move. She didn't want to stay still. The comfort of her bed, even in her un-air-conditioned room was impossible to leave. Ben lay beside her. His arm rested casually over her side. He was cool. He still hadn't fed. She wondered if he was thinking about her or her blood.

"I'm sorry, Elizabeth," he sighed heavily.

"Ben, I…"

"I don't know what I am supposed to tell you. Death is as much a mystery to me as it is to you. I don't know if you are supposed to know these things… if I should tell you or just let you lead your life."

"Do you want me to know?" Lizzie kept staring at the clock.

He stroked her hair tenderly. "I hoped you would remember something."

"To prove you were right about thinking I was Lily?"

"I knew you were Lily at Springs," Ben moved his hand quickly as she shifted her position to look at him. She sat up slowly and clutched a small pillow to herself. "You wrote a story for an English project and described a parlor with the exact detail of the Fulton House. Not like it is now, as a museum, but as it was in 1817."

"I did?"

"Do you really have odd sensations when you walk through there?"

"Sometimes," Lizzie looked at the pillow and picked at a frayed string. The first time she went through the Fulton House she thought it resembled all homes of the early 19th century. She figured she had seen pictures… not that she was actually there before. She looked at Ben and softened her eyes. "I went there today. But I didn't… nothing came to mind."

"It isn't important now."

"Isn't it? Isn't there some reason I've gone back there? That I was born in New England again and went to the high school in the town where you wanted to settle with Maria and brought Oliver to start over? Isn't there some significance to all of it?"

"Maybe… is it worth the worry to think about it so much?"

"I want to understand. I don't want to be afraid."

"You needn't be afraid."

"What about Oliver?"

"Oliver won't hurt you."

"But he…" Lizzie still couldn't bring herself to admit his contact on Facebook. "If I stay with you, he will stay away?"

Ben sat up straight. She saw a look of hurt in his eyes, although not completely comprehending her last statement. "Do you want to leave, Lizzie?"

"I haven't let myself think that," she looked back at the frayed string. "I don't know how I could because I love you more than I've ever let myself love anyone."

She said it. Not the way she hoped. Not in a happy or passionate moment. She was exhausted. She was confused. She could barely control her actions, much less what she said. It was a moment of clumsy truth. She was afraid to say anything else, afraid it would make her too vulnerable and too exposed.

Ben took her hand away from the pillow. He kissed the top of her fingers and turned it over, looking at the gauze taped inside her palm. She saw him swallow hard and moved herself towards him, moving her hand to take hold of his chin to pull him into a kiss. She felt the breathlessness and let him push her back against the bed. Lizzie moved her hands down to his belt and then her jeans. She moved her lips away from his and leaned her chin back to whisper in his ear. She kissed the outside of his ear and lifted her arms to press him into the curve of her neck. "Take my blood," she felt his breath and waited for the cut of his teeth as she writhed her hips against his.

He suddenly pulled back from her and lifted himself on the strength of his arms. She saw the burning look she yearned to satisfy, but with it was anger. Lizzie regained her breath and disregarded the anger. She lifted herself back up to meet his lips and moved her kiss down to his neck exposing her skin to him again.

Ben pushed her suddenly down on the bed, restraining her arms with a tight grasp above her elbows. The pain inside her hand awakened as the anger overtook the hunger. "No, Lizzie," he said harshly. She tried to move herself up again but he kept her down. "Don't."

"Ben," she cried.

"It isn't healthy," he glared at her, keeping her in his rigid grip. The sound of laughter came up the stairwell and could be heard beyond the door. Lizzie heard Jackie and Meg muffle their whispers, making their words unintelligible. She heard their doors close separately, not letting her eyes leave Ben. She tried to lift herself once more but he maintained his force. She finally wilted in resignation.

Ben stepped back and readjusted his clothing. "I should leave."

"Why?"

"Because," he took in a deep breath. "You need rest. You're anemic," he explained. "It hasn't been eight weeks. And you bled quite a bit yesterday."

"But what I just said… Ben… doesn't that mean anything to you?"

He looked at her, his eyes still seething. "It means everything. And that is why your safety is more important to me than it ever was."

"Do you fear my safety?"

"I worry about your health, Lizzie. Get some rest," he kissed her gently on the top of her head. "I'll go to the clinic after work tomorrow. Then… we can finish this," he attempted a smile.

"Not if you go to the clinic."

"I'll call you tomorrow," Ben breathed out slowly and quietly left her room. Lizzie shut her eyes and fell against her bed, resuming her stare at the green numbers of her clock.

Lizzie wasn't sure when she fell asleep. She watched the moon rise through the cracks in her blinds and knew at some point she faded out of conscious. She felt as though she was dreaming, but wasn't sure how much of it was her unconscious or her own speculation of all that had entered her mind. She saw Oliver standing by the fireplace in the kitchen of the Fulton House. He was wearing a bike shirt with an Adidas logo. She went through the entirety of her tour trying to think of something, anything that would prompt an idea or thought or memory of Lily. She thought of Harriet's glassy stare in her portrait but couldn't imagine the painted image as a flesh and blood human. She couldn't see Charlotte.

It was just before five when she saw the numbers of her clock again. She wanted to stay in her bed but the thoughts irritated her. She turned on her computer so she could play some music and offer her brain a distraction. Her eyes felt heavy but she decided to check messages she neglected from Sunday and Monday. A lot of birthday wishes and pictures from the party.

Lizzie looked at the happy images. It was a really wonderful night, when she realized how lucky she was to have such good friends and such an amazing, thoughtful boyfriend. She let those images warm and divert her. She switched to her wall and read through all the birthday wishes, including one from Oliver.

She went back to his page and clicked on his photographs. There was one of him in an Adidas biking shirt. It showed his tall muscular physique. He was very attractive, much more than Ben. He looked like one of the vampires from Meg's novels, with his dark thick hair and mischievous dark eyes. Lizzie felt her cheeks burn suddenly as she realized he had features very similar to Will.

She switched immediately over to Ben's page and looked at his few photos, including the ones Nora tagged from her wedding. Her tired eyes didn't resist the emotion. He wasn't as handsome as Oliver or Will. He was strong, but had an average height not much more than her own. His freckles dotted over the bridge of his nose. His reddish brown hair curled slightly but not like a great mane. She loved him. Those green eyes always looked at her with appreciation and concern… and love. She felt the bruises above her elbows, but knew he was trying to protect her at the cost of his own satisfaction. He had wisdom and kindness and a thoughtfulness she thought was imaginary for many years. Why would she let a few historic details allow her to question that? Why did she tempt herself with the doubt of his true feelings? She wasn't destined to go to California and be with Oliver. She made the choice to be with Ben. She made the choice to go running and seek him along the river to ask him out. She chose to offer her blood when he dared to tell her the truth. She made that choice, knowing what she felt and what she wanted in her heart. As Lizzie Watson. Lily had nothing to do with that. Lily and her heart's desires were in the past, faded away like the wallpaper in the Fulton House.

Chapter Twenty

Lizzie looked at the display of DVDs, wondering if any would appeal to impulse. She shifted the items in her arms to pick up a copy and read the short description. The words blurred as she caught sight of another customer walking swiftly by. She gasped on a lost breath as she mindlessly returned the DVD to the shelf.

The man stopped to pull a CD from the shelf. It was much more vivid in reality than her glance at Facebook pictures. It was as if she was standing a few feet from Oliver in his Adidas biking shirt. "Will," she was startled by the sound of her voice choosing to interrupt her stare.

"Hey Liz," he turned around slowly. "It's been ages."

"A year or two," Lizzie shook her head, readjusting the package of paper towels and sweater in her hand. She looked at the big package of diapers Will was carrying. "A lot has happened."

"I'll say so. A baby boy in June," he beamed proudly.

"I saw your pictures on Facebook," Lizzie realized that smile didn't warm her as it once did. "What's his name?"

"Brian."

"You and Lindsey must be happy."

"Yeah, I think we are. You look great."

"Thanks," Lizzie darted her eyes away from his gaze. She felt uncomfortable and guilty acknowledging the admiration she once craved from that face.

"How's Davis?"

"Pretty good. He and Andrew just got back from P-Town."

"Yeah, I'm sorry to have missed their last parties."

"I imagine you've been a little occupied," Lizzie looked towards another customer walking in her direction. She stepped out of his way and closer to Will.

"Indeed," Will nodded blankly.

Lizzie shifted her paper towels again and mimicked his nod. "Well, maybe we'll see you at the next party," she said quickly, stealing one last glance at his dark eyes. It really was uncanny… that two people who never met could look so similar.

"Yeah. Well, it was great to see you," Will retreated to his original direction.

"Great," Lizzie accepted the loose embrace he offered before turning away.

Lizzie watched him until he disappeared into the crowd by the registers. It wasn't that long ago… really… when the mere sight of him made her day. When she hung on his every word. When she wished and hoped that he would look at her with the admiration he just did. Only it wasn't… it was just applause for her achievement. A little lasciviousness… but nothing… really serious. And she didn't care. Only she did. Not because it was Will looking at her that way. Because it was like someone else looking at her that way.

Is that why she liked Will? The struggle for their ten or so lines of conversation made her wonder why her heart was so crazy for him. Was it just a resemblance to someone…

"Hey!" Ben came up beside her.

"Hey," she mouthed, still staring after the shadow of Will.

"Why did you get so many paper towels?" he set down a long heavy box on the floor.

"I need to contribute to my apartment, even if I'm not there all the time," she shook her head and saw the box. "What is that?"

"Some shelves to put in my closet. To give you some space to leave your things, if you want."

Lizzie warmed. She wondered if that was just an impulse buy because he agreed to follow her into Target. Or if it was something he had been thinking about for a while.

"Do you want to pick out another design?" he asked when she didn't respond.

"Weren't you a carpenter in one of your lives?"

"No," he laughed as he wrapped his arm around her waist. "Even if I were, I doubt I would have the time… are you okay?"

"Yeah, I'm fine," Lizzie straightened herself. "I just saw… I just saw Will."

"The guy you had a thing for?"

"Yes," she looked for any hint of jealousy. What would Ben have said if he saw Will and his resemblance to Oliver? He just looked back at her with those green eyes and a smile itching the sides of his mouth. She shook her head. "I like those shelves. Let's go."

"Let's go," he repeated and broadened his smile to hide another twitch. Lizzie glanced one more time to see if she would find Will. But he was gone.

*****

"You don't have to tell me," Ben said as he came into the kitchen with her dinner.

Lizzie took the plastic bag with the Chinese food. She pulled a plate out of the cupboard and started taking the food from the cartons. She looked at him, knowing perfectly well to what he was referring. She didn't know if she wanted to answer him. "What would happen if you ate this?" she stared at a stack of plates piled in the open cupboard.

"My digestive system no longer works."

"Yeah… but I don't really need to eat this Chinese food to survive. I eat it anyway."

"You use some of it," Ben closed cupboard door. She could tell this wasn't the conversation he wanted to have. "If you go running in the morning, you'll use more of it."

"Thanks, Coach," Lizzie muttered.

"Elizabeth, I didn't mean anything by that."

"No," Lizzie shook her head. "But… what happens if I put this in your mouth? Does it just sit in your body? Have you really NOT eaten for two and a half centuries? Don't you miss… chewing? Do your teeth even work?"

"The ones that matter do," Ben said blankly.

Lizzie pulled the beef teriyaki off the skewer. "I would miss food," she looked at her plate full of greasy vegetables, meats, and noodles. "What do you do for comfort food? Is there a type of blood that is bad for you but just tastes so good?"

"When I ate food, Elizabeth, I ate what the earth provided. I knew many winters with a few salty meats and moldy bread," he looked at her. "I never had affection for pizza or ice cream… I never knew."

"Wow," Lizzie felt sad and suddenly disinterested in her low mein and appetizer sampler.

"But the smell of bread baking is still… I sometimes get a phantom rumble in my stomach."

"Food is such an important part of my family," Lizzie pushed her plate aside. "How do you… do you miss having family?"

"I have you."

"Yes, but… there will be… at some point if this is really… you will have to meet all the crazy aunts, uncles, and cousins. Oh God," Lizzie really started to feel her stomach swim and moved away from the kitchen.

"Your parents?"

"My parents," Lizzie muttered and brought herself to the brown leather chair in the living room. She watched Ben follow her and settle on the couch.

"You aren't eating?"

"Do you ever wish you had a family, Ben?"

"Do you?"

She met his eyes. "Sometimes," she cast her eyes down, away from his gaze. "Will had a baby."

"Oh," he let out a heavy breath.

"When I had that stupid crush… I used to imagine having a child with him, a little girl with brown curls and green eyes."

"And now?"

"I don't want… his child," Lizzie left the chair, wanting to go back to her Chinese food. "But I don't know that I don't want any child… ever."

"This is an important conversation," Ben reached his hand in her direction.

"This is surreal," Lizzie shook her head. "I mean… I'm not going to have this conversation. You don't need to have children. You are forever young. You don't need someone to … take care of you when you're old."

"But there is more to having children than…"

"What do they say when they start to age passed thirty and it's evident that you will exist on this planet longer than them?" Lizzie said abruptly, realizing he probably had this debate with himself before… with Maria.

"Do you want children?"

"I want… I want my disgusting dinner," Lizzie moved towards the doorway.

"Elizabeth," he followed her.

"Maybe, I don't know," she paused. "It doesn't matter, if in the end, I choose you, does it?"

"It matters if you choose me and decide to give up something that is important to you."

"Haven't I already… Ben I chose you," she sighed, thinking of Lily. She managed to push those thoughts aside for nearly three weeks. She hadn't forgotten them, but was able to hide them in a neglected corner of her mind. Seeing Will knocked a lot of things out of neglected corners.

*****

Lizzie was lost in the ninth chapter of *Tom Jones* when Ben startled her from her concentration. "All done?" she watched him turn on the computer.

"Pretty much," he sat at his desk. "I should get some storage boxes for the things I cleared out of that closet."

"You didn't have to do that."

"There are clothes that have been in there for decades."

"Are you going to keep them?" Lizzie was surprised he had any packrat tendencies.

"Maybe not," he laughed at her reaction. She recognized the hunger behind his amused response. He saw her apprehension and looked at his computer screen.

Lizzie glanced back at her book. She went for a healthy run along the river that morning. She was tired but still felt the invigoration of oxygen coursing through her body. Did it tempt him? It had been ten weeks. They hadn't spoken of it since the night in her bedroom. She knew he was worried after she cut her hand… but the stitches had long since fallen out. She thought of her Chinese food and all the lipids working through her bloodstream. Maybe the run didn't matter so much when her blood wasn't as clean.

She resumed concentration on the book as he read his messages and typed a few things. After she finished the next chapter, she looked up and saw his eyes on her. She saw the burn that excited her hide behind the smile he quickly offered. "I have to run a few errands." Lizzie knew one of those errands. It was Saturday afternoon. "Do you want anything? I can stop at Starbucks on the way back."

"No, I went running this morning," she knew it was wicked to tease him like that. "I don't need caffeine."

"Okay," he got up from the desk and stopped to kiss the top of her head on his way out. "I'll be back in a few hours."

"See you," she pretended to read, but couldn't concentrate as the prick of disappointment overcame her. She heard him get his keys and walk through the door. She sat still, staring at page 116 for nearly twenty minutes, wrestling with the logic in her mind. The logic that told her to stop asking Ben every weekend since he held her so tightly above her elbows. She knew it was for her health and safety. She knew exactly what Ben would say if she did ask him.

Lizzie left the book on the couch and went to the computer. The screen saver danced from side to side, never bouncing into a corner. She moved the mouse and returned to his desktop. She opened the internet browser and habitually went into her email. She went up to the address bar to look for her Facebook link and saw a bookmark for cambridgeblood.org. Lizzie took a breath and decided to go to the page. The login screen she found in a Google search months before loaded. Ben's name was automatically filled in, as well as his encoded password. Lizzie clicked to try it. The screen paused for a few seconds and redirected her to the site.

The home page had several photos of healthy looking individuals representing both genders and a number of ethnicities. She honestly couldn't tell if they were supposed to be the donor or the vampire. She skimmed quickly over the welcome message. "Since 1948, the Cambridge Blood Clinic has been offering vampire humans a safe alternative for blood acquisition. All of our sources are screened to ensure healthy, relaxing, and satisfactory nourishment. Vampires are carefully matched to sources based on health requirements, preference, and history. To begin your match process, please click here.

"If you are a source, please click here.

Lizzie clicked on the source link and was redirected to a menu. She selected frequently asked questions:

What is the screening process? – The health and safety of vampires is our mission. All sources are required to come in for regular checkups between contributions. You will be tested for drug use, diseases, and cell count. For tips on keeping your blood healthy, please click here. To review the compensation policy, please click here.

Does it hurt? - Most vampire/source transfusions are no different than giving blood to a donor bank. You will feel the prick of a needle and a little swelling after, but no pain. Like donating blood at a hospital, you may feel light-headed. The clinic provides beverages and snacks before you leave.

Will I get bit? – Most sources and vampires exchange through a needle. We have some vampire clients who prefer a traditional method of feeding. You can make the choice on your match questionnaire as to which method you wish to give.

How long does the blood exchange take? – Expect to spend 90 minutes at the clinic for each appointment. This includes a screening, cleaning, transfer, and recovery time. All sources are welcome to stay in the lounge during recovery.

Is this anonymous? – Discretion is important to everyone at the clinic. We guarantee your anonymity. If you wish to use an alias, please click here to have one assigned to you.

Can I become a vampire? – The clinic is strictly a feeding service. We do not condone the transfiguration to vampire.

The last sentence made Lizzie's heart beat in panic. In spite of a curiosity to go back and click on all those links, she logged off of the site and switched the screen over to Facebook. She knew Ben was gone – and would likely still be gone for another hour or two. She didn't know why that last question more than any other rattled her. She never thought to ask him that question. She never wanted to ask that question. The fact it was something a source would ask disturbed her greatly.

The Facebook homepage showed a series of trivia of which she didn't care and didn't want to see. She scrolled all the way down to the end, about to log off when she caught the status update from Oliver – Oliver Cottingham is on sabbatical.

There were close to thirty comments beneath the status. Most of them were students bemoaning the fact that Professor Ol wasn't teaching for the fall semester. There were one or two colleagues wishing him luck on his research project and travel. Lizzie swallowed hard. Travel? She scanned back up the screen and noticed that Oliver had posted a note with the same title, "Oliver Cottingham is On Sabbatical."

To My Devoted Students:

It is with great regret that another semester begins at North California College and I shall not be teaching. As many of you know, I have been busy researching the environmental impact of tourism. In cooperation with the Museum of Science and many enthusiastic students, we have been visiting campgrounds and parking lots and amusement parks to measure... well, trash and a lot of, lot of smog. I intend to spend this semester finishing my research in California, as well as comparing results with colleagues in other regions of the country. In the spring, I hope to put all this random information into some form of writing. But, as you can probably tell from this rambling paragraph, that is not my strong suit. I will be back next fall teaching Environ Science 100 – 500 again. Have a great year. And seniors, I'll see you in May at graduation.

Professor Ol

Lizzie felt really stupid. Really stupid for thinking poorly of Oliver. He had changed. And not just because she knew the story of Lily and his unrequited love for her. She let herself smile fondly as she thought about his care for the planet. That was an impressive and noble pursuit for someone who saw two centuries of Earth's decline. Almost as impressive as creating a blood clinic.

She clicked out of Facebook and decided to leave his office. Her mind wouldn't settle back on Fielding. She wanted to look back on the clinic website. She couldn't... do that to herself. She made herself a turkey sandwich and sat in front of the television, but found that as compelling as the novel. She finished a half of her sandwich and fidgeted about the room. She took another perusal of his movie and music collection. Nothing settled her mind enough to keep her thoughts from the temptation to go back to Ben's computer.

Her eyes caught the white roses under the mirror. They were always fresh roses – except the two weeks he went to Chicago and Lizzie let them die. Were they Maria's favorite? She couldn't imagine any other reason he would have white roses on a Victorian table. She never saw him buy or replace them. It was some sort of ritual. Lizzie resisted the urge to go back to the computer, but not to return to the buffet. She opened the drawer with the silk napkins and found the photograph.

Lizzie forgot how sad she looked. She knew about Oliver and Eloise. Did she know about Lily? Would someone as Catholic as Ben said Maria was believe in something like Lily coming back to find Oliver? Lizzie paused as that floated in her head, feeling as though Maria's gloomy eyes were staring back and judging her. For being with the man she didn't have the courage to leave… and yet she left him in the most wretched way anyone could leave. She killed herself when he couldn't die. Ben said he took her blood only once and that she hated it. Why? Lizzie was Catholic once… she knew the hatred for bodily pleasure that dogma encouraged. And yet… nothing thrilled her more than the thought of her blood making Ben's heart beat rapidly.

There was no clinic when Maria was alive. Where did Ben go? Was she jealous of the sources? Did she think there was some other exchange beyond blood? How did she feel when Ben came home and put his warm body beside her, with the blood of another woman coursing through his veins? Was Maria really the only woman in two hundred years?

Lizzie put the photograph back in its place. She remembered him telling her he kept his books because they meant something to someone he liked to remember. Was that Maria? If she was so timid and superstitious would she read Keats and Byron and Henry Fielding? Lizzie went back to the office and pulled each volume off the shelf one by one. She flipped through the pages and looked at each title page searching for a clue. Any clue. Something to show to whom the books belonged before he decided to preserve them.

She opened a copy of Shelley's poems and took in the breath of old paper and the leather binding. She felt her head swim and looked up to stop the dizziness from pouring over books. She saw Ben standing in the doorway.

"Hi," he smiled.

"Hi," Lizzie blindly replaced the book on the shelf.

"Already finished with Tom Jones?"

"I have ADD today."

"So do I," he revealed the burn was still in his eyes.

"Ben," she started as he came towards her and kissed her passionately. The suddenness of it thrilled the speed of her heartbeat.

He unzipped her sweatshirt and moved his kiss towards her neck. He breathed in and lifted a whisper up to her ear. "Yes?"

"Yes," she barely breathed as he lifted her off her feet.

*****

Lizzie jerked her head up suddenly. Darkness settled outside the office window. She felt Ben's heartbeat pounding in a nearly normal rhythm beneath her as her senses gradually moved back into focus. Her throat was dry and the air was cool against her bare back. She carefully moved herself off Ben and stood up to retrieve the sweatshirt from the floor. She rolled her shoulders back and forward to reinvigorate her tingly arm.

There was something… something else in her mind before she opened her eyes. She closed them to try to prompt the dream back in her memory, but all she could remember was a sensation… but maybe that was a few hours ago when she was awake and Ben… he opened his eyes and smiled as if seeing that memory in his own mind. He sat up slowly and rubbed his eyes. "What time is it?"

Lizzie lifted her shoulders helplessly. "I don't know."

Ben slowly stood and retrieved a few pieces of clothing as he went to his computer. "It's 8:30," he moved back towards her. "It seems later."

"We both fell asleep," Lizzie coughed on her dry throat.

"Not for very long," he smiled at her.

"Long enough for me to dream something."

"Yeah?" he looked curiously.

"I don't remember what it was," she coughed again and went to get a glass of water. When she came back, Ben was back at the computer.

"We got an email from Jack," he said lightly and then sobered his expression.

"Yeah," Lizzie nodded, having read hers at work two days ago. "It's the Melissa Benson BBQ."

"Do you want to get dinner?" Ben avoided her eyes.

"No," Lizzie didn't hide her irritation.

"You need to eat something. Something better than that leftover Chinese food."

Lizzie set her jaw. "Okay, I'll order a pizza," she sat on the sofa. He looked at her for a few lengthy minutes of silence and then went back to the computer. "You're not going to the concert, are you?"

"I don't think I should."

"Why not?" Lizzie looked directly at him.

"Because I would have a difficult time looking at those parents, Elizabeth."

"Because you know how their daughter died?"

"So, apparently, do you."

Lizzie felt a burn in her cheeks that trickled down to the new wound at the side of her neck. "Then I feel more profoundly that I should go," Lizzie looked down at the glass of water in her hands.

"Then you can go for the both of us. Send Jack my regards."

"And that's it? You just end the subject?" Lizzie stood up and glared down at him. "You obviously feel guilty about this, Ben. Even though you say you don't know anything for sure."

"I feel guilty, Elizabeth, because every day I am thankful that it was Melissa and not you," he didn't look at her as he said it.

Lizzie's hands shook. She summoned the strength to rest her glass on the desk for fear she would drop it. She breathed in a sob and exhaled with tears. Ben looked at her and let go of his anger. He came to her side and pulled her into a strong embrace. "You don't have to go," he said softly. "You can tell Jack I made plans for us that can't be re-scheduled. Blame me."

Lizzie wrapped her arms tightly around him. "I have to go," she cried. "I have to…"

"Okay," Ben smoothed along the top of her hair as she slowed her sobs. "It's not your fault, Elizabeth."

Lizzie pulled herself closer to him. His body was so warm. His arms were strong. And safe. She felt as though he could shield her from anything that would harm her physically. But no matter how closely she pressed against him, she couldn't protect herself from the reality of what he was, what he would always be, and how inescapably her life was now entwined with it.

Chapter Twenty-One

Lizzie smiled as Jack set the beers in front of her and Jen. "Perks from sitting with the band," he winked as he took his seat on the other side of his wife. Lizzie smiled at the familiar faces around the table. Faces she knew from years of Jack's gigs. All of them were at her birthday party, but that was a whirlwind. A whirlwind when she could forget about Mike and their indiscretion on the back porch. But there he was with his girlfriend, Amy. How much had changed since that cold January night. And yet Lizzie was back to where she was a year ago… the only one at the table without a partner.

"Are you running that race again this year, Lizzie?" Jen asked.

"No," Lizzie shook her head, laughing at the fact her habit receded to three miles only three times a week. It was unlikely she could accomplish twice that much, never mind thirteen.

"You still look pretty good," Jen nodded as Lizzie peeled pork off of her ribs. She laughed to herself, thinking how Ben would probably disapprove of her food choice. He wasn't there to say anything. Besides, it was another seven weeks before he had any real say in her diet.

"Thanks," Lizzie dodged a look from Mike and the nasty stare from Amy.

"Lizzie!" a voice called from behind her.

"Sara," Lizzie almost choked on the ribs she barely swallowed. "I didn't know you were here."

Sara picked up the toddler walking in front of her. "Hi," she greeted the table. "Hi Jack. Excellent job, guys."

Lizzie could tell from Sara's extra polite tone that she really didn't like the music at all. Some things hadn't changed since high school. "We're playing another set in a half hour," Jack explained, oblivious to Sara's real opinion. Lizzie could tell from Jen's hidden expression that his wife was less clueless. "Is that Josie?"

"Oh no," Sara laughed. "Josie just started crawling. This is Timmy."

"He's so big," Lizzie smiled, feeling the ache Will had dislodged a week before.

"He's growing out of his clothes every week, I swear. Thank God I kept all his brothers' clothes," Sara shifted Timmy from one hip to the other. Lizzie slid over on her bench to offer Sara a seat and pulled a piece of pasta salad off her plate for Timmy.

"Lizzie, where's Ben?" Sara startled Lizzie as she offered Timmy a third piece of her pasta.

"He had a work thing," Lizzie said weakly. It was easier to lie to Jack and the band. Sara was a different story.

"So you guys are still dating?"

"Yeah," Lizzie found another piece of mayonnaise covered ziti for Timmy's eager hands.

"Dating?" Jen laughed. "They're practically living together."

"Oh," Sara pursed her lips. Lizzie knew she was wrestling between her high school ego and the Christian wanting to say something about the sanctity of marriage.

"How's your mom doing?" Lizzie opted to let it go, softened by Timmy's eager pudgy fingers.

"She's holding up," Sara accepted the topic change. "She always brightens when the grandchildren are around."

"I can see why," Lizzie smiled at Timmy and then Sara. "Are you visiting for the weekend?"

"Mom told me about the fundraiser. I thought it would be fun for the kids – and it's a good cause," Sara smiled at the table, relatively quiet as they ate their barbeque.

"Yeah," Lizzie felt the weakness tempt her.

"I remember the day she disappeared," Sara looked blankly in front of her. "It was one of the first days my dad let me drive to school. I was so excited I got to drive, I crammed too many people in that Ford Escort. Even you, Jack."

"I remember," he grinned.

"When we drove by the Bensons' house, there were three police cars. It was odd because that's probably all the police in this town," Sara laughed without any hint of humor.

"Yeah," Jack interjected. "We all stayed at my house to see what was going to happen. But nothing did."

"We played a lot of Trivial Pursuit that night."

"I think Lizzie won every single game," Jack laughed.

Lizzie blinked her eyes, hoping no one saw the tears that started to form in them. "That whole summer…" she returned her gaze to Timmy's hungry fingers. "We played a lot of Trivial Pursuit."

"Ben brought pizza," Sara smiled, no doubt thinking the pizza was just for her. Lizzie thought how she was often the one who ate seconds, filling her blood with unappealing lipids.

"Ha," Jack laughed. "Lizzie says he's a health freak now."

"So is Lizzie," Jen smiled.

"Except at barbeques when Jack's band is playing," Lizzie met her eyes.

Timmy grew restless when his supply of ziti ended. He turned around and patted his mother's lips with greasy fingers. "I think we'll go back to Grandma," Sara dodged a finger between her teeth. She lifted her eyes back to the band with another empty smile. "See you later, Lizzie. Jack."

"Jack," an older man echoed as he came over to the table.

"Mr. Benson," Jack turned around.

"I wanted to thank you again for all your help," the older man took Jack's hand then circled the table to the rest of the band.

"You remember my cousin, Elizabeth Watson? She was in my class at Springs," Jack nodded to Lizzie.

Lizzie stood up and nodded. "Mr. Benson."

"Thanks for coming to support my girl."

"I remember Melissa," Lizzie said flatly. "She was a great … person."

"She would have been 35 today."

Lizzie found the strength to make herself smile, even as the meat in her stomach started to curdle. Mr. Benson looked at Lizzie slowly. "You remind me of her a little," Mr. Benson's stare started to glisten.

"She was a lovely girl," Lizzie said blankly.

Mr. Benson breathed in slowly. "Yes. One of your classmates gave us a sizable donation this year. I think that will allow us to award two extra scholarships in June."

"Ben?" Jen asked.

"Benjamin Cottingham," Mr. Benson nodded. "They lived over on Scott Road. Big old house, he and his brother. I think one of them used to give Melissa a ride home from softball practice when I couldn't get there in time. They were good boys."

Lizzie put her hand against the table to keep her balance. "Lizzie knows Ben pretty well. He's her boyfriend," Jen offered. "He still is a good guy."

"He is a lucky guy," Mr. Benson nodded. "Thanks for coming."

Lizzie sat down as he walked away. She saw several eyes at the table look at her. Lizzie forced herself to concentrate on her plate and started to pull the meat off her ribs, even if she didn't have the stomach to eat any more.

"What a nice man," Amy commented. "How sad. You can tell he still grieves for his daughter."

"They never found the body," Jen sighed. "I can't imagine that he has had closure."

"How awful."

"Did you see how he looked at Lizzie?" Jack asked. "It was like he was seeing a ghost. You do kind of look like her."

"Kind of," Lizzie dropped the bones on her plate.

"That's creepy," Jen softened her eyes on Lizzie. "Did that ever freak you out?"

"I never really thought about it until recently," Lizzie looked up at her friends.

"Did they ever find out who did it?" the bass player asked.

"Nope," Jack shook his head. "No body. No suspect."

"They must have suspected someone?" the bass player's wife asked.

"I think they checked out her boyfriend. He was a real asshole," Jack rolled his eyes. "And then there was some guy who lived on Peabody Ave. that got arrested for molesting his kids. They tried to link him to this… but they couldn't prove it. Then it just kind of faded out of the public attention."

"That's sad. That must be difficult for Mr. Benson, too," the bass player's wife added.

"But think of the good he's done. All those scholarships that help students. He managed to turn his sorrow into opportunity," Jen offered.

"Good point," Jack patted his stomach. "Lizzie, you look like you could use that beer I got you."

"I would if a bunch of people just compared me to a dead girl," Jen touched her hand. "Are you okay, Lizzie?"

"I'm fine. I'm happy to be here. Alive, with my friends," Lizzie hoped the extra effort of her nod didn't give away her struggle. "I'm lucky I am able to complain about being 34 and growing white hairs."

"Here, here," Jen grinned back.

*****

Lizzie slid the tablecloth a little more towards her left and began setting the napkins and silverware in front of all the seats… except two corners waiting for Ben's chairs. She retrieved wine glasses from the bar and went back in the kitchen for trivets to set in the middle of the table.

"It looks lovely," Nora walked in with a vase full of flowers. "Do you want them in the middle? Or is it too tall for people to see one another?"

"It's perfect," Lizzie admired the arrangement Nora set in the middle of the table. "She'll like the cala lilies."

"Smells delicious," Nora breathed in. "I love your lasagna."

"It was her special request," Lizzie shrugged as she heard a clamor come up the stairs. Ben carried two chairs from his dining room, followed by Mark with a case of wine. Ben smiled as he passed Lizzie and directly delivered the chairs to their spots.

"Your black skirt," he unhooked a small bag and handed it to Lizzie. "Mark, did you get everything from your car?"

"A bag of ice," Mark finished placing the bottles on the bar. "I'll go get it."

"It smells delicious," Meg passed Mark in the dining room entrance. She put in her second earring and crossed the room to hug Lizzie.

"Happy birthday, Meg."

"I miss your food," Meg went to the bar and opened a wine bottle. "Ben, you don't know how lucky you are."

Lizzie looked at one of the settings and adjusted a fork that was askew. "I am," Ben put a hand behind her back as she stood up straight again. She didn't like the implication of the lie that he had any appreciation of her culinary skill. She knew he was aware she liked to cook, but he would never really know if she was good or not. Or care.

"Before I forget," Meg paused before pulling the cork from the bottle. "I want to thank you both – Ben and Lizzie – for your birthday gift. That was really… that was so thoughtful."

Lizzie felt Ben's hand tense suddenly at her back. She took it as a cue to smile even more broadly. "It's your birthday."

"But," Meg beamed as she poured the first glass. "That book must be so old. Of course you know, Lizzie. I'm not surprised you found it… but that was really generous."

"What book?" Nora asked.

"A first American edition of Byron's *The Vampyre*," Meg offered a glass of wine to Lizzie.

"I should get dressed," Lizzie took the bag with her skirt and turned to Nora. "There's cheese and cut vegetables in the fridge."

"I'll take care of it," Nora shook her head to a glass of wine as the doorbell rang.

Lizzie walked quickly up the spiral staircase to her room. She kicked aside the pile of clothes she left on the floor in a dissatisfied attempt to determine an outfit. She was annoyed that a few things were a snug around her waist. Ben entered a minute later and closed the door behind him.

"I'm sorry. I completely forgot I did that," Ben laughed at his clumsiness. "I happened to be purchasing something for you the day you called me about Meg's birthday. And I saw that, so I sent it here – from the both of us."

"You bought her a first American edition Byron?" Lizzie let the pettiness show in her face. But it wasn't petty. He gave Lizzie a book and that was special. It was less special if he gave Meg an antiquated book. A book about a vampire. A book that was their secret.

"I meant it to be from you as much as me."

"I can't afford that," Lizzie started taking off her t-shirt and jeans. "And… geez, Ben… she's not… she's not your girlfriend."

"It's just a book." Ben was in good spirits, enough to tolerate her moodiness. He fed before coming to Jefferson Park.

"Yeah," Lizzie went to her closet to find the shirt she wanted to go with her skirt.

"Did you want me to get her something else?"

"A bottle of wine would have sufficed," Lizzie muttered. "Or if you wanted to be special, rum."

Ben came beside her as she stared at the closet. He rested his hands on her shoulders. Lizzie remained immobile, even as he started kneading the tension from her joints. He slid down her right bra strap and slowly kissed her shoulder. "Ben," impatiently turned to face him. "I have to get dressed."

"Nora can handle things for a little while."

Lizzie looked at him and felt the stress return to her shoulders. "Endorphins?"

"She's a runner, like you," Ben smiled as though he had a few drinks.

"Oh yeah?"

"It was just a needle," he pulled her close to him. "But we can both benefit from it."

"Not now," she pushed him away in disgust and took her stockings from her drawer. He watched her roll them over her leg. In her agitation, she ripped a hole and drove a run down the length of her shin. "Fuck."

"Yes, let's," Ben laughed.

Lizzie glared at him, grabbed her clothes, and went into the bathroom. She got dressed rapidly and managed to not rip the second pair of hose in her haste. Ben's eyes softened to apology when she opened the door. "You know it was just a transfusion, Elizabeth."

"What happens if a cop pulls you over after you have an endorphin drenched transfusion? Do you get a DUI?" Lizzie growled as she looked for a match to her hoop earring.

"No," Ben smiled. "Come on, I'll make you feel better."

"For Christ's sake, Ben," Lizzie looked at him hard. "I have a lasagna in the oven. I know you don't care about such things. But it's important to me."

Ben immediately sobered. She knew he wanted to say something, but was either incapable or afraid of forming the question. He swallowed and let out a painful sigh. "You're right. I'm sorry."

"I'm going to get a glass of wine," she hissed as she threw on a painful pair of heels and left the bedroom.

*****

Two bottles of wine were empty by the time Lizzie cleared the salad plates and brought out the lasagna. Meg's friends from the university were a boisterous group, especially Didi and Tamara. Lizzie knew them from other gatherings they hosted at Jefferson Park. They both taught in the English department. They met there eight years ago and were married for three. And they both hated Alec McCaffrey. They were kind enough to avoid their favorite bashing – no doubt out of kindness to Jeff, Meg's date for the evening. Jeff was also a grad student, but not on his second thesis of his second masters like Meg.

"It's been too long since we've had a party in this house," Meg sighed as Mark opened another bottle of wine.

"Are you going to have a Halloween party this year?" Tamara asked.

"Of course," Meg didn't pause for Lizzie's agreement and listed her favorite costumes.

"It's not even a month away," Lizzie handed a plate of lasagna to Meg.

"It will give me something to take my mind off…" Meg took a quick bite after a glance to Jeff.

Lizzie swallowed any urge to protest she didn't want to cook and be unappreciated by Meg who took her for granted or Ben who just didn't care. She cut another slice of lasagna and handed it to Nora, who offered a smile of understanding to Lizzie's unspoken thoughts. "I have some good news," Nora looked at Lizzie and then the rest of the table. "Kind of appropriate to share at a birthday celebration."

"You're pregnant," Meg muttered into her wine. Nora looked at Mark and bit her lip. Meg set down her glass. "You haven't had anything to drink all night, Nora. And we all knew you were going to start trying the moment you got back from your honeymoon."

Lizzie swallowed her reply to Meg's tactlessness. It was her birthday… and the third glass of wine.

"Congratulations," Ben broke the weird silence with a lift of his glass. "You must be very happy."

"Of course we are!" Nora let the joy explode across her face and dissolved the displeasure with Meg. Mark smiled broader than Lizzie had ever seen him. "We're almost three months. I know I'm supposed to wait a few more weeks to tell anyone… but I'm just so happy."

Lizzie went over to give Nora a hug. "So… that's the end of April?"

"April 25," Mark said proudly. Lizzie turned and hugged him.

"That's really great you guys," Meg followed with her own embraces. "And good news to hear on my birthday."

Lizzie took her seat and finished serving the pieces of lasagna, making sure to give Ben a small piece with lots of sauce. Meg and Didi had lots of questions for Nora and Mark, allowing Lizzie to keep silent and drink her wine. She was happy for Nora and Mark, but that joy seemed to just sit in front of her and not go inside of her. Like the lasagna on Ben's plate that he would never eat.

*****

Lizzie looked at the steam clouding her reflection in the window. She shut off the faucet and took another wine glass to wipe out with the soapy cloth. "Elizabeth," Ben's voice called suddenly as he came into the kitchen. "Why aren't you in the living room with everyone else?"

"Because I won't enjoy myself knowing there are lots of dishes that need to be cleaned," she rinsed out the glass. "I actually like washing dishes. It's one of my favorite parts of a party."

"I don't believe you," Ben took the towel hanging on the oven railing. "Is that just your excuse to stay in the kitchen?"

"That's why it's my favorite part of the party."

"Are you okay?" he took one of the glasses and wiped it dry.

"I'm fine," she selected the greasy lasagna pan and decided to attempt to scrub off the melted cheese.

"I'm…" he looked around to find where to settle the glass.

"Just put it next to the stove," Lizzie didn't look away from the pan.

"You've worked hard today," he took one of the knives resting in the drainer. Lizzie opened her mouth to say something about how to dry it, but resigned herself to the fact he knew nothing about a kitchen and its maintenance.

"Meg means a lot to me."

"Which is why I… I shouldn't have gotten the book," he sighed.

"She loves it. She really impressed Didi and Tamara. That means a lot to her," Lizzie concentrated on a stubborn spot of crusted sauce. "It's okay, Ben. Your heart was in the right place."

"But you aren't. Was it … did Nora's news bother you?"

"No," Lizzie lowered her voice in case anyone could hear through the dining room and across the hall in the living room. "Why would it?"

"You were upset when you saw Will a few weeks ago."

"And I told you, I've made my choice."

"We could…"

"We could what?' Lizzie made a harsh whisper. "Before I could even think about any of this, we have to bring family into our … relationship."

"Why don't we?"

"You want to meet my family?" Lizzie looked at him in disbelief. "And have my family meet yours?'

Ben shut his eyes and started to speak, but Lizzie cut him off. "And what am I suppose to say? This is Ben, my boyfriend. He's a vampire. He lives off of peoples' blood. He can't die. He doesn't get old. And this is his brother, Oliver. He killed a teenager from my high school. And he was my lover in a former life. Oh – and he killed me, twice."

She held him there, as he helplessly clutched the dishtowel under her angry gaze. He had that same look of wanting to say something, but lacking the ability to begin the articulation of his thought. He shifted his eyes suddenly, prompting Lizzie to turn around and soften her expression to Nora. "Ben, please go rescue Mark. He's been on good behavior with

Meg, but I think he needs a little conversational distraction," Nora pleaded. "I'll help Lizzie. I know how to dry the dishes so she doesn't feel like she needs to wash them all over again… which I'm guessing is an art you still haven't mastered."

Ben managed a smile and surrendered the towel. "I guess not."

"Don't worry. It took me three years of living with her," Nora beamed broadly as he left the kitchen. "I'm assuming that's the source of the tension I walked in on? He didn't touch the knives properly?"

"It doesn't matter. I'm sure Jackie and Meg don't care when I'm not here," Lizzie felt badly for causing Nora's confused frown. "I'm very happy for you and Mark."

"I'm over the moon with joy and terrified," Nora lifted a glass to dry. "You'll find out someday."

"I might not," Lizzie looked back at the dirty pan.

"I know you've said you weren't sure you wanted kids," Nora looked at her. "But even now… with Ben? You guys must have talked about it."

"We talked," Lizzie hardened her shoulders. "He can't have children."

"Oh," Nora set down the glass. "Well there are other options."

"I'm not in any rush to have kids, Nora."

"Yeah, but…" Nora lifted the glass again and put it in the cupboard. "You are so good with kids. You had such a way with them at the Village. And when you nannied."

"I haven't nannied in years," she loosened a stubborn spot of cheese. "Maybe I'm great with kids because I'm not a parent. I'm planning on being the coolest aunt to your kid."

"You will be," Nora hesitated. "And Ben will be a pretty cool uncle. He's a good guy."

"He is a good guy," Lizzie looked to her reflection in the window, but it was lost in the cloud of steam.

*****

She knew he was following her. She didn't see him in the darkness of the damp evening, but she sensed he was close behind her. She sped up her pace and ran to the narrow corridor between the bushes and the carriage house. She laughed and leaned against the wall of the building as he came around the other side of the greenery. He caught her laughter and stifled it abruptly as he kissed her. His kiss was less tender, but sincere. So sincere she could feel it in her heart. Even as his roughened hands clutched awkwardly at her dress. He was so timid, for such a tall strong man. He was afraid of her.

Lizzie felt as though she was underwater. She faded away from the kiss and opened her eyes as the warmth dried her throat. It was still dark. Ben was asleep with his back against her. She didn't remember going to bed. She didn't remember… the wine swam in her stomach, swirling her brain. She got up quickly and went into her bathroom for some water. She drank two glasses quickly, but not enough to quell the urge to bow her head over the toilet. How much wine did she drink? She never drank that much… at least a bottle. She let herself cry as she fell to the floor and leaned her head against the wall. She brushed away the ends of her hair that clung to her cheek and pulled off her pantyhose throwing them on the floor. Ben clearly wasn't interested in her that evening… in whatever state he had walked or carried her up the stairs.

She knew he wouldn't be. She made the decision to stay up with Didi and Tamara after Mark and Nora made their exit. Meg disappeared with Jeff at some point. Lizzie drank more wine even though she knew she reached her threshold. She knew it would be distasteful to Ben and drank too much to remember when the party ended.

She remembered the dream, even though it lingered as fragments of the complete story. It felt… she felt the dewy air and the unevenness of his awkward fingers. She saw the glint of moonlight in Oliver's dark brown eyes. She shut her eyes to escape the glare of the bathroom light and felt the alcohol still swirling in her brain.

She threw up again, bringing herself back to the unpleasantness of the present. She didn't want to have that thought about Oliver in her head or the sensation of anything she would want to remember about… her head spun and ached with the dehydration. Why did she do that to herself? It was reckless… and she was beyond reckless damaging behavior to her body. And yet… she was sleeping with a vampire.

He took care of her. He always put her well being first. He wanted to make her happy. Why? Why did it mean so much to him? Why was he attached to her so completely when, by his own admission, he tried to stay away from her? Did he try to stay away from her simply because of Oliver? Oliver had more devotion to that separation. Even though he had more reason to be with her. Did Melissa Benson purge Oliver of the Lily fixation? Ben didn't think so. Lizzie knew he worried. Was he worried that Oliver would kill her… or that Oliver would take her away from him?

Lizzie didn't want Oliver. She didn't want another vampire in her life. She loved Ben. She was still angry with him because he just didn't think about things… that weren't important to him. That was no different than any other boyfriend… or friend. Meg always annoyed Lizzie with her oblivion. Every single day.

Her thoughts were a muddle. She was tired. She was still drunk. Her body ached inside and out. Her dream and its sensation filtered in and out of her thinking. It wasn't real. It couldn't have been real. There wasn't a carriage house at the Fulton property. It had to be the Harris carriage house. It made sense because Lily wouldn't want Annie to find her sneaking about with her sister's boy. Lizzie was startled awake by the detail that so easily entered her mind. In a panic she rose to her feet and opened the bathroom door. She went to the bed, ready to shake Ben out of his sleep. She stopped as she opened her mouth to call out his name. She didn't want him to know what she was thinking, what she remembered. She didn't want to know if the thoughts that entered her brain so suddenly were true. She didn't want him to know she dreamt of kissing Oliver… and that for a few dwindling moments, she liked it.

Chapter Twenty-Two

Lizzie set down the box of books on the floor and pulled out a couple volumes to place on the shelves. She readjusted the irritating tightness of her jeans. She pulled her sweater down, annoyed with herself for sampling so much of her cooking that week. She was nearing the end of eight weeks and needed to get back to running regularly and eating with more sense. She bent down and picked up a few more copies of *The Fulton Family Legacy*.

"Gerard Fulton came in here a few days ago," Paula entered the gift shop.

Lizzie laughed as she looked at his name on the binding of the books she placed tightly in the vacant space. "Did he have anything interesting to say?"

"No, but he was asking after Leslie, the lovely girl who works at the hospital."

"Well that's sweet. I don't suppose he left me a check for the hospital, did he?" Lizzie was dissatisfied with the shelf she filled. She pulled out the books and decided a better facing was necessary.

"No," Paula shook her head. "So you'll do the noon tour? You can take off after that."

"Thanks. I have to go help hang cobwebs," Lizzie explained. "We should have done something festive in the museum."

"I don't know how we could justify any mention of Halloween in this house, Lizzie," Paula tried to be serious. "No matter how many times you claim there are ghosts."

Lizzie managed another laugh to mask the chill she gave herself. She no longer believed in ghosts. She was afraid of memories. She half hoped her task of the day would be restocking the gift shop and not going through the house on a tour. Not on the day when supposedly the barrier between the living and the dead was weakest.

She shook her head, cursing herself for that thought when she heard the bell of the door. She finished arranging the books to avoid seeing what tourist walked in to force her confrontation with Lily. Then she heard a familiar voice answer Paula's ritual greeting.

"Oliver," she said almost inaudibly as she turned around.

"Hi Lizzie," he smiled genuinely. "How are you?"

"I'm well," Lizzie swallowed, aware that Paula was looking at her. "This is Oliver, Ben's brother."

Lizzie could tell by Paula's expression that she was scanning her memory for a detail. Lizzie hoped that she wouldn't remember the name Oliver from the information about Raleigh and Eloise Hutchins. "You look familiar," Paula increased Lizzie's panic. Was there a picture of Oliver in that pile of papers? "I know," Paula answered her own question before Oliver could explain anything. "I've seen a couple articles about you. You are working on a research project with the San Francisco Museum of Science. It's been in all sorts of museum newsletters. It has to do with tourism, doesn't it?'

"Indeed," Oliver grinned proudly, looking briefly at Lizzie. "Actually, I'm in town to compare notes with some colleagues at UMASS."

Lizzie felt her shoulders relax a little and looked at another shelf to rearrange.

"It's an interesting idea," Paula nodded, but Lizzie could tell she was impressed. "You know, I have a friend who works at your museum."

"It's not my museum. I teach at the local college. But I might know your friend."

"Joanne Bates?"

"I know Joanne," Oliver smiled. Lizzie caught herself admiring his smile. "I can tell her you say hello."

"Yes, definitely. Tell her Paula says hello."

"Oh God, I'm sorry," Lizzie realized her flub and left her concentration of the bookshelf. "Oliver, this is Paula. She's the education program coordinator."

"Nice to meet you," Oliver continued his sweet smile and held out his hand officially.

"The same. So is your visit here part of your research?"

"No, I," he lingered in a barely noticeable pause. "I was hoping I could take a tour."

Lizzie darted her eyes to the clock behind the desk. It was 11:30. There was a possibility some more public would come through to join them by noon. "Lizzie could take you," Paula offered generously. "If anyone comes at noon, I'll take that tour."

"The desk?" Lizzie asked.

"Donna will be done by then," Paula thought she was doing Lizzie a great kindness. "When you are done, you can head out to get ready for your party."

Lizzie hoped the burn wasn't evident on her cheeks. She wasn't going to explain there was a party at her house that night. It required enough effort to not freeze in terror at the thought of walking through the house alone with Oliver. On Halloween. "Are you sure?"

"Go on," Paula took the book from Lizzie's hands.

Lizzie offered a polite expression towards Oliver. She stopped to take a drink from her water bottle and then guided him out of the shop down the corridor into the house. She took in a deep breath and used all her ability to not tremble. She was glad to see him, but couldn't bring herself to show the affection of seeing an old high school friend. She didn't know if it was right to be glad to see him. She didn't know if Ben would appreciate her being glad or scared or knowing that Oliver dared to do what he would not do.

"You can't touch the furniture," Lizzie explained the rules flippantly, without the charm she used with tourists. "And if there are ropes in the room, you can't go beyond them. Turn off your cell phone."

She hoped she wasn't too abrupt. She wouldn't look at him. She couldn't. Not yet. Not in that house. She led him out of the stair hall into the great room. "The Fultons were…" she started and tried again. "The Fultons were a prominent Cambridge family in the early 19th century. They were loyal to the British in the Revolution and the War of 1812. John Fulton acquired his fortune…" Lizzie faded feeling ridiculous. "This is the great room," she said quickly and stopped so he could look for a second. Then she went back through the hallway into the parlor. "This is the parlor," she paused briefly before passing through. "And the dining room."

Oliver walked around the table, looking at the china laid out on the table and the paintings hung over the fireplace. He put his hands behind his back, perfectly obedient to the instruction to not touch. He lifted his chin back to her when he made a complete circle of the room. She hastened to the other side and went into the next room. "This is the kitchen," Lizzie continued her simplicity. She shuddered and stared at the fireplace, wondering why no one had lit a fire.

"You look great Lizzie," Oliver took advantage of her pause. "I like the red hair."

Lizzie immediately regretted her choice to dye her hair again. She hadn't thought until Oliver spoke it that she chose a resemblance to Eloise. "Thanks," she said weakly. She knew her heartbeat accelerated. She wondered if he could sense her adrenalin rush. She let herself glimpse quickly at his dark eyes, but looked away when she was confident there was no burn hidden in them.

Oliver circled the large wooden table with a few utensils laid out to look as though the cook might come in and start the next meal. Lizzie never realized how absurd it was to see a bowl and a couple wooden spoons. As though the cook would start with that. Besides, the table was always covered in flour and grease. She shook her head uncertain where that argument came from. She looked at her watch. It was only 11:40. She couldn't tell him they had to get out of the way of the tour coming through. If she took him upstairs, she would likely run into Donna.

"How's Ben?" Oliver broke the silence.

"He's good," Lizzie nodded mechanically. "He's great."

"Good."

"I know you are a vampire," Lizzie heightened her posture, fearing that would shed his friendly demeanor.

"I imagine you do," he maintained his gentility, almost amused. He looked at her briefly and crossed to the fireplace. He lifted his hand to touch the mantle but remembered the rule and put his hand behind his back. He looked back at Lizzie, revealing the search for a dozen answers in his eyes.

"I know about Lily, too," she said softly and let herself look at his face. He was really very handsome. Lizzie was surprised that he looked the same as the last time she saw him at Springs. It wasn't like he had grown into his looks in the 18 years since he… graduated. He didn't have the alteration of age to better define his features. He was the same as his photographs, with thick dark hair and intensely mysterious brown eyes. He was tall, but that didn't surprise her. She remembered that in her dream.

He started to smile but seemed to catch the thought that prompted it. Or maybe the memory of Lily was always bittersweet. "I imagine that is why you are here," he met her eyes.

"I worked here for four years before I…" Lizzie realized she answered his indirect question. "Before I knew I was her."

"Did you remember something?" he revealed hope in his eyes, though his face remained calm.

Lizzie felt her cheeks flush, remembering her wine soaked dream. "I honestly still don't believe it completely," she said hastily. She tried to force the doubt into her brain, even though it was more difficult to be a cynic now that she was dating a supernatural. "I've had dreams. They usually mix the present with the past. Or sometimes I would give a tour and say something that I had no way of knowing."

"Like what?" he revealed an impish amusement.

"One time I said the parlor wallpaper was green," Lizzie muttered, thinking of Paula's reprimand after overhearing that. "Obviously, it's not. But… we don't know that's not the original wallpaper."

"It's not," Oliver shook his head. "It was green. Lily… she always liked that color."

"Oh," Lizzie was relieved Lily was referred to in third person. "Do you remember this house?"

"I remember it well," Oliver looked up as if collecting the memories in his mind. "It feels strange to be here again."

"How so?"

"It's empty. *This* room was always full of servants. They were all such gossips about everyone who came in here, about every house in the neighborhood. The gentry and the servants," he stopped to recollect more detail. "The wallpaper is peeling and faded."

"Well, yeah."

"A lot of the furniture is different. It smells musty… not like smoky fires and the starch from Mrs. Fulton's linens. This room doesn't seem right without a big cut of beef hanging over the fireplace or the herbs from the ceiling… it's different. But the way it creaks, the way the light comes through some of the windows… it's the same."

Lizzie shook her head in the silence that followed his comments. "They are so god-dammed precious about that wallpaper."

"That's funny," Oliver laughed. "There are so many things on this planet that need to be preserved. And people get obsessed over wallpaper."

"It's nice wallpaper."

"Yes, but it's not as essential as the ozone layer," Oliver remarked. "Do you remember any of those things?"

"Nothing as specific as that. I once dreamt I was watching a string quartet play in the great room. But I was wearing jeans in the dream… so… I don't even know what she looked like."

Oliver let his eyes rest on Lizzie for a few silent moments. She felt the latent fear rise up in her throat. She glanced at the fire irons and wondered if necessary, could she use them to defend herself? She looked away from the fireplace as she heard the noise of Donna's small tour come down the main staircase. Their footsteps and voices quickly faded towards the gift shop. The silence set once more in the kitchen. Lizzie could hear the hum of the traffic outside the windows. "We should probably move our tour upstairs right now."

"Let's go," Oliver took himself up the servant steps into the master bedroom. Lizzie slowly followed him into the room. She saw him standing against the sun of the west facing window. She saw the outline of his strong build as he stared down to the parking lot. "Has Ben told you anything about Lily?" he asked the window.

"I know you killed her. And Eloise Hutchins. And Melissa Benson," Lizzie spat out, wishing she had taken that fire iron from the kitchen. She scanned the bedroom, but doubted the hairbrush on the vanity would be an effective tool of protection. She could break the washbasin on the nightstand.

"That's what he told you?" Oliver continued to ask the window.

"Some of it," Lizzie said weakly. "I figured some of it out on my own."

Oliver shifted his gaze to another direction of Brattle Street. "I loved Lily," he swallowed a memory Lizzie could tell was still painful.

"Ben said that."

"Lizzie, I'm not going to hurt you," Oliver turned to face her.

"Why are you here?"

"To see you."

"Are you going to see Ben?"

"I doubt it."

"You came to Boston just to see me?"

"No," he shook his head. "I really do have some professional work in the city. But while I was here… I wanted to see you."

"Why?"

"I found out about you and Ben."

"How?"

"There are pictures of you two all over the internet. At your friend's wedding. At parties and outings…"

"Right," Lizzie looked down. "What do you feel you need to tell me about Ben?"

"I…" Oliver looked back to the window. "Just be careful, Lizzie."

"What?"

"I can see that you are in love with him," Oliver clenched his jaw. "It's obvious in those pictures. It's obvious right now."

"You don't think I should love him?"

"I think you should be careful. You need to ask yourself how honest he has been with you."

"He has told me…" Lizzie wanted him to look at her. He kept staring out that stupid window. Brattle Street couldn't be that fascinating on the last day of October. All the foliage was gone. There was hardly any foot traffic this far down the street. "He hasn't told me everything. I haven't told him everything about my life – and I've only been on this planet for 34 years."

"He tells you that he is protecting you from me?" Oliver looked at her directly.

"Yes," Lizzie couldn't meet the eyes she wanted to turn.

"Do you think he should?"

"You killed those girls…"

"He killed, too, Lizzie. Do you judge him?"

"He admits that. He feels badly."

"You don't think I feel badly? I *loved* Lily."

"I'm not Lily."

"No, you are not. But what does Ben think?"

"I…" Lizzie lost her words in the look of his eyes. There was something familiar and warm about his stare, something she wanted to trust even as all the information of the past several months echoed in her brain.

Oliver approached her and touched her cheek softly. "Lizzie, I'm sorry. This isn't fair to you. There is bad blood, if you'll pardon the expression, between Ben and me. You needn't get caught in the middle of it," he focused his eyes on her, as if searching for a trace of Lily. Lizzie didn't feel as though he saw what he was looking for. He dropped his hand and breathed out. "I think I've said enough for now. I'm a little overwhelmed being in this house again. I will be in town for a while. Please… let's talk some more."

"You don't want to see Ben?"

"I think it would be best if I didn't. But if you think I should, then by all means, let's all have a chat," Oliver walked towards the door and smiled at her.

"I'm not sure that's a good idea," Lizzie suddenly looked towards the guest room, as if fearing someone might come in to John and Margaret's bedroom to disturb their conversation.

"It isn't fair to you, Lizzie. He should have let you be," Oliver sighed.

"No," she let anger overcome her. "I can take care of myself. I made a choice to be with him. He makes me happy."

"He thinks you're…" Oliver closed his mouth over his words. "Don't you have to go home and get ready for a party?"

"Did you want to see the rest of the house?'

Oliver gazed towards the door and the direction of the other bedrooms. "Some other time."

"Let me walk you out," Lizzie led him back towards the hallway and the main staircase. She heard Paula starting her tour in the great room.

Oliver laughed and whispered to her as they went down the stairs. "I used to sneak in and out of this house… and now you have to walk me out."

Lizzie looked at him curiously at the bottom of the staircase. She wanted to know what he meant by that, but wouldn't let herself ask. "It's the museum policy," she uttered plainly and led him back into the gift shop.

*****

Lizzie saw Ben's car in front of the house and panicked. Had she really taken that long with Oliver? No, it was hardly ten minutes past noon when she said goodbye to Donna. She stopped at the grocery store on the way home. She glanced at the clock before turning off her engine. It was only 1:30.

She pulled the bags from the back of her car, debating what to tell Ben about her morning. She didn't have to say anything. She knew… she knew almost completely that it was the better option. He was just another visitor. Except that she agreed to see him again.

She hadn't processed all of their conversation. What did Oliver mean by suggesting Ben hadn't told her everything? Lizzie meant what she said. She didn't expect that she would have known everything about Ben by that point. Really, it had only been six months. In those six months she learned a great deal of truth about Ben… and about herself. Was his version of the story about Oliver the truth? Or was it as jaded as her opinion of Sara?

"Hi," Ben grinned down from a ladder at the top of the staircase. Lizzie smiled back and went into the kitchen.

"Lizzie! You are off cobweb duty. Ben got here early and has been stringing them," Meg explained as she emptied a dust pan into the trash. "Did you have any ghostly encounters at the museum?"

Lizzie set the bags on the counter and started pulling out the things for the fridge. "Not really," she felt Ben enter the room.

"The hallway is all set, Meg. What's next?" Ben asked, though Lizzie knew he was watching her.

"Ask Lizzie if she needs help setting up the dining room. I'm going to leave that to her. She has a better eye for food arrangement," Meg took the dust pan out of the room.

"You got here early," Lizzie shut the refrigerator door.

"My appointment was canceled," he let her see the hungry look in his eyes. "There wasn't a backup available… so I just came here earlier."

"It… it's only been six weeks," she said in a low voice, not knowing if Meg was still in the dining room.

"I just wanted to see you," he pulled her close to him. "I forgot you were working."

She let him kiss her. She could tell he was hungry. Fortunately there would be a lot of alcohol at the party. Fortunately, he was too driven by instinct to be sensitive to the fact she was somewhere else. She wanted to give in to his desire, to lead him upstairs and push out everything troubling her brain since she saw Oliver exit the gift shop. But the reality of the dwindling afternoon overpowered her weakness. "I have to make artichoke dip," she loosed from his embrace. She got the pan from the cupboard and stopped suddenly. "Is Jackie home?"

"I haven't seen her," Ben shrugged. "Why?"

"So you were alone with Meg?"

"Elizabeth."

"You didn't eat."

"I helped your friend move furniture in the living room. Then I got up on a ladder and hung cotton that's supposed to look like a spider wove it. I wasn't… I didn't come here to feed."

"Yes, but, Meg," Lizzie opened another cupboard.

"What do you think of me?" he was irritated. "I wouldn't do that to you. Never mind Meghan."

Lizzie didn't like the fact he used her full name. She went back to the refrigerator and pulled out some more ingredients. Ben stopped her and forced her to look at him. "There's something else," he tightened his grip on her wrist. She didn't know what, if any, part of her could show she was with Oliver. Could Ben smell him?

"Nothing," she shook her head quickly. Lizzie knew he wouldn't believe her denial, but she released his grip and went back to the counter.

"Did you remember something at the house today?" he asked, almost hopefully.

Lizzie swallowed. "I… was giving a tour and thought it was strange the kitchen table was so clean."

Ben laughed. "Did that bother you?"

"Kind of," Lizzie sighed as she opened the can of artichokes. "I don't like to think about things that make no sense to me… but are coming from some place else. Especially today."

"Halloween?"

"Well, it is strange," Lizzie lifted the lid of the can, thinking again how it was odd that Oliver showed up.

"It's just another day, Elizabeth," he rubbed the back of her shoulders. She looked at him and figured if anyone would know that, he would. It was also a Saturday… and if Oliver wanted to see her when he was in town that would be the reason he showed up at the house.

"I need to start running again. It would make me less grumpy."

"If you…" Ben began but stopped as Meg came back into the kitchen.

"Ben, can you help me move the sofa again? I've decided I don't like where we put it."

"Sure," he followed Meg out of the room. Lizzie took in a breath to stop from screaming after him to not indulge Meg. She knew the anger was irrational. She knew it wasn't about Ben. And she had food to make.

*****

Lizzie wended her way through the crowd of guests back into the kitchen. She traded one dirty platter for the next round of appetizers from the oven. "Hey lovely," Andrew beamed as she set down the tray on the dining room table. "That was a phenomenal spread. What was it? Cranberries and Swiss?"

"And a little bit of OJ."

"Where's Ben?"

"In the living room… somewhere," Lizzie lost track of Ben in the constant serving of food and greeting of friends. She knew he struck up a conversation with Meg's friends an hour before and assumed he was still there convincing them he was drinking and eating like everyone else.

"Are you okay?" Andrew touched her shoulder.

"Of course," she tried to summon the energy for a smile, but skirted around the table to neaten the arrangement of dishes.

"You look upset about something," Andrew set down his martini glass while she wiped some crumbs off the table.

"I'm just tired."

"Something wrong with Ben?"

"No," Lizzie shook her head. "He's perfect. There's just… it's been a long day."

"I don't know why you went into the house today. I would have taken your shift," Andrew took up his glass. "Well, I'm glad there's nothing wrong with him. I like him too much to let him go if you split."

"I would have the same problem," she fingered a cracker and covered it with cheese. "Did you say your business trip starts tomorrow?"

"Yes. Davis and I are going to be early birds tonight so I can get up and be at the airport for six."

"LA again?" Lizzie remembered the location of Andrew's company's headquarters.

"Yes," Andrew rolled his eyes.

"Ben goes back to Chicago next week."

"Why don't you go with him?"

"November is busy at the office," Lizzie shook her head. Not that Ben extended the offer. Even though this time it was only a couple days. A couple days every week for the whole month of November.

"Well, I'm home on Thursday. We'll cook dinner for Davis."

"I'd like that," Lizzie managed a smile even though she didn't feel it. She didn't like to think about the fact Ben was going away. Because in spite of her protest, it wasn't perfect. He was going away for several days to Chicago. She was irritated that he helped Meg. And now on top of everything else, there was Oliver.

*****

Lizzie released a deep sigh as she let down her hair. Her reflection looked tired. There was possibly another ten pounds on her frame. The reflection looked unfamiliar, but maybe that was the makeup. She would start running… on Monday.

She heard a peel of laughter from downstairs as she wiped off the mascara. She wasn't interested in returning to the party, even without her costume. She could reasonably disappear. No one would notice. She was invisible for so much of the party, serving food and cleaning up. Andrew and Davis made their earlier exit. Even Ben seemed okay with her absence. She was glad to focus on a purpose and not have the idleness to let her mind fill with the thoughts that were tempting her now that her hair was down and her guests were gone.

She liked seeing Oliver. There was a terror she only admitted to herself when she speculated the fire irons. But… it was much more familiar than seeing an old high school chum. Seeing him in that house… she had to admit… made the idea of Lily a little less uncomfortable. Lily's thoughts were strange, but the way they ebbed into her mind so harmlessly…

She turned suddenly as her door opened and Ben entered. She smiled at him, pushing her contemplation away from immediacy. She saw the burn of his eyes, but knew she was safe with three of Andrew's martinis. He came immediately to her and started a passionate kiss. She lost all memory of whatever was irritating her about the evening and fell with Ben against the bed.

Lizzie stared at the green numbers, afraid to close her eyes and see the green hedges on the other side of the Harris' carriage house. She had enough on her mind to keep her wide awake, thoughts that slowly leaked into her brain after she heard the last of the guests leave and Meg climb the stairs to enter her room. She was exhausted. The alcohol was slowly wearing off. She didn't want to close her eyes and see…

"Elizabeth?" Ben whispered. Lizzie wasn't surprised he was awake. He hadn't fed and was restless. She stayed silent, uncertain why he wanted to start a conversation in the hour before dawn. He stroked down the side of her cheek. "I can tell by your breathing that you are awake."

Lizzie turned into him. She was too tired to show the worry on her face. He looked at her a few more minutes and kissed her lips gently. She reached a hand down between their hips, but he caught it and brought it back to rest on her stomach. She knew that wasn't what he wanted and felt the fear awaken her. "What is it?" she tried to think how she was going to explain her conversation with Oliver. It was a simple, friendly conversation. There was nothing for which she need feel any shame. They were old high school friends who caught up… about the Fulton House two hundred years ago.

Ben looked at her and then suddenly shifted back onto his pillow. He looked at the ceiling and took in a deep breath. "Right before I came up here…" he breathed out again. "Meghan kissed me."

Lizzie felt the relief of one worry turn into the bitterness of another. "What?"

He continued to stare at the ceiling. "I didn't realize you came upstairs. I went to look for you in the kitchen. She was there and she said a few things and then…"

"You kissed her back."

"Lizzie, I'm very sorry."

"Meg is vulnerable right now." Lizzie turned her eyes away from him and followed his gaze towards the ceiling.

"She was drunk," Ben argued. "I don't think she would have done that…"

"Did she apologize?"

"I apologized to her."

"Why?"

"Because it was wrong."

"Because she tempted you."

"Lizzie," he irritated her with that familiar name. Why was he using it? "I love you."

"You wanted to drink her blood."

"No."

"If she wasn't drunk, you would have."

"No."

"Do you kiss any of the others?"

"Others?"

"The women from whom you take blood every Saturday."

"No, Elizabeth. I haven't done that since… since I've had your blood."

"You did it after you slept with me?"

"You were sleeping with… Elizabeth," he turned back to her. Lizzie wouldn't divert her eyes to meet his. He propped himself up on his elbow and leaned over to kiss her again. She didn't respond. "Those women are… I find other women attractive. I find Meg attractive. But she isn't… none of them are… I love you."

Lizzie pushed him away and sat herself up. She knew she had less right to be angry with him with her secret, but the idea that he found Meg attractive made her ill. Ben sat up beside her and turned her chin back to face him. "Elizabeth, move in with me."

Lizzie pushed his hand away and turned from him. "Why are you asking me this now?"

"I wanted to ask you many times. I wanted to wait until the next time we shared blood… but… I…"

"Is this so you won't be tempted by Meg again?"

"No," he said angrily. "Elizabeth, come home with me. I miss you when you aren't there. I want to wake up with you every day."

"Why?"

"Because I love you."

"Why? Why do you love me?"

"For a lot of reasons."

"Because I let you feed from me when I have an endorphin rush? Or… is it vengeance against Oliver?"

Ben got out of the bed and walked across the room. He got halfway dressed and then looked up to glare at her through the darkness. "Why would you say that?"

"It seems to be the way of you vampires," Lizzie said cruelly. "Charlotte turned Oliver into a vampire to get back at him for stealing Lily. You obviously don't like Oliver. Is that because you are still loyal to Charlotte? You found out I was Lily and kept him away from me. Was that to avenge Charlotte's murder? Or because two hundred years ago Charlotte chose Oliver and cast you aside?"

"Don't you think I kept Oliver away from you because I was afraid he would hurt you?" he looked at her, the anger still fueling his eyes. Lizzie felt a chill shudder her body. She left the bed, searching amongst the pile on the floor for a shirt to cover her. Ben was still waiting for her answer when she was dressed. "What do you think, Elizabeth? Do you think I'm not capable of loving someone just for the sake of loving them? Don't you think that because I love you I want you to be safe? That I think of someone other than myself and my petty anger?"

Lizzie swallowed and walked towards her dresser, not ready to answer him. He grabbed her arm and forced her to look in his hungry eyes.

"Or is it that you don't know what it is to love someone that much? Maybe, Lizzie, you expect me to be unfaithful because cheating comes so easily to you."

Lizzie shoved him away from her. "Get out."

Ben took the rest of his clothes and headed towards the door. He paused before opening it. Lizzie wanted him to say something more. She was hurt by what he said, but she wanted him to say something… something to prove that Oliver was wrong. That Ben wasn't keeping things from her. That he… really loved her. She knew she hurt him… but hurting him was a way of proving that. He looked down after his pause and then walked out the door.

Lizzie collapsed onto the floor and stared out the window, watching the sun rise slowly into the day.

She didn't sleep. She gave up hope of finding its escape and comfort by 7 o'clock. She went downstairs and finished cleaning the remnants of the party Meg felt were acceptable to leave behind. She wondered if Meg was still awake when she and Ben fought. She wondered if Meg felt any guilt for kissing her boyfriend. Or if Meg thought Lizzie wasn't good enough for someone like Ben.

She was angry. She knew most of it was at herself. She knew she was a hypocrite for hating Ben and Meg for a moment. A moment he walked away from. A moment he would not conceal from her. Lizzie wouldn't tell Ben about Oliver, but she let herself make accusations based on what Oliver said. But the very fact that Ben … he didn't deny kissing Meg back. If he could do that knowing it would hurt Lizzie, what else could he do that would hurt her?

She didn't want to face Meg… whenever she decided to get herself out of bed. Lizzie took a quick shower and called Nora, who offered to get Lizzie and excuse Mark from helping to register for baby products.

Nora stared at the wall of baby strollers and clutched her scanner expectantly. She darted her eyes over the inventory and glanced down at her piece of paper before scanning a blue stroller. "Mark's sister-in-law uses that one. She loves it."

"I'm surprised you didn't ask her to come with you instead," Lizzie glanced at the baby swings as they turned down another aisle. "She probably has a better idea what to suggest than I do."

"She's less fun," Nora smiled. "Besides, you've been a nanny. You know a lot about kids."

"That was years ago."

"You needed to get out of that house," Nora looked down the aisle, but was satisfied with that section of the store. "I'm not surprised she did it."

"Ben did it, too."

"She was drunk and… Ben wouldn't do that to you."

"Meg has been my friend for fourteen years."

"And since when has that given pause to her libido?" Nora charged down the next aisle, hosting a display of feeding products. "Do you really think Ben would want someone like Meg?"

"Are you going to breast feed?" Lizzie distracted herself by pulling a breast pump off the display hook.

"Yes," Nora scanned it after a look at Lizzie. "It's weird to think about, isn't it?"

"Not really," Lizzie picked up some bottles to suggest to Nora.

"I suppose it's natural. Babies feed off their mothers while they're in the womb. It's just strange to think there is a little being who will be dependent on my bodily fluid for survival."

"There are alternatives if you don't want to do it, Nora."

"No," she looked at a set of breast pads. "It's a bonding experience."

"It is," Lizzie faded. She thought of her blood speeding up the rhythm of Ben's heart. Did Ben feel that bond with his other sources?

"This whole experience is fascinating… and weird," Nora scanned the breast pads and a package of membranes. "The fact that we can nourish another being… that sounds gross."

"No." Lizzie couldn't mask her dejection. Lizzie turned into the next aisle and found a diaper bag for Nora's approval.

Nora smiled broadly at the classic green appearance. "Mark won't hesitate to carry this around."

"Do you want to know the sex?"

"I'm scheduled for another ultrasound in two weeks," Nora let the grin escape her. "Mark and I are still debating if we want to know before delivery."

"Either way it's good news." Lizzie's eyes blurred the colors of the diaper bags together.

"Oh Lizzie," Nora touched her shoulder as Lizzie's phone rang.

"It's Ben," Lizzie didn't take the phone out to look.

"I can talk to him if you don't want to."

"I'll talk to him," Lizzie let the tears surface in her eyes. "I'll be right back."

Lizzie rushed towards the store entrance and answered before it went to voice mail. "Ben."

She heard the long exhale before he spoke. "Hi Elizabeth."

"I can't talk long. I'm shopping with Nora."

"Good," he paused. "I have an appointment at the clinic… but maybe you … will you come over after?"

"I don't know," Lizzie leaned against the exterior of the store and watched a young couple go in with two infants. "I didn't sleep very much last night."

"I was hoping we could talk."

"We're talking now," she blinked her eyes so the exiting customers wouldn't see her tears.

"I …" he cleared his throat. "I regret what I said before I left last night. I want you to know that. I don't want another day to pass with you thinking that I really think you are… Elizabeth, I don't want to be with you so I can hurt Oliver."

Lizzie breathed out. She couldn't form any words to respond to him. She knew this was the opportunity for honesty… but it was even less ideal to mention that she saw Oliver at the Fulton House, as neutral and amicable as their conversation was. She didn't want to say it on the phone, without him in front of her. Did that not make some of his harsh words ring true? She hadn't kissed Oliver as he kissed Meg, but wasn't she the one being deceitful?

"Ben," she stared at the sidewalk beneath her. "We both said hurtful things last night. I had no right to… say such an awful thing."

"You were hurt," Ben said with understanding, but not forgiveness.

"I was…"

"I shouldn't have told you that in the middle of the night…and followed it up with a plea to come live with me," Ben didn't allow her to finish her thought. "I want you to live here, Elizabeth. I meant what I said."

Lizzie dared to lift her eyes, catching the sun and making her head spin. "Ben, I'm very confused right now."

"You know I love you."

"I know," Lizzie took in a deep breath. "I don't want this to be a choice I make to avoid Meg."

"That's fair."

"I am thinking about it," her eyes softened as a cloud muted the glare of the sun. "I've got to make things right with Meg before... before I make any decisions."

"Okay."

"I... I think maybe we should attempt some sort of human relationship. Will you come to Thanksgiving and meet my crazy relatives?"

"Of course," his tone lightened. "My trips to Chicago will be over by then."

"Right," Lizzie sighed. She let herself forget he was spending much of his November screening blood donors in Chicago. How many would he sample personally? "You're leaving Tuesday?"

"In the morning. I'll be back on Friday."

"I want to see you before you go," Lizzie forgot all her anger with a pang of longing.

"I'll be home from the clinic around three."

"I'll have lunch with Nora and go home to get my car and some clothes. Although I might fall asleep when I get there," she yawned.

"That's okay. As long as you are here."

Lizzie said goodbye to Ben and went back to Nora, finished with her registry. Lizzie explained the apologies of her phone call over a leisurely lunch, but still managed to dodge every significant element of what was troubling her. She wanted to tell Nora... but how could she even begin to describe Lily and Oliver and all that?

Nora dropped Lizzie off without going inside. She was still angry with Meg. And much though Lizzie hoped to avoid an encounter, she knew she was just going to have to face it, especially when Meg was standing at the top of the stairs waiting for her.

"Lizzie, I'm so sorry," Meg began immediately. "I had too much to drink."

"You have too much to drink a lot," Lizzie took off her coat. "Anyway, it's done."

"But you had such an awful fight…" Meg looked down. "Ben is a really good guy. I am sorry I put him in this position."

"What about me, Meg? Doesn't it matter that you did this to me?"

Meg's lip trembled. "I'm a rotten friend."

Lizzie knew it was wrong to judge Meg. She felt her conscious sting from the hypocrisy. "You're lonely," Lizzie shook the anger out of her head. "We all do stupid things to stop that ache."

"So we're okay?"

"I guess so," Lizzie just wanted to get her things and leave the house.

"I love you, Lizzie," Meg hugged her. "I'll make it up to you."

"Yeah," Lizzie said absently and let Meg go. "I promised I would meet Ben."

Meg nodded and disappeared into the kitchen. Lizzie rounded towards the stairs but noticed the stack of mail she hadn't checked in a week. She grabbed the pile and brought it up the stairs. On top of a stack was a photograph that showed why Oliver was so familiar to Paula. He was on the cover of another museum newsletter. Lizzie scanned the caption and accompanying article. It explained what she already knew about his research and visit to Boston. He was giving a student lecture and collaborating with faculty at UMASS.

Lizzie shut her bedroom door and let herself look at his photograph, a random candid of him wearing a cap standing outdoors with a group of students. Ben was so angry at the mention of his name, at her suggestion that his worry was anything but a genuine desire for her safety. How could this Professor Ol in the photograph be menacing? He had an ill opinion of Ben. Was it not possible they both were lying about one another? Was it bad blood as Oliver had said? Was it really bad blood? Was it Charlotte? Was it Melissa Benson? Was it Eloise Hutchins? Or was it Lily?

Chapter Twenty-Three

Lizzie felt the burn of the cold November wind in her lungs as she climbed back up the stairs to Ben's door. It had been a while since she ran four miles. She was glad she made use of the daylight after she got home from the office. It was one less hour she was sitting alone in the apartment.

She was used to being there by herself. He worked late many nights when she would go there to cook dinner or read a book. Even so, she half expected him to be there waiting by the kitchen window as he was on her birthday. That he hadn't really gone back for a second week. That he decided he accomplished all obligation required in his previous visit.

She knew it was a month commitment to get the Chicago clinic on its feet. That his weekends home were his opportunity to catch up on the business of his Boston office. She knew it was less time he spent with her. He promised it was only a month. He told her, when he left early that Monday morning, that at the end of November he would come home, go with her to Thanksgiving, and never go back to Chicago.

She didn't think she would miss him as much as she did. She didn't like some unresolved tension about things that were spoken aloud after the party. Lizzie knew the wounds of those words could only heal with time. She knew the fact she missed him accelerated the healing process by letting her see what her life would be without him. After the first week, she wanted it to be the end of November. His bed felt cold without him at her side. Her day felt empty without seeing the gray green eyes. He tried to call or email her every day. But a five minute hello wasn't the same as having his conversation beside her.

It was different than the last trip he took, when the thing that most upset her was forgetting her birthday. Then she could distract herself by spending time at Jefferson Park, watching movies and drinking wine with Meg. Lizzie didn't want to go home. She didn't want to talk to Meg. She couldn't indulge her apologies or excuses. She didn't want to be in her bedroom where there was a recent memory of such an awful fight with Ben.

She took a shower and started a load of laundry before settling with her laptop in the living room. There wasn't a whole lot in her email that she hadn't seen at work, but she was able to linger voyeuristically on Facebook for twenty minutes. She didn't want to find Meg there. Or even Nora. She couldn't deal with them. She read through one of Andrew's surveys and then saw a status update from Oliver.

He didn't try to contact her since their hasty departure from the Fulton House. Maybe he said all he wanted to say. Maybe his work was keeping him busy in Boston, busy enough to realize Lizzie wasn't worth any further conversation. She was relieved and disappointed. She didn't understand what he told her. She wanted to know more. About him. About Lily. She knew Oliver would have those answers. She knew it would displease Ben. She knew that wanting it was worse than the thing for which she was avoiding Meg. So, perhaps it was best that the only news from Oliver was a ten word phrase about meeting with professors from UMASS.

She broke her concentration when several sirens echoed through the window, followed soon by flashing lights. She left the couch to see what was happening across the street. There were three police cars and an ambulance. She watched as a few pedestrians paused and started to group outside the house.

The sirens stopped, allowing Lizzie to hear the stillness of the apartment. She realized her laundry was done and went to move it to the dryer. She peered out the window again when she returned to the living room and saw an officer circling the three decker with yellow tape. She remembered seeing a young couple coming and going from the apartment. Ben told her there was another couple he met when he first moved in years ago. They assumed he was the grandson of the original Dr. Benjamin Cottingham. Neither the flashing lights nor the lingering officers showed evidence which couple was involved in the emergency. She got a chill and went back to her seat on the couch, noticing something strange about the wall with the mirror. There were no white roses on the Victorian table.

She picked up her computer again and saw the indication of a new message. She went to her inbox and saw Oliver's picture with the Adidas shirt tagging the unread message. Lizzie took in a deep breath to stop her hands from shaking. Her heartbeat accelerated as she moved the mouse to open it.

"Hi Lizzie,

I was glad to see you last week. I would still like to get together before I leave town. Please allow me to take you to lunch.

Oliver"

Lizzie breathed in again, aware of another siren and more flashing lights outside the window. Did he know she was looking at his status and thinking about him? Or was it just coincidence because they were both logged onto Facebook? She looked down from the window and typed quickly.

"Oliver,

It was nice to see you..."

She looked at Ben's office, as if he were secretly waiting there. As if he would come out and catch her typing a message to Oliver. As her eye moved back to the computer, it passed the buffet where Maria's things rested and watched over the apartment. What would she say to Lizzie, knowing what she knew about Oliver? He was bad news. She needed to stay away from him.

But she wanted to know. She wanted to know if Oliver was really... how could he be... he was Lily's friend. Her lover. Why wouldn't he want to talk to Lizzie? Why should she deny him the chance to explain himself? Lunch would be...

"I would like lunch very much. I work pretty close to Harvard Square. Does that work for you?"

She sent the message and looked at the buffet. Maria was stupid. She didn't love Ben. She killed herself and didn't care about Ben's feelings. Lizzie made the choice for Ben, knowing everything that she knew. She loved Ben. She got over her fear of relationships and being unloved and asserted herself to be with him. She knew that. No two hours with Oliver was going to take that away from her.

The response came onto her screen. *"I can come to Harvard Square tomorrow."*

Lizzie saw the empty table at the back of the room. The vase disappeared after their fight. Why did the white roses no longer matter after she accused him of loving her out of revenge? After he accused her of wanting to cheat? Was she cheating? It was just lunch. She would tell Ben about it... when he was home. If she told him, it wouldn't be wrong.

"Meet me at the Border Café at 12:30," she typed quickly and then moved her cursor to log herself out of Facebook.

*****

Lizzie made up an excuse about a doctor's appointment and convinced Richard to release her for the rest of the day. It was difficult enough to find any focus in the morning. She doubted she would have any ability to concentrate on work when she got back from lunch. It gave her the freedom to drink, something she felt a necessity for easier conversation… and safety.

She was early. She left the office with plenty of time to spare. She got a table and was halfway through her first margarita when Oliver walked into the restaurant. He stopped briefly to pause at the hostess station but then lifted his eyes as if expecting to see her. She waved weakly and watched him approach the table. He seemed even more handsome in his North Face winter coat and well tailored jeans. She didn't remember what he was wearing to the museum. Why did it intrigue her so much now? It's not like he ever worried much about the clothing he wore. He dressed in whatever was most useful and comfortable in the weather.

"Hello Lizzie," he smiled.

"Hi," she managed pleasantry as she tried to erase the comments from her mind.

"Already started?" he looked at her fruity drink.

"Well… I figured I'd be drinking alone, so I didn't think it would matter if I went ahead."

"Yes, that always is… I thought lunch would make you more comfortable… being in a public place," he took off his coat and settled into a chair.

"It's okay. I'm used to it," Lizzie swirled the straw through the slush. The tequila already turned her cheeks pink. "Ben usually orders my second drink for himself."

"Ah," Oliver picked up his menu and looked it over. "So I should order what you're having?"

"Yes, please," Lizzie laughed and sipped through her straw. "You should get fish tacos and decide they weren't fresh."

"You definitely know the routine."

"I'm getting the chimichangas. They are really bad for me… but I don't care."

"You look really good, Lizzie," Oliver sat up in his chair. "Are you still running marathons?"

"Hardly," she laughed at herself. "I'm lucky if I get in five miles a week these days."

"I bet you could still do it if you put your mind to it," Oliver smiled. His smile made her squirm in discomfort and in hope.

"It's all about the mind," Lizzie sat back from her drink.

"The mind is an amazing thing," he kept his gaze steady.

"Indeed," Lizzie nodded as the waitress approached and took their orders. Oliver followed her recommendation to repeat her margarita and the fish tacos. "I saw an article about the talk you gave at UMASS."

"I haven't given it yet," Oliver smirked.

"Oh," Lizzie felt her cheeks burn, hoping it was just the alcohol.

"It's on Thursday. You should come."

"I…" Lizzie grasped the neck of her margarita glass.

"I'll ask you again before we leave," Oliver put the straw into his glass of water that he wasn't going to drink.

"I never thought of you as a scientist," Lizzie took another sip, grateful for the pungency of the tequila.

"I was a lawyer once."

"That's why you were so good at debate club?"

"Yeah," he looked down with a pleased grin and then shifted back to her. "You were a fierce opponent."

"I was rather bull headed in high school," Lizzie fingered her straw. "I still am."

"Actually, it was a debate we had about municipal recycling that got me interested in environmental science," Oliver bit his lip.

"Really?"

"You were pretty passionate about newspapers and collecting bottles and cans," Oliver fiddled with the silverware. "It got me thinking."

"Well, you actually did something with those thoughts. I'm still wasting a lot of hot water when I take a shower."

"Nobody's perfect. Hell, I am researching the environmental impact of tourism and I fly in airplanes across the country. But… it doesn't make the issue less important. I realized that about ten years ago. When you are around this place long enough, you realize how … I've seen so much damage to the earth. I am trying to use my longevity for some good."

"That's… that is wow."

"I'm not a businessman like Ben. I tried that… it didn't work out so well."

"You aren't like Ben."

"Except for one pretty major detail."

"No, you aren't like Ben," Lizzie looked hard at the dwindling amount of liquid in her glass.

Oliver let his eyes go to the window and follow the blurred shapes walking down Church Street. "Didn't you go to college here?"

"Mm hmm," Lizzie answered through her sip.

"You like Cambridge, then?"

"I guess. Enough to work here and live close by."

"Mmm," he looked at her.

"You got married."

"I did."

"That's good," Lizzie hid the fact she felt a sudden letdown. "How did you meet her?"

"She was a student," Oliver took the wrapper from Lizzie's straw.

"You were her professor?"

"I was still in grad school – a TA," Oliver twisted the paper.

"When did you find out she was like you?"

"Like me?" Oliver looked up. "Lizzie… I … changed her."

"Oh," Lizzie felt the redness in her cheeks burn.

"I thought for sure Ben would have told you that."

"He didn't." Lizzie drank the rest of her margarita. She watched Oliver crumple the wrapper and toss a tight little ball onto the table. "How does that work?"

Oliver breathed in slowly. "I drank from her. Then she drank from me."

"So they get that part right in all the stories?" Lizzie played along with his levity.

"Pretty much," he didn't take his eyes off her. "You and Ben never talk about that?"

"Why would we?"

"I… I just figured."

"What's her name?"

"Alison," he smiled.

"Alison," Lizzie nodded to conceal another sink of her stomach. "Does she know about Lily… and all that?"

"Yes."

"And she knows you are here, seeing me?" Lizzie dared herself with the tequila warming her.

"No."

Lizzie looked up as the waitress landed the food on the table. "I didn't tell Ben I saw you," Lizzie picked up her fork and knife.

Oliver set his hands flatly on the table and met Lizzie's eyes. He looked away from her and picked up his own fork, only to move some of his food around on the plate. "Lizzie, I want you to feel free to ask me anything. I imagine you have a lot of questions."

"Will you tell me about Lily?"

Oliver swallowed and set the fork down. His eyes broadened with an intense pain, but an equally intense sympathy. "What do you want to know?"

"Everything. All I know is the few details that Ben told me and … how she died," Lizzie looked down into her food.

"What did Ben tell you?"

Lizzie bit her lip and lifted her eyes away from her food. "He just said that she was a maid. That… she was Horace Fulton's lover… and then Charlotte's," Lizzie watched his reaction to see if that stung him with any amount of jealousy.

"That's true," Oliver nodded as though they were discussing Abigail Adams or Marilyn Monroe.

"Where was she born?"

Oliver offered her his margarita and took her empty glass towards him. "Her mother worked – just like Lily – as a lady's maid for the

Jacksons on Brattle Street. Mr. Jackson took a fancy to her and… there was Lily."

"Margaret's maiden name was Jackson," Lizzie hesitated over her sip.

"They were half-sisters. Not that anyone spoke of such things. But to be fair, it was Margaret Fulton who arranged for Lily's mother to find a place when she was cast out of her father's home. Her housekeeper…"

"Annie," Lizzie swallowed Oliver's margarita. He paused, looking at her curiously. "Um, we learn at the museum that the housekeeper was named Annie."

"She was my aunt," Oliver breathed out slowly. Lizzie chose not to tell him she dreamt that detail. "Lily's mother was 8 months pregnant when she went to Margaret Fulton. Mrs. Fulton found a place for her to give birth. Lily's mother died in childbirth. Mrs. Fulton and Annie arranged for Lily to live with my mother. Before she was married, my mother worked for John Fulton and cared for his oldest son. My mother knew how to read. Margaret asked her to prepare Lily to return to the Fultons when she was twelve."

"So you grew up with Lily?" Lizzie set down her glass.

"She was a year younger than me. She helped my mother in the kitchen between her lessons. I worked with my father in his wheelwright shop. But we were … always together…" Oliver looked back towards the window. Lizzie wondered how vivid the memories of his childhood could be so many years… centuries later. Some of the details of her life faded after just a few decades.

"She went to the Fultons when she was twelve?" Lizzie brought his focus back from the window.

"To help my aunt and look after Margaret's children."

"Harriet and Peter."

"Yes."

"And Horace Fulton?"

"Lily resembled her mother's beauty. She was already imperfect with her illegitimacy. It wasn't difficult to think of her as a lover. Even for Horace Fulton. "

"Did she love him?"

"She loved that whole wretched family. Even when they treated her so… even Horace Fulton," Oliver shook his head. Lizzie felt another question form on her tongue as he started to speak again. "She was only there a year when he brought her to the garden and performed inappropriate acts."

"He molested her?" Lizzie wondered how loudly she asked the question.

"I guess… I suppose that's what it would be called today," Oliver breathed out. Lizzie was startled by his sudden sensitivity. She forgot they were discussing a different century with different sexual mores. She wondered if he was still that tender… or if he could excite her nerves as much as Ben. Her cheeks burned, realizing he was watching her thoughts wander. "He was older than her."

"Five years," Lizzie found the detail from a memory that might have come from the museum or her subconscious.

"Yes," Oliver nodded. "She visited my mother every Sunday after church. She said goodbye and then met me in my father's shop. She read me books she took from the library. She told me about all the people who visited the Fultons. She was always fascinated by the foreigners because they traveled from a great distance – places she wanted to go. I loved to listen to her, to just watch her think. She was so bright and… beautiful…" his voice softened from his professor vernacular. An impish grin slowly curved across his chin. "She was curious about so many things. Maybe it's because of what Horace did to her, but she didn't hesitate to show her affection. She was very, very sexy."

"So she became your lover?" Lizzie laughed, not sure if it was amusement or discomfort that prompted it.

"She was my first," Oliver smiled sweetly. "I wanted to marry her. My mother loved her, but didn't… my parents knew about Horace and didn't think she was good enough to be a wife. They wanted me to marry the daughter of another local businessman."

"What did you want?"

"I went to New York to fight the British in 1812. I asked her to marry me before I left, but she refused. She knew what my mother wanted for me and was ashamed of what Horace did to her. "

"But she loved Horace?"

"She thought it was her fault for tempting him," Oliver clenched his jaw. "But he died. Then she became devoted to his widow."

"Charlotte," Lizzie watched his reaction to the second pronouncement of that name. He was cool and calm, no indication that Charlotte took his life or that he took hers.

"They were friends. I didn't understand the depth of their intimacy until… what has Ben told you about this?"

Lizzie shook her head and lifted her shoulders. She wasn't sure what Ben could have told her. "Just that Lily went back to you until Charlotte discovered your affair."

"I decided to leave my family and marry her. We planned to go west," he looked out the window again.

"I'm sorry to ask you to remember this," Lizzie saw the cheese congealing on her plate.

"I remember it whether you ask me or not," Oliver said softly. "I… it is good to tell someone. To tell you."

Lizzie straightened her spine and went to her diminishing margarita. "So why didn't you go west?" Lizzie knew that wasn't how the story ended.

"She was worried about the Fultons," Oliver rubbed his hand against his chin and looked at Lizzie.

"Because of Charlotte?"

"Lily and Charlotte were friends. I can't speak for what Lily felt or wanted from that friendship," Oliver paused, revealing a glint of hurt in his eyes. "Charlotte admitted many years later that she loved Lily. Lily listened to her, as she listened to everyone in her life. Lily was the last human Charlotte ever let herself trust and feel anything for. She ended up killing Horace because he assaulted Lily. Lily knew what Charlotte was capable of. I think she believed she could keep Charlotte calm and so she stayed."

"Did she keep Charlotte calm?"

Oliver's face seemed to turn towards a frown, but suddenly forced a smile. "As long as Charlotte believed that Lily loved her."

"But in the end, she didn't take out her wrath on the Fultons. She took it out on you."

Oliver picked up his fork again to try the pretense of eating. Lizzie looked at her plate and took a forkful of rice. It was lukewarm and its taste didn't register.

"Ben said you…" Lizzie was conscious of the chatty lunch crowd around them. "He said… Charlotte deserved her end."

"He told you I was responsible for that, too?"

"Yes," Lizzie took another large sip of drink.

"It's true."

"Would Lily have thought she deserved it?"

"I hope so," Oliver looked at Lizzie as if expecting her to make an answer for Lily.

Lizzie took another bite of her cold rice. She slowed the movement of her jaw, hoping he would fill the silence. "They found a letter Harriet wrote to Charlotte. She probably didn't send it if they have it at the museum…" Lizzie wiped her fingers on the napkin in her lap. "It's strange to think that I was part of this… but I really don't remember much of it."

"Do you want to remember it, Lizzie?"

"I… I'm not sure."

"There was a lot of sadness," Oliver turned away from the table.

"But… isn't it a part of me?"

"I don't know. Is it?" Oliver looked at her.

"Isn't that why you and Ben are in my life?"

"You don't think you have control over your own destiny, Lizzie?"

Lizzie picked up her fork and stabbed it into the food. "I don't know."

"We all have a choice," he nodded as the waitress stopped to check on them. "I learned the hard way it is too easy to blame fate for making poor choices."

Lizzie looked at the fork sticking through her untouched chimichanga. His words echoed of Nora's constant advice. The fact he lived through much more horrific choices than Alec McCaffrey and came to that conclusion seemed like true wisdom.

"In the end it is my responsibility… for Eloise and for Lily."

Lizzie wanted to remind him of Melissa, but decided to not open her mouth. She was tempted to take another sip of margarita, but decided her blood was bitter enough.

"You ran a marathon, Lizzie. Can you give fate… or Lily credit for that?"

"A half marathon."

"The point is, *you* did it."

"I didn't kill anyone."

"No," Oliver nodded. "No."

"If you accept that you did those things… why are you sitting here with me? How can I not believe you won't do it again?"

"Is that what you believe?"

"I don't want to," Lizzie breathed out slowly… looking at him. "I mean… I changed. I like to believe anyone can change and make themselves better. Especially if they are on this planet forever."

"You aren't her," Oliver looked down sadly. "Lily was unforgiving."

"I have to get back to work."

"You've hardly touched your lunch."

"Neither have you," Lizzie caught his eye briefly and then looked for the waitress.

*****

She laughed as she ran through the hedges into the Harris' yard. There was just enough moonlight to define the shadows of the trees. She saw a candle in a window of the house as she waited. Suddenly his arms came around her, turning her into his kiss. He lifted her off the ground and held her against the wall of the carriage house. She heard one of the horses whinny in alarm, speeding up the rhythm of her heart. The thrill of potential discovery heightened the thrill of his touch…

Her heart beat rapidly as she opened her eyes to the darkness of Ben's room. She pulled the blankets over her head and cocooned herself in the warmth, but it wasn't the same as Ben beside her. Even when his body cooled at the end of the week. She closed her eyes, hoping to find sleep but was only able to see Oliver's dark eyes nearing her before a kiss.

She tried to fill her brain with other thoughts – of necessary tasks at the office, of groceries to buy on her way home from the hospital, Nora's baby shower – but the dark shadows of the crescent moon kept haunting her mind.

It was difficult to distract herself with the information Oliver gave her. She left the restaurant under the pretense she had to rush back to the hospital. She regretted letting Oliver pay for the meal… the meal neither of them ate. She didn't want to linger much more in his company to argue the point. Nothing he said was too startling or disturbing to her reality. She heard much of it as if it were a history lecture in college or a training summary from the preservation society. Not that the preservation society would educate her about the bedroom habits of the servants or the presence of vampires in the Fulton House.

She didn't know if what she learned should make her feel better or worse about Oliver. It was obvious he loved her – Lily. He still hurt from what happened to her… and what she did to him. She chose to marry him in the end, but she wouldn't leave the Fultons. What kept her in Cambridge? The friendship of a female vampire? She didn't want to stay. She wanted to be someplace else and with the one who could take her away from her cursed life. Did Oliver say that? Lizzie couldn't remember that detail in the midst of two strawberry margaritas. Was that something he said? Or was that her active imagination speculating about history? Or was it… something dislodged from her memory?

The idea of Lily was like the idea of Harriet – someone from a distant time she would discuss on a tour. Lizzie tried to put herself in Harriet's shoes, living in that house and then later as a grieving mother. It helped her to understand the history of the museum and present it in a way she thought was interesting to visitors. Lily was simply another version of Harriet, with a more salacious history. Except she knew people that Lizzie knew. Oliver knew her. He felt real emotion for her. Lizzie couldn't picture her from a glassy eyed portrait. She could imagine the thoughts in her head and the pains of her heart and the yearning to be someone other than what she is. She still didn't connect Lily with herself. She could sympathize with her hurts and motivations… but it wasn't her own. It wasn't her life.

The thoughts and details kept creeping back into her mind. She wanted to know more. She wanted to know if Lily liked Harriet. She wanted to know what Lily wore and what she was expected to do every day. Did Margaret like her… or was it guilt for her father's sins? Did she like the world of Brattle Street? It couldn't have been a whole hearted passion, if she kept visiting Oliver at the wheelwright shop.

Lizzie kept staring at the ceiling, watching the bleary November dawn creep into the room. She realized Ben hadn't called her that night. She knew he anticipated a busy day of meetings. He was undoubtedly exhausted… if he was well fed. If not, he was restless and would… would he seek out a source in Chicago? How was that different from feeding in Boston? It wasn't… except his words echoed in her brain. She knew she was not being completely honest with him about Oliver. She feared his trustworthiness because her own was lacking.

What good would it do to tell Ben about Oliver? Lizzie knew the moment she spoke Oliver's name, Ben changed his mood. Lizzie didn't understand that. Oliver was… he was so kind to her. He wasn't any more of a monster than Ben. She knew Oliver committed … he did horrible things. So did Ben, though she didn't know those as well as she knew Oliver's crimes. Oliver admitted he was wrong. He knew he should take responsibility and try to improve. To do good to compensate for the hurt he caused.

He ended a life. He ended her life… if it was hers. Was it really something to do with Lizzie? If Oliver didn't stop Lily, would Lizzie exist? How did she know to pick the next life that would lead her back to Oliver? Why go back to a horrible end? What if this time it wasn't going to end that way? What was it that Meg said? The next time it would improve? What if this time it was supposed to end with what Lily didn't have? Did that mean she was supposed to marry Oliver?

Was that why Ben said nothing of him? Did he fear Lizzie would go to Oliver? Is that what she was supposed to do? That didn't make sense. She liked Oliver. But Ben was… she loved Ben. She missed his warmth. She was jealous he was in the company of other people. Lizzie wasn't jealous that Oliver was married and unavailable. She wanted Ben. She wanted Ben to come home. She wanted him to tell her… she wanted him to tell her about Lily. She wanted Ben to come to the Fulton House and make her remember things. She wanted to dream about him. Why was he leaving it to Oliver?

Chapter Twenty-Four

Lizzie put away her groceries in the cupboards. She felt at home in Ben's kitchen, a room he seldom used except to read the Sunday paper in the morning sun. It was spacious, not quite as modern as Lizzie would hope for her own space. It could be her own space.

She was slowly starting to wrap her brain around the idea of Ben's apartment becoming home. She wasn't sure how ready she was to give up her spot at Jefferson Park. She liked that apartment and all its memories. Things wouldn't end well with Meg. Neither had made much effort to bridge the gap after Halloween. Lizzie figured that would pass eventually. It seemed trivial in comparison to the other thoughts plaguing her mind, even though Meg was a more important part of her life than Oliver.

The ring of her phone jolted her back to the present. Her heart sped at Ben's name on the caller ID. She felt a twinge of guilt that it rang just as another thought of Oliver left her mind. She took in a breath and greeted him.

"Elizabeth," she could hear the smile in his voice that suddenly made her wish he was there. She wouldn't let herself want that. It was only Wednesday. He wouldn't be back until late Sunday. "How are you?"

"I'm staring at your kitchen," she laughed, wondering if she should tell him she was contemplating improvements to it. No, she told herself quietly. She was going to wait until Thanksgiving, on the way home. "How's Chicago?"

"Cold," he said quickly. "Listen, I need you to do me a favor."

"Sure," she pulled out the last of her produce.

"Can you look for a file in my office and then fax me the pages?"

"Where is it?" she went across the hallway.

"In the right hand drawer of my desk. It should be a folder called Hemo Financial or something like that." Lizzie went to the drawer and searched through the files. "Are you having a good week?"

"Yeah," Lizzie kept looking through the tightly filled drawer.

"Anything exciting?"

Lizzie's cheeks burned as she thought of lunch with Oliver. Did he know Oliver was in town? How could he? Would Oliver go to the clinic for a source? "Found it."

Ben quickly gave her the number. She could tell he was in a rush to get off the phone. She heard a conversation behind him. He wasn't much interested in the small talk, and probably didn't want to hear the minutiae of her week. "Nothing really exciting, no," Lizzie sighed. She missed him. She wanted him to come home and fill her thoughts of something other than Oliver and his information about Lily. She knew she needed to tell him about Oliver. "You can't talk long, can you?"

"Sorry," his voice was genuine. "I will try to call you later tonight. You won't hold it against me, will you?"

"Don't worry, I'll still fax your file."

"Thanks," he paused. "I love you."

"Love you," Lizzie said before the phone disconnected. She went to his fax machine and watched as the papers slowly copied. She waited for the transmission to clear and then returned the file to its place. As she closed the door, she saw a hanging folder labeled "Green Falls, NY."

Lizzie pulled the folder out of the drawer and opened it up to four or five files. They all had property and estate information. Most of the papers were very old. Almost a hundred years. They detailed the sale of a local goods store from Benjamin Thomas to a Mr. David March. There was a deed of sale for a house on 124 Union Street. Lots of tiny print that Lizzie found a blur. She shifted through the papers of each folder until she came to the last, labeled Maria Thomas.

There were many more old pieces of paper. Lizzie didn't understand what half the documents entailed except the last. A death certificate. Lizzie scanned over the page and saw she drowned in the Hudson River on the 20th of May in 1915.

She closed the folder and put it back in the drawer. She let out a shallow breath to curb the sudden sadness curdling in her stomach. She caught the dim reflection of her face looking back at her from Ben's computer screen. Something about the shadows across her cheekbones frightened her. As though it was a ghost and not herself looking back.

She quickly pressed power on the computer to erase the image. She wasn't really curious about her email. She wasn't really going to see if

Oliver wrote anything. They said goodbye. It was done. She wasn't going to see him again. Maybe there was something from Ben. If he didn't have time to talk, when would he have time to write her an email?

She went to the address bar to find Facebook, but scrolled down to cambridgeblood.org. She clicked Ben's login and entered the site. A window popped up alerting Ben Cottingham that he was overdue for an appointment. She thought he went when he was home. Didn't he? She couldn't clear her thoughts enough to remember Saturday – or anything before Oliver filled her mind with details of Lily.

She clicked the prompt and was redirected to his profile page. It was kind of like Facebook, for someone who didn't idle so many hours in front of it as Lizzie. There was a photograph of Ben. It wasn't recent. His name was listed as Ben. His location Cambridge, MA. It said he has been vampire since 1779. She knew all that. She saw a small box for preferences. He checked off a number of options, as one might on a dating website. Clinical. Female. Athletic. Unmarried. He had no preference for ethnicity. Did that matter with blood? His preferred blood type was AB positive, but accepted all varieties.

Her eyes blurred. Why did it matter if the woman was married? Was that because he used to sleep with them? Did it matter now that he was in a relationship? Lizzie wasn't AB positive. She was O negative. Did that mean her blood wasn't his favorite?

She saw a blinking icon on the top of the page. She pulled her eyes away from his profile and clicked it, switching her over to a mailbox. The top message was a reminder for his missed appointment. She opened it. It was a generic email informing Mr. Cottingham that his appointment with Samantha Wells was canceled. If he was unable to find an alternative, the following sources were available for appointments this week.

Lizzie clicked one of the options. She was young. Much younger than Lizzie. She was athletic. Apparently the recommendations paid attention to his preferences. Fair skinned. Blue eyes. Blond hair. Lizzie shut her eyes. She reopened them and went back to the inbox. She opened the reminder from a previous week. There was a link to the appointed source, Genevieve Coulson. She had red hair, brown eyes, and was 25. Just like Ben.

She logged off the website. She paused for a few seconds and shut off the computer. She didn't want to know any more. She didn't want to think about what Ben wanted. About what she never was. Young and athletic. He didn't want her until she ran that half marathon. He always knew where she was, but he never cared for her until her body fit his preference. All those women… she only saw two… but she knew all the rest fit his profile. She knew they were the ones he would unofficially date. The ones whose blood he wanted to drink. The ones with whom he was surrounded as he screened sources for the Chicago clinic. When he was far away in another city and didn't have the time to talk to her, not even to tell her to stay away from Oliver. So she wouldn't.

*****

Lizzie received Oliver's email at work. He didn't mention lunch at all, but simply encouraged her to come to his talk at UMASS that evening. She thought very quickly about inviting Andrew, but immediately talked herself out of it. She wanted to keep Ben's brother out of any part of her life that involved Ben.

She was intrigued by the topic. It appealed to both her professional world in museums as well as her passion for the environment. She would have gone if it weren't Oliver Cottingham. She would have gone if there wasn't a chance that the evening could end with another piece of the Lily mystery colored in. That's what she kept telling herself as she took the train ride across Boston.

They were in a small lecture hall. She was impressed by the full audience. She noticed a crowd of giggling coeds in the front row. Were they fascinated by the topic or by visiting Professor Ol? She wondered if anyone knew what he was. Could one of them be a willing source? Maybe one was even a vampire, for all Lizzie knew.

She hid in the back row and found herself compelled by his statistics. Her thoughts focused on his topic and didn't wander to speculation about vampires or Lily. She was impressed that he was a good teacher as well as politician. She wondered if that was the lawyer coming through.

Lizzie got up slowly from her seat and waited in the back of the room as Oliver greeted all the eager young women. They left in a flurry of giggles. She caught his eyes following them until they met hers. She waved slightly as he turned to a handful of professors. Lizzie collected her coat and approached slowly. He turned his eye to her in between breaths of conversation. After several minutes, the professors headed out of the hall.

"Hi," Oliver smiled warmly with a direct look at Lizzie.

"Hi," Lizzie returned as Oliver gathered his papers and shut down his laptop.

"I'm very glad you came," he said with the same extra charm he offered the giggling girls. "Shall I take you to dinner?"

"I'm not hungry."

"At least a drink," he zipped his carrying case.

"Very well," Lizzie agreed. It was just a drink.

*****

"You know, truth be told, sometimes I think I am just full of it," Oliver cast his eyes up as the waitress set down two glasses of wine at their table.

"No, it was really fascinating," Lizzie hastily took a sip. "You know your material well. You know how to make it interesting. Not just some flat scientific facts. You could give Al Gore a run for his money."

"I doubt that," Oliver laughed. "I'm glad you liked it."

Lizzie set down her glass gently. She looked at Oliver's enthusiastic expression. She was surprised he was so pleased by her good opinion of his lecture. After her pathetic excuse of a tour she gave him, he couldn't be much impressed by her notion of good public speaking. He was very upbeat, energetic. Lizzie expected there was a sense of accomplishment. She also imagined he fed before the lecture.

"So how is Ben?" he broke her concentration with a sudden, but still friendly question. "I'm almost surprised that you didn't drag him down here with you."

"Really?" Lizzie coughed and stifled it with another sip of wine.

"Almost."

Lizzie bit her lip and lingered with the wine glass not too far from her lips. She breathed and set it back on the table. "Actually, Ben is out of town."

"Hm."

"He's been," Lizzie looked about to measure the noise of the surrounding crowds. "He's been helping with the final stages of a clinic that's opening outside of Chicago."

"He's gone back to that?"

"He still has his computer company. I don't know how he is managing both right now."

"Ben works very hard," Oliver rested his fingers on the base of his neglected wine glass. "He always has."

"Yeah," Lizzie hoped her discouragement wasn't obvious.

"You know, I think I got an invite to their opening," Oliver looked up to try to catch a memory in his thoughts. "Yes, it's on my desk in San Fran," he laughed to himself. "It's next weekend, right? Is he taking you to that?"

Lizzie shook her head and swallowed almost half her glass.

"Yeah… probably not," he looked at her. "That would be an interesting party. The who's who of the vampire world. Some of the guests might surprise you."

"I've had enough surprises this year," Lizzie met his eyes. "I'm not sure how amazing the next one might be."

"True enough."

"Do you go to the clinic?"

"Not very much," Oliver said slowly. "I prefer a more organic method."

Lizzie's eyes widened as she reached for her glass. "Oh?"

"Don't get me wrong. I appreciate the importance of the clinics. Everything that Ben and his friends achieved is really very important. Especially with the escalation of AIDS and malaria and … all those diseases. But it isn't… it isn't natural."

Lizzie took the last large swallow from her glass, not even tasting the wine. She let out a deep breath as she landed the empty glass on the table. Oliver leaned a little closer and lowered his voice. "Ask any vampire and they will tell you that they prefer teeth to needles." Oliver sat back and slid his full glass towards Lizzie. “It’s like your wine. It’s as much about holding the glass and taking a sip – savoring the flavor and feeling the burn. It wouldn’t be the same if someone hooked you up to an IV and just put the alcohol into your bloodstream.”

“No,” Lizzie put the stem of the glass between her fingers. “If you don’t go to the clinic… and your partner is already a…” she lowered her voice under the hum of the bar conversation. “… a vampire – what do you do?”

“I have loyal sources. I go to the clinic on occasion. But I’ve been around long enough to know the good from the bad.”

Lizzie took a sip from the wine glass. “I suppose that’s true,” she managed a smile as her mind wandered to Ben’s office in early September. “Do you like endorphins?”

Oliver couldn’t stop the grin creeping across his cheeks. “Of course I do.”

“Then… if your wife isn’t a source… do you,” Lizzie stopped herself from finishing the question she didn’t censor herself from starting. “I’m sorry. That was very inappropriate.”

Oliver looked away from the conversation towards the bar. Lizzie felt naïve and foolish. She was still so new to this world. Ben was only one personality of vampire. Apparently they weren’t all as he was. The definitions of their right and wrong altered, even amongst brothers… or whatever they were. Oliver turned back from the bar, the smile still evident in the corner of his lips. “Do you have to work tomorrow?”

“What?”

“I’m heading to New York on Saturday. I thought I might do a few tourist things tomorrow. Somewhat research. Somewhat genuine curiosity.’

“The Freedom Trail?” Lizzie realized how absurd that would be for Oliver who fought the British.

“There is a pretty interesting exhibit at the Science Museum.”

“I haven’t been there in ages.”

“You have to work?”

“I’ll see how I feel in the morning,” Lizzie answered coolly. “I should probably head home.”

Oliver disappeared briefly to take care of the bill. Lizzie had her coat on and purse ready by the time he returned. "Can I walk you to your car?"

"I took the train."

"Then let me give you a ride home."

Lizzie followed him quietly back to the UMASS campus. There was a cold November wind distracting her thoughts from saying anything other than how frigid the temperature felt. Within ten minutes they were in a parking lot beside a silver Jeep Wrangler. "Rental?" she asked as he searched for the keys in his pocket.

"Actually, it's mine. I keep it here for the few times I visit," he unlocked the car.

"How often do you visit?" Lizzie shuddered as the wind leaked under her coat.

"Not as much these days," he got in the car and leaned across the seat to open her door. "But… things change. Eventually I'll be too young to stay in California."

Lizzie sat herself beside him and shivered again as she pulled the seatbelt across her. "Are you planning to come back soon?"

"No," Oliver started the ignition. "Although, a colleague wants me to come to UMASS and fill an open position next fall."

"You're not considering it?" Lizzie's teeth chattered.

Oliver paused before pressing on the gas. "No. I like my work right now. I don't look too shockingly young. I like California. I'm glad I went back."

"You were there before?"

"I was there until…" he stopped and cast a glance at Lizzie. "I was in LA until Charlotte was gone. That's when I came back here."

"Oh," Lizzie looked out her window into the blackness of the Charles River.

"Where am I taking you?"

"Cen… to Newton," Lizzie decided that she didn't want to lead him to Ben's apartment. "Can you find your way to Storrow?"

"Sure can."

Lizzie let the silence fall between them as she slowly recovered from the chilly wind in the warmth of his car. She only spoke to give directions to Jefferson Park.

"You guys live in Newton?"

"My apartment is here," Lizzie said quickly. "I… didn't want to stay at Ben's place tonight. There was a murder across the street the other night."

"Really?" Oliver pulled in front of the house.

"Yeah," Lizzie looked down at her purse. "A crime of passion."

"He's still in that place near the hospital?"

Lizzie lifted her eyes back to look at him. He gazed out the window with disinterest, as if making small talk before she decided to get herself out of the car. "Yes," she unbuckled her belt and felt the exhaustion of a long day suddenly mingle with the glass and a half of wine. "What did you do to Melissa?"

Oliver snapped his head to look at her. His eyes were very sad, as if he didn't have the ability to summon a mask to hide it. "I didn't kill her, Lizzie."

Lizzie shut her eyes. She was waiting to hear that answer. She knew… she always knew that was what it was. Ben never had the determination to quiet her insane doubt. "You know what happened to her," Lizzie said with a calm of which she didn't know she was capable.

Oliver hardened his grip on the idle steering wheel. "I do," he returned with equal calm but no apology.

"Will you tell me?"

Oliver looked at her briefly and then back through the windshield of his Jeep. "I am responsible," he continued that calm tenor of his voice. "I don't deny that."

Lizzie looked down at her hands. She knew there might be some reason she should be afraid and want to leave the car. He wasn't keeping her there. He wasn't forcing the story into her mind. She asked the question. She was the one hesitating before going to the apartment. Lizzie lifted her focus back to his concentrated stare through the window. Oliver turned his head quickly and offered his gentle grin. "I used to give her a ride home every once in a while. She was a good kid. Smart. Definitely very pretty," Oliver hid his smile from Lizzie. "She knew what I was."

"Did you tell her?"

"She figured it out. She paid a lot of attention … she had a crush on me."

"Oh," Lizzie fiddled with the strap of her purse.

"I liked her. I…" Oliver shut his eyes. "I indulged her. We had a quiet affair the summer before I went to Amherst."

"You went to Amherst?"

"Just for the freshman year," Oliver breathed out. "I intended to stay close to help Ben with the property, but…"

"Melissa died."

"She visited my dorm. Then when I came home on breaks…"

"But she was dating Kyle Granger."

"Yes, I know," Oliver looked down. "It wasn't that sort of relationship. If you could call it a relationship. Melissa was attracted to the vampire. If she thought she had a chance with Ben, she would have pursued him."

"She thought Ben wanted Sara."

"Yeah," Oliver laughed quietly. "Melissa wanted to become vampire. She didn't believe Ben would use her as a source, much less change her."

"Would you?"

"She was my source…but I … she was too young and emotional. I didn't think she knew what she was giving up. Plus, there are so many other…"

"You changed your wife."

"That was different, Lizzie."

"So what happened to Melissa?" Lizzie thought of Ben's comparison of Oliver to Meg. Meg didn't know her limitations. Oliver's conversation and demeanor didn't resemble Meg's mania at all. Was Melissa something that just got out of control?

"She knew the science of it. She knew if she lost a certain amount of blood she would only survive if I fed her blood," Oliver faded and then shook his head back to the present. "I was home for the summer. It was the weekend before the Springs graduation. I hadn't seen her since March break. I was hungry and stupid and… I didn't pay attention. She cut herself before coming to see me. She let me feed on her even though she already lost a lot of blood. I stopped when I knew what was happening. She was upset, irrational. She wanted me to finish. I offered to take her home and made a whole bunch of promises about later in the summer. She left the house in a fury. I didn't know what to do. I didn't know if I should follow her. I knew she wasn't well. She lost too much blood. I should have taken her to a hospital. I ..."

"What happened to her?"

"She used to come to our house by an old wagon road in the woods."

"At the start of the state forest."

"Yes," Oliver nodded. "There is a brook that runs through it. It was a rainy night. It was a very rainy spring so the brook was overflowing. I don't know for certain, Lizzie, but I'm pretty sure she fell or fainted in the brook."

"But you don't know."

"I know she didn't make it home that night."

"Do you think she threw herself in the brook?" Lizzie surprised herself with her question.

"That is a possibility."

"They never found a body," Lizzie kept looking at the strap entwined in her fingers. "So nobody knows for sure."

"I found footprints in the mud very close to the creek. It looked like she skidded at the water's edge."

"Why didn't you tell the police? Or Mr. Benson?"

"I thought about it. I still think about it, Lizzie. They searched those woods. They looked in that water. They didn't find her."

"So... how do you know someone else didn't come and take her? Or... that she didn't run away?"

"I don't know that. But I'm pretty confident that she fell."

"Then her body is still in those woods?"

Oliver nodded quietly.

"If they found her, they would have seen her bite marks," Lizzie suddenly realized. "That's why you..."

"Ben had his eye on MIT. He was happy at Springs. He was happy to be in Coldbrook again. I didn't want to take that away from him."

"Nobody would have believed that you were…"

"But any hint of scandal…" Oliver shook his head. "He thought I did it. He still does, apparently. I don't blame him after… everything else. So I transferred to a college in California and started a new life plan."

"But that family… doesn't know what happened to their daughter. Her falling in the brook is a lot less horrific than thinking somebody raped and murdered her."

Oliver met her eyes. Even in the dim shadows of the street lamp she could see the guilt that lingered there. "You're right."

"You and Ben had an opportunity to have a new life. Melissa didn't."

"Ben… he didn't have anything to do with this. He didn't even know that I was seeing Melissa. He knew I gave her rides and jumped to the worst possible conclusion because you…" Oliver stopped himself. "Funny thing is, he thought he was protecting me."

"No. He was protecting himself, too."

"And you."

Lizzie felt the cold of the November wind leak through the car door. "Did you think that Melissa looked like…"

"I thought she was very pretty," Oliver decided to answer the question he thought he heard.

"Oliver," Lizzie tightened her grip on her purse. "When you came to the Fulton House, you said I should be careful of Ben. Why did you say that?"

Oliver looked back at the windshield. "You should be careful, Lizzie," he said sincerely. "You should be careful sitting here with me. You should always be aware. Ben sees me a certain way and expects me to do things that will prove his opinion correct. I don't blame him entirely. I don't think it's fair all the time. I'm glad that you are asking me questions so that I can give you a different version of the story."

"Is that all?" Lizzie held her breath.

"My wounded ego is a pretty big deal, Lizzie," he laughed. He looked out the driver side window at a car that passed along the street. "You know, the thing is, Lily was as much a sister to me as a lover. I could talk with her about anything. She always listened to me. She just listened and never passed judgment. When she was gone, I didn't have that any more. I didn't have anyone who would listen to me."

"That's because you killed her," Lizzie hardened her jaw.

Oliver looked at her. "She also never hesitated to tell me when I was losing perspective," Oliver smiled, softening Lizzie's harsh expression. "I don't know how this reincarnation thing works, Lizzie, but that's the part of Lily that seems to be living in you."

She managed a confused smile. The conversation was so surreal, talking about deaths with which Oliver had a hand, direct or indirect. She wanted to know those details. She did think at the end of the day that he was a good soul, who meant well … but, like Meg, got in trouble by making the wrong decision. Meg's trouble usually only involved too much alcohol or a poor taste in men. Oliver's resulted in consequences far more severe, that affected and hurt other people.

She knew he paid her a kind compliment. He attributed something that he admired in Lily to something he… respected in her. He thought of Lily as a sister. Did that mean that was how he saw her? It wasn't an inappropriate thought, even with Ben. Especially with Ben.

His smile weakened with her silence. "I'm sorry. I shouldn't have said that?"

Lizzie lifted her shoulders. "I don't know what the rules are for this," she said helplessly even though she was pretty certain she was breaking them anyway.

"It's late," Oliver fingered the keys hanging from the ignition.

"Thanks for the ride," Lizzie opened the door.

"Let me know about tomorrow."

"Good night, Oliver," Lizzie left the car. He waited until she closed the door of the house behind her.

Chapter Twenty-Five

Lizzie leaned her head back and looked up to the T Rex towering above them. "I remember this from when I was a kid," she lowered her chin and smiled at Oliver.

"It is pretty impressive."

"Did you ever come here on a field trip?"

"I don't think Springs brought us here."

"No. Elementary school. We had a sleepover here." Lizzie stopped in front the exhibit on fossils. "You never went to elementary school."

"I didn't even know how to read when I changed."

"Is that why Lily read to you?"

"Yes," Oliver looked down at the description of the Mesozoic Era. "I learned how to read so I could remember her books."

"How many times did you go to college?"

"Twice. Law school took a long time," he rolled his eyes.

"Where?"

"Stanford," Oliver moved to the next placard.

"When did you go to California?"

"After Eloise," Oliver walked into the next gallery.

Lizzie pretended to read more on dinosaurs but the words didn't sink into her brain. She followed Oliver's path and saw him staring at another glass case. "I didn't go right to California." Lizzie saw his reflection in the glass. "I took my time getting across the country. I was in New York for a few years first."

"What were you doing?"

"I was an actor," he winked and moved to the next case. "I enrolled in Stanford University in 95. I graduated from law school in 04."

Lizzie bit her lip. That wouldn't be too unusual a phrase coming from someone who looked Oliver's age. But Lizzie knew that the century was different from what any casual eavesdropper would surmise. "And you became a lawyer?"

"Indeed."

"For how long?"

"Fifteen years or so," Oliver led her towards the next display. "Then I invested in the movies."

"You're kidding?"

"Nope," he laughed. "I lost a lot of money."

"You didn't get rich?"

"I told you I don't have Ben's head for business," he glanced briefly at the levers and pulleys. "But then Charlotte came back."

"Oh."

"She was successful as an actress. They loved her youthful appearance. It was perfect for silent movies. She loved Hollywood in the 20's," Oliver looked at the empty gallery around them. A guide entered with a group of school children in the room, filling the air with a hum of sound. "She liked all the chorus girls."

"Charlotte was a lesbian?" Lizzie said as the guide came to a lull, fearing it echoed over the tour.

Oliver laughed and put his hand behind her to direct her to the next gallery. "Charlotte had more female lovers. When it came to blood, I don't think she had a preference."

"You were her lover?" Lizzie looked at a photograph of cells, realizing they were in an exhibit about blood.

"On and off for several years," Oliver looked at her and not the exhibit.

"Did you love her?"

"Yes."

"More than Lily?" Lizzie said it before thinking.

"No."

Lizzie sat on the bench in the center of the empty room. She looked at the map she picked up at reception, not registering her location in relation to the giant T Rex. "Why did you…"

Oliver sat beside her and looked up at the ceiling before fixing his eyes on her again. "Charlotte was a monster, Lizzie. She was here too long. She lost her humanity. I think she lost it even before she met Lily, even though she claimed to have human emotion for her. She was cruel."

"Women are cruel," Lizzie thought of her own heartlessness to Mike's girlfriend. "Was she unfaithful to you?"

"Always. As was I to her. But that wasn't…" Oliver took the map from Lizzie's hands and stared at it. "It was about Lily."

Lizzie wanted to ask him to explain, but she heard a voice telling her to let him be.

"I don't ever want to be like that," he shook his head.

"Like what?"

"Like Charlotte. I don't want to live too long," he stood and went back to the display.

"Why would anyone want to be a vampire?" Lizzie asked as a couple walked into the room.

Lizzie felt her cheeks burn but managed a pleasant smile as they walked over to read the placards. She felt Oliver's hand gently touch her shoulder and urge her out of her seat. "Want to get out of here?"

The November wind softened to a milder, but damp temperature. Lizzie appreciated it as they walked silently along the Charles for a half hour. Lizzie had too many thoughts in her head to know when or how to start the next conversation. "Are you okay?" Oliver finally turned to her. "You looked a little green in there."

"I don't know what I feel," Lizzie kept walking. The rhythm of her steps was a healthy distraction from letting any thought take hold and develop an uncomfortable emotion. "I still don't know how Lily is me. How do you know that she is me?"

"You called me Thomas."

"What?" Lizzie stopped her distracting paces.

"My given name is Thomas Oliver."

"When did I call you Thomas?"

"During a debate on euthanasia. It was... I think our first debate."

"Was there anyone in the debate club called Thomas?" Lizzie searched her memory for any Thomas she knew in high school.

"No," Oliver shook his head. "You looked at me to argue a point for it. You addressed me – quite respectfully – as Thomas. Nobody else noticed."

"Ben said I wrote an essay and described the Fulton parlor in vivid detail."

"Yes. He told me that."

"So you both knew… and I had no idea."

"No idea?"

"Well, I didn't know what those things meant. I always had vivid dreams. I also have a theatrical imagination… so I've never thought very much about it."

"You probably didn't believe in it."

"I didn't believe in vampires."

"How did you find out?"

"Ben told me."

"Did you believe him?"

"No," Lizzie shoved her hands in her pocket and went to a nearby bench. "So I stuck out my wrist and told him to drink my blood."

"Really?" Oliver laughed and slowly sat next to her on the bench. "I thought he was married."

"I was surprised he started seeing you."

"Why?"

"The Melissa thing freaked him out. He kept telling me we needed to leave you be and let you live your life."

"I'm glad he changed his mind," Lizzie sighed. "My life has … it's like a completely different reality before Ben told me what he was. I didn't like that reality. I wanted to get rid of the life I had."

"You have the same job, the same apartment… the same city."

"That's all just scenery," Lizzie fingered a piece of paper inside her pocket. "I was so unhappy… and lost. I kept falling for these real jerks. I was a jerk, too. I still am."

"Why do you say that?"

"Because Ben doesn't know I'm sitting here."

"Right," Oliver nodded. "Will you tell him?"

"I will," Lizzie breathed out. "I will. On Thanksgiving."

"Why Thanksgiving?"

"Because he is coming home to meet my parents. Then I'm going to tell him that I will move to Cambridge," Lizzie felt a breath of relief telling Oliver. She told someone. She drew the line in the sand.

"Congratulations."

"Thanks," Lizzie smiled. "Do you think the two of you will ever… speak again?"

"Do you want us to?"

"Of course."

"I'll be here briefly after Thanksgiving. Maybe we can get together."

Lizzie breathed out through another smile. "Good," she rose to resume their walk along the Charles. She let the silence fill the moments between their steps. The buzz of approaching rush hour sped along Memorial Drive. She thought of her runs along the river and seeing Ben.

Oliver looked at the Harvard buildings. He took a few thoughtful steps and shifted his eyes back to Lizzie. "Before Ben, were you dating anyone?"

"Not really."

"Not at all? No boyfriend since high school?"

"I wasn't… I wasn't the most attractive person, Oliver," Lizzie felt the drive to speed up her pace.

"You didn't see yourself as attractive."

"I suppose that's true. I never had a real interest in dating anyone. My friend Meg always had enough romance for the both of us… and I've never really had a lot of faith in happily ever after."

"Why's that?"

"I always thought it was because of my parents…" Lizzie stopped and looked at Oliver. "But now I'm starting to think there were other memories."

"Something changed your determination," Oliver stopped alongside her.

"I met this guy…" Lizzie looked at Oliver's dark hair and eyes, seeing the resemblance to Will right in front of her. "I had a devastating infatuation with him. I thought he was my…" Lizzie faded as so many other thoughts in her mind started to fade under the gaze of Oliver's dark eyes. "I thought Will was my soul mate."

"He wasn't?"

"Hardly," Lizzie shook herself out of her lapse and started walking again. "He was just very charming. It turned out he had a thing for someone else."

"He broke your heart."

Lizzie felt the sympathy of his glance. A silent understanding she neither asked for nor was surprised to find in his eyes. "I think it was the first domino of many changes. It provoked me to run and shed the hated weight I battled my whole life. That gave me confidence enough to ask Ben to dance and… come find him here." Lizzie felt a sudden chill as the wind shuddered across the river. She realized the warmth of the sun had nearly disappeared behind the horizon. "It's getting cold."

"Where do we go next?"

"I should get some dinner," she cleared her throat, almost hoping he would take the cue.

"Let's go find some," he smiled, making her relieved he didn't get the hint.

*****

Lizzie was grateful Oliver received a phone call and excused himself from the table to answer it. It allowed her the chance to take four bites of her hamburger and a few fries to absorb the pint and a half of beer she consumed while sharing details of the past fifteen years. She did most of the talking, sharing stories of her days at the Village with Meg and Nora, almost all of Meg's agony and ecstasy in the name of love, and the trivia of gala planning at Mt. Elm. She realized as she finally chewed her lukewarm burger that she hadn't felt that at ease in a conversation in many years… or perhaps, ever. She felt she could tell Oliver anything. That he was, in fact, like her brother.

"Sorry about that. I had to finalize some of my New York plans," Oliver returned to their booth.

"No worries," Lizzie set down her burger.

"You should keep eating," Oliver laughed. "Don't stop because of me."

"I'm just a little hungry."

"Okay."

"Are the friends you're meeting also… are they vampires?"

"Yes."

"Did you know them when you lived in New York?"

"Yes."

"Good friends?"

"One is a former lover," Oliver touched the perspiration on his untouched beer.

"Oh."

"I changed her."

Lizzie felt her cheeks burn. "How many have you changed?"

"Just two," Oliver lowered his eyes. Lizzie wondered if he was remembering their conversation in the museum or the explanation of Melissa Benson.

"But..." Lizzie felt the thought escape before she completely registered it in her mind. "You ... you don't want to stay with them forever?"

"Forever is an awfully long time," Oliver looked to the stage where the band was checking sound.

"Yes, but... why did you change them?"

"Rachel was also an actress. She was in the silent movies, first in New York then in Los Angeles. She didn't want to grow old. She's a little vain, actually. I thought I was in love with her. I thought I wanted to spend – well, yes, maybe I did think I wanted to spend forever with her. But after five years, we really didn't have very much to say to one another. Plus, there was still..."

"Charlotte?"

"Yes. Charlotte," Oliver glanced back at the stage as a high pitched chirp came from the microphone. "She went back to New York. I stayed in LA until I came back to go to Springs."

"What about Alison?"

Oliver let out a smile, showing affection Lizzie almost wished didn't exist. "Alison was a surprise. She was in a seminar I was teaching. She knew what I was. I didn't have to explain anything to her," Oliver faded into his smile. Lizzie felt suddenly foolish. Melissa Benson knew. Oliver's wife knew. Neither was as oblivious as Lizzie to this sub-culture. They didn't feel the need to reveal a wrist and make the vampire prove it. Supposedly Lizzie knew vampires in not just one life, but three. Was she really that dense? Or was she trying to protect herself from something she didn't want to know?

"Was she a source before you changed her?" Lizzie forced herself to ask another question for which she didn't really want the answer.

"She was," Oliver explained slowly as the band tested the bass. "I miss the taste of her blood."

"Then why did you?"

"Because I thought … I saw us together for a long time."

"But not forever?"

"No. Not forever."

"So why isn't she here with you?"

"Because she fell in love with one of her sources," Oliver answered as the band revved into the first song.

Lizzie looked at her hamburger and forced herself to take a bite of her cold meal. She swallowed it down with a large gulp of stout and turned her attention to the music playing. She didn't know the band. She couldn't follow the lyrics as her head clouded with all the information of the past two days and the deafening pulse of the speakers. She mindlessly consumed the rest of her beer and half of Oliver's as the band completed their first four songs.

"So… are you still with you wife?" Lizzie asked the question she held on her tongue.

"No," Oliver answered as the lead shouted out the start of the fifth song.

Lizzie reached for Oliver's beer and swallowed the remaining half. Her cheeks flared with the warmth of the alcohol and the lingering wind burn. She barely noticed the detail of the remaining four songs. For two of them, she dared herself to observe Oliver bouncing his head. He didn't seem upset by his revelation. Did he not care? Why did he not care? Had Alison hurt him by leaving… or was he relieved? Did that give him the freedom to pursue other interests? Like his doctoral thesis? Or the chance to meet what Lily had become in a new century?

She was still lost in the whirlpool of her thoughts when the band cleared the stage. Oliver took the bill on the table and paid it with a credit card or cash… or something. It was all a blur. The day started to meld together in a strange cocktail of emotion and memory. She didn't feel herself emerge until they stepped out into the brisk evening.

"Shall I take you home?"

"I can take a train," Lizzie hadn't decided if she was going back to Jefferson Park or Ben's empty apartment.

"There are strange creatures walking about," he winked. "Let me take the train with you."

"Why did she fall for one of her sources?"

"Why? I can't tell you why, Lizzie."

"How long were you together?"

"Ten years."

"That's not too long."

"No."

"Did you want it to end?"

"No."

"Then why…"

"I think my obsession with work had something to do with it. Alison wanted to take advantage of her perpetual youth. A number of her friends have children and are getting gray hairs… I imagine a part of her wanted to get away from that. She is still new to this."

"Is she still in California?"

"No, she is in Japan with her lover."

"Oh."

"I will see her again. We still own a house together. I don't… forever is also too long to condemn to never."

"Mmm," Lizzie started a quick walk towards the T station. She still wasn't certain where she was going to get off. She had to move. She didn't want to pause long enough to think about another readjustment to her reality.

She walked quickly down the steps into the terminal. Oliver was like a shadow behind her. She couldn't hear his steps, but felt his company. She paused to look down the dark tunnel, as if that would hasten the arrival of the train. There was nothing but the long echo of darkness. There were a handful of other expectant passengers, but not a large enough crowd to allow herself the silence of not thinking of what to say.

"Why did you marry her?"

"I loved her."

"Ben says you fall in love easily."

Oliver laughed lightly as the fume ridden air ruffled through the tunnel. "I suppose I do."

The echo of the approaching train whispered like a ghost. "I am very reluctant."

"Why?"

"Because… it …" Lizzie faded as her purse slid off her shoulder. She readjusted her arm to put it back in place as the wind of the tunnel increased and the train approached. She looked back and saw Oliver's dark eyes watching her. She smiled briefly and nodded her head towards the train. She took a small step forward as the doors opened, following the other passengers. Oliver suddenly reached for her hand and pulled her towards him. She heard the bell warning the close of the doors as he pressed his lips to hers. She felt an instinct to push him away but forgot it as she lost awareness of the station and the train pulling away. She dropped her purse and abandoned all sense of time and place. She only felt his warm, passionate kiss. It was familiar and comfortable. She thought of his hesitant hands by the side of the carriage house. He was no longer tentative. His kiss thrilled her and made her want more. She didn't want to pull away even though she knew there was something she should remember about why she shouldn't stay so close to him, why she shouldn't let him indulge that intimacy. No, he was always hers. No matter what other choice she made. No matter how many lovers he had. How many vampires he made. Oliver was always hers.

Another train thundered into the station. A large noisy crowd left the train and pulled Lizzie back to awareness. She let go of Oliver and picked up her purse. "I should… get on this train," she said quickly. Oliver put his hand at the lower part of her back. "No. Don't come with me," she walked to the open doors. She regretted her harshness and turned quickly. "Have fun in New York." She got on the train just as the doors slid shut. She saw his dark eyes watch her as the train started to move. They looked confused and sad, just like her own.

Chapter Twenty-Six

Lizzie stared out the window across the yards of the neighboring houses on Brattle Street. She didn't know which belonged to the Harris family two hundred years ago. Most were likely built long after the Harris family left Brattle Street. There was no carriage house attached to any of them, not even as a converted garage. It was entirely possible the carriage house and the Harris homestead were no longer.

"What is this room?" one of the visitors called Lizzie back to the present.

She shook herself out of her reverie. "This is the guest room," Lizzie said with the monotone effort she produced for most of her tour. Her rhythm was off. She knew she wasn't interesting and that she was making her three members and two student guests bored with her relation of elementary facts. "The four poster bed is made of mahogany and was purchased by Margaret Fulton in 1811," Lizzie was losing interest in herself as she stared at the bed and felt the sensation of Oliver's kiss. She smiled again and tried to put some more intonation in her explanation of the London expatriate who crafted the wood posts. She was glad when she filled her three minutes in the room, neglecting to mention any of the guests who actually used it, and was able to take the tour back down the stairs to the gift shop.

She was glad Paula and Andrew were locked in a conversation about some reality show. Lizzie had little inclination to be social for most of the day. She almost made the phone call that morning to Paula saying she felt ill. She realized she didn't want to be stuck at Ben's apartment, or even worse, her own. She knew the idleness and solitude would allow her head to fill with the question she wasn't ready to answer. She didn't want to think about Oliver and his kiss, even though it returned to her mind every other silent moment. It was one thing to remember the sensation. It was another thing to think why she kissed him back.

She hoped there would be a phone call from Ben, or even a message to tell her he was thinking of her. Anything to prove she was on his mind, even if it only made her feel guilty. She wanted to feel guilty, anything to stop her from wanting... from wanting it to happen again.

"Lizzie, you will be here Thanksgiving weekend, right?" Paula asked her suddenly.

"Mm hm," Lizzie reached for her water bottle.

"I'm going to New Jersey for the holiday," Paula explained. "Andrew can only work in the morning. It will probably be you and Donna to close the house."

"Okay," Lizzie tried to focus her thoughts on Thanksgiving and Ben. Maybe she could convince Ben to come to the house. She wasn't sure why the absence of Paula and Andrew would suddenly make it more appealing… but maybe… She had plans for Thanksgiving. She was determined to keep them. She wasn't going to let a few moments after three beers change her mind. Once Ben was back she would forget everything. She missed him. She missed having him to talk to, to hold her close, to be at her side… to take her blood.

"Is that okay with you Lizzie?" Andrew asked as though he repeated himself.

"What?"

"That if things aren't too busy I leave an hour earlier that day?"

"Yeah, sure," Lizzie answered with little concern.

"I might bring my mother here," Andrew explained. "But I know she would like the afternoon to do some more shopping."

"Of course," Lizzie managed a smile.

"You must be excited for her visit," Paula offered when Lizzie decided to focus on the sign in book. She couldn't read the names and addresses scrawled over the lines, but it was a preferable pretense to avoid listening to Andrew's trivial details.

Lizzie sat at the reception table and looked for something to distract her mind. She picked up a volume of *The Fulton Family Legacy*. It was open to a chapter about the family's involvement in politics at the end of the 20th century. Lizzie flipped back to the introductory chapters about the earlier Fultons. She already knew Margaret and John were crammed into a scant twenty pages. There were portraits of both of them, as well as one of John Fulton's son from his first marriage, Horace. Lizzie looked closer at the grayscale copy of the portrait.

He wasn't smiling. The bulk of his cravat diminished any suggestion of a neck and made his head look disproportionately large compared to the rest of his body. He had dark eyes – or so they seemed in the black and white copy – that had very little white in the irises. His hair was shortly cropped, but showed the subtle hint of a curl with the two or three strands captured on his forehead. He had tiny ears and a long narrow nose. She saw the resemblance to his father. She supposed he could be handsome, especially if the contour of his muscle was poorly rendered by the portraitist. She wasn't sure why she thought it might be… except that… well of course it was. It was just a painting. A painting of a man long since turned to dust. Had she once… really… was he really the one Oliver said took Lily to the garden and…

"Is the boyfriend home yet?" Andrew leaned over the edge of the desk.

Lizzie felt her cheeks burn scarlet. She couldn't imagine even Andrew would conclude the thoughts she was supposing about the illustration in the book. "No," she kept her eyes on the book.

"Do you want to have dinner with Davis and me?" Andrew picked the book up from under Lizzie's gaze and flipped through a few pages. "Gerard Fulton is a blowhard. I can't believe he gets people to pay to read about how great he thinks his family is."

"I was reading it," Lizzie dared to lift her eyes to Paula.

"Yes, but you didn't buy the book," Andrew set it down irreverently. "Do you want to come for dinner?"

"Sorry," Lizzie managed a pleasant expression. "Nora and Mark already invited me."

"When is he back?"

"Tomorrow night," Lizzie sighed. "But just for a few days. He has to go back for some event next weekend."

"How did Ben's brother like the house?" Paula approached the desk.

Lizzie darted her eyes quickly to Andrew's expectant face. She hoped more red stayed away from her cheeks. "He liked it," Lizzie cleared her throat. "He's a scientist. I think he just came to be polite."

"When did Ben's brother come here?" Andrew asked.

"Halloween," Paula answered before Lizzie could supply her own. "The day of your party. Did he go?"

"No he didn't," Andrew looked hard at Lizzie.

"Ben and Oliver don't get along very much," Lizzie found enough cool to offer up a level of honesty without divulging the worst details. "He was in town and has an interest in museums… so he decided to check out the Fulton House."

"And his brother's girlfriend?" Andrew raised an eyebrow.

"Shut up Andrew," Lizzie rolled her eyes. "We went to high school together."

"Oh yeah, that's right."

"He just gave a lecture at UMASS," Paula added.

"Really?" Andrew looked at Paula.

"Yeah," Paula searched amongst the papers on the desk. "See."

Andrew took the museum association newsletter and looked at the photograph. "Professor Ol is kinda hot," Andrew looked at Lizzie.

"And kinda married," Lizzie took the newsletter out of his hands. She felt her heart speed up as she looked briefly at his photograph.

"Did he like the house?" Andrew repeated Paula's question.

"Yeah," Lizzie muttered quickly. "He even noticed the wallpaper."

*****

Lizzie was tired after a day of walking aisles to look at changing stations and cribs with Nora. She thought about going home to Jefferson Park to see if Meg was all right. Lizzie didn't want to keep excluding Meg from her life… not after she committed the same sin. It was an effort and emotional honesty she wasn't completely ready to confront. She had to talk to Ben before anything. She had to tell him. She had to come clean about seeing Oliver and what… what liberty she allowed him to take.

She settled on the couch to wait out the hours before Ben's taxi would bring him home. She drank two sips from her wine and leaned against the pillow as she clicked through different television stations. She hadn't decided to watch anything when she set down the remote and resigned to the fact she wasn't tired enough to sleep, but lacked the energy to do anything else.

She was impatient to see Ben. Impatient for his company. She dreaded the truth she had to reveal. She told herself she could wait until he came home from Chicago for good. Would the delay make it more difficult to reveal? He told her about Meg. He didn't tell her the moment after it happened. He seduced her and waited until she was too tired to… think logically. The fight was awful. That was Lizzie's reaction. Would Ben be any more forgiving? Or would he take off somewhere – would he leave early for Chicago? Would he seek comfort amongst all those athletic, young, unmarried sources? She didn't want him to go away again. She didn't want the loneliness and jealousy to fill her heart and make an excuse for indulging Oliver. For indulging herself to fill the vacancy left by Ben's absence. That's all it was. She associated Oliver with Ben. She missed Ben. She wanted to be with Ben.

But when she was with him again, would she be able to forget Oliver?

She was at ease talking to him, even about things that were uncomfortable. Or surreal. Not that she felt ill at ease discussing them with Ben. Well, no more than… it was an unusual set of circumstances that seemed to belong more in a science fiction series than her own life. But… for some reason, Oliver was more familiar. As if she had such conversations with him before. Which she had. But not as Lizzie. As someone else.

How did that work? Where in that brain did Lily survive? Even though Lily's own mind was dust and decayed for centuries much like Horace Fulton. And yet here was Lizzie on the couch warm and breathing and thinking thoughts from another body… but the same soul? Did Lily ever have Lizzie's thoughts? How could that happen? How could Lily see the future? Lizzie was remembering the past.

If Lily's past was her past, did that mean that Lily's feelings were hers as well? If that was the case… she loved Oliver. Oliver meant less to Elizabeth Watson. He was the older brother of the kid who followed her best friend around. Except that kid was really a perpetually young man, with a soul that was older than the country. What Ben was in high school was irrelevant now. She loved Ben. She loved the man who bought her books and carried her home after spraining her ankle. The man who built her shelves in the closet and wanted to protect her... from Oliver.

Lizzie shut her eyes to push out the next thought that Oliver was a threat to her safety. It was all a horrible misunderstanding between the two men – fueled, no doubt, by a rivalry over Charlotte. Was it Charlotte? Or was it something – someone – else?

Lizzie jumped and opened her eyes in a panic. Her eyes slowly shifted into focus on Ben's smile. "Hi," he touched her cheek as he tucked a few stray hairs behind her ear.

"Hi," she answered in a raspy voice. "What time is it?"

"It's almost midnight," Ben explained. "My plane had a delay because of snow squalls."

"It's snowing?" Lizzie propped herself up weakly.

"Not now," he sat beside her.

"I fell asleep."

"I didn't mean to wake you," Ben rested his hand beside hers. "I just wanted to look at what I've been missing this week."

"I'm glad you woke me. How was Chicago?"

"Busy. Very, very busy. How was your week?"

Lizzie was glad her cheeks were already red from sleeping close to the radiator. "I had dinner with Nora and Mark yesterday. Today we went shopping for baby furniture."

"Oh," Ben wasn't very much interested. Did he suspect there was something else? Lizzie leaned towards him and wrapped her arms around his neck. He turned into her embrace and kissed her passionately, but briefly. "I have to get some work done tonight. I have a meeting tomorrow morning and spent little time preparing for it. I'm sorry, Lizzie."

Lizzie rubbed her eyes at the sound of her nickname. Her thoughts were too cloudy to think about his meaning. She didn't want to worry about any confessions and would much rather find a comfortable pillow. She shook her head and rested her forehead against his shoulder. "I'm tired anyway."

"Come on," he suddenly scooped her off the couch. Lizzie was already asleep when he got to the bedroom.

She didn't see much of Ben in the following days. He was leaving for Chicago again on Thursday. He spent most of the days in between at his business, or working on the computer in his home office. She read her book on the couch while he worked, but always went to bed long before he left his desk. She woke up in the middle of the night with his arms around her, but he was gone by the time she got up to get ready for work.

It was difficult to keep her mind focused with his absence, even as he sat in the same room as her. The memory of Oliver's conversations and his kiss kept seeping into her brain. She was idle at work and let herself look up articles about his research project. She found an actor bio – with no photo – on imdb. There were pictures of him on his college's website. She found a page the students created about the projects. She could tell from that and his Facebook that many of his female students were smitten – not to mention a few of the males. It was very easy to understand why.

He hadn't contacted her at all since she watched him from the train. Maybe he realized the error of his impulse. He didn't want to create more tension with Ben. Or maybe he simply respected her and didn't want to cause her more confusion. Yes, he would want her to be happy. He always did. Except when he went to Charlotte.

Lizzie lifted her eyes from her book and watched Ben at his computer. The glow of the screen reflected off his pale skin. He was very pale. He had the look of exhaustion under his eyes, making the freckles of his skin glaringly obvious. Lizzie wondered if he fed before he came home. She thought of the calendar and realized it was beyond eight weeks.

She looked back at her book, knowing she hadn't run in over a week. She wasn't conscientious about her diet and imagined her blood less appealing than the multitudes he was screening over the past three weeks. Then again, if he was that hungry it meant he hadn't fed on his last visit to Chicago. Maybe he was hoping to wait until he came home.

"What are you reading?" he asked suddenly.

Lizzie looked up as he rubbed his forehead in a break from the computer screen. He lifted his eyes to her and offered a smile. "Just some chic lit."

"Do you mind if I interrupt you for a few minutes?"

"No," she shook her head with an impish grin.

"Come here," he held out his arm and folded it around her as she approached the desk. He gently eased her onto his knee as he clicked the mouse to bring up a website for a bed and breakfast. "What do you think?"

"It looks pretty. What is it?"

"An inn in the Berkshires," he kissed her cheek lightly. "I was thinking we could go there after we leave your parents next Thursday.'

"The whole weekend?"

"Why not?"

"I promised Paula I would work at the museum on Saturday."

"Tell her you changed your mind."

"I can't."

"Then we can drive back Saturday morning," he kissed her again.

"When will you be back?"

"Wednesday night."

"Jack emailed me yesterday. He and Jen are having people over for drinks that night. Do you want to go?"

"Why don't you pick me up from the airport and we can head to Coldbrook?"

"You don't want to come back here…"

"I want to be with you," he turned her chin towards him and kissed her. She felt the thrill of his hunger as he pulled her closer to him and then lifted her towards the desk. He pushed aside the pile of papers before unfastening the top of her buttons. Lizzie reached for his buckle as the phone rang loudly. Ben paused and rested his forehead against hers momentarily before deciding to take the phone call. She saw the burn in his eyes focus on her half opened shirt and knew that was why he left the room.

Lizzie got off the desk and picked up the papers off the floor. A lot were clinical reports of some nature. Several O's, A's, and B's. She arranged them in neat piles, hoping she hadn't put them out of essential order. As she straightened one pile, a thick vellum envelope slipped out. She sat in the chair and pulled the invitation inside. The paper was glossy – imprinted with the image of red blood cells. Inside were the logistical details of location, time, and the cost of the tickets. Lizzie was startled by the number of zeroes in the cost of one ticket.

Lizzie looked through the RSVP card and return envelope. It seemed as though Ben hadn't paid any mind to the materials. He was probably going to be there regardless and wasn't required to RSVP. The last item in the invitation was a slick card with a photograph of a porcelain skinned female body. A strip of red velvet rippled across her torso, barely covering the nipples on her breasts and just reaching the space between her legs. On the back was an additional invitation to a VIP reception where key patrons would be matched with the prime sources. Lizzie couldn't imagine that all those important contributors would sit around a room hooked up to IVs to get their dose of blood. Judging from the photograph, she didn't think that was what the party entailed.

She heard Ben come back into the room and shoved the invitation back into the envelope. "Sorry about that," he grinned as he set a glass and bottle of wine on the desk.

Lizzie forced a smile to mask the disappointment she felt come over her. If he was offering her wine, he didn't want her blood that evening. Was he saving his appetite for the VIP reception? "Are you going to this party?" she held up the invitation.

"I doubt it," he laughed. "I have to get all the sources screened and prepared for the first day of feedings on Sunday. I doubt I'll have any mind for socializing."

"But you've been working so hard," Lizzie argued to hide her relief.

"I will be glad to be done with Chicago," he uncorked the wine. "I don't think any clinic was this disorganized."

"Why is it?"

"My friend started this venture with her partner. He was supposed to manage the lab and oversee all screenings and source evaluations. Six months ago, he left her."

"Why?"

"He fell in love with his source, ironically," Ben shook his head. Lizzie felt her cheeks burn. "She couldn't turn back. They need this clinic in Chicago. But… it is a different city."

"What do you mean?" Lizzie accepted her wine and reluctantly took a sip.

"There is a great resistance to clinical methodology. Too many organics," Ben sighed. "This is probably boring you."

"No," Lizzie shook her head, knowing he was going to stall with conversation until she finished her wine anyway. She wanted to ask him if he preferred organic over clinical, but thought that might indicate to whom she had been speaking. Lizzie felt an overwhelming irritation with herself. How could she be upset with him for wanting to feed at the clinic when she was lying to him for nearly a month? How could she accept his invitation to the bed and breakfast when she was so dishonest with him? How could she say she wanted to live with him when she kissed his brother?

"It will all work out. It has to. I'm not going back there after this next trip."

"Ben," she drank a large sip of wine but lost her nerve under his watchful gaze.

"I'm not going to work anymore tonight," he took her hand and pulled her out of the seat.

"I'm glad," she leaned to kiss him.

Ben was gone when she woke the next morning. She knew he would be. She knew he was only gone for a week. She knew when he came back he wasn't going away again. But this time when she saw his empty pillow and felt the cold at her side, she didn't completely believe it would be warm again.

Chapter Twenty-Seven

Lizzie traced along the margin of the legal pad and then started to color it in. She didn't think the tangent about Thanksgiving menus was necessary for the minutes of the planning meeting. She was surprised Richard asked her to sit in. It was better than sitting at the desk waiting for the last tedious minutes of Wednesday morning to pass by.

"Can you think of any other Fultons, Lizzie?" Dr. Chiang brought her attention back to the table.

"Pardon?"

"Any other members of the family who will come to the opening reception?" Richard finished the question.

"There is an aunt or something that lives in Connecticut," Lizzie was aware of Dr. Chiang's stare. She was always intimidated by those young eyes. Certainly Dr. Chiang knew far more interesting people than Gerard Fulton. "She is pretty old."

"Do you think the museum would give us a mailing list?"

"It wouldn't hurt to ask," Lizzie shrugged, as the thought of Charlotte Fulton suddenly appearing at the opening of the Fulton Cardiac Center amused her. Not that it would happen. Charlotte was long since dead. It would be amusing if she was there - a vampire helping cut a ribbon to a part of the hospital concentrating on the pulmonary system.

The meeting faded into another tangent. Richard, Dr. Chiang, and the marketing director were clearly already on vacation. It seemed premature to be planning a reception for the end of March when they still had the gala to get through in February.

Lizzie managed to conceal a breath of relief when the meeting broke up. She returned to her desk and saw the red light indicating missed phone calls. "Have a good Thanksgiving, Lizzie," Dr. Chiang said kindly on her way out the door. Lizzie watched her walk down the corridor and swallowed back her silent envy. She wondered if Eric was still interning, if Dr. Chiang ever knew about them. If that was the reason she paid any attention to Richard's admin.

She scrolled through the list of missed calls. She saw Ben's number twice. She went to her cell phone and saw three missed calls from him and a voicemail. She quickly dialed into voicemail and typed in her code.

"Elizabeth," he began and paused, creating a lump in Lizzie's stomach. "I can't leave the lab. It's… it is very important that I stay. I feel awful. I know how important tomorrow is. I have a flight on Saturday. Pick me up after you leave the museum and I will make this up to you. I promise. I'm sorry. I love you."

Lizzie shut her phone as the lump in her stomach chilled her entire body. She didn't call him back. She didn't want to talk to him. She didn't want to tempt the ache of disappointment by making her thoughts vocal. She simply texted she would pick him up at the airport Saturday night. She didn't wish him a happy Thanksgiving.

*****

"It's too bad Ben's stuck in Chicago, Lizzie," Jen sat beside her.

"It sure is," Lizzie stared at her beer bottle.

"What is he going to do for dinner tomorrow?" Jack took a handful of chips from the coffee table.

"Probably nothing," Lizzie muttered.

"I would like to do nothing," Jen laughed. "It would be better than a house full of our relatives."

"You like hosting," Jack argued.

"That's why you have chips and salsa tonight. I'm not cooking anymore."

"We invited Sara and her husband to come tonight," Jack shrugged. "Sara said she's busy helping her mother."

"Probably," Lizzie looked at the conversation between Jack's band mates. She was careful not to focus on Mike, lest he would think she was trying to catch his eye. "Jen, do you need any help with anything tonight? I'm happy to help while I'm here."

"Are you kidding? Sitting here and drinking is the best thing we can do right now," Jen smirked.

"Okay," Lizzie sipped from her bottle.

"Hey, did you hear?" Jack took more chips. "They think they found Melissa Benson's body. Or what's left of it."

"What?"

"You didn't hear it?" Jen exclaimed. "It's all the local papers have been writing for a week."

"I guess it didn't make the Boston news," Lizzie wished she hadn't spent all her idle time on Facebook.

"Yeah, some hikers from New York or New Jersey were following the old springs last week. A woman in the group found a bone. The cops came. They think they found her whole body. They're still doing DNA tests. But there was a Springs Regional sweatshirt."

"Where was it?"

"At the edge of the water," Jack interjected, as the conversation on the other side of the room went quiet. "They think she fell in the creek closer to her house where there is a significant drop. They say the currents carried her quite a ways. There wasn't as much rain this year, so the water level dropped. That's why they think the remains were found."

"So they think it was an accident?"

"Either that or she jumped," Mike snickered.

"I don't think that's the case," Jen shook her head. "They say it was rainy the night she disappeared. It was probably just a really unfortunate accident."

"You remember my mom used to freak out when we played in the woods? She always thought we would fall in that brook," Jack looked at Lizzie.

"That poor girl," Lizzie let the tears form in her eyes, thinking of Oliver's story and how badly Melissa wanted to become a vampire. How she felt rejected for not having her blood taken. How stupid she was for trying to trick a vampire.

"Now her parents know," Jack pursed his lips.

"They can't hope anymore," Jen sighed.

"Now they can move on," Lizzie lowered her eyes. Now she knew. Now she could move on.

*****

Lizzie looked at the clock. Donna would return to the gift shop within fifteen minutes. They could close the door and start counting out the register. It still gave her four hours to idle about until she went to the airport. She agreed to meet him outside of Terminal B at 9:15. Part of her still wanted to tell him to get a cab and then go home to Jefferson Park. She knew it wasn't his fault he was delayed in Chicago. She knew that… and yet… she didn't feel it at all. She anticipated the honest conversation, where she would come clean about Oliver and say she was ready to leave Jefferson Park. She no longer had the energy to tell him the truth, much less the desire to forgive him enough to offer a commitment.

It wasn't his fault. She kept repeating that to herself throughout the past two days, when her relatives looked across Jen and Jack's dining room table. She knew they were wondering if Lizzie really had a boyfriend, or if she was just making it up. Or if they believed she had someone, he clearly didn't love her enough… to meet her family. He didn't love her enough to leave that stupid clinic in Chicago and all its prime sources. If the clinic was open, what was there left for him to do? Was he going to more exclusive receptions? Even though he told Lizzie he wouldn't have time to go. Or maybe he went and that was why he had to stay in Chicago longer. And miss Thanksgiving.

The bell of the gift shop heightened her irritation. She didn't want to deal with a stubborn tourist trying to get a visit after the last tour began. Or worse yet, it would be some Christmas shopper who would linger too long over history books.

"Hi Lizzie."

She looked up and met Oliver's dark eyes. "What are you doing here?"

"I'm sorry I didn't call. But…" he breathed out. "I promised you I would get together with you and Ben before I went back to California."

"Oh," she looked down and then back up at him. "Well, Ben is still in Chicago. I don't think that's going to happen."

"That's too bad," he looked uncomfortable and then met Lizzie's eyes. "So you haven't… he wasn't home for Thanksgiving?"

Lizzie remembered she told Oliver her plan. "I haven't seen him for nine days."

"I'm sorry," he sobered his expression.

"I went home to Coldbrook anyway," she couldn't tell if his expression was sympathy or hope. "You know they found some bones in the state forest, by the old springs."

"Did they?"

"Some hikers from New York… were you with them?" she asked what was on the periphery of her brain since Jen told her.

"I thought a lot about our conversation, Lizzie," he hesitated. "I didn't know if we would find anything. I convinced Rachel and some friends to go for a hike. They were able to see things I wouldn't let myself see."

"The body?"

"Yes," Oliver muttered as voices from Donna's tour started to echo down the corridor. "My friend Ian knows a lot about water currents. We looked over two days."

"And then you had Rachel call the police?"

"Yes," Oliver bit his lip as the voices neared the gift shop. "I thought about… I wanted to give the family some peace. I knew enough to find the answer."

"How do I know that you didn't just…" Lizzie lowered her voice as Donna appeared. "put it there?"

Oliver looked up and smiled at the tour as they entered the shop. Lizzie smiled at Donna. "Donna, this is Oliver. This is Ben's brother."

"Ben's brother?" Donna held out her hand. "I actually haven't met Ben… but I've been told he's a good guy."

"So have I," Oliver glanced at Lizzie.

"Are you going to bring him through the house?" Donna suggested. Apparently, she didn't know Lizzie already did that.

"Um," Lizzie darted her eyes to Oliver. "I think so. Is that okay?"

"I'll take care of any sales and then lock up the shop," Donna agreed. "Do you mind closing the house as you go through?"

"Not at all," Lizzie left the desk and led Oliver quickly down the hallway into the parlor. She closed the door out of habit and looked at Oliver.

"I didn't put the body there, Lizzie."

"I know," Lizzie turned to the window. "I just… I needed to doubt you for a minute."

"Why?"

"Because…" Lizzie faded and pulled the shades. "I have to close the house as we go through."

"So… we're alone here?"

"Not yet. Donna is going to close the gift shop and then… yes," Lizzie nodded as she pulled the last window to darkness. She crossed the space quickly and went into the dining room.

"It's odd the way they set it up. You can tell no one eats in here."

"Kind of like a dining room for vampires. Plates that never get filled," Lizzie pulled more shades.

"Lily and one of the other girls… I can't remember her name… used to finish the wine glasses as they cleared dinner," Oliver walked towards her.

"How was New York? When you weren't taking hiking trips in Coldbrook?" Lizzie abruptly went to the kitchen.

"It was fun," Oliver closed the door for her.

Lizzie let out a breath. "Good," she paused at the fireplace and felt the draft coming down the chimney. "I can't imagine what this… It must be difficult to return to this."

"Why do you say that?"

"Because this is where… Lily was the cause of so much sadness for you. Your life as a human was brief… and yet had so many consequences that…"

"Lizzie," he touched her hand.

Lizzie stepped away from him. "What else do you remember? Other than herbs and meat hanging?"

"Smells."

Lizzie wanted to know more. She wanted to know less. She walked out of the kitchen and up the stairs. She went directly into the master bedroom. She pulled the shades and noticed Oliver didn't follow. She returned to the hall but didn't see Oliver. She went to the guest room where he was pulling the second shade.

"I saw Donna walk down the street."

Lizzie inhaled several slow deep breaths. The dim light of the lamps cast shadows she never noticed before. Oliver looked different… and more familiar in those shadows. She was aware of his height and strong muscles from working in his father's shop… only, no, he was hiking and cycling. He wasn't a wheelwright any longer. Lizzie looked away from him and darted her eyes about the room.

"We should… I need to finish closing the house," she caught her breath but couldn't move.

"Lizzie, I keep thinking about you. About our conversations," he paused and lifted his eyes, daring her to meet them. She tried to focus on the worn carpet but felt compelled to glance at his dark pupils. "About that moment in the train station."

"That was wrong," she swallowed air.

"Was it?"

"Yes," she took a weak step backwards. "I love Ben."

"This isn't about Ben," he took more deliberate steps forward. "It's about you and me."

"Oliver," she wanted to cry. She thought of the eager kisses behind the carriage house. His lips were at hers again, making that flash of dream a reality. She lifted her arms to push him away but wilted as he opened her mouth and made the kiss more intense than the last. Ben. Ben. Ben. She tried to think of Ben, who no matter how much he hurt her didn't deserve this. Oliver moved his lips away from her mouth and across her cheek, down to the nave of her neck. His hand reached for the waist of her skirt. Lizzie jerked herself away and left the room.

She went back across the hall to Harriet's room. She pulled the curtains shut and in her agitation walked into the dresser. She watched a bud vase wobble back and forth, fearing it would land on the ground with a destructive crash. She breathed out in relief and faced the doorway where Oliver stood watching her.

Lizzie looked at the floor. "What's so special about that chair?" she tried to think of Gerard Fulton.

"That's where you died."

Sound and the focus of the floorboards at her feet started to blur. She felt the blood drain from her head and leave the strength of her knees. Oliver caught her and guided her to the edge of the bed. "I'm sorry," he said softly. "Should I get you some water?"

"Did it really happen here? In this room?" Lizzie clutched his hand.

"Yes," Oliver swallowed.

"How?"

"I…" Oliver sat beside her and looked at her hand in his own. "I was a fool, angry and consumed with my own selfish rage. I didn't want it to end the way it did. I just wanted her to be with me."

"Why were you angry?" Lizzie felt she knew the answer but didn't know where to find it in her mind.

"Lily chose someone else."

"Charlotte?"

Oliver stood up and walked over to the chair. He stared at it in silence for several minutes. "Has he really told you nothing?" Oliver didn't move his eyes from the chair.

"About what?"

"About Mr. Chester and the plans for Harriet?"

"No," Lizzie shook her head as it started to muddle again with blurred shapes and sounds.

"What do you remember? About her?"

"I remember running into the Harris' yard and hiding behind the hedges. I remember you coming out of the shadows and …" she stood up slowly. "I remember that I loved you."

Oliver grasped her hand and pulled her into another kiss. She felt the cloud of her mind dissolve as the warmth of his kiss provoked her own. The room spun into another reality. The lamps were lit by flames. The wallpaper had no water stains or cracks. The wood on the bedposts glowed with a fresh sheen of oil.

Lizzie pulled herself away from Oliver. A quiet voice in her thought about closing up the museum, but she ignored it as Oliver took apart the buttons of her sweater and unhooked her bra. She felt his hand press against her left breast. He grinned as he felt her heart pound through her skin. He kissed her again and moved his hands to the waist of her skirt, slowly sliding it over her hips as he lowered in front of her. She became aware of the cold when he removed her stockings but resisted the urge to shudder as she watched him slowly undress. She saw the muscle she imagined, that she knew from all those meetings in the shop. He was exactly as she knew he would be. Tall and strong. The scar at his side was worn and faded, but still noticeable. He came back towards her and kissed her warmly. She pressed against him for the heat she felt escaping her body. He moved his hands down along her back and behind her hips as he pushed her towards the bed. He lay down with her and slowly began his rhythm. She breathed in deeply, silencing herself for fear that Charlotte – not Charlotte- would hear in the next room. She arched her back and turned her neck as the sensation warmed her spine. She felt his breath move to the base of her shoulder and the slight prick of fangs as the sensation flooded through her brain and the blood pumped out from the veins of her neck.

His body warmed on top of her, diminishing the cold drafts of Harriet's room. She pulled the warmth closer to her as he moved away from the inside of her shoulder and rested his head against her beating heart. She saw the gleam of the oiled bed posts before she closed her eyes and everything in front of her blurred…

There was no moon as she walked around the path to the front of the house. There was a candle burning in the kitchen. Annie was still awake. Would she notice the creak of the front door? She tucked her loose hair under the cap and checked her apron strings. Someone took her hand away from her back and turned her around.

He was in shadow, but even in the darkness she could see the green of his eyes. She wanted to move away from him. She felt badly indulging him, indulging herself after visiting Tom. After the decision Tom made to leave Boston. She couldn't resist as he pulled her lips towards his.

"Lily," he whispered her name as no one else ever had, with respect and admiration. Not to call an order or refer to her as some sort of pet.

"I don't have much time," she pulled away from him. "She will be back soon."

"I know," he kissed her again.

She didn't want to stop. She didn't want to go back into the stuffy room with Harriet. She wouldn't be able to sleep. Not after his kiss. Not after another complication to her escape. "I have to go inside," she attempted weakly.

"You don't have to do anything, Lily. They don't own you," he pressed his forehead against hers.

"Stop," she put her hands around his and stepped back from him. "I don't want you to hurt them. I don't want you to… please take her away and go."

"You don't want me to go."

"I am going to Kentucky with Tom."

"You don't want to go to Kentucky. You want to go to Prussia and Turkey and France. I can take you there, Lily."

"She won't let that happen."

"I told you there is a way," he rested his hands against the sides of her face. "I can make you like her, like me. Then we can be together. We will go to the countries you read about. You will see all those places with me."

"But how?" she fought the tears she felt surface in her eyes.

"I have money."

"Without her? What about Harriet?"

"We shall let Harriet be," he kissed her forehead. She looked up and saw the green visible in the shadows.

"What if she tries to stop us?"

"She won't," he caressed her cheek. "She has Horace's fortune. She has what she wanted."

"She won't have me."

"She has others. You know she has…"

"Will it hurt?"

"No," he kissed her again.

"Will I become like her? Will I be cruel and … will I be a monster?"

The green eyes looked at her. "You will never be her," he touched her brow. "You have a heart that is full of love, Lily. You will not be a monster."

She rested her head against his shoulder as he pulled her into an embrace. "Will you love me?" she asked into his ear.

"I will always love you," he kissed her again.

Lizzie shook with the cold and sat up suddenly. "I have to finish closing," she looked for the clothing on the floor.

"We can go somewhere," Oliver stood behind her and turned her back into his kiss. Lizzie couldn't resist and let him touch her lips again. She was still somewhere between awake and dreaming. She saw the image of shadows outside the front door and felt the movement of her mouth. She wasn't sure how many minutes passed before she pulled away.

"I have to get Ben at the airport."

"Oh," Oliver watched her reassemble her sweater and skirt. She shoved her tights in her pocket and then looked to the historic bed. The cover was ruffled. She straightened it out and hoped it wasn't obvious someone had touched the precious furniture. She watched Oliver zip his ski jacket. He was still so handsome and eager to be near her. She turned away and rushed from the room down the servant steps.

Oliver followed right behind her. Lizzie quickly gathered her things and went to the alarm. She set the code and ushered him out of the building. "Let me get you something to eat," Oliver touched her back.

"I have to meet Ben," Lizzie faced him.

"You are beautiful."

"I'm..." Lizzie felt the sadness overtake her.

He kissed her again. He stepped back as her breath nearly gave out. "You should go."

"Goodbye," Lizzie turned in the opposite direction. She hastened her speed to a run and let herself cry all the way to the train station.

*****

Lizzie went directly to her car when she got to Ben's apartment. She contemplated going inside for the remaining two hours. She didn't want to be surrounded by Ben's things. Maria's things. Were any of them Lily's things?

Lizzie looked at the marks on her neck in the rearview mirror. She thought about getting a turtleneck, but there was no point trying to hide it from Ben. Even if she could justify the distance of one night as punishment for abandoning her on Thanksgiving, she wouldn't be able to hide it for the weeks it would take the marks to fade. She tied her scarf around her neck and tucked it inside her jacket. It was a temporary solution, at least until they got back to his apartment.

She wasn't sure she wanted to hide it. She wanted him to know. She didn't feel the need to lie about Oliver. Ben should know. Not because Lizzie wanted to be fair to Ben. Because she wanted to be fair to Oliver. She made a conscious choice to accept Oliver – Thomas – back in her life. Is that what she was doing? Hadn't she made that decision by letting him seduce her and take her blood? Ben chose to stay in Chicago. He chose to put his career before her. He chose to deceive her about Lily.

Why didn't he tell her that he knew Lily? That he … loved her. He loved her enough to want to stay with her forever. To make her a vampire. Lizzie kept trying to shake that detail from her mind. Oliver was proof that changing someone into a vampire didn't necessarily bind them to that person forever. Forever was a long time. But that was Oliver. Ben was more steadfast and determined. He only left the women he loved because they left him by dying. She didn't want to die. She didn't know she wanted to leave him. She couldn't stay. How could she trust him again? How could she not know he was hiding something from her? About her? He said he didn't know what he should tell her. But to not tell her that he knew Lily, that he loved Lily, that he stole Lily from Oliver and Charlotte, that he wanted to make Lily what he was… that was a heartless attempt to withhold the truth. Why? Why tell her that Lily was in love with Oliver but not him? Why wouldn't he want Lizzie to know to whom her heart once belonged?

She didn't say much at the airport. She let him kiss her cheek, but pretended to focus on the traffic making its way back to the Pike. They drove in silence. She knew he was tired. She knew he knew she was upset. He had no idea about Oliver. No idea at all.

Ben brought his bags to the bedroom and Lizzie went to the couch in the living room. She glanced to where the vase of white roses used to be. Lily was the reason for white roses. She didn't know how or why. She knew the roses were for Lily… for her.

"Do you want to go get some dinner?" Ben asked from the doorway.

"No," she set a hard stare on him.

"You are still in your coat." Lizzie took off her coat, but kept the scarf tied around her neck. "You are angry with me," he sighed heavily. "I don't blame you. I… I know this weekend was important to you."

Lizzie looked away from him. She didn't want his false sympathy. If he was really sincere, he would have been there. He wouldn't have made another choice. He preferred to be with other vampires and not at the eating frenzy of a bunch of regular humans.

"Are we going to talk about this?" he sat beside her and took her hand. She pulled it back and hid it under the cushion beside her hip.

"Oliver came to see me."

Ben turned away and let out a cool breath. "I thought he might."

"What?"

"I knew he was coming to town to give a lecture."

"You knew?"

"Yes, Elizabeth," he looked at her not showing any anger or impatience.

"He came to the Fulton House," she tried to provoke him.

"Did he take one of your tours?" his question was almost too light and frothy to be sincere.

"No, he did that a month ago."

"A month?"

"Halloween. The day you kissed Meghan."

"So is this retaliation?"

Lizzie fingered the ends of her scarf. She looked back at Ben. "He told me things about the house and the Fultons…"

"And Lily."

"Things you wouldn't tell me."

"What did he tell you?"

Lizzie let out a breath and walked behind the couch towards the empty table under the mirror. "Do you know they found Melissa Benson's body?"

"No," Ben let his confusion show.

"They are pretty sure she fell into the brook and drowned," Lizzie watched his brief distraction from focusing on her.

"I'm sorry to hear that."

"Why?"

"Because it must make her family sad."

"But relieved to know what happened," Lizzie hardened her jaw. "Oliver helped find the body. He probably could have found her seventeen years ago, but he didn't want them to see the fang marks on her. He didn't want any suspicion to come near the Cottingham household."

"That doesn't make him any less guilty."

"He didn't kill her."

"I never said he did, Elizabeth," he went behind the couch to face her. "You were the one who made that conclusion."

"You didn't stop me. You didn't want me to … you wanted to keep him from me."

"Did I stop him from going to the Fulton House to take your tour?"

"No," Lizzie felt her anger muddle with confusion.

"Did he tell you how he killed Lily?"

"He showed me where she… I died," Lizzie's voice cracked.

"And you still think he is someone you can trust and feel safe with?"

"No more than you," she turned away from him.

"How many times have you seen him?" Ben asked slowly, still not letting any anger into the tone of his voice.

"He took me to lunch and I went to his lecture. Then we went to the Science Museum. Today he came back to the house," Lizzie stared at a window across the street decorated with red Christmas tree lights.

"I'm glad he was able to answer your questions about the Fultons and Lily."

"I had a dream, Ben," she turned to face him again and let the hardness return to her eyes. "A very vivid dream about Lily. You were there. You kissed her. You…" her breath quickened as she tried to form the words. "You told her you were going to make her like you."

Ben stopped his breath and softened his eyes. "You remembered?"

"You didn't tell me you were a part of Lily's life."

"I didn't… I wanted you to remember that."

"What?"

"Then I would know that…" Ben stepped closer to her.

"What?"

"You remembered that?" he looked at her hopefully. "He didn't tell you?"

"No," Lizzie shook her head in disbelief. "You wanted to change her. You wanted to drink her blood and feed it back to her so that you could be with her forever."

"Yes," he nodded and smiled.

"Is that what you want to do to me?"

"I… Elizabeth, this isn't," he shut his eyes, struggling. He hadn't fed. "I think about that. But I would never… ask that of you."

Lizzie closed her eyes to let the tears fall. She felt Ben come close and pull her into an embrace. She resisted, but couldn't summon enough energy to push him away. She didn't let her arms respond and stood lifeless in his hold. He pulled away and smiled at her. He smoothed down the sides of her hair, tracing a few fingers along her cheek to wipe away her tears. "I don't want that," she breathed through a sob.

"No," Ben caressed her hair again.

She raised her tear stained eyes to his. "It's all because of you."

"What?" he dropped his hands and stepped back.

"You made that promise to Lily. She accepted it and Charlotte found out. Then she took," Lizzie paused on a thought she couldn't tell if it was her own. "She took Oliver's life. He didn't know anything. You destroyed him. You made him into the monster that you say he is."

"Oliver made his choice."

"He wouldn't have had that choice if you didn't want Lily. Charlotte would never have found Lily if it wasn't for you," Lizzie heard the last sentence echo in her brain. She didn't understand what made her say that. Was it the irrationality of her anger? Or was it something else she couldn't remember?

She went back to the couch. She felt the itch of the wool at her throat and ripped off her scarf before dropping her head into her hands. She wanted a drink. She wanted to not be there, having that conversation. She wanted her life back, her thoughts back to her own. Being so close to Ben wasn't a comfort. It made it all worse. She looked at him standing over her, hesitating whether or not to offer his hand.

He bent his knees and came to her eye level. "Lily made me want to be human again."

"What does that mean?"

Ben couldn't mask the struggle of what to say. He moved her hair from where it stuck to tears on her cheek and tucked it behind her ear. He moved his hand away from her slowly. She saw a strange sneer and the hint of his fangs very briefly. Lizzie sat straight against the sofa, knowing he saw the bite marks on her neck.

"Is that all he did?" Ben stood up slowly, looking at her un-stockinged legs.

"No," Lizzie swallowed.

His shoulders collapsed and his eyes revealed more fear than anger. "Why, Lizzie?"

"I don't know."

"Now he... he won't let you be."

"Will you?"

"What?"

"Will you leave me be?"

"Do you want me to?"

"I can't trust you. You keep things from me."

"You knew I wasn't telling you everything."

"This is different," she swallowed. "You didn't want to admit you had anything to do with Lily's unhappiness. "

"I thought I made her happy," Ben looked at the empty spot on the table beneath the mirror.

"She died because of you," Lizzie stood up to interrupt his gaze.

"Yes," Ben reached for her shoulders. "I know."

"Then why didn't you tell me?"

"I didn't know how to tell you."

"That's not good enough," she hissed.

"Elizabeth, I love you."

"You loved Lily. You just see me as... you see her, not me," she couldn't breathe through her nose.

"That is not true. You are confused," he tried to pull her closer for another embrace.

"Stop it. You should be angry with me. You shouldn't be this kind," she broke away from him.

"I am angry with you," he stiffened his lip. "But I love you too much to not see you are hurting right now."

"You don't love ME. You love her!" Lizzie shoved him and headed towards the door.

"She is part of you."

"I'm going home," she found her purse and opened the door to the stairwell.

"Elizabeth, don't leave," he grabbed her hand.

"Please, Benjamin. Please let me go," she cried as she pried her hand loose. "I don't want this anymore."

"Elizabeth," he heaved a great sigh and dropped his hand as she turned towards the staircase.

Chapter Twenty-Eight

Lizzie stared at the crack edging across the plaster of her ceiling, not wanting to get off the bed. She tried getting up a few hours before. She was discouraged by the fact all the clothes in her dresser were too small for her. She left the clothes that fit her extra twenty pounds at Ben's apartment. All her things… she had to go there to get them. She chose not to think about that and went back to bed. She tried to sleep, but couldn't let go of her mind.

She turned on her side and heaved in another sob. She couldn't believe there was anything left in her tear ducts. She already cried most of the night, only stopping when she briefly found sleep. The longest interval was only two hours. She dreamt of Oliver's teeth at her neck and woke herself to stop the memory from coming back. She didn't want to think about Oliver, about what she did or why she did it. She knew it was wrong. It wasn't as wrong as Ben deceiving her. Was it? He lied about Lily. He lied about who she was and why he wanted to be with Lizzie. He didn't want her. He never wanted her and her flawed body. He just wanted what Lily had become, to get back at Oliver.

She shut her eyes. That wasn't her anger. It wasn't her bitterness. And yet… it was. She always feared Ben had an ulterior motive to their relationship. Beyond blood. There was always something… like the white roses.

She heard a gentle knock on her door and felt panic motivate her to sit up. She touched her throat and was confident in the frumpy turtleneck she found at the bottom her dresser. She was surprised to see Nora on the other side of the door.

Lizzie thought about her red eyes, but knew it was too late to try to hide them. Nora's glance of sympathy was worse than any other thought that went through her mind all night long. "Ben?"

"It…" Lizzie sighed and nodded her head. She cried again as Nora squeezed her arms around her.

"Meg called me," Nora whispered in her ear. "She heard you crying last night. And this morning," Nora pulled away. "She was afraid you wouldn't talk to her. She is worried about you."

"Just because I was crying?"

Nora glanced over Lizzie's shoulder at the chaos of clothes and miscellaneous clutter. "Why don't you come downstairs? I brought brownies and wine. Meg got Chinese food."

"I'm not hungry," Lizzie lied. Why was she lying? It didn't matter if she ate crap now. It didn't matter what she did to her blood or her body. It was never enough anyway.

"Come on," Nora pulled her hand and led her down the spiral staircase.

Meg stood up off the floor from where she knelt arranging all the cartons on the coffee table. She paused awkwardly for a second and then clutched Lizzie with another hug. "Oh Lizzie, what happened?"

"I broke up with Ben," Lizzie left the embrace and sat in front of the feast on the table. She hadn't eaten in twenty-four hours, even though she fed another creature.

"What happened? I mean… I was pretty sure you were on the marriage track. I thought you would be telling me to look for another roommate."

Lizzie saw Meg's expectant eyes and took in a breath, contemplating how much she was going to tell. She wanted to tell her everything. But … she couldn't. She couldn't tell her best friends that she broke up with her boyfriend because he lied to her about loving her in another lifetime. Because she let another vampire take her blood. Meg didn't see the flaw in demanding the suspension of belief about love and its otherworldly powers. Maybe Meg would understand past lives and… vampires. Nora wouldn't have that empathy. Not even for stupid mistakes. But the stupid mistake was real and easy to explain. "I cheated on him."

"What?" Nora didn't waste a beat.

"With his brother," Lizzie forced her tired eyes to meet her friends' glances.

"He doesn't get along with his brother," Meg remembered a detail Lizzie was grateful to not retell. "And isn't he married?"

"He's separated," Lizzie took a Crab Rangoon and started to pull apart the corners.

"When did it happen?"

"He came to town a month ago. I went out with him a few times and then yesterday… before I picked Ben up from the airport…" Lizzie touched her turtleneck, fearing the marks burned through the woven cotton of her sweater.

"Are you in love with him?" Nora asked bluntly

The tears pooled in the rim of Lizzie's eyes. "I'm not sure."

"Do you love Ben?" Nora continued.

"Yes, but he," Lizzie closed her eyes. "I can't be with him anymore."

"What do you mean you can't be with him anymore?"

"Did something happen in Chicago?" Meg asked before Lizzie could filter an answer to Nora's question.

"No. I don't know. I …"

"Lizzie… this isn't because… you didn't cheat because of what happened on Halloween?" Meg still wasn't waiting for Lizzie's answers.

"That seems so long ago," Lizzie faded into a stare at the dark television. "No."

"Well, Lizzie, that was really stupid," Nora decided as she sat on the other side of the coffee table.

"It was stupid," Lizzie took a gulp of wine that Meg offered her.

"How did Ben find out?"

"I told him," Lizzie rested the wine glass on her knee.

"He is a good guy," Nora glanced briefly at Meg. "I don't blame him for breaking up with you."

"I left him," Lizzie took another sip.

"To be with his brother?" Meg sipped from her own wine. Lizzie wondered how much her friend hated her now. She never knew if Meg was jealous of her for having Ben. Would she resent her for throwing it away? Or would she be relieved Ben was out of both their lives?

"Meg," Nora hardened her voice. "Lizzie, he loves you. You love him. Why … I honestly don't understand why you would do this."

"He doesn't love me," Lizzie shook her head.

"Did something happen to make you think that?"

Lizzie met Nora's eyes briefly and then consumed the rest of the Crab Rangoon in her hand. She couldn't explain it. Not to Nora. Not even to Meg, who might understand. To tell the story of Ben would require the distraction of telling Meg her fantasy world was real. "It's complicated."

Nora let out an irritated sigh. She lifted her own Crab Rangoon and chewed it slowly. She took a napkin and patted her lips slowly. "Lizzie, I love you," she crumpled the napkin and reached across the table to grab Lizzie's hand. "I will be here for you even if you are determined to self-destruct."

"You'll get through this, Lizzie," Meg put her hand on top of theirs. "If I can get over Alec McCaffrey, you can get through this."

"Are you over Alec?" Lizzie dropped her hand and picked up a greasy chicken finger. She wanted to ask if Meg was over Ben, but that was like rubbing salt in a wound for them both.

"I take it one day at a time," Meg shrugged and let an impish grin leak from her mouth. "And I've got good friends to help me through."

"I haven't been a good friend to you," Lizzie shook her head.

"I deserved it… it doesn't matter now. We need to eat this before it gets cold," Meg avoided Lizzie's eyes and picked up a carton of low mein.

Lizzie managed another weak smile. Meg's cure for everything was grease, chocolate, and alcohol. All in the company of her oldest best friends. Lizzie subscribed to that belief when she was disappointed by Will or frustrated with her job. But this dull ache within her was unlike anything that ever caused her misery. She didn't believe her wounded soul would heal.

*****

Lizzie and Meg finished two bottles of Pinot Noir when Nora left with the remainder of her frosted brownies. Lizzie felt the nausea when she finally went to bed. She didn't know how she managed to pass four hours with her friends, but there was enough distraction to keep her mind away from Ben. Or Oliver. Or Lily. It all felt better by the last glass of wine anyway… until the final sip when she struggled to keep her eyes open and her stomach swam with all the fermentation.

She walked away from the house, following the patterns of the lit windows on the grass. She went to the garden and breathed the heavy scent of summer blossoms. She knew young Master Fulton wouldn't follow her. She hoped he wouldn't. His fiancé was in the house. What a silly little thing she was. She was pretty and good. Good enough to distract him from temptation in the shadows of the chestnut tree.

She saw the white blossoms reflect the brilliance of the moon. The petals were soft and perfect and pure. Like the silk Mrs. Fulton ordered for the wedding gown. She pulled the long stalks off the bush, until a thorn cut her finger. She winced with the sharp pain, knowing it opened her skin. She lifted her finger to her mouth to clean the wound. The evening sounds hummed her into calm, dissolving the pain from her finger. She pulled more stalks until she had a small bouquet for the young mistress.

A new sound interrupted her thoughts. She knew it was him. The brother. The one who gazed over the shoulder of Mistress Harriet. She turned around, dropping her torn finger, and allowed his stare. He had the hungry gaze of young Master Fulton in his green eyes. It was shameless and unrelenting. He wanted her, more completely than anyone ever could. She didn't fear he would hurt or strike her to alleviate his want. She waited for him to speak or move. Something stopped him, holding him in place away from her. She handed him the roses and laughed on her way out of the garden.

*****

Lizzie was relieved Ben didn't answer the door. She rang the bell a second and third time, waiting ten minutes after each attempt. She let herself in, unwinding her key as she closed the door behind her. She set it on the table inside the doorway and walked straight into the bedroom with her empty bags. She filled them quickly, clearing off the shelves in the closet. She grimaced as she realized the summer clothes were all too small for her, but didn't think it was reason to leave them behind. She tossed out her toothbrush and gathered up all the toiletries from the bathroom. She collected the books by the bed and stuffed them into the top of her bag.

She didn't take her time in that room. She didn't fear Ben would walk in. She deliberately took the day off from work and came when she knew he wouldn't be there. She wanted him to come home and see the emptiness. That way he would know… he would know she wanted it to be over.

She went to the kitchen. That room was more hers than his. Even though he purchased all the dishes and appliances. She used and cleaned them. She didn't think she should leave food in the refrigerator. He wouldn't eat it. It would spoil. She didn't have that many hands. Nor did she wish to do him any favors.

She brought her bags to the dining room, noticing all the bottles of her favorite wine. He bought that for her. So he wouldn't be tempted to take her blood when he was hungry. So she wouldn't be coherent enough to understand his deceit. Her eyes wandered over the drawers of the buffet. All that beautiful, untouched china. The photograph of Maria buried under silk napkins. Did he have anything of Lily in that house? Anything he held onto to remind him of her?

Lizzie shook that from her mind. She wasn't going to think about Lily. Her mission was to erase herself from Ben's apartment. She went through most of the rooms. She retraced her steps back down the hallway towards his office. The blinds were drawn, leaving a shadowed light against the bookshelves. So many beautiful books. She only read five, maybe six of them… they were beautiful books. From the early 19th century… when Lily was alive. Without breath for another thought, she went to them and started pulling volumes from their resting place. She looked again at Keats and Shelly and was about to replace Byron when she noticed the front page stuck to the inside of the cover. It had gotten wet, making the pages wrinkled and creating a sealant against the leather. With a little effort, she pried open the page. There were a few lines scribbled in ink that ran, but weren't erased. She didn't recognize the handwriting. It was like letters she saw in the museum archives, an attention to script that disappeared with the proliferation of keyboards. It took some effort to decipher the blurred blue. It wasn't Byron. It was Shakespeare.

"*Let me not to the marriage of true minds*
Admit impediments. Love is not love
Which alters when it alteration finds,
Or bends with the remover to remove:
O no! it is an ever-fixed mark
That looks on tempests and is never shaken;

It is the star to every wandering bark,
Whose worth's unknown, although his height be taken.
Love's not Time's fool, though rosy lips and cheeks
Within his bending sickle's compass come:
Love alters not with his brief hours and weeks,
But bears it out even to the edge of doom.
If this be error and upon me proved,
I never writ, nor no man ever loved." L

Lizzie dropped the book in a loud thunk on the floor. She reached down to retrieve it and saw it as though it were under a half foot of water. She heard the footsteps in the grass behind her and stood up to see Ben standing in the doorway.

She saw the color of his cheeks and knew he fed recently. "Elizabeth," he startled her stare with his quiet voice.

She recoiled against the bookshelf and folded the book against her side. "What are you doing home? Aren't you supposed to be at the office?"

"I went to the clinic this morning. I decided to take the rest of the day off," he turned on the light and made a step into the room. "I'm glad you are here."

"I just came… to get my things," she looked away from him. "I didn't want to see you."

"You didn't have to … I could have done that for you," he still looked at her.

"No."

"Very well," he lowered his eyes to her hand and then up at the empty spot on the shelf. Could he tell what book she held? Did it matter? She returned it to the empty spot, not bothering to fill the uncomfortable silence with any conversation. She walked to the door when she heard the alarm of her phone sound. She pulled it from her pocket and felt her neck burn as she turned off the sound.

"That was him, wasn't it?"

"Does it matter?"

"It does if you leave here to meet him," he blockaded the door.

"You can't keep me here."

"I could," his face was calm but his voice indicated anger.

She put her phone back in her pocket and let out a deep sigh, hoping to calm the rapid beat of her heart. "Ben, please, let me go," she hoped the crack in her voice didn't make her fear too obvious.

"Elizabeth," he stepped closer and tried to take hold of her hand. Lizzie jerked it back and crossed her arms across her chest. "I don't want to lose you."

"Me? Or Lily?"

"I lost Lily," Ben turned his glance away from her.

"You've lost me," Lizzie clenched her jaw. "You deceived me."

"How?" Ben looked up at her. "I was honest with you from the beginning about who I was."

"Not about whom I was."

"I told you. I don't know if it is for me to tell."

"It is when it is part of who you are," Lizzie moved closer towards the door.

Ben pulled her back into the room. "Why were you looking at that book?"

Lizzie saw the green glint in the reflection of the moonlight. No, the artificial ceiling light. She shut her eyes hearing the crickets buzz in the tall grasses. She rubbed her forehead, but couldn't stop the spinning sensation as the hum of the crickets buzzed even louder in her ear before it all went black.

"Here, drink this," Ben offered a glass when she opened her eyes. The water was cool. "Have you eaten anything?"

"I don't remember," she muttered a lie she knew he wouldn't believe.

"It doesn't matter," he took the water glass and replaced it with a stemmed goblet. "That will make you feel better."

Lizzie glanced at the clock noting the half hour before noon as she took a sip of red wine. She wondered if he was going to get her drunk to keep her there. Or if he was indulging her bad habit to win her favor.

"What do you want to know?" he moved to the other edge of the sofa. "I will be completely honest with you, Elizabeth. You can still leave me. At least give yourself the opportunity to know more than what Oliver told you or what you saw in a dream."

"This isn't about Oliver."

"Yes, it is about Oliver," Ben pulled the chair from behind the desk and placed it directly opposite her.

She took in a deep breath and let herself drink the entire glass of wine. His mood was better than it would have been had he not just come from a feeding. She saw the bright look in his eye and wondered if she had an endorphin rush. Was it simply a runner's high or... she couldn't bring herself to ask that question. It was difficult enough to form her mouth around the words pertaining to Lily. "You were Mr. Chester."

"It was said I was Charlotte's brother."

"Paying flattering attention to Harriet Fulton?" Lizzie felt a surge of protectiveness over the glassy eyed portrait.

Ben looked toward the window briefly, emitting an irreverent laugh. "I suppose you could call it that," the green slowly hardened to the gray.

"Why?"

"It was all part of the plan."

"What plan?"

"The Fultons were already a distinguished family of good fortune when I was a farmer in Lincoln. They never gave up their loyalty to the British. Not during the Revolution and not even when there was another war forty years later. Only by that point, they had more money and more local authority. You know their history. I don't need to tell you all the details."

Lizzie made her breaths quiet and calm. None of these details were startling to her, but she felt a protectiveness claw at her heart. It was as if Ben told her such conniving details about Meg and Nora. "You wanted their money."

"Well of course."

"What was your plan?"

"Charlotte married Horace."

"Then she killed him."

"Yes."

"And then you were going to marry Harriet?" Lizzie felt very sad. A small part of her felt she should go to the Fulton House immediately and tell someone.

"Yes."

"Were you going to kill her, too?" Even with his hard stare, he was unable to answer the question. She looked at the empty wine glass and then his colorless eyes. "What were you going to do to Peter?"

"Many young boys didn't survive to adulthood," his voice had no expression whatsoever.

A chill resonated from the surface of her skin to the marrow of her bones. She never saw the vampire in Ben. Even when he took her blood. But now, as he told this story, it became very clear to her that there was a part of him that was cold and dead to the world.

"But Peter did survive," Lizzie argued the history of her Saturday tours to herself. "He survived and had children, who had children all the way down to Gerard Fulton."

"The plan changed."

"Lily."

"Lily was just a maid. Neither of us suspected the maid would be an impediment. That a girl… the bastard child of Margaret Fulton's father would undo everything."

"How?"

"We both fell in love with her," Ben turned away.

"Enough to forsake the Fulton fortune?"

"In the end I would have given anything to be with her."

"Why? What was so special about Lily? She laughed at you," Lizzie said blankly. Ben jerked his head and stared at her directly. He was eager for her to say something else. She knew he wanted to test her memory. If it was her memory or just something she repeated back from Oliver. "The white roses."

"The white roses," the calm in his voice grew very quiet.

"They were supposed to be for Harriet," Lizzie didn't know if she should tell him the details of that wine drenched dream. She ached to tell someone, to know that it wasn't just the coinage of a sick brain. "You followed her into the garden."

He offered a knowing look. She couldn't tell if it was amusement or disdain. "She was waiting in that garden… probably waiting for Horace. I didn't care. I followed her. I assumed Lily was a… I thought she was an obedient servant who knew how to keep quiet about dirty deeds. I had every intention of taking her and her blood that night. Then she looked directly at me and laughed without any concern at all."

"Did you take her blood?"

"Not then."

Lizzie shut her eyes, wondering if any more thoughts that weren't her own would suddenly surface. She opened her eyes back at the glass in her hand and contemplated if more wine would ease her into Lily's conscious. It seemed important to remember that detail. She couldn't reconcile it to what she remembered. There was nothing about vampires in those memories. Just… two men between whom she felt herself divided now.

"What about Charlotte? When did she fall for Lily? Did Lily laugh at her too?"

"You were right. If it wasn't for me… Charlotte would never have paid any attention to Lily," he waited again, as if she could add something to that part of the story. "Charlotte realized I was distracted from our purpose. She discovered I had the same interest as her husband. She sent me back to France to get it out of my system. She went after Lily herself. Her intention was to kill her, but she fell for Lily's charm just as easily as I did."

"How?"

"I wasn't there. I know Lily cared about her. I know Lily liked… just as you do… the thrill of feeding. It wasn't just a physical … Lily saw herself as a monster because of what Horace did to her. I think she saw something in Charlotte that made her feel less horrible about herself. But then… Charlotte killed Horace. Lily saw the ugly side of Charlotte and wanted something else."

"You?"

"She went to Oliver first."

"But she wanted to protect Harriet… from you."

"Charlotte told her the plan. Charlotte never believed she loved the Fultons, least of all Harriet. Harriet treated her miserably. Maybe that was because Harriet knew how I felt about Lily."

"Were you in love with Lily?" Lizzie asked a question she couldn't remember forming in her mind.

"I thought she was just… I thought I could get away from it in France…" Ben looked at the bookshelves. "I never stopped thinking about her. How fearless she was. How she let me…I knew I would see her when Charlotte summoned me back to marry the daughter. I bought her presents. I bought her that volume of Byron you were holding."

Lizzie caught the wine glass as it fell out of her hand onto her lap. "Did you woo Harriet?" Lizzie didn't want more details about the book. The book was on the shelf, with its water smudged quotes scribbled on the inside cover. She would never have to look at it again.

"I pretended to. I liked it because Lily had to be the chaperone most of the time. I believed she had forgotten me. I knew about her and Charlotte. I knew she was sneaking out behind Charlotte's back to see… Oliver."

"She loved Oliver," Lizzie argued as much to justify her present actions as Lily's past ones.

"She wanted escape," he looked at her. "He was a way out."

"So were you," Lizzie looked at Ben, wondering if he still thought of the shadows outside the front door and the promise of France and Prussia.

"I can't tell you what she felt," Ben swallowed. "I kept her secret about Oliver to gain her trust. I gave her those books. I promised I would leave Charlotte and take her away," Ben's voice was still cold. "I wanted to take her to Europe. She wanted to come with me. She told me she loved me."

Lizzie closed her eyes, feeling the tight embrace at the end of her dream. "You wanted to make her into a vampire."

"I did," Ben looked away. "But then… she changed her mind."

"What?" Lizzie was startled to finally hear a detail that went beyond her dreams.

"She said she was afraid Charlotte would hurt Oliver if she ran away with me. She suddenly became very protective of that boy – more than she ever was of the Fultons," his voice was still calm, but the disdain in his reference to that boy revealed the heart of his feelings for Oliver. Lizzie felt her stomach turn to stone as she dreaded the completion of the next few sentences. "Charlotte knew Oliver was her friend. I think she even knew his family disapproved of a marriage. She didn't know he wanted to run away with Lily. She didn't know… I told Charlotte that Lily was sneaking off to meet him. I sent a message to Oliver that Lily wanted him to come to the house. The boy couldn't read. He had no idea it wasn't from her. I knew he would find Charlotte instead. I knew because I asked Lily to meet me down at the river."

"You…" Lizzie saw the book under the water again. She remembered Ben coming behind her and kissing her in the marshes. Her eyes filled with tears and barely had the voice for her next sentence. "She loved you."

"I thought Charlotte was going to kill him, like Horace. I didn't think she was going to change him."

"But you…" Lizzie felt her whole body swim. "But you aren't like that. You aren't a murderer."

"I was," Ben didn't unlock the eyes that stared at her. "I never pretended that there aren't things in my past of which I am ashamed."

"You deceived me," Lizzie hardened her jaw as the swimming of her insides shifted into fear.

"If you didn't remember Lily, who was I to tell you?"

"I did remember her."

"In pieces. You didn't remember her connection to Oliver without my help. You didn't even know her name."

"You didn't tell me you wanted to kill Oliver."

"No. I did not."

Lizzie stood up quickly. She looked down at Ben, but decided to walk briskly from the room when the dizziness of her brain affected her balance. She went to the living room and the table where the white roses used to sit. She paced back and forth to consume the agitation of her limbs. She paused in front of the mirror catching the reflection in the shadows of the unlit room. She saw her brown eyes looking back, but all the other features blurred. She squeezed out the tears and rounded back to Ben, standing silently on the other side of the sofa.

"Did you know Oliver went after Lily?"

"Charlotte wasted no time telling me what she did. She told me that he went to see Lily."

"You could have saved her," Lizzie tried to rub the cold out of her arms.

"It's possible." Ben shifted his eyes away from Lizzie.

Lizzie walked through the archway back into the dining room. She looked at her bags resting in front of the buffet. She looked for her coat, not remembering where she left it. She needed to get out of there.

"Elizabeth…" he came behind her and after a pause dared to enclose her in his arms. The pace of her breath increased as he tightened his embrace and rested his chin inside her shoulder. "Don't go. Stay with me."

She took hold of his hand and then used the grasp to unravel herself. "You aren't…" she allowed tears to be the answer to her confused emotions. "Why on earth would Lily come back to *you*?"

Ben dropped his arms and looked at the floor. Lizzie grabbed her bags and walked towards the door, hoping her coat was there. Ben suddenly took hold of her shoulders and forced her eyes to focus on his. "You are not Lily," he said sternly. "You were. Right now you are Elizabeth Watson. What Lily did and what she felt has nothing to do with you."

"Doesn't she?" Lizzie raised her voice, dropping her bags and wrestling free from his firm grip. "I am still an employee of the Fulton House, cleaning furniture and protecting the name of that family. When I'm not there, I am essentially a servant to the hospital. I have her heartlessness with people who love me, when I let myself be loved. Maybe I've been running from it so long because Lily had such tragic consequences to the love in her life… and yet it didn't really matter, did it? In the end I am with the same two men. I suspect if Charlotte were still on this planet, she would also be... The fact is, Ben, even though I didn't know her name until a few months ago, I have been living Lily's life for over thirty years."

"No," Ben took hold of her again.

"Ben," she lost the strength of her anger as he pressed his lips to hers. She couldn't resist him. She wanted him. She wanted to stay with him. She knew she should not. She kept her arms lifeless at her side and allowed his kiss until he pulled away. Lizzie shut her eyes and let the oxygen plunge into the depth of her lungs. "You aren't telling me the whole story, Benjamin. Lily didn't choose you. She went back to Oliver. She went to him and let him close enough to kill her. It's not you."

"Oliver is dangerous, Elizabeth."

"So are you," Lizzie took her bags to the door. She paused for a second, worried that her next step would be too final. She trembled on another sob and walked out of his apartment.

Chapter Twenty-Nine

Lizzie pressed her thumbnail on the edge of the plastic lid and watched it bend under the pressure. She took her next sip and went back to fidgeting her idle hands. She was trying not to think about… to not talk herself out of her offer to meet Oliver. Coffee was harmless. A public place, where she could consume a beverage and not feel awkward while he did nothing… except stare at her.

She glanced at her watch. She was early. Of course she was. She was the one who took off on 128 for two hours before texting him to mandate a location on her drive back. She didn't have a book and didn't think to buy a magazine. There were some well read newspapers, but she couldn't be bothered with current events when so much of the past disturbed her present.

"Hi," his warm voice coaxed her eyes away from her cup.

The pit in her stomach didn't impede the smile that rose to her lips. "Thanks for driving here."

"I imagine you don't want to risk running into anyone, but … Beverly?" Oliver took off his ski jacket and sat. Lizzie liked his zipped sweater. He always looked like he was ready to hike up a mountain.

"I just needed to go some place less familiar," Lizzie looked at the few people in the store. If she was trying to avoid anyone she knew, inevitably she would know someone. But neither the student bent over his laptop with headphones or the group of ladies discussing a recent novel looked familiar.

"Everything okay?" he reached across the table and took one of the hands prying at the plastic lid.

"I…" she met his eyes, knowing he already knew. He knew things about her without her having to speak a word. "I left Ben."

She saw the smile he concealed very quickly. "I'm sorry, Lizzie," his sympathy was genuine. "I imagine that was very difficult for you."

"You were right," Lizzie took back her hand and used it to lift the cup to her lips. "He didn't tell me the whole truth."

"Did you remember something about Lily?"

"I see so many things now," Lizzie looked down. "More vividly than ever."

"What did you see that made you so angry with Ben?"

"That he was there. He was in love with Lily, too," Lizzie had nothing left in her red cup with which to fill the pauses. She took the holiday themed sleeve off the cup and started to tear apart the seam.

"What did Ben say?"

"I can't… I don't want to talk about this right now," Lizzie looked at his dark eyes, feeling their familiarity and warmth. Lizzie glanced at the laughing book group and student still distracted by earphones. "Can we leave here?"

Oliver smiled and followed her lead out of the store. Lizzie wasn't sure where they could go. It was too cold for a walk. Oliver motioned to his Jeep. "It's warm."

Lizzie sat in the passenger seat and watched as he turned on the ignition but left off the headlights. "When do you go back to LA?"

"I have a flight booked for Friday," he turned to her. "But…"

"What?"

"I'm on sabbatical."

"You have a life there."

"I could have a life here."

"What are you saying?"

"I'm saying things are…" he rested his hands against the steering wheel. "I have a job offer."

"Your students…"

"There are students in Boston."

"Oliver… this isn't," she felt a hard lump in her throat. "I don't know what I want. I don't want you to change everything simply because…"

"You know what? I was invited to attend a fundraiser for an environmental non-profit this Friday. I wasn't going to attend. But I'll stay through the week and you can come with me."

"A fundraiser?"

"Would it be too much like work?"

"I don't know," Lizzie swallowed, not really worried about any similarity to the Mt. Elm gala.

"There's dancing," he showed a full out grin that charged the nerves in Lizzie's stomach.

"Dancing is nice."

"We can get dressed up," he touched her hair.

"That sounds…" Lizzie let herself meet his eager gaze. He leaned closer and kissed her lips. Lizzie heard her mind say it wasn't right. She walked out of Ben's apartment only five hours ago. It was easy to lose those thoughts with the sensation of Oliver's intoxicating touches. She remembered the thrill of his lovemaking at the Fulton House. She moved her hands to his waist and fingered the zipper of his jeans until the image of blue ink running under water flashed in her memory.

"I need to go home," she gasped as she pulled away.

Oliver sat upright and caught his own breath. "We can go somewhere."

"It's too soon," Lizzie's voice trembled as she clutched the door handle. "I'll see you Friday."

Oliver warmed his smile and covered the look of frustration. "I'll pick you up at 7."

"Yes," she grabbed her bag and went to her car filled with belongings from Ben's apartment.

*****

Lizzie bought a new dress for the fundraiser. She only had two that fit her. One was the red dress she wore to her reunion, the night she met Ben – the vampire. She couldn't bring herself to wear it again or throw it away. Her other dress wouldn't conceal the marks on her neck or her recently returned flaws. The new dress wasn't ideal, but it had a high collar and impressed Meg when Lizzie opened her bedroom door. "You look nice."

"I'm going out."

"The brother?"

Lizzie nodded, afraid anything else would inspire the guilt she pushed from her mind.

"So you are going to date him?"

"I don't know."

"You look like you are pretty serious about dating him right now."

Lizzie's cheeks burned. She didn't make up her mind if there would be anything after this night. She had more questions to ask him. Things she felt she should know before she could decide what she wanted… what she felt. If she should love him. Did she? Or if she should feel guilty for hurting Ben. She did. In every quiet moment of the day.

Meg paused in silence for a few minutes. She breathed out and straightened her expression. "Um, listen, Ben stopped by today."

"What?" Lizzie felt her knees weaken.

"I didn't have class until two. This morning he brought over a box of things he said you left behind. I didn't know what to do with it. I put it in my room. He said it's just clothes and books."

"Books?"

"I'll go get it."

Lizzie pulled in a deep breath to swallow the urge to cry. She held the door to stop from losing balance while Meg went around the corner into her room. She came back within a minute and put the box on top of Lizzie's bed. Lizzie opened it without hesitation. She saw a couple sweaters and several of the leather bound books. On top was Byron. She lifted it and dared to look at the blurred blue sonnet. Why did he give that to her? What was the point of that?

"You probably want to finish getting ready," Meg looked at Lizzie carefully and left the room. Lizzie kept staring at the book, hoping the image of the water and grass would come back to her. She knew there was something more to that, something Ben wanted her to remember. She closed her eyes and only saw blackness.

The doorbell rang and disturbed her focus. She scurried through the chaos of her bedroom and down the staircase. She opened the door and saw him dressed in a long black coat, erasing all the images of the outdoorsy Oliver.

"I need my shoes and a coat," she shuddered as the air blew across her bare forearms.

"So this is where you live."

"Yeah," Lizzie stopped at the top of the stairs. She turned to say she was going to run upstairs, but he used the opportunity to kiss her passionately on the lips. She wrapped her arms around him and quickly lost awareness until she heard a door open at the top of the stairs.

Lizzie stepped back and quickly checked the mirror for smudged lipstick. She faced Meg as she landed on the bottom step. "Hi."

"Hi," Meg's eyes moved beyond Lizzie to Oliver. "You must be the brother."

He offered the charming smile that must have endeared so many young students to Professor Ol. Lizzie wondered if Meg was in any way susceptible. "I'm Oliver."

"Meg," she accepted his hand. "Where are you taking Lizzie?"

"A fundraiser for an environmental coalition."

"Lizzie knows all about fundraisers."

"There's a baseball star hosting."

"Lizzie doesn't like sports."

"I like the environment," Lizzie was surprised by Meg's bitterness. Apparently she determined to channel Nora that evening. "I need shoes."

When she returned down the stairs, Meg still looked at Oliver without saying a word. "It's supposed to snow, you know," Meg muttered as Lizzie put on her coat. "You shouldn't stay out too late."

"I'll take care of her," Oliver was undeterred by Meg's smarminess. Lizzie didn't say goodbye as they went down the stairs.

"You do want to go to this thing?" Oliver broke the silence as he opened the door of his Jeep for her.

"Yeah," Lizzie sat in the car as he walked to his door.

"We could just skip it and go to the hotel room."

"Hotel room?" she felt his eyes looking over her.

"No, that's a bit presumptive," he turned on the ignition.

"I like dancing," Lizzie shrugged. "No one has ever taken me out to dance before."

"Excellent," Oliver smiled as they pulled away. Lizzie watched the blur of Christmas tree lights they passed. Ben didn't take her out to dance. But they danced at the reunion and there was… there was another time she couldn't remember…

*****

"Your honest opinion?" Oliver shut the closet door where he hung their coats.

"I told you," Lizzie gazed down onto the lights of Boylston Street. The blanket of snow made the Christmas decorations of downtown Boston look more festive. "I thought it was a good event. Better than anything we could do at the hospital."

"I doubt that," he rested his chin on the top of her head.

Lizzie thought about turning from the window into him. She wasn't ready to kiss him. Not yet. There wasn't much conversation over the loud band or polite talk with Oliver's colleagues. "Where do you stay when you come east?"

"A friend's apartment."

"Another vampire?"

"A source." Oliver removed his sports coat and loosened his tie. She didn't realize she was so blatantly watching until he smiled after unclasping the third button of his shirt. She still wasn't ready and found a chair and finally removed her heels.

"I thought the band was excellent," Oliver stopped at the third button and settled into the chair opposite. "I had fun dancing."

"That was the best part."

"It was," Oliver didn't attempt to shield the lust in his eyes. She already noted there was no burn there and felt comfortable he fed recently. Except that Oliver wasn't… he wasn't Ben. Did that mean he did something else recently?

Lizzie looked at Oliver. He was so handsome. So very, very handsome. And charming. Like Will. Like Meg. How long before his attention would be diverted from her? "Why did you fall in love with Charlotte?"

Oliver expressed a knowing smile and exhaled a deep breath.

"Why," Lizzie continued, "if you loved Lily so much, would you fall in love with the monster who interfered in your happiness?"

"I asked myself that question many times," he avoided her eyes. "Especially when it ended. In the beginning, she was the only vampire I knew. Benjamin went back to France. Charlotte brought me with her to New York. It was a volatile friendship. There was physical attraction.

There was a lot of hate that made that attraction even more… strangely enough… exciting."

"Is that why you let Charlotte change you?"

"Charlotte was waiting for me. I thought Lily would be there. I knew someone in that house was using her, the way Horace did. I knew it made her unhappy. I didn't know it was a … I didn't believe that she loved him. She wanted to leave. She was going to marry me."

"Charlotte convinced you that wasn't true."

"She showed me a book he bought her. There were things scribbled inside, but I couldn't read them. I was never educated enough to impress Lily. I knew she was intelligent, something those Fultons refused to appreciate. The fact another man bought her books and appealed to her mind… Charlotte knew my weakness. She convinced me Lily was lost. I let her seduce me and take my blood. I don't remember that night clearly. It's a horrible, thrilling dream."

Lizzie saw sadness creep across his face, as if Charlotte's revelations were a recent conversation. She tried to think of the book under the water and the kiss in the marshy grass. No detail surfaced. She couldn't think of anything to prove or disprove what Charlotte told him.

"She manipulated the truth," Oliver's expression changed from sad to something both uninterested and intensely angry. It was as though he could distance himself from the reality of Charlotte, but not her trickery. "Lily was telling Benjamin that she was leaving him."

"What?"

"He didn't tell you?" Oliver had no sense of alarm.

"No."

"He told me after Charlotte died," Oliver looked at her briefly. "I didn't know that when I saw Lily. I… didn't know."

Lizzie knew the next part of the story, but didn't want the detail. "What did the Fultons do when Lily died?"

"The Fultons never knew. Charlotte had her buried in a common grave. She told Margaret and John she and ran off with me to Kentucky. It was one of Charlotte's cruel jokes. The world thought we were together, when I was the one who…"

"She had the last laugh."

"No, she didn't."

"Because you killed her?" Lizzie asked lightly, even though the thought terrified her.

"Because you are here with me," he lifted her from her chair. "Let's stop talking about the past, Lizzie. Let us focus on the here and now."

Lizzie took in a deep breath as he lifted her chin gently and pulled her towards his mouth. She moved her lips against his and forced the questions from her mind. He didn't want to talk any longer. She knew the answers to her questions still hurt him. His hurt more than anything tugged at her heart. She didn't want to hurt him again. She chose Ben and broke his heart. She chose him again without even giving Oliver a chance to tell her the truth, the truth of his sadness. Ben denied Oliver the opportunity to tell her. Ben hurt him. Ben hurt her. So she didn't let herself think about how she was hurting Ben as Oliver's hands reached around for the back of her dress.

*****

Lizzie loosened herself from Oliver's arms and slipped into the bathroom. She let the steam of the luxurious shower fill the room. She knew she dreamt something in those few hours, but nothing remained after she opened her eyes. Nothing except a feeling of loss. She hoped the sound of water would refresh her memory – just to let her know if it was something of Lizzie or of Lily.

She knew there was a reason she didn't remember. Maybe it was a bad dream. If she woke with such a depressed feeling, how could it have been happy? She was happy… wasn't she? She was with a man who was in love with her. He didn't say it – but Lizzie was quite certain he was - and had been for centuries. It was different from Ben's emotion. There was something more human about Oliver's love for Lily. It was almost as if his attraction to Lizzie was an attempt to be his old self again.

Was it Lizzie? Or was it Lily that made Oliver enclose his arms around her in a contented, sleeping embrace? Lizzie convinced herself that Ben only wanted Lily… but was Oliver any different? Was he at all aware of Elizabeth Watson? Were they separate? Or were they really the same? Whose thoughts were floating through her mind? Who agreed to go out with Oliver and follow him back to a hotel room? If she was Lily, did she have the right to hurt Ben for what he did to her? Isn't that why she was upset with him? Why she no longer felt she could be with him? Did Lily just realize what he did to Oliver? Was it Lily telling her to stay away from Ben and go back to… go back… she wasn't going back to Oliver. Elizabeth was never with Oliver. Elizabeth didn't love Oliver. Did Lily?

She was attracted to him. It wasn't difficult to leave her mind when he kissed her. Was that Lily taking over… or just a baser instinct reacting to his good looks and seduction? Lizzie was attracted to his vampire. Her heart bled for the broken soul within him, but her desire to be close to him made her forget her conscious and go to some other place in her thoughts. Where her shame and fear couldn't stop her. She didn't fear him, in spite of Ben's repetitive warnings. How legitimate could they be? He just wanted to keep him from her, to keep her from knowing the truth. To keep her from knowing the monster Ben really was.

Lizzie's thoughts halted as she rinsed the shampoo from her hair. Was he a monster? She loved Ben. He never hurt her. He promised to never hurt her… physically. He kept the truth from her. But how much did she want this truth? Did she want to know all this? Wasn't it easier, wasn't she happier when she didn't know Lily? She always knew Lily. Lily was always a part of her. But not… not the part that chose Oliver.

The tears mingled with soapy water that ran from her hair. She loved Ben. She missed him. She missed his arms. She missed the freckles under his eyes. His gray green eyes that were always full of … what did Meg say once? Something about love and insatiable desire. If he was looking at her, he saw Elizabeth. Not Lily. He didn't tell her about Lily because he loved Elizabeth. She didn't let herself believe that. She let the doubt register in her mind when he went to Chicago. She let it be her excuse to hurt him.

But Oliver… he was still there. He wanted her. He wanted Lily. He fell in love easily. He could fall out of love just as easily. Could he with Lily? Or was Lily his soul mate? If that was the case, why didn't Lizzie feel that? Why didn't she ache for the embrace of his arms and leap out of the shower to seek them for comfort? Why did Lily choose Oliver if it wasn't for love? Was it really just an escape? How could an escape to Kentucky be preferable to Europe? Why did Lily hurt Ben so that he made sure Charlotte took out her wrath on Oliver… on Thomas? Tom. Her Tom. There was something else, something missing. A detail that was in the corner of her memory, but hidden in the shadows of a lost dream. What was it? To whom would it lead? Oliver? Ben? Or back to herself? Maybe… maybe that was what Lily wanted all along. Lizzie liked her solitude. She liked having time to herself. She liked her room at Jefferson Park. She liked her runs in the quiet of the morning. Maybe that was all Lily ever craved. Maybe Lily realized the monsters that both men were and wanted no more of it. That was why she chose to die.

Lizzie washed away the tears by the time left the bathroom and was back in her clothes. Oliver waited in the hotel robe looking out at the view of Boylston Street. "We got a lot of snow last night," he turned to her and smiled.

"Oh?" Lizzie noticed a room service cart in the corner of the room.

"I ordered a couple options for breakfast. I didn't know what you…"

"That's very sweet," Lizzie poured a mug of coffee and looked over the assortment of fruit and muffins.

"I think we're trapped here," Oliver looked at her dress, not shielding the disappointment in his eyes. "They haven't cleared the roads very well yet. Do you have to be at the Fulton House?"

"Not today," Lizzie shook her head over the mug and sat in the chair she found the night before. She knew why he was asking. She couldn't think of any real reason she had to go anywhere. She was only half certain she wanted to stay.

"Do you like the snow? We could build a snowman on the Common."

Lizzie smiled without thinking. "That would be… I dressed for dancing. Not for snow."

"Right…" Oliver looked at his scattered suit. "My students would laugh at this situation. Professor Ol too dressed up for the outdoors."

"You are fond of your students," she mulled over her coffee. "Would you really give them up to come back to Boston?"

Oliver sat in the chair near her. "It would be a pretty big choice, Lizzie. But if… I would consider it, yes."

"Why?"

"Because life is too short to listen to doubt."

"Life isn't too short for you."

"No. But my time with people is."

"Is that why you've changed the women you fell in love with? This sense of urgency?"

"I never thought about it that way."

"Then when you have forever, you realize you don't want it."

He looked away from her. "With some… but not with all."

"How many have there been, Oliver?" Lizzie knew the answer would be different than Ben's.

Oliver shook his head and laughed with another mischievous glance at Lizzie. "I really couldn't say."

"How many did you love?"

"Most of them."

"How many did you kill?"

Oliver straightened his spine and stood up from the chair. "Did you ask Ben these questions?"

"Yes."

He walked towards the giant mirror by the closet. "Charlotte was a bad influence on me, Lizzie."

"I don't care about Charlotte. I want to know about you."

"Too many."

Lizzie saw the saddened expression in his reflection. "Did that change after you… after Charlotte died?"

"Yes," he looked at her.

"I never see her. Not once in my memories or dreams."

"You are lucky."

Lizzie wanted him to finish his thought. What was so painful about that vampire that he couldn't tell her? What did it have to do with Lily? What did she do to make him eliminate her from this earth? What did it have to do with Lily's final choice?

She saw the pain on his face and in the sag of his shoulders. She felt her own cruelty for pressing the issue, for diverting him from his happiness. Happiness that he waited two centuries to find again. Happiness she was about to take away.

"Charlotte told me you would come back," Oliver was looking at her, but his mind was somewhere else.

"What?" Lizzie felt a chill on her shoulders.

"She told me about reincarnation. She was obsessed with it. She always believed Lily would come back to me. "

"To you? Not to her?"

"She told me Lily would come back to kill me because I killed her."

"No," she shook her head fervently. "I am not a killer."

"She was wrong, Lizzie," he knelt in front of her. "I have karma coming at me from so many directions."

"But Charlotte took your life and then you…"

Oliver pried one of her hands away from the mug. "Charlotte could only see hate and evil acts. I told you, she was here too long. She had no perspective. She didn't understand forgiveness because she never gave any."

"I don't want to kill you," Lizzie's voice trembled.

"I know."

"I…" she tried to speak but Oliver pulled her into a kiss to stop her words. He slid his hand under her dress, burning against her thigh. She felt her mind slipping away once more. She couldn't do it. No matter how good it felt in the moment, she knew the moments after would make her cry. She shut her eyes and stopped moving her lips against his. He pulled away a few inches without removing his hand.

"We can't go anywhere," his breath was warm against her face.

She opened her eyes to meet his gaze. "I need to go home."

"It will take forever to get my car out," he touched her cheek with a gentle kiss.

"I'll take the train," she clenched her jaw.

"Don't go," he moved his hand closer. She grabbed it and pushed him away.

"I can't do this," she stood up quickly.

"What?" Oliver reached for her hand.

She shook it off and found her stockings on the floor. "I can't be with you, Oliver. Go back to California."

"Lizzie, let's talk about this."

"I don't want to talk anymore."

"Are you going back to Ben?"

"I …" she lost her breath over another sob. "I need to be by myself."

"You are frightened. I shouldn't have told you what Charlotte said."

"It isn't about Charlotte."

Oliver nodded slowly and went back to the view of Boylston Street. "You still love him."

"Of course I still love him," she raised her voice. "I never stopped. I don't think I ever will."

"Even though he lied?"

"We all lie," Lizzie started rolling her stockings up her legs. "Maybe in this life, Oliver, Lily finally breaks free from vampires." As the words left her, a strange cool clarity seeped into her mind. "Maybe I came back this time to release you."

"Release me," he repeated quietly to the window.

"Maybe, Oliver," she found her heels under the chair. "Maybe you keep looking for Lily in all those women you fall for. When they aren't Lily, you lose interest."

"But you ARE Lily."

"I don't want to live the life that Lily didn't finish," she felt the confidence of her emotion. "I want my own life."

He left the window quickly and pulled her tightly into his hold. She felt trapped beneath his strength. "This is your life. It has always been your life, Lizzie. Maybe you don't know it yet. This is where you are meant to be."

She let the tears form in her eyes, afraid to make the slightest movement from the clutch of his arms. "I want… I want to figure that out for myself, Oliver."

"You want to be alone," he dropped his hands and stepped away.

"I'm sorry," she went for her coat in the closet.

"I will wait Lizzie."

"Don't," she walked out the door.

Chapter Thirty

Lizzie took the straw out of its wrapper and swirled it around in the ice water. She was accustomed to awkward silences with Sara. They slipped into their conversation frequently. It wasn't much different from every other annual meeting they had to catch up. Only this time, Lizzie carefully ordered the salmon and was mimicking Sara's sobriety. And yet there was Sara, as skinny as ever, ordering a steak. How could she achieve that after a fourth baby?

Sara was happy. Lizzie wasn't going to discredit the smile, even with the hint of sorrow about her dad's absence at the holiday. Sara may have lived in a cloud of reality Lizzie didn't accept. But the truth was, Sara was genuinely happy. She may not know the thrill of a vampire's kiss or bite. She would condemn it if she would let herself believe in such things. But Sara knew the thrill of a husband who loved her and children who claimed her as a mother. She had a happy, normal life.

Was anything really normal? Most years she looked at Sara's smile and condemned it as ignorant. This year she couldn't help but envy it.

"It's really too bad about you and Ben," Sara didn't waste any time after the waitress set their food down.

"It is too bad," Lizzie took a sip of her water. "I really… loved him."

"Well, God never closes a door without opening a window."

"I suppose not," Lizzie felt as though she was trapped without any doors or windows.

"Is anyone else a possibility?"

"A possibility?"

"Lizzie," Sara shook her head and took a sip of her iced tea. "Before you know it, you will be forty. Don't you want to be married and a mother by then?"

Lizzie looked at her, uncertain what to say. She didn't want to get married. She didn't want to be with anyone. How could she explain that to Sara, who lived and breathed her role as doting wife and mother? How could she tell Sara she had enough of relationships, not just in this life but in two? "Not everyone needs to get married to be happy," Lizzie picked up her fork.

Sara laughed in disbelief. "You don't really believe that, do you?"

"Why wouldn't I?"

"Well what else … it's not like you have a career, Lizzie," Sara shut her mouth and took up her knife to slice the sirloin. Lizzie watched the juices run out of the meat and seep into the potatoes. "How's Jack doing?"

Lizzie's eyes left Sara's plate and met her eyes. "He's doing well," she breathed out slowly, surprised something Sara said could sting her so profoundly. "His son Zach is starting to play guitar."

"Kids are amazing," Sara took a bite of her steak.

Lizzie slid her fork into her salmon, debating whether to indulge a jab or let the conversation fade into the hum of other voices talking around them. If she was still with Ben, there would still be an awkward conversation about marriage and children. If she was still with Ben, she would be living with him without a ring on her finger. If she was still with Ben… why did she let the idea enter her mind?

"How is Josie?" Lizzie filled the silence between the bites. She wasn't able to leave the subject of children.

"She is growing so quickly," Sara's sour attitude brightened immediately to a smile. "She is such a joy. She has been a perfect comfort this first year without Dad. Especially the first Christmas."

"I can imagine," Lizzie looked at the pink flesh on her plate. "And Ted?"

"He might be getting a promotion at the bank."

"Very good," Lizzie felt the sharpness of Sara's comment about career and wondered if the inspiration for pleasantries had dried up.

"Did you hear about Melissa Benson?"

"They found her body," Lizzie stared at her untouched food, wishing the conversation would revert to marriage and children.

"They say it's difficult to determine the cause of death at this point."

"It was raining the night she disappeared," Lizzie muttered the detail she heard several times in recent months.

"I think it was foul play," Sara put the knife through her steak again. "She grew up in those woods. How would she not know where the brook was?"

"Maybe she wasn't in the right frame of mind."

"True," Sara closed her mouth over her next bite. "She was an unusual girl."

"I didn't know her very well," Lizzie breathed in slowly and looked directly at Sara. "I can't say I remember if she was unusual or not."

"She used to date Kyle Granger. Jack didn't like him."

"Yeah, well, Jack didn't like pretty much everyone in high school."

"Kyle was into D & D and all that stuff. Don't you think he might have had something to do with it?"

"With Melissa?" Lizzie made herself raise her eyebrow in alarm. She didn't want to show she had any knowledge whatsoever of why Melissa was not in her right mind the night she fell and drowned. That she knew Melissa had her blood drained by a vampire. That she tricked the vampire. "No, I don't think Kyle had anything to do with that."

"But she was cheating on him."

"What?" Lizzie lost the reserve of her pretense.

"She used to sneak around with Ben's brother," Sara looked at her. Lizzie wondered if her revelation was really about Melissa or just an attempt to say she knew more about the Cottinghams than Lizzie. Not that she had any clue about the Cottingham boys or how they were connected to Melissa's death.

"How do you know that?"

"She told me on the bus one day. She wanted to know what I knew about Oliver and Ben. She mostly wanted to know about Ben."

"What did she want to know about Ben?"

"Just trivial stuff. I don't remember. His favorite color. His favorite food."

"Why would she ask *you* that?"

"I assume she wanted to get on his good side to impress Oliver. I don't know, Lizzie. It was so long ago. That was really the only time I ever had a conversation with her."

"Did you tell Ben?"

"I don't think it matters," she hesitated over her next bite and then set it down. "You know, I wondered if Oliver might be a suspect. But he was already in Oregon or wherever it was he went to college."

"California."

"Well wherever it was, he wasn't still in Coldbrook. Maybe she got all depressed because he moved away," Sara shrugged. "She didn't understand why I didn't like Ben."

"Why didn't you like Ben, Sara?"

"He wasn't my type," Sara said lightly. "He always seemed… I don't know… old. I suppose that didn't bother you, Lizzie. You always liked history and stuff like that. But Ben just wasn't that much fun in high school. Anyway, I'm kind of relieved you aren't seeing him anymore. He always made me uncomfortable."

"In what way?"

"Well, he was always there. Watching things. He was weird, too. Just like Melissa. And Kyle Granger. I bet he was into that D & D stuff as well."

"He…" Lizzie began a thought and lost it as the tears tempted her again. Why didn't she remember Ben so well in high school? Why hadn't she paid attention to him if he was someone she knew and loved in another lifetime? Why didn't she recognize him when she was the age that Lily was when she met him?

"It is too bad that she died so young," Sara concluded the topic. "But she is at peace now."

"She is now," Lizzie scooped up some rice on her fork. Who was to say that Melissa Benson wasn't going to come back someday?

"You know, Lizzie, Ted's cousin just got divorced last year," Sara slowly patted her lips with her napkin. "He lives in Boston. I could give him your phone number."

Lizzie breathed in and stopped herself from rolling her eyes. She simply smiled and took another bite of her meal.

*****

Lizzie held a small paper plate in her hand, hesitating over the table of hors d'oeuvres. She picked up a few vegetables and let her eyes wander to the window. She could see the apartments across the street and a few buildings behind them. Just a few streets over was Ben's. It was the closest she was to his place in nearly three weeks. Those three weeks seemed like three months in a lot of ways. She ached to see him again, to see the freckles under his green eyes smiling at her. She could tell him she was missing something. A shoe. A hairbrush. And she did just happen to be in the neighborhood.

Three weeks wasn't enough. It was two weeks since she walked away from Oliver. She wouldn't open his message. She left it amongst the other neglected messages of her inbox. The confusion was still swirling in her brain making everything unclear. The only clear thing was that she had to resist taking every tempting piece of food off that table and scarfing it down.

Lizzie heard a conversation swell as Davis led some of his theater friends towards the table of food. She didn't have to turn to recognize the fact Will was among them. She couldn't face him. Not when Oliver's teeth marks were still red beneath her collar.

She found Andrew in the kitchen, stationed with Davis' martini shaker plus a table of food to stop her from repeating her party habits. He was in a crowd of work friends. Lizzie lingered by the empty kitchen table, contemplating a plunge into the seven layer dip. She hoped she could hold it together for just one more hour. A half hour. Then she could leave. If she couldn't… if she fell apart in the next ten minutes, she would run to Ben's apartment. She didn't care. She needed someone who wouldn't think she was crazy or some pathetic loser who couldn't keep a boyfriend. But Ben… Ben wouldn't want to see her. She was worse than crazy or pathetic to him.

"So what's this Paula was saying?" Andrew put an arm over her shoulders. "You aren't coming back to the Fulton House?"

"I just thought I'd take a couple months off is all," Lizzie pulled her confidence out of thin air.

"You will come back?" Andrew pouted. "You're the only one with a sense of humor in that place."

"I'll be back," Lizzie didn't want to think about the Fultons or the impulse that prompted her to say something to Paula an hour earlier. She wanted a few extra Saturdays. She wanted a break from… Lily.

"Are you okay?" Andrew rubbed her back.

"I've been better," Lizzie let her eyes rest again on the seven layer dip. It would taste so very, very good.

"I have something for you," Andrew coaxed her out of the kitchen towards the bedrooms.

"Oh really?" she managed some sarcasm.

"Davis will be upset that I gave it to you without him. But he invited Will, so whatever," Andrew pulled her hand into their room. He opened the closet door and pulled out a gift bag. Lizzie took the cue and pulled out a circle of tissue paper. She unraveled it to reveal a small hinged painted box.

"This is exquisite," Lizzie almost feared to touch it.

"We went antiquing this fall. It's an old powder box. There's even still some powder in it."

Lizzie opened it up to a dusty puff of air. "All I need is a beauty mark."

"Careful, that stuff is toxic. Probably has mercury or lead," Andrew laughed. "Just don't eat it."

"Okay," Lizzie realized she no longer had as much risk touching lead as she had two weeks ago. "Andrew, this is really sweet. It's beautiful."

"I wanted to give it to you as a .... Christ, I wanted it to be your something old when you married Ben. But even if you aren't marrying him, it's yours."

"Thanks," Lizzie couldn't stop the tears.

"Not that I don't think you'll get married," Andrew said quickly. "It's just... well, I can't give that to you when it's someone different."

"It's okay, Andrew."

"I'm disappointed you won't be living in the neighborhood, Lizzie," he sighed. She remembered Andrew's fondness of Ben, but knew his loyalty was with her. She hadn't told him about Oliver, but knew there would be a night when she would indulge in one of Davis' martinis and tell all. They would forgive her, just as Meg and Nora had. They were her friends, even if they were her critics. They would help her get on her feet again, even if she didn't know where to go when she got there.

Chapter Thirty-one

Lizzie rolled up her spine and collected her breath before stepping into the store. It was three miles to the one and only store in Coldbrook from her parents' house. She went inside to buy some water and returned to the mild January air. She went behind the store where some picnic tables overlooked the water. They were abandoned for the winter but a good height to stretch her hamstrings before running the three miles back.

There was a sweetness in the unnaturally warm air. The water was normally covered with ice at that time of year. Instead it reflected the gray cloudy sky like platinum film. There was just the soft rattle of a few branches in the lilting trees. She wondered if any of the lake fed the springs. Did it have the same mystical waters that lured Maria to Coldbrook a hundred years before?

She was surprisingly calm. She spent the holidays and the weeks after concentrating on running and not eating. The focus provided release from the confusion of her emotions. She was happy in her solitude. She was satisfied with her choice to go back to herself. Relieved to longer have thoughts that didn't belong to her life.

She was fortunate to have the gala fast approaching and leave her with fewer idle moments at the hospital. She withdrew from her friends and social activity. She didn't have to answer more questions about what happened with Ben. It was easier to run herself into exhaustion and go home to bed. It made her dreams quiet. Lily went back to whatever dark corner of her mind from which she was disturbed by Ben and Oliver.

She was aware of someone watching. She took in a deep breath as she dropped her leg back to the ground and turned around slowly to see Oliver. Lizzie looked away from him and breathed in to contemplate her reaction. She couldn't deny the thrill of seeing his tall, strong physique and moody dark eyes. But it disturbed that calm she recently realized.

"Hi," he entreated quietly.

Lizzie picked up her water bottle. "Hi."

"I didn't mean to startle you," he bit his lip, keeping a wary distance from her. "I saw you walk out of the store as I drove by and… I just … I wanted to say hi."

"Okay," she felt her nerves enliven as he took a step closer. She hadn't been with anyone since she walked out of the hotel room five weeks before. She ran off that frustration and loneliness every day. Was it desire that excited her so suddenly? Or was it something else? She stepped back from his advance. "Why are you in Coldbrook?"

"I was checking on the house."

"The house?"

"The one Ben and I still own on Scott Road."

"Right," she nodded to hide her complete ignorance. Ben never told her they still owned property together. In Coldbrook.

"Ben wants to sell it."

"Oh," Lizzie felt a sudden letdown. Did that mean Ben didn't want to come back to Coldbrook?

"It's good to see you."

"Yes," Lizzie couldn't make an expression of joy or frustration. She took another sip of water and looked at the lake.

"Are you visiting your family?"

"I am," Lizzie let herself look back at his hungry dark eyes.

"It's a good day for a run," he took another hesitant step towards her.

"I'm training for the Boston Marathon."

"Good for you," he took one more step.

"Did you talk to Ben?"

"I did," Oliver stopped moving towards her.

"And he told you he wants to sell the house?"

"He wants to sever ties with me, Lizzie."

"Oh," she twisted the cap back on the water bottle. Tightly.

"He told me to stay away from you," Oliver continued. "There wasn't a lot of sentiment."

"He told you… why?"

"That isn't for him to tell me. You don't want that, do you?"

"Oliver," Lizzie felt a strange apprehension settle over her. "I told you before. Nothing has changed since I left the hotel."

"You've had time to think about it, haven't you?"

"I miss…" she shut her eyes, thinking of the sensation of her blood flowing out of her neck and warming another strong body.

Oliver put his arm around her waist and pulled himself closer to her. "You left him," he kissed her. Lizzie dropped her bottle and let him open her mouth and captivate her lips for several minutes. The exhilaration of her run sped up her heart and aroused her senses to his touch. It felt so good, so warm, so familiar. Like the dream that left her. It came back with his kiss. Oliver lifted her off the ground and carried her towards the back wall of the store. She saw the green hedges and felt the sensation of that long forgotten memory. She breathed out as he moved his kiss from her lips and down to her neck. She leaned her head against the wall as Oliver inhaled a warm breath from her skin. She knew it was the sensation she craved, but the panic she didn't let enter her mind before suddenly motivated her.

"No," she unclasped one of her arms and pushed his head up to face her. "It's too soon."

"What?"

"It hasn't been two months," she felt suddenly frightened, still pinned against the wall. "My blood isn't… Ben says it has to be two months."

"Ben is a fussy eater," Oliver growled.

Lizzie pushed her hands against his shoulders and managed to get her feet back on the ground. He paused for a few seconds, his hands still holding the side of her hips. He looked into her eyes, showing the burn of his hunger and the lust for her. She wanted to be touched, to feed him. She wanted to make the sadness buried beneath the hunger leave his eyes. She let him kiss her lips and neck again. He started gently but let his hunger propel his aggression. He lifted her legs again, startling Lizzie back to reality. "No," she pushed him away. He pressed against her resistance, forcing her head against the wall.

Her eyes watered and looked away from him, unable to make any other movement within his strong hold. "Lizzie," Oliver let her down gently, making the shame evident in his voice.

She walked away from him, feeling the intensity of the pain resonate on her skull. She wanted to cry and have someone hug her to make it go away. Not his arms. She preferred to suffer it alone. "I have to run home. I can't… I need that blood more than you do," she forced her kindness, more out of fear than empathy.

"Let me drive you home."

"No." Lizzie picked up her water bottle.

"I'm sorry, Lizzie. I didn't mean to hurt you."

Lizzie looked at his sad eyes. She could tell he was sincere, but no longer believed he could control himself. "I think you should go, Oliver."

"It was an accident."

"Why are you here?" she asked abruptly. "Why aren't you in California? Couldn't you have made a decision about the house without coming back to Coldbrook?"

"I wanted to … I hoped that I might see you."

"I don't live here. How did you know I would be here this weekend?" she gripped the water bottle tightly.

"I…" he faded, but looked at her with the answer in his eyes. An answer he was too ashamed to admit.

"Please leave me alone. I don't want to see you any more, Oliver."

"Are you worried about Ben?"

"I'm worried about me."

"No. I would never…"

"Oliver, you just hurt me," Lizzie walked towards the front of the store.

He took her arm and held her back. "I didn't want to hurt you."

"You didn't want to hurt Lily either," Lizzie let her fear show.

He released her wrist and let her turn away from him. "Lizzie," he called in a voice that was barely audible. She let herself look back at him. He was crumbling. She saw the terrified boy from the hedges looking at her. "I'll go back to California. I will leave you be."

She shut her eyes. "Thank you."

"I'm… I am very sorry, Lizzie." She heard his footsteps pass her. She opened her eyes to watch him get into his Jeep. He paused and gazed through the windshield. Then he started the ignition and pulled away.

The silence of the winter air descended around her again. He was gone. Lizzie knew she should feel relief. Instead she felt a deep penetrating sorrow. Muted only by fear.

*****

Lizzie took a breath as she went up the stairs. She almost felt guilty accepting the open door from the downstairs neighbor. She was a sweet woman who remarked something about not seeing her lately. Lizzie smiled and managed a polite answer about being busy. Nothing too suspicious. Hopefully … hopefully he wouldn't be angry for her intrusion.

She hesitated at the second floor landing. She allowed another doubt to enter her mind. There was no contact since December. He wouldn't want to see her. He wouldn't want to see her if she was upset because she let Oliver attempt to seduce her again. Wouldn't Ben tell her she deserved the consequence? She made her choice. She made the choice that Oliver wasn't … she walked away from Oliver. In the end she told him to go. Oliver went. He didn't attempt to call her or send an email or make any contact in the week since.

The apprehension didn't go away. No matter how many miles she ran on the tread mill. No matter how long the days were at the hospital. There was still something at the back of her mind left by the fact he hurt her. Not with any desire to bring her harm. She couldn't completely deny that she wanted him to go further. He let it get out of control. Her runner's high and his hunger blurred their judgment. Her poor judgment for allowing his intimate touch. His instinct overtook him, a haste and fury to get what he wanted without stopping. Lizzie understood absent-minded fury. She didn't understand how the sweet sad eyes could hurt her without thinking.

Perhaps she was making a bigger deal than necessary. It allowed her to make the trip back to his street. To walk up the stairs and knock on his door. It wasn't a decision to go back to him. She just… wanted to see him. To say she was sorry. Because she was wrong. She made a horrible mistake. Would Ben forgive her when she explained what happened? Could he look at her and not have hurt in his eyes?

She knocked fervently at the door. He might not hear it if he was in his office. If he had any inkling it was her, he might not answer it. It was seven weeks. Seven weeks since she left this apartment that was almost her own. Seven weeks since she let Lily cloud her head and motivations. Seven weeks since a vampire took her blood.

She knocked again. She had to… she had to see him to make things right in her own mind. She held her breath as she heard the unclasping of the chain and the door opened. She didn't recognize the young man standing in front of her. "Is Ben here?" her voice and her courage faltered.

"No," the young man managed a smile.

"Will he be back soon?" It took a lot of effort to bring herself to that street, to walk those stairs, and to knock on the door. She didn't know if she could do it again.

"He's in Chicago," the boy explained. Who was he? Why was he in Ben's apartment while he was out of town? Lizzie stared at him and noticed a bandage on the inside of his arm. He was a donor.

"But he'll be back?" Lizzie continued, as a woman come down the hallway towards the door.

"He's in Chicago indefinitely," he looked at the woman, who was holding a book. One of Ben's books. One of her books.

"Are you staying here?" Lizzie glared at the girl, who was wearing a turtleneck.

"I'm staying here until he sells it," the boy … he was too young to have such a nice apartment as Ben's… looked at her softly.

"How? How do you know Ben?"

"I work for him," the boy answered kindly.

"Can we help you with something?" the girl finally spoke, much less pleasantly than her friend. Lizzie swallowed hard thinking of her using the kitchen and not keeping it in the right order.

"I was … I just wanted to talk to Ben," Lizzie managed to explain without crying.

"I have to call him later. Is there something you need me to pass on?"

"Um," Lizzie bit on her lip, fully aware that she was just as capable of calling him herself. He was gone. Gone from Massachusetts. Gone from the city he stayed in or near for most of his two centuries. Because of her. Because he didn't want to see her. "Just tell him that Elizabeth said hi."

The girl looked at her and then the boy standing in the doorway with a knowing smirk. Her name meant something to them. "I'll do that," the boy lifted his smile.

"Thanks," Lizzie swallowed and rushed down the stairs out into the cold January evening.

Lizzie couldn't feel the movement of her legs as she walked into the gym and changed her clothes. She didn't remember leaving the locker room and getting on the treadmill. She merely watched the animation of her mileage go around the virtual track again and again until her mind was too tired to resist returning to the boy in Ben's apartment.

Chicago. He left Boston. For good? No. No, he left before. He went to France to forget her. Her? Not her… Lily. Lily was her. He tried to forget Lily. But he didn't. He came back for Lily. He would come back for her. She didn't want him to come back, did she? She walked away from him. She left him. Not to choose Oliver. In the end, that wasn't what it was about, right? It was about not being with one of them anymore. It was to set herself free from those monsters.

Then why was she so sad? Why did she go to his apartment? Was she really that upset by Oliver? Oliver still wanted her. Oliver still loved her. Would he ever stop loving her? Would he love her enough to not hurt her?

She watched the virtual track fill into the next mile marker. It was better without him. Them. She was going to be all right by herself. She was… well maybe not happy, but okay. She had her friends. Her family. She was taking good care of herself. For herself. Not just to become good food.

She picked up her pace as she thought about the teeth at her neck. Not Oliver's… that summer night in Ben's apartment. Sitting with him on the couch, feeling her pulse. Staring into his green green eyes as the freckles faded from his skin. The rapid beat of his heart and the warming of his flesh with her blood. It was intoxicating in a way nothing else ever was. Empowering. Thrilling. Would she never feel that way again?

*****

Lizzie climbed the stairs slowly, hearing laughter and voices from the living room. She paused at the landing to rest her weary leg muscles and hang up her winter coat. She glanced into the crowd circled around the room, blocking the television set. Meg glanced away from the conversation and waved without interrupting the discussion of Byron's *Don Juan*. Meg was hosting another study night, something Lizzie knew she did to divert her broken heart from Alec. Most of the time Lizzie was at the gym, but even with her thwarted errand and extra mileage, she was home early enough to observe the end of the meeting.

Lizzie smiled back at Meg and was about to turn away when she caught the stare of a student. Lizzie knew she recognized the young, dark haired woman. She mindlessly returned the blatant gaze as she summoned the oxygen back to her brain and memory. It was that young thing who was on Alec's arm in Starbucks. The snippy brunette Alec sent to get coffee while he made suggestive remarks to Lizzie about… Ben.

Lizzie shifted her eyes quickly with the realization. Was she one of Meg's undergrads? Did Meg have any clue? Did… what was her name? Claire. Did Claire remember Lizzie from Starbucks? She heaved a quick release from her lungs and headed towards the kitchen.

Lizzie filled her water bottle and then stared into the refrigerator as all her thoughts swirled in her head. Ben. No, not Ben. Not Chicago. Alec's little minion. Glaring at her. How dare she. She was only what? Eighteen. Maybe nineteen. Lizzie was going to tell Meg. Not that she had much of a right. She and Meg still didn't talk much. Things weren't bad between them. But they still weren't back to good.

Lizzie retrieved an apple and shut the fridge. She was startled to see the dark haired Claire standing in the kitchen entrance. She offered a short lived smile before bringing a half full wine glass to the sink to empty it down the drain. Lizzie soured her lips, wondering which of her bottles Meg offered that group. Not that Lizzie was drinking any more… but… she froze as Claire's dark eyes focused on her once more.

The look was familiar and frightening and made her think of all the reasons she ran and ran and ran on the treadmill. Claire was hungry.

"You don't like wine?" Lizzie dared herself the question.

"Not very much, no," the girl shifted her lips to a smile of mutual knowledge. How had Lizzie not noticed it before? In those scant moments of irritation with Alec during a heat wave? Was Alec one of her sources? She wasn't eighteen or nineteen. She had the age in her eyes, age well beyond her skin or lips or slender figure.

Lizzie felt the movement of her blood flow, the runner's high muted by the frustration she tried to rid from herself. She knew her cheeks flushed with color, revealing the recognition that increased Claire's smile as two other students brought empty wine glasses to the sink.

Lizzie nodded and smiled as Claire turned to the conversation about Byron's poetry. She capped off her water bottle and swiftly exited the kitchen. Did Meg know one of her students was a vampire? Never mind the association with Alec. Never mind Alec. Did that mean… did Meg know? Did she… did she know they were real?

Lizzie paused again in the stair hall, peering into the living room where Meg was laughing amongst the crowd rising from their seats. Did she know? Could Lizzie talk to her when everyone left? Could she… could she tell her everything about Ben and Oliver… and Lily?

She heard voices moving out of the kitchen and darted up the stairs. She didn't want to face Claire and her hungry eyes. Not with the endorphins still powering the oxygen in her veins. She slipped in her room and waited for the din of conversation to die down.

She turned on her computer to distract the remaining minutes until the students left the house. She stared mindlessly at the desktop as the voices quieted. She turned away from her neglected keyboard when she heard giggling come up the stairs. Meg didn't ascend the stairs alone. She couldn't identify the other laughter. There was no conversation, just the sound of the door closing and the sudden vibration of music coming through the wall between their rooms.

Lizzie took in a breath. That was the reason Meg hosted study sessions with her class at the house. She wanted one of her students to stay. If she couldn't be with Alec, Meg was going to be him.

It wasn't… no, it couldn't be… Claire… who went into that room. It wasn't the vampire. That girl, woman, thing wouldn't have come into the kitchen with that knowing look if Meg was her source. Right? Lizzie felt her head swim. Too many thoughts. Maybe she made it up. Another dream to distract her conscious from the fact she never told Meg about seeing Claire with Alec that summer day at Starbucks. A distraction from the more depressing reality that Ben moved away and left Boston. He left her.

She turned back to her idle computer screen. She pulled up the Internet and went on Facebook. She didn't visit as frequently since Ben stopped being a part of her life. She didn't take down the pictures of them together. She didn't want to. She didn't know if she ever could. She looked through her friends list and was relieved to see Ben hadn't deleted her. Not that it mattered. He never went on there. But just in case he broke his routine, she clicked on his profile.

He was on recently, accepting friend requests. She saw a few comments from a pretty redhead named Cecilia. She was the CEO or whatever of the Chicago clinic. The comments were relatively harmless. A few notes of appreciation for all his work… and delight in his relocation to Chicago. Lizzie looked at his info page. He changed his current location to Chicago. Nothing else changed. He didn't have a relationship status. He never did.

She saw the option to send a message. She clicked it and opened the window. She watched the cursor blink, not sure what to say or how to begin. What could she say? Please don't move to Chicago? I just met a vampire in my house? Come back to Boston to be with … someone who didn't have enough self control to be faithful to a man who loved her for two centuries? Maybe… maybe Ben didn't want to be near her. Maybe he realized it was best for them both to be separate. He moved away. To Chicago. To a redhead named Cecilia.

She was tired but felt agitation in her limbs as she shut off her lights and tried to close out her thoughts with music from her computer. She couldn't run more miles at that hour to shake the anxiety out of her head. She would go for a long run the next day. Along the Charles. He wouldn't be walking there. Not in the middle of the week. Not… not when he was in Chicago. But she would run. She would run all the thoughts and agitated energy into the ground.

She ran. She kept running. The music on her iPod pressed her forward in a rhythm as steady as her heartbeat. She had her back to the Museum of Science and kept running, running, running towards the Mass Ave. Bridge. The people on the path were a blur. The river faded into the gray mist of the clouds.

It started raining. Softly at first and then suddenly a downpour. Her clothes soaked through. But she kept running. She wouldn't run on the grass. She would slip on the mud and hurt her ankle. Ben wouldn't be there to take her home. It was a long way back to the train. A long walk back to the kitchen with its warm fire and Annie's fresh bread. She wasn't hungry. She wanted to keep running. She saw a path of white rose heads leading her out of the yard. There were more and more and more all the way down the path to the marsh. She ran to shelter herself from the rain, where the green eyes turned and smiled in expectation. She didn't hesitate and kissed him. He unzipped her sweatshirt and then she was lying on top of him in the library. She felt his heartbeat slowing underneath her own. She felt the vibration of its rhythm in her bones, as it reverberated from the walls, the music in the walls…

Lizzie opened her eyes and adjusted to the sound of her walls pulsing. Her playlist ended, leaving vacancy for the iambic vibrations of Meg's music to occupy her ears. Like the feel of a rapid heartbeat and increasing warmth of skin against her skin…

She shut her eyes again and tried to quiet the fury of her senses, but was unable to find ease to relax back to her subconscious. Lizzie opened the door into the dark and empty hallway. She went down the stairs and found her way in the blackness to the dining room. There was a half a bottle of wine left at the bar. She poured a glass and felt it immediately warm her veins.

She sat in the chair where she faced Ben and dared him to prove he could drink her blood. Where he looked at her with sincere green eyes. The green eyes that were waiting for her in the rain… the rain… the marsh… the water. The book under the water. Why did the book fall under the water?

Chapter Thirty-Two

Lizzie pulled her sweater as the board member and his wife walked away from the reception table. She knew the black cardigan hid the features of her dress, but it was cold so close to the outside door. Most of the guests arrived, allowing Lizzie to put the remaining seating cards into a neater arrangement.

"Hi Lizzie," Dr. Chiang approached the table with Gerard Fulton.

"Good evening."

"You know Mr. Fulton," the blue eyes smiled at Lizzie as she indicated the familiar donor. "I have some more guests coming shortly. But I suppose we should get to our table before they start serving dinner."

"They just began the salad course," Lizzie felt herself fluster. Was it because of Dr. Chiang? Or was it Lily's deference to a Fulton? "I believe you are sitting with Richard. Table 6."

"Thank you, Lizzie," Dr. Chiang's smile was too warm to justify the intimidation. She watched the pair enter the reception hall, wondering if Gerard was as smitten with Dr. Chiang as Richard. Even Lizzie was awestruck by her beauty in a brilliant blue gown. It made her black sweater feel even frumpier.

Lizzie took out her phone to fill the next lull that descended into the lobby. She pulled up her text mailbox, which was cluttered since before Christmas. Her most frequent correspondent was Nora, with unrelenting invitations for dinner, to which Lizzie often found the excuse of training to decline. She deleted Nora's most recent text, as well as Meg's inquiries to her arrival home, all the way down to her last text from Ben, saying his flight arrived. She didn't want to think about him. She stared at his number and wondered if she should erase that from her phone. She couldn't bring herself to do that. Not yet.

"Lizzie," a familiar voice lifted her attention away from the phone.

"Eric," she managed a smile to conceal her surprise.

"How are you?" his return grin had no awkward or bitter sentiment.

"Well," she nodded, glancing to her guest list.

"I'm sitting with Dr. Chiang," he rested his fingers on the table. "How have you been?"

"Running lots."

"Yeah, I heard you were training for the marathon," he lifted a flirtatious eyebrow.

"Are you still working for Dr. Chiang?" Lizzie assumed she was the source of the piece of gossip.

"I got a residency at MGH, but I keep in touch with her. In fact, she wants me to come back and work for her when the new cardiac center opens."

"The opening is next month," Lizzie tried not to show apprehension of seeing him in the cafeteria.

"Well, it might be a year or so… but she is very persuasive," he offered another knowing smirk.

"That's very… good for you, Eric."

"It's good to see you, Lizzie," he smiled. "Do you know where Kate and Mr. Fulton are sitting?"

Lizzie stopped at the familiarity with Dr. Chiang. Maybe his exuberant charm had nothing to do with Lizzie and was all about the department head trying to woo his medical talent. "Table six," her voice quieted.

"Thanks," he turned towards the reception hall. "I'll probably see you at the opening."

"Probably," Lizzie watched him leave and wished she could avoid that event.

It wasn't that she didn't want to see him. There was a part of her that was glad to see her former… fling. He offered her the chance for something else. She didn't take that chance because she wanted Ben. What if she accepted his offer a year before? Would her life be better? To have avoided all this heartache? To not know Lily. To have a somewhat normal life. Did she really have any other option than Ben and Oliver? Wasn't it obvious that Eric had a thing for Dr. Chiang all the while? Lizzie was just a distraction.

She didn't want a relationship with Eric. She always knew that. Even before Ben came into her life. She found him attractive. And maybe if she was in a better frame of mind, she would see how far he was willing to go to distract himself from Dr. Chiang. But she wasn't. She was miserable. There was nothing about her life that lifted her spirits. Not her job. Not the solace of her room.

She packed up the registration table an hour later, peering in to the ballroom where the dancing already began. Eric had his arm around Dr. Chiang in an enthusiastic turn. She never realized how well he could move on the dance floor. Maybe she misjudged him. Maybe… maybe she really wasn't who he was after in the long run. She decided not to go in and sit with the other staff to eat a cold extra meal from the caterer. She wasn't hungry… and she wasn't sure she could sit in that room and be pleasant.

*****

Meg was typing on her laptop when Lizzie came home. . "You're home early," she looked up and smiled.

"You're home," Lizzie sat in the chair without removing her coat.

"Did you expect I wouldn't be?"

Lizzie wondered if she would confess the reason for the pulsing music. Maybe she didn't want to know. Secrets were not fun, but sometimes they were easier than knowing the truth.

"I saw Eric tonight," Lizzie sighed.

"Oh," Meg took a sip of her wine.

"Maybe I made a bad choice."

"Seriously?"

"I don't know," Lizzie sighed and looked at the muted television screen. The costume epic made her think of Lily. "Maybe I didn't have a choice."

"Is he still interested?"

"He's a surgeon. I'm sure he has better options."

"Oh Lizzie," Meg sighed. "We're quite a pair, aren't we?"

Lizzie met her eyes, wondering much they knew. Did Claire… say anything to her? Why would she? Lizzie didn't want to know. She was tired of finding things out that made life more complicated and less happy. "Well, I was thinking of a long run tomorrow. I suppose I should go to bed."

Meg took another sip of wine. "Hey, you know my friend Didi published her book. She's giving a reading tomorrow night. If you aren't exhausted by your run, you should come."

"It would be good to get out of the house…"

"There's a little party at her place after. I said I would help set things up, but if you want to meet me at the book store, you can join us for some wine and cheese."

"Okay," Lizzie paused. "Meg, I'm sorry we… I'm sorry that we don't talk much any more."

"Well, we have a baby shower to help plan. So we better start talking soon."

"Right. Tomorrow sounds good."

*****

It wasn't quite twelve miles, but close enough. She probably could have run more. She had so much energy that wasn't going any place except into her running. She didn't want to sit at home and think once again of a path she chose a year ago. A path away from a normal life – a normal life with a man who once said something to her about having a family. It was really just a suggestion for dinner. But he was interested. Maybe he wasn't that interested if his ultimate goal was Dr. Chiang. Then again, she lost track of him after Ben came to her apartment with a bottle of wine.

It was no use dwelling. No use sitting in her apartment wondering the whatifs. She wasn't really that enthusiastic about Didi's book. She vaguely remembered conversation of it on Meg's birthday. Some cheesy, oversexed novel, with a paranormal element. God. That was… she wondered if she would be able to sit through the reading without laughing outright.

She didn't laugh outright. Because, there in the second row, was Claire. There were a couple other students Lizzie recognized from the study sessions. None of them had that hungry look in their eyes. Well, none from what Lizzie could see in the back row of added chairs where she snuck in as Didi took the podium.

Lizzie didn't even pay attention enough to laugh. She was focused on the long dark hair of that vampire. Maybe she imagined it. She certainly had the physicality of an 18 year old. Again, from what she could tell ten rows back in the crowded reading room of the book store. Why why why why was she deciding to think about those things? She didn't want those creatures as part of her life. She walked away from Oliver because he hurt her. She wanted to go back to Ben… but Ben didn't want her. So she was better off.

But there was… Lizzie forced the detail of her run out of her mind. It would be too easy to get confident about her endorphins, easy to forget everything she knew she should think about. Easy to forget, as she did that winter evening on Jack's back porch with his drummer.

She shook herself back to the present when everyone clapped at the end of Didi's reading. Meg was seated next to Tamara in the middle row and asked a couple questions to get the crowd started. As if sensing Lizzie's concentration, she turned around and waved quickly before returning to hear Didi's answer about her favorite writing habits.

Lizzie didn't want to go to the party. Especially not if the students were invited as well. She waited until the questions ended and the line started for book signing. "You made it," Meg wended her way through the crowd.

"Yeah," she couldn't stop herself from looking to see if the dark hair was still in the second row.

"Are you coming to the party?"

"I intended to," Lizzie sighed. She wished she brought her car and didn't take the train. Oh well. She could deal with a walk. "But I'm tired. I think that run took more out of me than… I think I'll just get a book and congratulate Didi."

"Well, if you change your mind, you know the address, right?"

Lizzie nodded, even though she really didn't know where Tamara and Didi lived. She watched Meg follow Tamara out of the store and bought a book. It was the least she could do. Maybe she might even read it for distraction. Didi was pleased to see her… so that was… something.

As she hastened to leave the store, her eye caught a glimpse of the New Age section, and a large, glossy book about reincarnation. She stepped in front of the shelf and scanned through the hefty volume. So many words about regression therapy and hypnosis. Too much work. She put it down and saw a whole shelf on the subject. None of them had answers about Lily or books that fell into the water. But… it was something… something to pretend had an answer. Something to occupy another lonely evening.

"That book isn't any good," a voice startled her so much Lizzie dropped it. "Most of these aren't."

Lizzie allowed herself to take in the dark hair and dark eyes and slightly olive skin. Even under the loose form of a peasant blouse, it was obvious Claire had a perfect hourglass. The right proportion to her waist, the lift to her round breasts. She smiled at Lizzie's concentrated glance and then pulled another book from the display. "This one is all right. Mostly because the author uses personal narrative. It could be a load of crap, but I always found it insightful."

"You've read it?"

"I've read a lot of things," she replaced the book. "Although, truthfully, I probably won't read that book."

Lizzie looked at her signed copy. "Then why did you come here?"

"Professor Lewis asked the class to come support her friend." It was odd. She almost spoke like the eighteen year old she was pretending to be. But Lizzie knew that was an act. She could see it in her dark amber eyes. "But I think I'll skip the party. I doubt their crudités will do much for my appetite."

Lizzie felt the scarlet on her face as those amber eyes locked with her own. She pulled her concentration away and found another book in which to feign interest. "Are you going to the party?" Claire persisted.

"Didi is a good friend," Lizzie replaced the book and moved along the shelf, putting her in the women's studies section.

"Hm," Claire still looked, waiting for Lizzie's eyes to turn. She pulled out a book about female physiology and didn't pretend very long to look at it before taking one slow step away from Lizzie. "I might be able to tell you a thing or two myself. I don't think my personal narrative is as compelling as that book, but I do have some experience with that sort of thing."

Lizzie couldn't stop herself from meeting the amber eyes or the blood rush from appearing once more across her cheeks. She knew Claire was hungry and could probably sense those twelve miles that pushed the oxygen through her bloodstream. She didn't want to go to Didi's party and sit around with Meg's friends and students. She didn't want to go home. She wanted what she knew she shouldn't want. She… "What can you tell me?"

"Why don't we go somewhere that's better for this type of conversation?" Claire's voice changed, dropping the teenager façade. Lizzie didn't answer. She merely followed her out of the bookstore, across the parking lot towards a red Volvo Coup. Her heart accelerated as she took the passenger seat and Claire silently drove out of the parking lot.

"How do you know Alec?" Lizzie spit out after five minutes of silence made her too jumpy to sit still.

"He's an old friend," Claire focused on the drive.

"Is that all?"

Claire laughed and pressed her directional. "Alec and I were freshmen together many years ago."

"How many years ago?"

"Before I changed. We are the same age – technically."

"Oh…" Lizzie thought of how seeing Alec and Meg together made her squirm. But… Ben was no different. He was… older. And for that matter, so was Oliver. "Why are you in Meg's class?"

"I went back to the university last semester. Thought I'd major in a different genre this time. Alec said she's a good teacher," Claire darted her eyes briefly to Lizzie. "I can't deny I was slightly curious about you."

"Me?" Lizzie clenched the book in her lap tightly. What was she doing? This couldn't be any more sane or safe than kissing Oliver behind the store in Coldbrook.

Claire laughed again. Her laugh wasn't youthful. It was wise and wicked. "My husband knew Ben Cottingham. They weren't particularly friendly. Matthew never understood the point of the clinic. Neither did I for that matter. I never met him, but I knew of him. I knew he kept to himself. I was curious about the woman who changed that. And why."

"I don't want to talk about Ben," Lizzie set her jaw. She did want to talk about him. But this woman clearly didn't like Ben. She didn't want to cry in front of this vampire, who was eerily confident in her eighteen year old body. Lizzie felt the weakness of a five year old in her body that was twice Claire's age.

"Fair enough," Claire pursed her lips as she turned the car again, leaving the main road. Lizzie hadn't paid attention to their direction or where they were going, but suddenly the number of trees increased and the sizes of homes got noticeably larger. "He wasn't my main interest anyway, Elizabeth."

She turned her head back at her full name. She remembered their hasty introduction at Starbucks and was certain Alec called her Lizzie. "What is?"

"I saw a picture of you in your living room," Claire lightened her voice to admiration. "You've changed so much. You reversed your aging process. By sheer force of will. Not because someone bit you and infected you with a strange form of DNA. I envy that."

"Is it the change or the endorphins?" Lizzie breathed out in annoyance. Were vampires that shallow? Was it all about athletics and youth and neurological chemicals? What about love?

"I admire the change," Claire sighed. "I won't ever change. I can't get worse. I can't get better."

"But you are beautiful," Lizzie said impatiently as she allowed herself another glance in the glow of the street lights.

"That gets boring, doesn't it?" Claire turned the car into a driveway. "But I thank you for the compliment."

"What do you want from me?" Lizzie saw the grand house.

"Isn't the question, Elizabeth, what you want from me?"Claire shut off the car and locked eyes again.

Lizzie swallowed, unable to answer. Claire smirked and left the car, leading the way up the front path into the house. They left their coats in a carefully decorated foyer, and walked past darkened rooms from which Lizzie briefly observed pristine furniture and immaculate carpets. Claire suddenly stopped and entered a darkened space with lots of books. It smelled more like the Fulton House than the modern décor of the other rooms they passed. The books were old… like Ben's. There were shelves from floor to ceiling full of them. An elaborately carved desk was at the back of the room. In the center were two high backed couches.

Claire turned on the light and glanced back at Lizzie. “Are you hungry? Or thirsty? Some water perhaps?” she smiled. Lizzie knew there wasn’t going to be an offer for wine. Maybe water would be a good idea.

Claire left the room quickly, leaving Lizzie to admire the shelves and read the bindings. American fiction from the 19th century. Alcott. Hawthorne. Twain. She pulled out a volume of Emerson and read the first page of *Self-Reliance*.

“This is my favorite room,” the amber eyes stepped across the threshold and held out a glass of water. “It reminds me of my husband.”

“Where is your husband?” Lizzie wondered if he was in college too.

The strong dark eyes shifted. “He died.”

“How did he die?” Lizzie drank some water to swallow the regret of her reactionary thought.

“Stupidity,” she swallowed. “Or arrogance. I change my mind every day.”

“Oh.”

Claire eyed her momentarily then took in a breath. “This room is cold. I am going to start a fire,” she went to a fireplace between the tall bookshelves. Lizzie was impressed how quickly she lit the large logs and created a warm blaze.

“How old are you?” Lizzie found herself admiring her perfect figure again.

“I was 18 when I changed,” she rolled back on her feet and stood up.

“Do you feel that young?”

“Some days,” she eyed Lizzie and took a few steps towards her. “Mostly it’s a strange in between. Not old enough to be old. Not young enough to be young.”

“When did you change?”

“1968.”

“You could be my mother,” Lizzie tried not to confuse herself with the fact that physically she could be Claire’s.

“I suppose I could,” Claire’s grin curved wickedly. “It’s all relative, don’t you think?”

Lizzie tried to smile back, but nerves weakened her knees. She went to one of the high backed couches and looked at the fire. "Did your husband change you?"

"He did."

"You were in love with him?"

"Yes," Claire softened her voice and sat slowly beside Lizzie. "We were together for more than forty years."

"What happened to him?" Lizzie felt rude, but she still didn't know if she should even care about offending that woman.

"He fed from a tainted source long before I met him. He was able to clean up his blood. But the fool drank bad blood two years ago. He got ill again and died."

"Tainted... by what? Lead?"

"Yes," Claire looked at the cracking flames. "He fed from someone living in an old house. He should have known to consider the paint."

"What did that do to him?"

"Burnt up in the sunlight. Just like some old novel," Claire turned back to Lizzie. "But it's done. I can't undo that."

"Have you been with anyone else since he died?"

"A lover?" the wicked laugh focused on Lizzie.

Lizzie felt the pace of her heart increase. "You chose forever but you lost it."

"I will see him again," Claire smiled confidently.

"What do you mean?" Lizzie's heart leaped.

"We can talk about that later," Claire touched Lizzie's hair. "You ran today."

Lizzie's body tensed as she saw the hunger in the eyes. "Yes."

Claire slid her finger along Lizzie's ear and rested on her pulse. "You like giving blood?"

"I do," Lizzie met the hungry eyes.

"I did, too," Claire moved her hand away from her pulse and started to unbutton Lizzie's sweater.

Lizzie slid off the sleeves of her sweater and watched the long fingers start at the buttons of her blouse. "Is the sensation of taking it better?" Lizzie stopped her and looked back at the dark eyes.

"It's different," Claire froze close to Lizzie, so close that Lizzie was taking her breath and giving it back. "But not better."

"Do you miss giving life to him? To the one you love?"

Claire pulled a little further back, still eyeing Lizzie. "Yes. Do you?"

Lizzie shut her eyes, feeling a storm of thoughts fill her head and spin her around. "Yes."

She opened her eyes and saw the dark eyes waiting. Claire bowed over the curve of her shoulder. Lizzie felt the softness of her lips press against her pulse and then pull away. The air felt cool against the skin where Claire kissed her. She waited for her to bend over her neck again but saw the dark eyes meet her own once more.

Lizzie allowed her to push her shoulders gently back against the couch. She looked up at the shadows of the ceiling as Claire traced the curve of her body with her warm breath. She didn't move as the vampire felt for the zipper of her jeans and pulled them off her legs. The coldness of the air disappeared as the breath warmed the top of her thigh and the long black hair brushed across her knee. Lizzie deepened her lungs when suddenly she felt the fangs strike the vein beneath her left hip. She felt a rush of blood coursing to her pelvis. The color of the ceiling warmed into a blurred focus as her breaths heaved from the base of her stomach.

She saw Claire's satisfied smile appear above her eyes. She sensed a warm kiss atop her forehead and felt the whisper, but didn't hear it. Lizzie closed her eyes and let the smile and color of the ceiling and the rush of blood all blend into darkness.

*****

The ferry faded into the shadows. The moonlight was obscured by the increasing clouds, leaving a murky reflection of the sky on the river. She knew the rain was coming. She smelled it in the air. It would be a relief to the heat of the past several days, a relief to her mind that was as crowded with thoughts as the house was crowded with guests when she left.

Her heart skipped as she thought of the brother. His eyes never stopped following her. Not even when it was evident the new Mrs. Fulton wanted him to direct his attention towards Harriet. Harriet was too young for those green eyes.

He came from the shadows of the trees, still dressed in his layered suit. His broad hat shielded the green eyes. She knew it was him. He had the white rose in his hand. She commented about the weather. That it was about to rain. He said he didn't care. She watched him loosen his cravat before taking a seat beside her. She let him take her hand as she talked of the wedding. He didn't care about her gossip. He didn't care about the river or the darkening sky.

He lifted her hand and kissed it. She didn't giggle or blush as all those silly girls. It was an endearing kiss, but not the most passionate she knew. He understood that. He was aware of her stained soul. She knew he wanted more than just a kiss on the back of her hand.

He set her palm back down on the log and walked away. The skies opened up and rattled with thunder when she stood to follow him. The water blinded her eyes. She couldn't see but felt the cloth of her dress press against her skin. As she drew in a breath and tried to discern the shadows from the trees and his dark figure, strong arms lifted her off the ground. The water dripped from the rim of his hat down along her nose. He carried her until suddenly the rain stopped blinding her sight.

They were under the awning of the ferryman's cottage. He let her down slowly, keeping his arm against her waist. Her stomach was close enough to feel the buttons of his heavy coat. She saw the green eyes again, level with her own. She drew in a breath and pressed her lips to his. She felt her whole body warm with his kiss, drowning out the chill of the rain. She opened her lips as he lifted his hands to her wet hair. She reached for the coat of his suit and then his vest, but stopped when something cut inside her mouth. She pulled away and saw the intensity of his green eyes watching her. He opened his mouth to a hungry grin, revealing teeth that were sharper than any human teeth should be.

She stepped back. He was not… he was not human. He could hurt her. Fear overcame her as she understood why he was there, why he looked at her, what he wanted from her body. Those green eyes that followed her to the garden, that made her laugh… those green eyes froze against her own. She couldn't move or speak a word but felt the look of that stare. His eyes were not like those of young Mr. Fulton, full of hate and disgust for his desire. The green eyes looked at her with something else. Something that wasn't monstrous. The eyes were as human and full of yearning as her own. She knew those eyes. She knew them a long time before and would know them forever. She dared herself to move back to his embrace. She lifted her chin away from him to expose her neck. He pulled her back to a kiss and brought her into the cottage.

*****

The sound of the fire cracking alerted her eyes to open. She saw the shadows of the flame dance on the ceiling. Lizzie slowly took in the details of the room, remembering the dark library and the dark haired beauty who brought her there. She shifted herself to sitting, causing a blanket to slide off her onto the floor. She felt the cold air, in spite of the fire. Her jeans were neatly arranged on the opposite couch. She stood slowly to retrieve them, feeling the gradual return of blood to her brain. She glanced down at her thigh, seeing the two marks inside her left hip. She touched them briefly, not feeling the pain she always expected from those wounds. She gave another shudder from the cold and quickly replaced her jeans.

She went to the fireplace to absorb some more of its heat. She needed to dry off. No. No, that was a dream. She shook her head and looked at the mantelpiece. There was an ornate wooden clock and several small statues. A sword hung from chains beneath the shelf. Something from the Revolution. Something the Fulton House would relish as an acquisition. She peevishly touched the metal, knowing Claire wouldn't chide her for leaving fingerprints.

She jumped as she heard the door close. Claire walked into the room with a pitcher of water and a warm smile. "You closed your eyes and went somewhere else."

Lizzie watched her refill her glass and took a sip quickly. She didn't know what Claire expected her to say, if she expected her to say anything at all.

"That happened to me. Alec brought me to a party. I took something that made me out of my mind anyway. I hooked up with a Harvard law student. That's all I knew. Not even his name. Then I went home and dreamt about him for weeks. Not about that night that I hardly remembered. It was more vivid than any dream I had. I heard things and smelled them. I remembered the feel of fabrics… and I knew from the design of those fabrics it was a different time."

"You," Lizzie set down the glass, as so many idea rose to her lips. "You knew him before?"

"I didn't understand it until he showed up at another party three months later. We barely spoke. That time he took my blood. I had another dream when I realized I was his lover in England in 1601."

"I knew… I knew Ben before."

"Did you see him just now?"

"I was me. But not me," Lizzie watched her go to a cupboard and get a small tin canister, a green bottle, and a spoon. She sat on the floor as she settled everything on the table before Lizzie.

"Mmm," Claire opened the pretty green bottle and poured some liquid into the empty water goblet. She looked up at Lizzie. "Were you happy?"

"I…" Lizzie sighed. "I was happy when I was with him. As me. Elizabeth Watson."

"But you are not with him. You just fed me. What happened?" Claire rested the spoon on top of the glass. She concentrated on the spoon and pulled a sugar cube from the tin canister.

"There was another vampire."

"Was he in the past as well?" Claire poured some water over the sugar cube.

"Yes," Lizzie watched the liquid in the glass foam into a cloud.

Claire lifted her eyes to study Lizzie's expression as she searched her mind for something. "There was another of Charlotte Fulton's. Was that him?"

"You knew Charlotte?"

"Matthew spoke of her. She's gone, isn't she?"

"She was in the past," Lizzie still looked at the cloud in the goblet. "But I never see her."

"Three vampires?" Claire's grin shined with the giddiness of her body's youth.

"No," Lizzie shut her eyes. "One of them became… he was cursed because of me."

The giddy expression fell from Claire's eyes. "It is a curse."

"I didn't mean that."

Claire lifted the glass and sat beside Lizzie. She shifted the hair that fell in front of Lizzie's forehead. "No wonder your eyes are sad."

"I love Ben. I know I loved him then. But I ruined another life. And I think I must pay for it."

Claire handed her the goblet. "You have free will, Elizabeth. You have determination to change your physical self. Don't you think you have the will to overcome this?"

Lizzie fingered the cool goblet and met the dark eyes. "I… I'm not sure."

"Drink that. Maybe you will see the answer."

Lizzie took a small sip and rested the glass on her knee. Claire said nothing. Lizzie didn't know what else to say without further pushing her sanity on the subject of Ben. The silence in the room deepened, only disturbed by the cracking of logs on the fireplace. In agitation, she took another deep swallow of the cloudy liquid.

"I feel like I'm living that other life," Lizzie broke the silence with her mindless sigh.

"Do you want to change that?"

"I don't want to be a servant for the rest of my life."

"Then don't be."

Lizzie looked at the remainder of the green cloud.

"You have the determination to run a marathon. Why can't you determine a new path?"

"I always end up with the same people. I don't know if I want anyone else," Lizzie met the dark eyes and took the last of the green liquid. She put the glass on the table and felt the atmosphere shift into sharper contrast. The tick of the small wooden clock on the mantelpiece echoed. She heard the movement of the warm air from the flames waft up the chimney. The ridges of the upholstery's brocade grew under her fingertips.

"Decide what you want, Elizabeth. Decide and then choose to make it happen."

Lizzie let out a breath as the warmth of the fire colored her cheeks. The sad fortitude of those dark eyes burned something within her. Impatience. An urge to go somewhere. Do something. Move. Feel. Not somewhere else. That moment was so vivid. So real. So important. Like she was on one side of the door about to unlock it and see what was on the other side. Something in her mind was waiting to reveal itself. Something… something that would explain everything.

Her dream was so vivid. The dream after she gave her blood to that vampire. That blood was coloring her cheeks and … making her heart beat. Lizzie looked at Claire's peasant blouse and wondered if the heart slowed back to normal. She turned to Claire and untied the top of the blouse and slid her hand across the left breast, finding the pyrrhic rhythm. She saw the dark eyes staring with admiration and sorrow and a new hunger. Lizzie leaned towards her and gave in to the kiss that met her lips.

*****

She fastened the buttons of her dress with agitated fingers. Even with the half moon, a silver light crept into the room, enough to find her shoes and cap without bumping into the furniture. The bed was left in shadow, provoking her agitation. She didn't want her to wake and stop her from leaving.

She crept through the door, careful to take her time and not provoke the creak of the bottom hinge. She silently pulled the latch into place and let out a deep sigh with her escape. She didn't know how to face the morning, but staying through the evening was impossible. Her fingers still shook in the kitchen. Annie's fire was low, but still burning. She added another log to the flames and found the pitcher of water. She drank all of it, resolving to go back to the well after allowing a few moments in front of the growing flames.

He was standing in the unlit corner of the room. Her heart leapt and increased its rhythm. He was waiting for her. She knew he would be, but didn't think he would have remained so long.

She reached her fingers to her neck, making certain the collar of her dress concealed the marks. He knew they were there. He gave her marks like that. He wanted to do it again. She could see it in the glare of those gray green eyes. She didn't want him. She didn't want…

He stepped into the light of the fire. She shut her eyes. Vile, vile creature. They were the same. She couldn't let herself think differently. She knew their plan now. Charlotte made it very clear why he came back. It wasn't for her. It was to marry and murder Harriet. Like Horace. They were using her, making her part of their contemptible plan. She had to leave. She couldn't leave. She couldn't leave those green eyes that haunted her dreams since the night of the wedding.

He muttered something about her silence. She said nothing to break it. He asked her about a book. She didn't want to know about a book. He asked some trifle about the weather. The fury burst from her lips. She told him what Charlotte explained. About Mr. Fulton's niece and the truth of her consumption in France. About the larger plans for the Fultons… her family.

She lunged out of her chair to strike him. She was angry that he didn't say anything to argue against her, to say he wasn't a monster. Her hand landed against his face with more pain for her than him. She lifted her other arm to try again, but he took hold of it and held her still. He looked with those green eyes, forcing her to cry the tears that reflected his sadness. She saw his struggle. He didn't want Charlotte any more than she did. He wanted escape. He wanted her. He wanted her more than the money. More than blood.

He let her go, took his hat, and left the room. She cried again, afraid that she drove him away. She wanted the green eyes to come back. She had to protect Harriet, but would risk her safety if it meant those eyes would look at her again.

*****

Lizzie saw the dead leaves rustle in the wind across the driveway. It was the only sound on the street. Strange for a Saturday afternoon in early March. She glanced at her phone and checked the time she called for the cab. It had been fifteen minutes. They said ten. She figured it would be twenty. She wasn't in a panic. She just didn't want to linger forever outside the house.

The night and the morning were a blur. She felt the stiffening of muscles she hadn't stretched in a long time. She knew she slept a little – enough to dissipate the alcohol from her bloodstream. Probably just over an hour to quiet her mind and fade out the tornado of images. The night and the morning were a blur. When she opened her eyes in the guest room… she assumed it was a guest room, she found her clothes neatly arranged by a pile of towels. She didn't find Claire in the big house after she showered and dressed. She wasn't in the library or the foyer or any room below, none of which showed the remnants of the night before. Not even the pretty green bottle and spoon.

She found her coat on a table in the foyer with a number to call for a cab. It was written on the back of a calling card for Claire Chamberlain, with her phone and email. There was an option, if Lizzie decided to take it, to contact her again.

On it was a date Lizzie calculated to nine weeks. Lizzie couldn't process that thought. She couldn't move forward to think about the future. The past became so vividly apparent at that house. Images that had nothing to do with the female vampire. What was it about that night that made Lily's mind so clear? Was it the surreal circumstance of the evening? Was it the absinthe? Was it that Lizzie abandoned her conscious and just gave into her body? Had her encounter with Claire opened up that part of her mind? Did she just need something else to put her into Lily's head and feel her sensations, feel her joy, feel her pain?

She glanced at her phone again. She wanted to call Ben. She wanted to ask him if he understood this. If he was as aware of Matthew Chamberlain and his wife as they were of him. If he knew other vampires who mated with lovers they had in several lifetimes, in the form of different bodies, but always the same soul. Maybe the Chamberlains were unique. Maybe more were like Oliver who went from mate to mate to mate looking for something they would never find. And when they realized what they wanted that person to be and she wasn't… she died.

The stillness of the air settled as the leaves stopped moving. Why couldn't she see all of Lily's thoughts? Why did they only come in pieces? Why didn't she have the complete memory? There was more, more than she had ever seen or known or felt. But there was still something missing. Something the absinthe didn't let her see. What was Lily hiding? Why did she agree to marry Oliver if the green eyes haunted her thoughts as much as they haunted Lizzie? What did the green eyes do? Why didn't Lily want to remember the reason she chose Tom? Was she ashamed? Or was she scared?

She heard the car come down the road and saw it slow in front of the driveway. She looked back briefly to the house. A small part of her wondered if there was still a key to Lily's thoughts inside. Was there enough of the green bottle left to bring her back to the Fulton house again? She saw the cab idling and decided to go home.

Chapter Thirty-Three

Lizzie lifted a piece of asparagus from the plate and carefully wrapped it with pastry dough. She set it on the baking sheet and stopped before picking up the next slender green stalk.

"So when are you coming back to the Fulton House?" Andrew carefully cut his scones into small triangles.

"I like having Saturdays free."

"Free for what?" Andrew raised an eyebrow. "You're less cranky. Are you seeing someone?"

Lizzie picked up another slender green stalk and pursed her lips. "No."

"Are you screwing anyone?" he laughed and took another section of dough to shape.

She looked at him briefly, knowing of all her friends Andrew wouldn't raise his eyebrow at her night of absinthe the previous weekend. Well, leaving out the part about the blood and flashbacks to another life. "Andrew," she set another finished piece on the baking sheet. "I'm less grumpy because I'm having fun. I enjoy cooking with you."

"I enjoy it, too, lovely," he leaned across the island and kissed her cheek.

"Then why don't we do it more often?"

"Cook for your friends' baby showers?"

"Or any shower. Or any wedding. Or any party," Lizzie took in a deep breath. "Why DON'T we start a business, Andrew?"

"We've always said …"

"We've always said. Why don't we do it?" Lizzie wiped her buttery hands on a towel and got the pile of papers from her bag. "I've been doing some research. I think we could qualify for a business loan. We'd have to start part time to keep our jobs… but, Andrew, we could do it."

"You're serious."

"Yes. Yes, I am," Lizzie added determination to the thoughts she let roll about in her brain since she decided to change the resemblance of her life to Lily's.

Andrew froze a look towards her. "I'd have to talk to Davis."

"Of course."

"But, he does his theater and doesn't make any money. I can do this and… hell, we could make money."

"That is the point."

"God, I hate my job."

"It would be hard work, Andrew," Lizzie looked at the papers. "But, I've planned so many events at the hospital. You have an exquisite eye for presentation. And we both know flavor. We should… we should at least try."

Andrew broke into a broad smile. Lizzie knew it was not just a twist of his charm. "Let's do it."

"We could cook Davis dinner tonight and sweeten the deal."

"I'll make his favorite pasta alfredo. You want to make that torte he loves so much?" Andrew winked. "He won't be able to refuse."

"I like the way you think, Andrew," Lizzie returned to her asparagus.

Andrew took his full tray and put it into the oven. He paused and turned carefully. "I saw that Ben's place sold this week."

Lizzie swallowed, losing the glow of confidence. It was information she was going to have to process sooner or later. "Oh?"

"I saw the sign … no word from him?"

"He moved to Chicago, Andrew," Lizzie concentrated on her hors d'oeuvres.

"Yeah, but … never mind," Andrew shook his head. Lizzie wished he finished his thought. She knew she had no right for that expectation. Not when she left out so much information with her friends all the time. They knew nothing, nothing about what plagued her mind. She couldn't even tell Andrew the primary motivation for her sudden devotion to starting a business. And yet… if it succeeded, hopefully she could go back to having a life where she didn't have to lie to her friends. Where she could just be Elizabeth Watson and not have to worry about what her friends might say if they knew what she did after a book signing. She hoped, but she knew no matter how much she threw herself into this project, she could never go back to what it was before she knew Lily.

*****

"I don't know what I'm going to do with all this," Nora sighed as they entered the condo after the third trip back to Lizzie's car.

"You will find a place for it," Lizzie dropped the gift bag by the coffee table. "You'll keep yourself busy for the next few weeks arranging it all."

"Mark will help me," Nora went to the kitchen. Lizzie followed and accepted a glass of seltzer. "Do you want to stay for dinner?"

"Your mother's cake filled me to the brim."

"It was a good cake, but not as good as the rest of the food," Nora put the seltzer back in the refrigerator. "I'm glad you and Andrew are finally putting your talents to use. I told my aunts of your plans. They want to hire you."

"One of them took my phone number," Lizzie let the smile and not the lump in her throat overtake her.

"I imagine I am going to see you even less if you are working and starting a business," Nora walked back towards the living room.

"I will make time for you Nora," Lizzie sat between the bags on the couch. "Especially when the baby comes."

"We've haven't seen you very much lately," Nora sat on the one chair in the living room not covered with presents. "Are you seeing someone?"

"No." Why did all her friends make the same assumption? They knew she was training for a marathon.

"Not even one of the doctors?" Nora looked over her seltzer glass.

"I thought you didn't approve of casual affairs with Mt. Elm personnel."

"I don't," Nora sighed. "It's just… you look lonely, Lizzie."

"I'm where I have to be right now, Nora. I'm training. And you're right. It will be a lot of effort to get the business started. I don't have time to date."

Nora caught herself and stopped the frown. "Are you still in love with Ben?"

Lizzie looked at Nora. She blinked her eyes quickly to stop tears from forming. "Yes."

"Then why don't you go back to him?'

"Because he moved to Chicago."

"He did?"

"Yeah," Lizzie breathed out. She avoided sharing that detail with Nora, knowing she wouldn't be as sympathetic as everyone else.

"But I just saw him."

"You saw Ben?"

Nora narrowed her eyes at Lizzie as if trying to determine the reason for a falsehood. "Yes, I saw him at the grocery store."

"The grocery store?"

"Yes," Nora continued without any clue why that detail should be so odd.

"What was he doing there?"

"Buying groceries, I assume."

"Are you sure it was him?"

"Yes, I'm sure," Nora was almost irritated at the answer. "We spoke for a few minutes."

"What did he say?"

"He asked about the baby. And he asked how you were. I told him about your running."

"Did he say anything else?"

"Well, I said that you and Andrew were thinking of starting a business."

Lizzie tried to calm her breath without making it look too obvious. Why was he back in the Boston area? Why was he in a grocery store where Nora would shop? Why didn't he try to see her? "Did he look well?"

"He looked tired. He said he was working a lot, so I imagine that had something to do with it. He's still… Lizzie, I really don't understand why you ended that."

"No," Lizzie picked up one of the overly packed gift bags and started pulling out bottles and burping cloths to put on the coffee table. "I don't think you would."

"You hurt him pretty badly."

"I know."

"Why?"

"I can't explain it."

"Was it the… was it about kids?"

"What?"

"You said that he couldn't have children. And I wondered if… seeing me… did that make you want a baby, Lizzie? Did that make you have second thoughts about Ben?"

"Children…" Lizzie looked up blankly. "Children were one of the thoughts I had… but a very small reason compared with the rest."

"Which is?"

"Nora, you wouldn't understand."

"Try me."

Lizzie's eyes watered and looked away from Nora. She wanted to say something. It was easy to tell Claire. But she was a vampire. She knew about past lives. How could Lizzie tell *Nora* about Lily? "I can't talk about it."

"That's lame," Nora was annoyed. "I think you were a real shit to him, Lizzie."

Lizzie looked at Nora blankly. She didn't know what to say.

"I know that was harsh. But he… would you think about giving it another try?"

"I have thought," Lizzie swallowed. "I think about it every day."

"Then why don't you call him?"

"It isn't that easy."

"It is easy," Nora grabbed Lizzie's purse and found her phone. She opened it up and then stopped suddenly. "Are you worried about Meg?"

"Meg? No," Lizzie exclaimed, realizing Nora probably wasn't privy to Meg's study sessions. "Why does this matter so much to you?"

"I don't know," Nora shrugged. "I guess… well I think you two were meant to be together. I don't normally buy into that sort of thing… but it just seemed so … like you were waiting for him all that time. And then when you were ready, he was there. And when he was there, he made you so happy. Like you found the perfect fit for your unique self."

"That's what I think about you and Mark."

"Yeah," Nora glanced down. "I feel that way about Mark… and maybe I need you to work this out to prove that perfect fits stay together."

"Are you and Mark…"

"No," Nora shook her head and smiled. "This baby makes it even more perfect. But… Lizzie… it seems to go against nature for you to not be with him. It just doesn't seem right."

"I thought you didn't believe in fate and destiny and all that."

"I don't … most of the time. I want to believe it about you and Ben. You are miserable without him. It's like you've lost a part of yourself."

"I'll get over it."

"No, Lizzie. I don't think you will," Nora looked down. "You could always adopt, you know."

"It isn't… I know," Lizzie sighed. "Nora, it's more complicated than children."

"If you love him, you will work it out."

"I want to believe that, Nora," Lizzie let out a sad sigh.

"Then make it happen," Nora gave her the phone with Ben's number ready to dial. "He will forgive you."

"He came back and didn't want to see me," Lizzie protested. "I hurt him too much, Nora. He doesn't want me back."

Lizzie looked at the number on the screen. It would be easy to press send. But then what would she say? She had too much to say. Things didn't make sense to her yet. He could help her understand. Suddenly the phone vibrated indicating a call from Andrew. Lizzie dodged Nora's eyes and took it to indulge his questions about the food.

*****

Lizzie felt the relief of the cool evening air. She was glad to escape and bring the signs and lingering paperwork to her car. The stuffy corridor of the Cardiac Center started to make her head spin. Well, that, and Eric's arrival. Maybe it was because Dr. Chiang was preoccupied with keeping Gerard Fulton company… or maybe he was still interested.

She paused in the driver's seat and inspected her reflection on her visor. She saw the fatigue of her long day in the image staring back at her. She wore the shoes she hated and felt them squish her already blistered toes. She touched up her lip gloss and flipped back the visor. She didn't want to get back on her feet. Her poor feet. Well, at least there would be no more occasions for heels before the marathon. She managed to find the strength to walk on them as she clicked the remote key for her car.

"Elizabeth," a voice called as she turned the path from the parking lot.

A mix of relief, happiness, and fear overcame her. "Ben."

"I… I'm sorry that I… I don't mean to scare you."

"What are you doing here?" she held onto her breath. Was she awake? Had she fallen asleep in her car? Was she dreaming? Was she Elizabeth? She wanted to see him. She had so many things to say, to tell him. She didn't know where to begin and remained mute with the end of her question.

He lifted a shiny postcard in his hand. It was the invitation to the Fulton Center opening. Every major medical industry was invited. She would have noticed his company on her address list. One of the doctors must have sent that invitation. "I knew you would be here. I wanted to talk to you."

"Then why not call? Or write an email?" she stepped back, almost losing her balance on her heel. He offered an arm she immediately refused. She couldn't stop the anger from hardening her words. It wasn't anger. It was hurt. Hurt she couldn't express since he disappeared to Chicago.

"I don't know. I thought you wouldn't answer," he let out a low breath. "You look… amazing."

"I've been running a lot."

"Nora said…"

"Why did you go to the grocery store?" Lizzie let the anger form the question.

"I needed some batteries," he laughed to himself. "I can't lie. I knew I might see her. I wanted to… I wanted to know how you were."

"I thought you went to Chicago. That boy said…"

"Keith told me you came to the apartment," Ben restrained a smile.

"He told me you were gone indefinitely."

"It was more difficult to leave than I thought," he rested the pause with a focus on her.

"You sold your home. You let strangers in the apartment. In our… she was reading my book."

"Did you get the books I brought to Jefferson Park?" he looked confused at her anger.

"Yes," Lizzie shook her head as her own confusion clouded her sense of conversation. "What do you want?"

"I wanted to see that you are okay."

"Well, I'm okay," she breathed out impatiently.

"I miss you, Elizabeth."

She lifted her eyes to him. She hoped she wouldn't cry, but it was very difficult to not lose strength with that last phrase. She didn't know how to answer him. If she should tell him how much she missed him. Everything she remembered about Lily. About the green eyes that were full of love. That followed her everywhere. That frightened Lily, but only for the moment before she realized she would love him forever. Why did she change her mind?

The ring of her phone broke the stillness. She tried to ignore it, but she set her volume too high. She silenced the ringer and noticed Andrew's repetition of unfortunate timing.

"You have to go."

"I don't…"

"Someone is waiting for you," he looked back to the hospital building.

"No, Ben, I – "

"I just hope that means you are staying away from Oliver," he said it. Why did he have to say it?

"I… he went back to California."

"I'm glad you are staying away from him."

"I'm not with him," she summoned the courage to tell him what she waited to tell him since that December morning in the hotel. She didn't want to be with Oliver because she still loved him. "It's not because he is a bad person, Ben."

"No?"

Lizzie's thoughts clouded with the memory of hitting her head against the back of the country store. That was a mistake. An unfortunate mistake. Why did Ben have to make such an awful assumption about

Oliver? He was crowding her head with things that had nothing to do with the emotion swelling within her heart. She wanted to tell him about her dreams. Why was he making it so difficult to say anything? Why did he just want to talk about Oliver? "I decided to be alone," she let the words escape her without thinking. "I needed to get away from both of you to clear my head."

"Good," he nodded and shortened his breath. "That is how it should be."

"Ben, now I know…" she began without softening her voice.

"You should go back inside, Lizzie. I imagine he's anxious to take you home."

Lizzie wanted to throw her purse. She was so infuriated with him and herself. Why couldn't she say what she wanted to say? Why did he have to bring up Oliver? Oliver was gone. He didn't visit her dreams. Lily didn't want Oliver any more than Elizabeth. Why didn't Ben stay? Why did he come at all if it was only to tell her to go back inside and be with someone else? There wasn't someone else. She looked once more in the shadows to see if he would come back. All she could hear was the buzz of the light at the edge of the parking lot. She turned around and went back into the hospital, where Eric was waiting with a glass of wine.

*****

Lizzie appreciated the light from the street. It made it easier to find her stockings without having to turn on one of the lamps. She took in a breath as she sat on the edge of the sofa and stared at her unfinished wine glass. She didn't want to leave in such a rude rush. But he was asleep. She wasn't going to stay through the morning. This wasn't like that.

She shut her eyes to squeeze out the tears. She was tired. Just tired. It was a long night. She wasn't going to think about Ben. She wasn't going to think about how she just… she just did it to him again. She went to someone else. Ben didn't want her. He walked away. He told her to go inside. Then why did he just show up like that?

She needed to leave if she was going to get to the train before service stopped for the evening. She didn't want to walk in her heels. She should have taken her car. Why… why, why? She was supposed to be moving forward and making improvements in her life. Not stepping back into her old bad habits.

She rolled her stockings up her thigh and noticed the red blemishes. What would Ben have thought of those? Would he care? Would he look down on her because she was so reckless? She pushed down her skirt and stood up to grab her shoes.

"I was wondering about those," Eric stood in the archway of his living room. Lizzie lost the strength to stand on her sore feet and sat back down on the couch.

"Those are pretty recent, aren't they?" he didn't leave his stance, but looked at Lizzie strangely. She couldn't tell if it was judgment or ... something else. It wasn't... the light in the room was too dim. He couldn't possibly be one of them. She just saw him eating shrimp at the opening. And... there were just too many in her life now to make sense. She was tired and was imagining things again.

Did he think it was a disease? Was that his concern after a lapse of precaution during their hasty seduction? He didn't say anything then. He wouldn't be looking at her that way if he was threatened by those marks.

Lizzie swallowed and tried to keep her face cool. She reached for her abandoned wine glass and took a sip to thaw her frozen reaction. "They're just bug bites," she made a strong effort to be calm.

"No they aren't," he sat beside her.

"Then what are they?" she forced a smile.

"Something else bit you. Or I should say someone," he took the wine glass and helped himself to a sip.

"There's no such thing as vampires," she tried again to laugh. Maybe she said too much.

"How long have you been a source?"

"I..." she tried to begin but still felt trapped by the confusion between relief and fear. "Are you a source?"

"I am," he met her eyes. It wasn't as intimidating as Claire, but Lizzie did not feel in control of the situation. She always felt she knew exactly how to identify Eric and his confident surgeon personality. A vampire feeder was not part of that. She looked at his neck exposed by his unbuttoned shirt. "I go to the clinic."

"Oh," Lizzie heaved out a deep breath.

"That's not where you got these," he slid his hand up her thigh. "Are you dating one?"

"I was," Lizzie looked at the liquid in her wide mouthed glass. She imagined the vampire world wasn't that large. If Eric went to the clinic, he knew Ben. She was tempted to explain Claire, but stopped herself. He wasn't moving his hand. She knew that was deliberate, but she was too curious to indulge it. "How did you find out about them?"

"I dated one while I was a student. But it didn't work out. It never does."

"So you are still…" she didn't finish her question as he leaned in to kiss her. She felt his hand go the rim of the stockings, but she wasn't ready to stop the conversation. Having someone in her normal day to day life who knew about vampires, who knew about the clinic, who wasn't Alec McCaffrey made the dreams less surreal and everything of the past year more believable. She pulled his hand away from her hip and slid away from his kiss.

"I am her source at the clinic," he pushed back Lizzie's disheveled hair.

"Does she bite you?"

"Not these days," he looked at her thigh.

Lizzie studied him, wondering if it was someone at the hospital. Someone ageless and beautiful and more accomplished than her age would imply. "It's Dr. Chiang, isn't it?"

He smiled briefly as his answer. Lizzie thought of those brilliant blue eyes and tried to remember if there was any hint of her hunger or what she really was. She glanced back to Eric to see if there was any emotion in his revelation. He leaned to kiss her again, stopping any question from escaping her lips. She decided to let it go and gave in to the hands that slid back up her thigh.

Chapter Thirty-Four

"If we sell coffee, we could have a nice little shop for our baked goods," Andrew mused over his Starbucks cup.

Lizzie laughed, not sure they could compete with the industry giant two blocks away. Hopefully the secret would be Andrew's pastries. She had to admit the space was growing on her. With a decent clean up and a new stove, the kitchen would be a good work space. "Nora's aunt called me yesterday. She would like to hire us for her book club tea."

"I hope we get the loan so we have a kitchen."

"We can do that out of my kitchen…" Lizzie faded, knowing Andrew was excited about the idea of renting a space like this.

"Yes, but this is better," Andrew repeated again. She was glad to see him so excited and wasn't going to argue against him. She knew Davis was encouraging the idea of a storefront. If they got the loan and the ability to pay for it, she might be convinced.

The landlord returned from a phone call in his office. Andrew immediately went to his side with another flurry of questions. Lizzie wasn't much interested in the ability to paint the walls, knowing full well Andrew would have the final say to the interior design. Lizzie didn't much care as long as she had say over the kitchen. She looked to the window and watched the foot traffic, wondering how many passersby were the type to stop in a cute little bakery for a cup of coffee or would solicit their services for a party.

The April sun brightened the sidewalk, exposing some of the dingy color of the urban street. There were a lot of college students crossing back and forth. They weren't likely to want a caterer, but they would come in for coffee – especially if the shop was open late at night. Granted, it was the middle of the day. There were likely young professionals in the neighborhood who might visit on the weekend or older couples like the one across the street from Ben's old apartment.

She took another sip from her coffee and refocused on the passing foot traffic. Everyone seemed to enjoy the burst of spring sunshine. A few pedestrians locked into the concentration of an iPod or cell phone oblivious to the weather. She liked the diversity, the vitality, the… she saw someone pass the window and almost dropped her coffee. Will? No, it wasn't Will. She was sure when he came back and looked at her through the window.

"Hi Lizzie," he let himself in the door.

"Oliver," Lizzie looked briefly at Andrew who cast his eyes on the tall dark haired man. "What are you doing here – in town?"

"I was invited to give another lecture at UMASS. I put some more research together… so it seemed like a good opportunity to see if my theories make sense to the general public," he smiled and nodded at Andrew.

"Andrew, this is Oliver," Lizzie lowered her voice, knowing Andrew understood who Oliver was.

"Nice to meet you," Andrew's appreciation of Oliver's physique was not subtle.

"Andrew and I are starting a business," Lizzie explained. "We're hoping to rent this space."

"Not a bad location. Not far from the university," Oliver nodded.

"We're going to get lunch," Andrew offered. Lizzie could sense a bit of mischief in his voice. "Would you like to join us?"

Oliver looked at Lizzie. He would have welcomed the invitation if it was just her making it. "I just ate," Oliver wasn't lying. She saw the color in his cheeks. Did that mean he had a source in the neighborhood? Did that mean she would see him in the neighborhood whenever he came to town?

"That's a pity," Andrew looked back at the landlord as he hung up his phone again. "I will finish things up and we can head out. Oliver, at least join us for a drink."

Lizzie watched Andrew return to the other side of the vacant shop. "You don't have to."

"I actually have to be somewhere," Oliver sighed. "A business, huh?"

"The hospital is boring," Lizzie shrugged. "I wanted to do something more interesting with my life."

"You're running another marathon."

"Yup," Lizzie realized he paid attention to her Facebook. "Did the lecture go well?"

"I think so. I hope this research will qualify me for a federal grant."

"Wow. That's great, Oliver. Really great."

"I'm seeing someone."

"Oh?"

"I've known her for a few years," he lowered his voice so she was the only one who could hear. "She was actually a source for Alison. She works at the university and is a big help with my research."

"You are going to meet her?"

"Yeah," he pursed his lips. "What about you? Are you seeing someone?"

"Nothing serious," Lizzie glanced at Andrew who started asking questions about paint again.

"Are you happy?" Oliver looked at her, almost unraveling her cool.

"I'm trying."

"Do you see Ben at all?"

"I saw him a couple weeks ago," Lizzie forced the emotion to stay in her stomach. "He went to Chicago for a little while. But now he's back in Boston."

"I knew he went to Chicago…" Oliver faded. "I didn't realize he came back."

"He has a business here," Lizzie shrugged with the logic she repeated to herself over and over.

"Yes. Yes, he does."

"It's good to see you," she said blankly as she heard Andrew affirm the fact they would have a decision by the end of the week.

"Yes," Oliver smiled. "I'm glad I happened to walk by when you were here. I felt very badly about how things ended when I last saw you. I'm glad that we were able to… say hello."

"Yes, it was nice," Lizzie nodded as Andrew returned to their side.

"So how about that drink, Oliver?"

"I'm afraid not," Oliver shook his head. "It was good to see you, Lizzie."

Lizzie watched him walk out the door and heaved a giant sigh of relief.

*****

Lizzie didn't make it to the shower before the contents of her stomach rose to her throat. She rinsed out her mouth and washed her face as she determined to call into the office. She froze at the look of her reflection when she thought about the date. Stupid. Stupid. Stupid. So stupid.

Meg was on the other side of the door when Lizzie left the bathroom. "Are you okay?" Meg asked with genuine concern. Lizzie didn't want to answer. She had to go to her room and calculate the weeks. She nodded hastily and left the bathroom. "Are you pregnant?" Meg called down the hallway.

Lizzie turned. Why would she make that assumption so rapidly? Was it on Lizzie's face? "No," she denied too emphatically. "It was just something I ate."

Lizzie went back up the stairs. She couldn't talk to Meg. The last thing she needed was Meg's council about options. She didn't want to think about options. She didn't want to think about what this could mean. She knew she had been foolish. Why didn't she go back on the pill? She was too lazy. Too greedy. Too stupid.

She made the call into Richard, using the same excuse of bad food. She didn't remember what she ate in the past 48 hours. She stared at her phone, contemplating another person to call. She thought about Nora. Nora would know… at least how to stop the sick feeling in her stomach. She knew Eric was probably in surgery. She couldn't call him yet. He was a doctor. She knew another doctor… no that wasn't a possibility.

She put down the phone when the knock came to her door. She opened it and saw Meg standing in a towel, with wet hair dripping over her shoulders. "Here," she handed Lizzie a box. "I had a scare of my own a few weeks ago. I got a couple extra."

"Really?"

"Yeah really," Meg looked hard.

"Thanks."

"It doesn't take too long. If you need anything, I'll be here," Meg touched her arm.

Lizzie managed an expression of appreciation and shut the door. She threw up a second time before taking the test. Was she supposed to vomit that much? She needed to run. How on earth was she going to get through this?

She left the stick on the back of her toilet. She returned to the phone and opened up her contact list. She saw Ben's name. She ached, ached to talk to him. But… how could she … if she was going to have another man's baby? A baby that he could never give her? It would be wicked – and some level of satisfaction to hurt him with that fact – but she couldn't do that to him.

A baby. The panic ebbed away. She gave up thoughts of ever having a child. She wasn't going to have that possibility with Ben. Now, she figured her child would be her business. She didn't think she would commit to someone as she had with Ben. She didn't think the one night reunion with Eric was more than one night. Now there was a possibility for something different. It wouldn't be… she didn't want him to give her a ring. He would support her. At least she assumed he would. Maybe he wouldn't. Maybe a baby would erase the desirability quotient she earned with fang marks on her thigh.

She really didn't feel very good. Maybe it was a fever. Maybe it was the fish she ate for dinner. The idea of food made her stomach swim again. She went back to the bathroom, but the nausea subsided. She picked up the stick resting on the back of the toilet. It was negative. She felt the swift energy drain of all her lost food. Her stomach wasn't happy. She was very, very tired. She tried to drink some water, but she only had the ability to go back to her bed and fall asleep.

*****

Her head was a cloud when she went back to the bathroom. She didn't know how long she slept. The sun was outside, but the light was so dull in her room. She looked at the test again and readjusted her eyes. It wasn't a minus sign. It was a plus sign. She knew it was. She knew it was wrong. She knew that truth for weeks. Now she had to tell Ben.

First she had to go back to the store. Andrew was waiting to discuss paint colors. She didn't want to discuss paint. She didn't want to talk with all the people who came in looking for coffee. They weren't ready. The store wasn't open. She saw Ben, but couldn't talk to him there. Not amongst all the people. Not when she had work to do. She left a note for him to meet her at the end of the day, when her work was complete. He watched as she hurried about filling cups of coffee, those green eyes weakening her resolve to tell him the decision she had to make.

She knew Oliver was waiting outside the store. She felt badly for ignoring him. She couldn't take time away from the kitchen. She would go to him after… and tell him that he was going to be a father.

She walked past the cars, down the hill towards the river. She took her shoes off and put her feet in the water, letting the grass wave over the tops of her toes. Her feet ached from the long day. She hoped he would find the rose and come to her. She knew if he didn't come that night, her courage would fail. She would leave without telling him.

She had the book he gave her. The book she was going to give back. She opened it and read over the words she wrote inside the front cover. They blurred together and didn't distract her from worry. A baby. She didn't think she would ever have a baby. She had to marry him. Thomas would do the right thing. Even though she never did the right thing.

The book fell from her hands into the water. Ben grabbed her from behind and kissed her. He didn't give her the opportunity to speak first. She didn't want to tell him. How could she tell him? He expected her to go with him. He expected her to become…

She watched the pain change the green eyes to gray. She told him she wanted this baby. She told him she had to marry the father. He was angry. He wanted to hurt her. She saw the look that terrified her when she first saw his teeth. She knew… she knew she couldn't be with this monster. She looked at the book under the water and walked away. She pretended not to hear when he said she would change her mind. She kept walking to stop the swirling of her stomach.

*****

Lizzie sat up and ran back into the bathroom. Was there really anything left in her body? She felt weak, barely strong enough to stand, but she left her room and went down to the living room. She went to the coat closet and pulled out the box she pushed there four months before. She found the leather books and opened the volume of Byron to look at the water-stained sonnet on the inside cover. She clutched the leather binding and shut her eyes repeating the lines, "love alters not with his brief hours and weeks, but bears it out even to the edge of doom."

Lizzie fell on the couch, clutching the book in her hands. All the images of her dream shifted into place. Lily was pregnant. With Oliver's baby. But Ben had already sent Oliver to Charlotte. The sorrow overwhelmed her. Lily's sorrow.

She shut her eyes and saw Harriet's room. She smelled the air, the heavy scent of flowers from the garden drifting into the open window. She was sitting in the chair waiting to tell him the happy news. Oliver came through the door as she knew he would. But he wasn't… he wasn't Tom. His eyes burned with that otherworldly intensity. Benjamin's threat made sudden perfect sense. Thomas muttered something about being with her forever. The baby. The baby. She couldn't have a baby with a vampire. She couldn't have a baby without him. She went to him. She kissed him. She let him have her. It wasn't love. It was fierce and intense, not the clumsy movements from their secret meetings. She moved her head to expose her neck. She knew he should have stopped. She knew the point came and went when she should have pulled away. She knew her release would come soon.

"Lizzie," someone shook her shoulder. Lizzie opened her eyes and saw Meg leaning over her. "Are you okay?"

"I'm not pregnant." Lizzie sat herself back up. "I think it's food poisoning."

Meg took the book from her clutches and looked at it. "Did you call a doctor?"

"Why?" Lizzie knew she was too weak to blush.

"Because you are going to run a marathon next week. You should know if this is serious," Meg felt her forehead. "I think you have a fever."

"I'm fine."

Meg pouted, but didn't push the subject. "Can I get you anything?"

"I just need to get it out of my body," Lizzie took the book back from her. "I'm pretty sure I've done that."

"Well, maybe this will make you feel better," Meg offered a brief smile and an envelope.

Lizzie wasn't too feverish to not recognize the return address of the bank. She lifted a weak pair of arms and managed to open the letter. She scanned the short paragraph and felt her brief burst of adrenalin plummet. "We didn't get it."

"Oh Lizzie."

"I knew we were aiming too high," Lizzie was unable to care when her head felt too light for any emotion. She couldn't process the dream much less the reality of that letter.

"Remember when you started running? You were in agony the first time you ran two miles. You said you were never going to do it again. But you got up and ran two miles every morning. Then it was three. Then it was four. And now it's a marathon. You'll get up and try again."

"Mmm," Lizzie smiled weakly, impressed by Meg's wisdom. Somewhere in the past five months Meg grew up.

Meg left the couch and went to the closet to get another blanket. She tripped over the box of books, knocking a gift bag off the top. Meg picked it up and pulled out a small hinged box. "This is pretty," she opened up the compact and showed the white powder.

"Careful, that stuff is toxic," Lizzie slid back against the sofa.

"Was this from Ben?"

"From Andrew," Lizzie thought about the possibility of lead and her weak stomach stirred a little. It didn't really matter any longer. "It was a Christmas present."

"Do you want this valuable antique in a box in the closet?"

"Keep it there. I should probably get it cleaned or something," Lizzie shut her eyes again. "Right now I just want to sleep." She felt for the leather bound book that slipped to her side and clutched it to her chest as she fell asleep.

She slept a lot. The dreams didn't play out in such vivid detail, but they presented encores of the feverish images that stayed in her mind since the summer. The hedges by the carriage house, promises whispered in the moonlight, sitting in the kitchen, and the green eyes that were always there.

She faded back into coherent thought by noon the following day. She was able to follow the tedious plotlines of a soap opera. Of course there was a story about an unwanted pregnancy. Of course… Lizzie let herself wrap her brain around the past 24 hours. She hated the fact she had food poisoning. She didn't know how she would get enough strength by the weekend to do her last ten mile run. She hated being confined to the couch without much energy to even take a shower.

There was a small part of her that wished it wasn't food poisoning, that wished the test wasn't negative. She didn't know how she would support a child when she couldn't qualify for a business loan with a partner. She didn't love the father. But Eric would have done the right thing. Just like Thomas.

Maybe it wasn't Lizzie who wished for the test to be different. Lizzie didn't want a baby. She had that pang when she saw Will and then when she found out about Nora, but it really was okay with her that Ben couldn't provide her with a child. Maybe it wasn't. Maybe that was Lily protecting her. Protecting her from the memory of a lost child. A child she wanted to have, to stay mortal, to make herself … to make herself human again. That child was her hope to start her life over. To get away from the Fultons who treated her poorly because she was a bastard. To get away from the parasites who used her for her blood. Tom gave her that choice. He gave her that way out. Not just to another place, but to another reality of herself. Ben, even with those eyes that loved her so completely, could not give her that. And when Thomas became a vampire, he took away that choice… leaving Lily with only one option for her escape.

She reread the inside of the book again and again. To the edge of doom. She loved Ben. Lily loved him so completely. Did she love Oliver? Did she love him enough to come back to him in another lifetime? Lizzie wondered if Lily's affection for him was any different than her affection for Eric. She liked his company more once she understood he knew about vampires. He was good to her. He liked her. If there was a baby, it wouldn't have been a bad partnership.

But Oliver was more to Lily than a thoughtful doctor. He was her best friend. He loved her – as much as those green eyes. Not enough to stay human. Not enough to resist Charlotte. So Lily took his child without even telling him.

Would Lizzie tell him? That secret went with Lily to the grave. Two hundred years ago. What good would it do to tell him now? Especially if he had someone… someone new? That source. He didn't love Lizzie. He got swept up in the idea of Lily, just as she had. They both lost sight of the present and tried to make the past work in the 21st century. It didn't.

Lizzie knew the answer now. She knew the missing piece to Lily. She understood it all. Enough, anyway, to finally put her to rest. Now Lizzie could live in her present and not constantly wonder why things ended as they did. She could direct better attention to herself. To not be discouraged by a bank's refusal. To rewrite her business plan and start cooking for Nora's aunt out of her own kitchen. To make herself better and strong enough to run 26 miles.

Chapter Thirty-Five

The night before the race, Lizzie shut herself away in her room. In her sleep she saw her food poisoning dream all over again. There was no coffee shop. It began with a wedding of the narrowed faced boy and an innocent young girl. She felt the teeth sink into her neck and opened her eyes. She wanted the dream to stop there. She couldn't feel the despair. Not that morning. She needed hope.

She opened her eyes before dawn. It was too early, but not worth the effort to go back to sleep. She read all the messages of encouragement her friends sent and posted on her Facebook wall. She knew it was foolish, but hoped there would be a note from Ben. He knew she was running. Even if he didn't want to be with her, Lizzie was certain he wanted her to succeed.

But… as the memory of her dream lingered, she realized she didn't just want a note on her Facebook wall. She wanted him. She went to his dormant profile, which still said Chicago was his current location. She quickly typed out the lines of Sonnet 116 and posted it. It was silly, especially when he rarely went onto the social network. But it provoked enough anxiety to propel her energy for the start of the race.

She didn't think about Lily as she ran. Her mind faded into the crowds of encouraging spectators. She remembered the race and why she was really there. To prove that her body overcame three decades of neglect and could do this impressive thing. She listened to the beats of her music and pressed herself forward. She looked towards road signs and supporters offering oranges and camera crews, pushing towards each mile marker. As Elizabeth Watson. As the 34 year old woman who got up and ran to do something for her heart. Not the 21 year old girl who ran away from it.

At mile 20, Meg jumped into the road. Lizzie took out her headphones and paused to greet her and Nora on the grassy side of Com Ave. She caught her breath and took a drink from the water bottle they gave her. She was empowered by their support to make it up Heartbreak Hill. Then she let herself think about the end, when it would all be over.

She crossed the finish line amongst crowds of cheering and accolades. She felt the sudden relief of no movement and an overwhelming pang of yearning. No one was there to congratulate her. She was alone. She found her way to a tent to get water and relief to the end of her momentum.

Lizzie left the tent an hour later, feeling the plunge of her isolation. All around her were accomplished runners with their friends, their children, their lovers. Hugs and kisses and words of praise. Why had she insisted her parents stay home in Coldbrook? She found her phone and dialed the number to her mom. She spoke briefly, giving the details of her time. Then she made the excuse that friends were waiting for her. But they weren't. They were back in Newton because Nora was too pregnant to deal with the crowd on Boylston Street. Was no one close by to congratulate her accomplishment? She felt the exhaustion fuel her emotion.

She wondered if Ben checked his Facebook. If he saw the message from her and thought… anything except a desire to ignore it. It was a foolish impulse. She would go home and delete it and hope he didn't see the message. She ran the marathon. She did something Lily would never do. She loved Ben. She wanted him. But maybe he was right. She was better off without them, living the life Lily never had the chance to complete.

She gathered her wits and summoned the strength of her runner's high to walk to the train. Maybe Meg and Nora would meet her at the next station so she wouldn't have to walk to Jefferson Park. She looked up to see her way through the crowd. A few yards away, Oliver's dark eyes smiled at her. "Well done, Lizzie."

Lizzie felt her tired heart leap. "You're here."

"I didn't go back to California."

"You came here… to see me."

"Of course I did," he put his arm around her.

"Will you take me home?" she let herself lean against his shoulder. It felt strong and comfortable. She lost notice of the crowd as they walked to his Jeep. She was grateful it wasn't far away and didn't mind that she had to sit beside him as they sat in the slow crawl out of the city.

"How are you feeling?" he broke their silence when he finally made it to the Storrow exit. They could have walked faster than the car moved, but the idea of standing on her feet didn't inspire her.

"Tired," she breathed out. "Exhilarated."

"I bet," he grinned wickedly.

She wouldn't meet his eye to show she knew what he was thinking. She didn't know if she wanted… She was glad to see him. To have her old friend there. Not the vampire who would celebrate her endorphin rush. "I did it."

"I knew you would."

"Yeah," she looked out the window, letting the thought sting her that Ben wasn't there. Why did Oliver come? Wasn't it just as well for her to stay away from him as well? "Why didn't you go back to California?"

"I think I'm going to take a job out here," he let out a happy breath and turned to smile at her. "After the last lecture, they made me an offer I couldn't refuse. I met the team working on the research. I will miss the NCC students… but I suspect I can recruit a couple of this year's graduates."

"Wow."

"And…" he turned his focus back to the slow moving traffic. "I've done a lot of thinking since January. Since you said you didn't want… if you don't want to be in a relationship, Lizzie, that's fine. I would rather have your friendship than nothing at all and a whole country separating us."

"Us? What about that other… the source you were dating?"

"You said I kept looking for Lily in all the women I've been with. You were right. I do look for her, for you."

Lizzie took in a deep breath and focused on the New Hampshire plate on the car in front of them. "Oliver…"

"I just want… I want to see you and be able to talk with you – about your work, about your crazy friends, about books, about the world. Is that inappropriate?"

"No," she read the 'live free or die' logo and thought of Lily. "I don't think it is."

"Good."

"I got really sick last week," Lizzie thought she could see a break in the traffic in the distance.

"You did?"

"A couple days after I saw you, I got food poisoning," Lizzie could tell he didn't understand her swift conversation shift. She didn't know if she wanted to finish the impulse. But the oxygen flow to her brain was still too slow to stop her. "I thought I was pregnant for about a half hour."

"A baby," Oliver's voice was barely audible. "I didn't think you were involved in a serious relationship."

"I'm not. I don't know if that would have changed the situation. But then I had a fever and a lot of vivid dreams. I dreamt… I remembered… Lily was pregnant when she died." She saw him tighten his grip of the steering wheel and moved her eyes to see the expression on his face. It was cool and calm. The heave of his chest showed a slow deep breath. "That's why… that's why everything happened, isn't it?"

"You remembered that?" his voice was as calm and cool as the stillness of his face.

"It was a dream. But I've had it twice. The first part was when Lily told Ben she wanted to marry you because she wanted the baby. Then Lily was waiting for you. She wanted to tell you so you could run off together. But when you came you were…"

"She didn't tell me."

"Because Charlotte changed you," Lizzie's eyes drifted away from Oliver and back to the road where the cars were thinning and picking up speed. "Did you know?"

"I know that she was pregnant, yes."

"Did you know then?"

"No."

"Who told you?"

"Charlotte," he set his jaw. Lizzie could tell from the speed of his articulation that he was done talking about the subject. She touched a nerve. A very sore nerve. It was the reason for everything. It was the reason she was sitting beside him now and not Ben.

She retreated into silence as he picked up speed and brought her home. He stopped the car in front of her house and didn't attempt to restart the conversation. "I'm going in," Lizzie said finally.

"Are your roommates home?"

"I… I'm not sure," Lizzie looked at the cars in front of the house. Nora's car was there. Meg's was missing. Maybe they were still watching runners… or maybe they went to lunch.

"Can I come in?" he looked at her, his emotion still expressionless.

She nodded and left the car to lead him up to the apartment. There was a long awkward silence as they stood at the top of the stairs. Lizzie knew she couldn't begin the conversation. She was impatient to hear more details but decided she wasn't going to press him. "I'm going to take a shower," she decided and disappeared into the bathroom.

The steam of the water relaxed her. She let her thoughts wander back to the glee and satisfaction of her accomplishment. She wasn't going to push the subject with Oliver. His company was still tentative. It was the right thing, wasn't it? After all he went through, didn't he deserve Lily? But what did… what did Lily deserve … after dying… twice? What did Elizabeth deserve?

She changed into a sleeveless summer dress. It would be too cool in a few hours, when the blood rush left her skin. She checked her email before going back down to Oliver. She saw a handful of congratulations from relatives who got the message from her mother. Including Jen and Jack. There was nothing from Ben. Nothing.

"Lizzie."

She turned around quickly. Oliver was standing in the doorway. She leaned back over the chair and clicked out of the internet. She returned her attention and smiled at him. "Thanks for driving me home."

"Do you want to get something to eat? You must be famished."

"I ate something in the tent. Maybe later," she smiled, uncertain if she should be alarmed he walked up to her room with no invitation.

"Charlotte knew."

"What?"

"She knew before… she knew even before Ben went to her. She could… you can taste it in the blood."

Lizzie let herself lean against the back of her desk chair. "When did she tell you?"

"It was a stupid fight. We always fought about ridiculous things. This time she was determined to win and told me what she was saving for decades. She told me that Lily was pregnant. She wanted me to feel… she wanted to undermine my confidence and tell me I killed my own child."

Lizzie bit her lip, unable to stop the tears from forming in her eyes. It was one thing to think that in the quiet of her mind. To hear it articulated in Oliver's voice made the pain of it very real.

"Ben told her Lily was sneaking out to see me. She already knew about me. Lily told her. She didn't think that Lily loved me enough to…" he clenched his jaw. "… to actually leave the Fultons. Then she tasted the estrogen. She knew Lily would want to be a mother more than a source."

"So Charlotte punished Lily and went after you."

"And she punished Ben with the belief that he was responsible."

"Did she know about Ben?"

"Charlotte wasn't a fool. After Ben told her about us, she figured out he was still in love with her. He could have saved her," Oliver muttered confusing Lizzie again. "He didn't love her enough."

"What else did she tell you?" Lizzie asked, uncertain about his last comments.

"Nothing. I was so angry I stabbed her in the heart. The heart she really didn't have."

Lizzie gulped a big swallow of air. He was so emotionless and cold as he explained that last detail. She heard him describe her death filled with remorse. She saw the repentance in his eyes when she confronted him about other fatalities of his vampire life. But none struck her with as much heartlessness as his description of Charlotte. "But you loved her."

"It was a lie. It was all part of her wickedness. She never cared anything for me. She kept me because she always thought Lily would come back. She believed Lily would come back to me. She wanted to cause her heartache and pain, as she felt for Lily. She believed in the end Lily would take my life as I took hers. But she thought she could take away her happiness first."

"She's not here now," Lizzie thought how she managed to take away her own happiness without any help from the ghost of a vampire.

Oliver heaved a deep sigh and sat on the edge of her bed. "I didn't believe Lily was coming back to me. I hated her so much. Even though I mourned her death, I believed she died loving someone else. She loved Ben more. She loved Charlotte more. I didn't think she really loved me until Charlotte told me about the baby. Until I found out she left Ben and wanted to marry me to start a family. Then you were at Springs… and I could finally remember the part of Lily that made me happy."

"Why didn't you say anything at Springs?"

"Because of Eloise."

"Eloise," Lizzie whispered, annoyed that Eloise even existed. What did she have to do with anything?

"But … these past few months. You remembered. You remembered me. You didn't remember the baby. I thought… I thought that meant that Lily forgave me."

"Forgave you?"

"I saw the hate in her eyes. Right before she kissed me. She knew what I did. I was too driven by instinct. I took her blood. I didn't understand any of the rules. I didn't… she offered herself to me. She knew what would happen. She wanted me to kill her."

"Do you still hate her?"

"I was angry that she could leave this hell. But she came back. You left Ben and came back to me."

Lizzie swallowed, unable to say anything to validate that opinion. She still wanted Ben. She didn't understand why Oliver was there. She knew she owed it to him… to give him Lily's forgiveness. But she wasn't… she wasn't going back to him. "What about Eloise?"

"Why don't you remember her?"

"I don't know… but I must be. There are things from that time I know that I shouldn't know."

"You don't remember how she died?"

"No."

"Good."

Lizzie felt herself squirm with that answer. Was she supposed to remember? Why did only Lily return to her thoughts?

"That was a lost opportunity to make things right. But now," he walked to her. "Now I can do that. I don't believe what Charlotte said will happen. She was so full of hate and vengeance, she didn't understand forgiveness. She didn't understand the beauty of our longevity is that we evolve and improve. We don't have to stay monsters. Our power can be used for good. We can find redemption."

Lizzie stared up at the tears in his eyes. He was the same strong, unbelievably beautiful Oliver. The beauty came from his vulnerability. From the humanity within him. She didn't see the vampire any longer. She saw the young wheelwright who was given the time and decades to improve his luck in the world. Not just for himself, but those around him. But even with that power and limitless time, he still had the weakness of a human heart. The need to be loved by the one he loved at the beginning.

She saw what Lily saw. The sweet boy for whom she would have given everything to raise a family. The boy to whom she could say anything, with whom she was at ease without any effort - who was willing to give up everything to be with her. He gave up his life when he believed he couldn't have her. He was forced into that position by the one Lizzie thought she loved. The one she let herself forgive. Why? He didn't care. He wasn't there. He disappeared into the shadows and faded out of her life. He didn't try to come back to her. Oliver was there at the finish line. He was the one who wanted her.

Why did Ben try to keep him away from her? The question faded as she focused on Oliver's sad eyes. She saw the echo of her sadness and ache for love. He loved her. He loved her forever. "Thomas," she whispered and stood strong on the strength of her calves to meet his kiss. He lifted her off the floor and landed her on the bed. She felt the swim of her exhausted senses as her head rolled against the pillow. She asked herself again why Ben didn't call. Why he wasn't there. She closed her eyes and didn't stop as Oliver slowly came down to the bed with her.

He rested his head against her chest. She let the breaths plunge into her stomach and made her ribcage rise and fall under the weight of him. Her mind was in a different place as he touched her. She was too tired to think and remember the 26 miles that exhausted her limbs and made her throat dry with thirst. Everything from her morning - from Hopkinton to Meg and Nora at Heartbreak Hill to the crowd at the finish line - left her mind. She kept thinking she had to get home. She had to be there before everyone woke up. She felt his nerves, his clumsy hunger. The depth of emotion in his kiss. Thomas would always love her, no matter what she did. He would always forgive her. He would always be there for her. Even if she didn't love him.

He lifted his smile and indulged a kiss on her lips before going back to lean against her heartbeat. Even through her dress she knew he felt the healthy rhythm. He took her hand and interlocked his fingers through hers. "Children don't matter if there is eternity," he brought her hand to her lips.

She let him hold her hand there, against his kiss. She didn't know if that was endearing or startling. Her senses were too tired. He moved his mouth away from her palm towards her wrist. He paused, looking at her veins through the translucence of her white skin. Lizzie touched his cheek with the tips of her fingers, but he stayed focused on the interior of her wrist. "You can give me life," he kissed her arm.

All too quickly, he lifted his head and shifted his concentration from her wrist to the inside of her neck. "I could…" he breathed against her shoulder. The instinct thrilled her and then memory froze her. She felt the tips of his fangs and the sensation of her blood rushing towards her shoulder. She lifted her hands and attempted weakly to push him off. He was too strong, too powerful, too intoxicated to notice.

"Oliver," she whispered but her voice was too tired and weak. He stayed at her neck. It was too long. It was too long. He was draining her. She felt the strength of her eyelids wane. She tried her hands against his shoulders again. He was locked into drinking. She shut her eyes and felt herself fall backward. In the fade to darkness she saw the green eyes watching her, waiting for her. She forced her eyes open and managed to summon the strength to jerk her legs and shift to her side.

Oliver rose and looked down at her. She could see the blood on the corner of his mouth. "It's bad blood."

"Lily," he looked down at her hungrily.

"No," she sat up, feeling very, very weak. "I'm not…"

She saw the fear in his eyes slowly melt into a different expression she had never seen. It was hunger and madness and illness. Lizzie wanted to shut her eyes, but was energized by a fear that crept from her stomach and inched out to the edges of her fingers. "Leave," she couldn't breathe. Her heart was beating too quickly. Something was wrong. Very. Very wrong.

"I can fix this," he tried to take her hand.

She couldn't look at him. It required too much effort. She needed her phone. "Get out of here," she managed the words between her struggled breaths. She found the strength to go back to the desk. She saw him leave as she heaved the next huge gulp of air to pick up the phone. She found Ben's number and pressed send.

Lizzie felt a cloud come over her and faded out of the moment. She saw Lily's body crumpled on the floor of Harriet's room. Benjamin came in and saw her body. He turned her over and leaned to feel the breath coming from her lips. He bit his wrist and let the blood drop from the veins. He held it to Lily's immobile lips and stopped. He let her head gently down and forced himself to stand. He walked away and faded into the cloud.

Lizzie opened her eyes weakly. She was extremely thirsty. And sleepy. The sleep was warm and comfortable. She wanted to go back to the cloud, back to the Fulton House. Back to Lily.

"Elizabeth," a voice whispered in her ear. "Elizabeth!"

Lizzie fought against her eyes opening again. She wanted to go in front of the fire in the kitchen. It was more comfortable there. There was a pitcher of water she could drink and listen to Annie sing songs while she made stew.

"Elizabeth," Ben called. Lizzie looked through a gauzy film at his sheer green eyes. She felt something sharp stab into her arm. She was cold. Very, very cold. She needed her petticoat. No. It was April. She wanted some water. She really wanted some water. She couldn't feel her legs. Her legs were so tired. She was running, running, running all the way to Fulton House. Away from the Fulton House and green wallpaper and Gerard Fulton talking about a chair. She was running, running, running back to her warm comfortable bed. Hearing Ben's voice telling her it was going to be okay.

Chapter Thirty-Six

Lizzie opened her eyes. Her senses adjusted slowly to the beep of a machine and the feel of something attached to her arm. She inhaled the sterile aroma of the hospital as the room took shape. She lifted an arm with a tube taped to her wrist. Something moved out of the shadows. "Lizzie," Meg stood from her chair. "You're awake."

"What happened?" Lizzie's voice cracked with dryness.

"Ben said you were dehydrated and anemic."

"Ben?"

"Yeah," Meg smiled. "He came right away when you called him… at least that's what he said. You don't remember?"

"It's kind of fuzzy," Lizzie tried to see if there was anyone else in the room. The bed next to her was empty and lit only by the street lights outside.

"I didn't call your parents. Ben and the doctor said you were going to be fine. That you just needed rest. I figured I would wait until you woke up. I didn't want your mom to freak out."

"No, that's… that's good," Lizzie managed a smile. "Where is Ben?"

"He had to make some calls to his office," Meg offered a knowing look. "He only left after I promised to stay here with you."

Lizzie sat herself up, again feeling the tubes and wires attached to her. She realized a wire was conveniently taped along her neck. She felt as though moving from horizontal to vertical was as challenging as 26 miles.

"How long have you been here?" she looked for a clock.

"A half hour," Meg beamed again. "Although I've been in the hospital all afternoon."

"What?"

"Nora had her baby girl."

"She did?" the smile let her forget the other obvious details of the moment.

"Rose Emily," Meg explained. "Nora's water broke as we were walking back to the apartment."

"Did Ben call you?"

"I saw him in the hallway. I came to get a cup of coffee for Mark. Ben explained that you fainted and were here under observation."

"What else did he say?'

"Just that you need a lot of rest and fluids. I think they are going to keep you here overnight. I can stay if you want."

"That's okay, Meg," Ben said from the doorway. "I'll stay with her."

Meg looked at Lizzie for approval. Lizzie nodded her head mutely. Meg looked toward Ben and stepped back from the bed. "Then I am going to get one last look at Rose and go home. Call if you need anything, Lizzie. I can give you a ride tomorrow… if you need one."

"Thanks," Lizzie watched her leave the room. Ben lingered in the doorway and stepped closer to the bed. "Meg said you told her I was dehydrated and anemic."

"You were," he breathed out as he took the chair from the shadows and brought it closer to her side.

"But… there is more."

"You had a transfusion, Elizabeth. Your blood loss didn't result in anything worse than dehydration and anemia."

"It could have been worse."

"Much worse."

"Thank you for… coming and getting me…" she looked down, wondering how on earth he got her to Mt. Elm and was able to explain her blood loss or the wounds in her neck.

"I'm glad you called me," he took her fingers and held onto her hand. She saw his green eyes, but was too weak to let her mind think about all the images of those eyes since December. She wanted to ask him so many questions. She wanted to say so many things. She was glad he was there beside her, after wanting his presence for so long. She wished it wasn't a hospital. She wished that it wasn't because Oliver…

"I'm … I'm sorry I let this happen."

Ben let go of her hand and folded it back against her stomach. "You need rest, Elizabeth. You should try to go back to sleep."

"I just woke up."

"You aren't well," he sat back in his chair.

"No," she clenched her jaw and felt the anger drain a lot of energy. "I have to tell you…"

"You don't have to tell me anything."

"I saw you. When I was… I suppose I was unconscious… I saw you with Lily. I never saw Lily before. But I saw her dark curly hair and her pale skin. You were there. You had the opportunity to save her life at the end. You could have made her a … like you and had her with you forever. But you didn't. You let her go. You let her die."

Ben locked his eyes on her. They revealed no emotion. Just frozen but rapt attention. "You loved her enough to let her go," Lizzie allowed herself to relax into the tears. "You weren't… you weren't a monster."

He touched the hand he left on her stomach briefly before walking to the window on the darkened side of the room. His focus was not on her but whatever was happening outside the window – on the Charles River.

"I… a month ago I dreamt about the thunderstorm after the wedding. I've had so many vivid dreams, Ben. I saw you in the Fultons' kitchen," Lizzie said to make him turn his eyes back to her. She wasn't sure if she was going to tell him what she did to prompt one of those dreams. She wanted him to know she saw him. She saw the monster and the man that loved Lily. Now she knew which one survived her death.

He finally turned his eyes back to her and let out a quiet sigh. "You really should get some rest now, Elizabeth. Even if you don't sleep, it is important that you don't use too much energy."

She lowered her eyes away from him, feeling the sting of his refusal to discuss these very important images. "Ben…"

"I'll be here," he insisted and looked back to the river. "You don't need to worry. I think we should just… you must try to sleep."

Lizzie relented and lowered herself back against her pillows. In spite of the frustration, she closed her eyes and felt the wave overcome her. It was a deep, deep sleep. She knew she was dreaming, but the images embedded themselves in the dark corners of her memory as she moved to the next one. She felt she should wake a few times, but told herself it wasn't important and let her mind roll into another wave of sleep. Finally, the brightness seeped under her eyelids and was unable to disappear into the darkness. She felt the wane of an emotion… a happy emotion, but the circumstance of the dream that prompted it was gone as soon as she opened her eyes.

She heard the soft click of a keyboard as she adjusted her eyes. Ben sat on the empty bed. He saw her open eyes and closed the laptop. "How long have you been here?" she brought herself to sitting. It was still an effort, but not as traumatic as the night before.

"It's just after three. You slept through the morning," he smoothed the hair across her forehead.

"I was tired."

"Yes," he looked at the machines to which she was wired. "I'm sure they will take you off the saline. Then we can get you some dinner."

"Mm," Lizzie looked down at her hands. She felt better enough to feel frustrated with her limited movement.

"I'll tell them you are awake," he quickly left the room.

Lizzie sighed and looked up at the ceiling. She noticed an arrangement of flowers on the table next to her. She was able to reach the card with her unrestrained arm and saw they were from Richard. News traveled fast in the corridors of Mt. Elm.

Ben came back into the room with another smile. "Who is my doctor?" Lizzie wondered if anyone she saw in the cafeteria was going to come in and ask her why she had two red marks on her neck… or if for any reason they happened to notice… her thigh.

"I have a friend who works here and at the clinic," Ben sat in the chair that was still close to her side.

"Dr. Chiang?"

Ben eyed her carefully and smiled in amusement. "She didn't think you knew."

"I figured it out a few weeks ago. She… a friend of mine has a thing for her," Lizzie looked down, feeling odd with the reference to Eric as her friend. He really wasn't, even though he knew more about her than the people whom she did label as friends.

"Eric Drummond," Ben lost his smile.

"You know him?"

"I know that you and he…" Ben gazed at the door.

"It's not…" Lizzie looked at her hands and then tried to make eye contact again. "What happened yesterday?"

"You lost a lot of blood."

"I know that. But how did I get here? How did Dr. Chiang become my doctor? How did Richard find out to send me flowers?"

Ben drew his fingers into his palm and tightened a fist. Then he released it and shook it out. "I was outside your house when you called."

"What?"

"I saw you leave with him. I came to watch you at the race. You made a better time than I thought, so I missed seeing you cross the finish line. By the time I found you, you were getting into his Jeep."

"You came?"

"I thought you wanted me to."

"I did… I didn't think you would."

"I started to go home but then I went to your house. I sat outside debating whether or not to go in and talk to you. I didn't want to act on my anger, Elizabeth. You made a choice to be with him. You invited him in. But… I didn't want… anything to happen to you."

"Ben…"

"I saw him leave. I knew something was wrong. I was going to go after him but then you called. I found you on the floor of your bedroom," he shut his eyes as if trying to stop himself from seeing. "The ambulance was there in ten minutes. They were the most terrifying ten minutes I've lived through in a long time."

Lizzie saw the sadness he tried to mask with a hasty smile. "Ben, this is my fault. I shouldn't have…"

"He should have known better," he drew in a slow breath, almost prompting his voice to growl.

"Known what?"

"He knew you just ran 26 miles. You were dehydrated and anemic already. But he lost control again."

Lizzie looked away from him, feeling the sensation of her head hitting the back of the country store. She let him kiss her. She let him come close to her when she knew better. When she knew her blood wasn't good enough. "Ben, I…"

"It isn't your fault Elizabeth," Ben hardened his voice. "Charlotte poisoned him."

"What? How can you poison a vampire?"

"I told you we have adverse reactions to certain elements in blood."

"Lead," Lizzie looked at the wires dripping liquid into her veins. She thought of Claire's husband and all the details Ben revealed in Quechee. "But he… you said that lead poisoning causes porphyria… or whatever it is that makes you sensitive to light. How can that be when he goes hiking and… he loves the outdoors?"

"He removed most of it from his system. But it never goes away completely. There is no complete cure. So when he doesn't keep a schedule and drinks weak blood, there is enough lead to cause symptoms to return."

"What symptoms?"

"Aggression. Mania. Delusions."

"Why didn't you tell me?"

"I tried to warn you about him. You didn't want to hear me. You thought I was keeping him from you out of spite."

She heard the echo of all the unpleasant conversations in November and again when he saw her outside of the Fulton Center opening. He was trying to tell her something she didn't want to hear. She kept the truth from Ben about all her encounters with Oliver. How could he warn her if she was seeing him behind his back? "How did she do it? How did Charlotte get the lead into his blood?"

"She convinced him to feed on contaminated sources," Ben paused for another lengthy minute. "The mill girls were all exposed to lead paint."

"Eloise Hutchins." The energy left her as the name left her lips. She leaned her head back and gazed at the ceiling. "So it was me all along. I am responsible for making him a vampire. Then I made him crazy. So… does that mean I will destroy him in this life, too?"

"No, Elizabeth." Ben rubbed his chin in his hand. "Eloise Hutchins was a fourteen year old girl. She didn't paint the walls of her home. She didn't have any choice in what happened to her. For many years I didn't even believe she was Lily. I didn't think you had anything to do with Eloise until you remembered she had red hair. And even if you did, it doesn't justify what he did to her… or you."

"He's … when he's like that, he's not the Oliver of Lily's memories. He's not… Thomas," Lizzie blinked her eyes, hoping her weakness wouldn't give way to tears. How could the Oliver who was so tender, so kind, so concerned about the environment, who listened to her… how could he be a manic, deluded monster? "If he drinks good blood, he will be all right, won't he?"

"He doesn't always take good blood."

"My blood wasn't…" Lizzie looked away from him. She could feel the plastic of the wire against her neck. "It hadn't been long enough."

"Long enough?"

Lizzie drew in the oxygen to summon her courage to be honest. She didn't tell Oliver her blood wasn't good enough. He drank it and went mad. "I was a source to another vampire."

She saw the tension harden his jaw. "Who did you feed?" The anger in his eyes was unmistakable. She never saw him bare that emotion so boldly. Not even when she told him about Oliver.

"Her name is Claire Chamberlain."

"Matthew Chamberlain's widow?"

Lizzie swallowed. She wanted to tell him it provoked vivid images of him and Lily. That she went there because she missed the sensation. That she wanted to be with a vampire… like him. None of that came to her mouth. The shame numbed her speech and crept down her throat. "It was…" she tried to begin a sentence when a familiar dark haired woman walked into the room.

"Hi Lizzie," Dr. Chiang greeted as she picked up the chart at the foot of her bed. There was no pause to acknowledge their mutual truths. That Dr. Chiang was a vampire or that Lizzie was a source. "How are you feeling?"

"Better," Lizzie couldn't look at Ben.

"You've got some color back," the doctor smiled at Ben.

"Ben says we should let you have some dinner tonight. So I think we can take this off," she removed the IV from her arm. "But I'd like to keep the heart monitor on you for one more night."

As she stepped back to the foot of the bed, Ben rose and whispered something to her. Lizzie couldn't understand all the words he was speaking, but knew he was telling her about Claire. Lizzie felt Dr. Chiang's eyes look over her again. "Actually, Elizabeth," she startled

Lizzie with the change of her name. "I would like to have you stay at the clinic for a couple days. I want to keep you under observation."

"I don't think that's necessary, Kate," Ben interjected. "She can stay with me. I can keep an eye on her."

Dr. Chiang smiled at Lizzie and cast a knowing glance towards Ben. "That's all right with me. Is that okay with you, Elizabeth? No need to occupy one of our beds when you have a chance to stay at that swanky new apartment." Lizzie forced a grin of agreement even though she felt a sting at the fact that Dr. Chiang knew more about where Ben lived presently than she did. "You're a very lucky girl, Elizabeth. You have some very concerned doctors looking out for you."

"I am lucky," she sank back against her pillow as Ben whispered a few more sentences to Dr. Chiang. Her head was too clouded to understand if she should be worried about the doctor's added concern or about Ben's anger. Did he really want her to come to her new apartment? Or was he just protecting her from Oliver until he had a clean source of blood?

"Kate is going to have them bring you some dinner," Ben's voice pulled her focus back after Dr. Chiang left.

"Great," Lizzie didn't have an appetite for food, especially Mt. Elm food.

"You are going to be okay," Ben rested his hand on her arm as he sat back in the chair. "I'm sorry if I was too bold saying that you would stay with me. But I can promise you that it is much more comfortable than the clinic."

Lizzie looked at the flowers by her bed. "If you knew Oliver was dangerous, why did you go to Chicago?"

"Because you left me, Elizabeth. I thought that was what you wanted. For the first time you remembered me with Lily… and instead of staying with me, you went to him," his eyes weakened from anger to the sorrow she had never seen.

"Why did you come back?"

"Keith told me you came to the apartment. I knew something happened. I knew it was Oliver. I wanted to be here the next time you needed me."

She looked at his eyes, feeling shame and guilt for ever doubting him. For ever doubting he wanted anything except her wellbeing. "I… I'm sorry."

"I'm just grateful you are okay. That he didn't…" he reached for her hand. She wrapped her fingers around his hand and felt the comfort of his grip. It was real. Not a dream. Not a ghostly meeting in a parking lot. He was there beside her, holding her hand and looking at her with the green gray eyes.

"Ben, I…" she began as a nurse entered with her food. Ben let go of her hand and arranged the table in front of her. He went back to his laptop to cue her focus on the meal. Lizzie took a half hearted bite of spaghetti then lifted her eyes to see him looking at her. He shifted his glance quickly, but she was certain it held the intensity of the stare he gave Lily.

Chapter Thirty-Seven

"Wow," Lizzie couldn't contain her amazement as she followed Ben into the apartment. It was a big open space, with no walls separating the living, dining, and kitchen areas. The stylish furnishings and shiny new kitchen were lit by floor to ceiling windows revealing the Charles River below. A spiral staircase went up to a loft on the second story.

"I wanted a new place when I came back from Chicago," he bit his lip. "I was rather self-indulgent."

"It's a nice space," Lizzie walked to the windows and admired the budding leaves on the trees along Storrow Drive.

"I didn't bring much from the old apartment," he bit his lip. "Just a few boxes."

"I like it," Lizzie turned back to him, wondering what happened to Maria's china.

"There are three bedrooms upstairs," Ben paused. "Do you want something to eat? I'm afraid there's nothing in the kitchen. Not even plates. But, there are a couple places that can probably deliver lunch."

"I'm not that hungry," she looked towards the kitchen with its polished marble counter and stainless steel appliances. "Why am I here, Ben? Is there something wrong with me?"

"You just need to take it easy," he guided her away from the window to one of the couches.

"I could take it easy at home. What are you and Dr. Chiang afraid will happen?"

"It's just a precaution, Elizabeth," he brightened his eyes.

"A precaution for what?" she folded her arms across her chest.

"Sometimes when a source has a low red blood cell count, there are additional risks."

"Additional to bleeding to death?"

"The chemical in our teeth – that anestatizes the pain of the cut – gets into the bloodstream of all sources. If there aren't sufficient red blood cells, there is a risk of mutation."

"Mutation?"

Ben met her eyes and nodded. "You had a lot of healthy blood pumped into you, Elizabeth. It has been well over 36 hours, when most symptoms manifest themselves."

Lizzie unfolded her arms and touched the wound at her neck. "When you say mutation, do you mean that I could become … one of you?"

"Not entirely," he shook his head, as if to conceal an unpleasant thought. "But often the only cure is a transfusion of blood from one of us, which means… the mutated source would…"

"Become a vampire," Lizzie swallowed. "Does this happen often?"

"No – not with regulations for source feeding," Ben hardened his jaw.

"Why didn't you explain this to me before?"

"I never thought it would become an issue, Elizabeth. I didn't think that you would… be a source for anyone else."

Lizzie felt her cheeks flame. It was a fair remark. He made it with a very neutral tone and without a hint of nastiness. "Ben, when you came to my room on Monday and you found me… you could have saved me, couldn't you?"

"I did save you," he left the couch.

"Yes, but if… if the ambulance didn't come in time, you could have given me your blood."

"That wouldn't be saving you."

"You said you thought about it."

"I did. I have. I don't know if I could ever do it," he faced her. "I know I would never do that without giving you a choice, Elizabeth. I would hate for it to be a choice you have to make."

"Why did you change, Ben? Did Charlotte trick you?"

"She did… but… it was a long time ago."

"Was there someone else – was there a Lily between you?"

"Charlotte seduced me when I was a drunk in a tavern. She fed on me for nearly a year. I had a head for money and figures that was very useful to her. I was a business investment," Ben's voice had the anger she heard when she mentioned the Chamberlains. "I wanted her power."

"Is that what you were like when you were a farmer?"

"I don't remember," Ben shook his head. "I honestly don't remember very much about those years before the Fulton scheme. I don't want to remember."

"Not even your own life? You were married and had children. You said you loved them."

"It's a distant dream."

"What's the point of living so long if you can't remember the life you want to last forever?"

"I didn't want to remember it when I changed."

"But you choose to remember…"

"Yes, I choose to remember her," Ben crossed back to entrance where he left his briefcase.

"Will you remember me?"

"I don't… I don't think about it that way. You are here right now."

"You want me here?" she stood from the couch and took a hesitant step towards him.

"Yes," he clutched his briefcase and watched her take slow steps towards him.

"I know why Lily chose him." Ben didn't respond. He kept his focus, but left the silence for her to fill. "I know why Oliver killed Charlotte. That's what we were talking about before he…" Lizzie stopped moving. "Charlotte told Oliver she knew Lily was pregnant. Lily told you. She told you first… you were the only one she ever told."

Ben took in a breath and walked away. She watched him disappear through a door under the spiral staircase. Lizzie waited a few minutes, expecting him to return. Did he go get something? Did he need to collect himself before he told her the complete truth? Several minutes passed and Ben did not return. Did something distract him from coming back? She went through the door under the stairs and found him behind a computer at a desk. "Don't you have anything to say?"

"What is there to say, Elizabeth?"

"That's why – that's why it all happened."

"It was two hundred years ago, Elizabeth. There are more current events that have bearing on the present," he looked at her intently.

"It has everything to do with the present, Ben. It's why I'm here. It's why I … it's why I let him…" she looked down and touched the spots on her neck again. "He needed to know Lily forgave him for killing their child."

"You aren't Lily," he went back to typing.

"I didn't want this, Benjamin," she snapped back. "Do you think I want her memories creeping into my brain at night? Or when I'm sick with a fever? Don't you think I want to be in possession of my own feelings and make a choice based on what my heart wants and not what some poor girl who died miserably never got to have?"

"I didn't think you wanted to have anything to do with her," he still looked at the computer. "You were the one … you made the decision to let her make your choices."

"But you loved Lily. Isn't that what you wanted? Isn't that why you were with me? So YOU could have your second chance? So you could feel as though she forgave you for taking Oliver away and making him into the creature that took her child? You didn't spend time with Sara and me at Springs because you had any interest in Elizabeth. You were waiting for the day that I remembered Lily. You told me you wanted me to remember that you were with her. You wanted me to be Lily."

"No," he looked away from the computer. "I wanted you to be Elizabeth. I didn't want to tell you about Lily and how she felt about me. I didn't want to force that thought into your mind and make you see it that way."

"But you told me about Lily. You told me about Oliver. Didn't you force those thoughts into my head?"

"Did I?"Ben stood up from his chair and came in front of her. "I told you because you asked me. Because you wanted to know."

"Are you going to blame me for all of this?" she felt the exhaustion of her body start to tease her. "Are you going to blame me for the fact that by sleeping with me you prompted whatever part of my mind hid Lily's existence? That for thirty-three years I had no idea about this? It wasn't until you came into my life again that I had any… desire to know a thing about Lily. It wasn't until you came into my life again that Oliver felt he could…"

He grabbed her by the elbows. His thumb pressed against the wound left by the IV, but she wouldn't let him see the pain she felt. "You came to me. You came to me by the river. You wanted this as much as I," he looked at her intensely. The anger she saw with mention of the Chamberlains crept back into his expression. "You made the choice to leave. You went to him. You, Elizabeth, made the decision to become his lover and give him your blood. You can't blame Lily for that. You can't use her tragedy as an excuse for your cruelty."

Lizzie's lip trembled and the tears pooled in her eyes. He released his grasp of her arms and pushed her away. "Do you want me to go back to him?" she rubbed the inside of her left elbow.

"No, I do not," he said bitterly with his back turned to her. "He loves you."

"He loves Lily."

"If that is what you want, I am not going to stop you."

"You aren't worried for my safety?"

He turned and laughed as he faced her. "What does my concern for your safety matter when you have none for yourself?"

She felt the energy drain from her head. A coolness came across her cheeks as her knees weakened. She retreated to a chair and sat as her ears clouded. Ben left the room and came back quickly with a glass of water.

"You should go upstairs and get some rest," he said distantly.

She shifted her hurt, angry eyes to him. "I would go home right now if I had the strength," she swallowed the water.

"Get some rest and we will talk later," he touched her shoulder and went back to his desk.

She waited until the blood came back to her cheeks. She stood and quietly left the room, knowing that Ben's eyes were watching her. She went up the stairs into one of the bedrooms. It was well furnished like the rest of the apartment, but clearly uninhabited. She lay down on the bed and tried to sort through all the heated words of the past half hour. Nothing made sense as her mind whirled between Lily and Lizzie. Somewhere between the images of white roses and blurred blue ink, she fell into a deep, dreamless sleep.

It was dark when she woke. The clock in the room read 2:15. She was too wide awake to go back to sleep. Her body was restless from sleeping so many hours. She felt the itch of her limbs from being idle for several days. She wanted to do something. Something more than stare into the blackness and see Lily's memories.

Her bag was on the chair by the dresser. Ben must have brought it up while she was sleeping. She decided to take a shower in the adjoining bathroom and change out of her jeans. It felt good to wash away the dried tears from her cheeks, but the steam reminded her of her empty stomach.

She left the room. The doors of the other bedrooms were closed. She wondered if Ben was in one of them, or if he was still in his office downstairs. There was no light at the bottom of the stairs – just the glow from the lights along the river. She went down and saw the office door was open and dark. She walked around the open space of the apartment, drawn almost immediately to the dining area and the sideboard. She opened the cabinet doors and found them empty. Until the last which hid a rack of wine. She pulled out one of the bottles and saw her favorite Malbec.

She was tempted and remembered her empty stomach. She looked at the kitchen and noticed a bowl of fruit that wasn't on the counter earlier. She walked toward the shiny apples and saw a receipt by the bowl for a grocery delivery. She opened the refrigerator and cabinets to see Ben's afternoon purchase of her favorite ingredients. Not a bad memory for someone who knew so little about 21st century food. But there were still no plates.

She made a turkey sandwich and ate it without much thought for flavor. She satisfied her stomach and felt the vacancy of the apartment overwhelm her. She returned to the bottle and was pleased to find a pair of wine glasses and a corkscrew. She wondered how long they were there, if they were always meant for her… or if there was any other source he brought home.

She walked back to the large windows, letting the warm burn of the Malbec relax her. She stared out onto the river, noticing the lights from Cambridge reflected on the dark water. She wondered where the marshes were centuries before. Where Lily sank her feet into the grass and lost hold of the book…

"Elizabeth?" she heard his voice at the top of the stairs. She looked up and saw him leave the doorway of her room. Even in the shadows, she saw the relief relax his brow.

"My clock is messed up," she looked back at the river. "I couldn't sleep any more."

"I got some groceries," he came down the stairs. "If you are hungry, there is food."

"I know," she showed him the wine glass and took another sip.

"Are you…" he stopped a foot away from her. "Are you okay?"

"I'm fine."

"I mean," he breathed out. "I don't mean physically."

"I just slept too much," she took another sip of wine.

"Elizabeth, I said a number of things this afternoon that I regret."

"A lot of it is true. I can't let the memories of Lily make my choices," she exhaled a staggered breath. "I don't love him. I realized that a week after… I always knew that. I just felt guilt. Like I had to do something to make it right. All I did was make everything worse."

"Elizabeth…" he came to her side.

"Do you wish I didn't remember Lily?"

"Sometimes," he pulled her hair back from her shoulder, exposing the marks Oliver gave her. "She knew me when I was something else. I loved her. I loved that she made me want to be different from what I was. Even though she died… and maybe because she did, I tried my best to become what I thought she believed I could be. But I destroyed her, as I fear I've..."

Lizzie saw a light move across the water – a boat or something… like a ferry. She drank from the wide rimmed goblet. She swallowed it after letting the flavor linger on her tongue for a moment. She didn't feel the warmth in her veins. She immediately took another lingering sip and set down the glass. "You would have killed her child if you kept her with you that night. You saved her from a lifetime of heartache. You set Lily free."

"Have I?" he turned her to face him. She saw the hunger in his grayer eyes. "Or have I destroyed her – you all over again?"

"You set me free. I was living this life blindly, unaware that I was trapped in Lily's misery. Confined by her lack of self worth, her paralyzed ambition, her inability to trust love. But I… I broke through that. I determined to fix myself, to face the things that make me unhappy. I want to live a better life, not die to escape misery."

"Do I make you unhappy?"

"Only when I'm not with you," she smiled through her tears.

He stroked her cheek and cupped her chin in his hand. "Once you told me I was what you were running to. You don't need to run any more. I want you to be with me. I want you to stay with me."

She lifted her hands to his chin and kissed him. She walked him towards the couch, gently pushing him to sit. She sat across his hips as his hands were at her shoulders, then her waist, fumbling for the end of her shirt and lifting it over her. "Ben, I love you," she kissed him lightly and then pressed against his forehead. "I never stopped loving you."

"I always loved you, Elizabeth."

Lizzie curled her lips into a smile and kissed him again.

*****

Lizzie walked back into the room and sat on the chair opposite the bed. Ben opened his eyes and smiled at her. "I knew you were awake," she laughed as she bit into one of her orange pieces.

"I knew you were more likely to feed yourself if you thought I was asleep," he sat up against the headboard. She breathed out as she saw the afternoon sun highlight the curve of his biceps.

"I was famished. Surely that must mean I'm not developing an appetite for blood."

"It's a good sign," he laughed. She missed his smile. She missed that open look of admiration he forced himself to hide until last night.

"How will I know for sure?"

"I will take a sample of your blood to the clinic today. They can do a final test. Then you should be in the clear."

"Then?"

"Then what?"

"I go home?"

Ben's expression sobered. "Do you want to go home?"

"No," Lizzie thought about her bedroom and the last time she was there… with Oliver. "Do you think he will try to see me?"

"He shouldn't," Ben swallowed.

"How do you know?"

"I spoke to him after you woke up. I told him you were… that you survived and that he should keep his distance."

"He won't do that if you tell him, Ben."

"Do you want to tell him?"

"No," she took the last piece of orange.

"You can stay here as long as you want," he reached his arm and pulled her to his side. "I would like you to make this your home. It would make this monstrosity less empty."

Lizzie smiled to herself. It was still so new and strange, all part of the dreamlike quality of the past six months. She liked the new apartment. She liked it a lot, with the marble countertops, the stainless steel appliances, the magnificent view of the Charles. It was almost surreal to think of it as hers… theirs. But she couldn't imagine leaving, even to go home to Jefferson Park. "I could start my business here," she let the thought escape her lips without recognition.

"The catering business with Andrew?"

"Nora told you."

"I think it's a brilliant idea. But you know, you could rent a space."

"No," she said firmly. "We tried that and didn't get a loan. Besides, I think we need to start small. Less responsibility. Especially if I'm working at the hospital."

"Why would you still do that?"

"To make money."

"You said it was dull."

"It is."

"If you come here, Elizabeth, you won't have to worry about living expenses."

"I have a car."

"And I'm certain by the end of the year you will have some income to take care of that," he fingered the ends of her hair.

"I still need money for startup expenses."

"Leave the hospital. If you need extra income, go work in a museum."

"Is this about me giving up a job I don't like very much or about a certain doctor?" Lizzie looked at him. "What exactly did Dr. Chiang tell you about Eric? How long has she been telling you things about me?"

"When I found out you worked there, I asked if she knew you. She never said much. But when I went to Chicago, I asked if she would keep an eye on you."

"Does she know Oliver?"

"Yes."

"Does she know about Lily and … the Fultons?" Lizzie half laughed at the fact Dr. Chiang's cardiac center was funded by Ben's thwarted pillage.

"Some of it," Ben touched her arm. "She's a friend."

Lizzie intertwined her fingers in his. She didn't really want to go back to the hospital and see Dr. Chiang regularly and have to wonder the thoughts behind those brilliant blue eyes. She wasn't eager to see Eric again. He was good to her. But it was done, like everything else that came before last night. "Maybe I'll take the summer off. I have some money put away. Not a lot… but enough to give me a couple months to start our business."

"Good," he grinned and pulled her back to the bed.

Chapter Thirty-Eight

Ben had to go to his office the next morning. Lizzie decided to test her endurance and take the train back to Jefferson Park to get some more clothes and her car. She appreciated the walk in the warm spring air. She breathed in the sweet blossoms along the sidewalks and admired the green starting to show on the grass of the park. As she followed the traces of emerging color, she saw a silver Jeep Wrangler parked on the other side of the street. Someone was sitting in the driver's seat. She didn't have to meet his eyes to know it was Oliver. She hastened her steps, locked the door, and went directly to her room. Lizzie saw the disheveled blankets on her bed and shuddered at the memory of Oliver standing in the doorway. Was there blood? Or was she imagining it? She couldn't stay there long. She heard Ben's warnings creep back into her mind. She wasn't afraid of him… and yet… he was outside her apartment. Waiting for her.

She opened several drawers of her dresser, pulling out all sorts of clothing. She didn't want to have to confront Oliver. She wasn't ready. Ben said the test results showed no mutation, but it would be three months before her blood was worthy of being a source. Oliver's madness would thrive on her poor cell count. Madness that let him believe she wanted him, that Lily came back to him. If he had the delusion, he could believe that. If he drank her weak blood, he could have her forever.

She found a suitcase and shoved all the clothes and her laptop and toiletries into it. She would come back later, to talk to Meg. With Ben. She brought the suitcase to her car and realized she forgot her coat with her wallet in her room. She rushed back to the door and let herself in, but didn't hear the slam of the screen door shut.

"Hi Lizzie."

"Hi," she struggled to keep her face calm as she turned back to face Oliver. Her heart beat so quickly and loudly she feared he would hear it and be tempted by her blood flow.

"You're okay," he smiled, but it required a lot of effort.

"No thanks to you," she started to close the main door. He put up his hand to stop it and stepped into the vestibule.

"Don't … just let me come in for a few minutes."

The space in front of the door was narrow. She turned quickly and went up the stairs to get away from him. "I have to be somewhere in a half hour," she began the lie and determined to fuel it with more information. "I have to go to the clinic."

"To see Ben?" he reached the top of the stairs.

"To make sure you didn't ruin my blood," she glared at him. She wanted to see his reaction – to see if he knew what he did.

"Lizzie," he reached out his hand. "I didn't want to hurt you."

"No?" she felt exposed standing so close to the stairs. She walked into the living room and crossed her arms in front of the couch.

He waited a few moments and then followed her. He went to the fireplace and stood awkwardly at the mantle. "It was an accident. I was… I was so happy that you… that we were together. That you made the choice to be with me."

"I didn't make that choice."

He left the mantle and went to her. "You told me that Lily forgave me. You kissed me."

"I made a foolish decision. I was confused. I thought I was supposed to... that it was what Lily wanted. Maybe it is what Lily wants," Lizzie tightened her fist. "But it isn't what I want."

"You let him manipulate you," he took hold of her cheeks and turned her face to his. "You let him convince you that Lily doesn't matter."

She pulled herself away as he tried to kiss her. "I know you loved Lily. I know she broke your heart. I know that she … I know the baby… it wasn't fair what happened to you, Oliver. But it isn't for me to make it right."

"This isn't about making something right," he went to her again. "This is about what is right. Us."

"There is no us."

"You don't want this?"

"I want you to leave," she looked directly at him.

"Please, Lizzie."

"You left me to die."

"You told me to leave."

"You could have done something."

"Yes," he nodded. "I could have saved you."

"You knew… didn't you? You knew that my blood wasn't right. You knew if you took too much I could change."

His dark eyes smiled at her, but she could see the deceit of his charm. "You knew… you did this to Melissa Benson."

"I didn't kill her."

"No," Lizzie walked towards the door. "But you knew when you took her blood she wouldn't be well enough to get home. You knew she would die."

"She tricked me."

"You knew she wouldn't survive without a transfusion. From you. So you didn't take her to the hospital. You didn't want her to mutate and turn into… you didn't want Ben to know what you did."

"You weren't there. You don't know what happened."

"I was there a few days ago. You did to her what you did to me. You left me to die."

"I don't want you to die."

"I don't want to live like you," she tried to walk passed him, but he took hold of her arms again and pushed her against the wall. He let go but stood in front of her, blockading her exit. "Did your wife have a choice? Or did you infect her blood by feeding from her too soon?"

"We made the choice to let it happen."

"No you didn't."

"You're confused," he shut his eyes. "You are overwhelmed. But you will understand… I know you will see that this is what should happen."

"What?"

"Why else would you keep coming back?" he touched her hair. "It doesn't make sense that you should die again."

"Oliver, I don't love you."

"You aren't supposed to be with him. Lily..."

"Oliver," she shut her eyes. "Why are you doing this? You are a good man, Oliver. Why can't you accept that this is what I want?"

"Because he doesn't deserve you," he took hold of her chin.

"He would let me go if I didn't want him," Lizzie made herself meet Oliver's sad manic eyes. "He wouldn't force me to stay with him because some vicious vampire told him lies about karma."

He let go of her arm and stepped back. "It wasn't a lie. You came back."

Lizzie pushed him aside and went down the stairs. She took her keys from the door and stepped out onto the porch, knowing Oliver was right behind her. She stepped onto the porch and felt him take her arm. "Oliver, this has to stop. I need to live my life now. Not… the one you and Lily never had," she looked away from the eyes that seemed to burn into her soul with accusation and challenged her goodness. "Please go."

"She asked you to leave, Oliver," Ben appeared at the bottom of the porch stairs.

Oliver let go of her arm and turned to face Ben. She had not seen them together since high school. Both sets of eyes burned with an intensity that frightened her. She saw Ben's fists curled tightly at his sides. She wondered what he was going to do when Oliver didn't leave. Oliver was taller. He was probably stronger than Ben. He could hurt Ben. He could… "Ben," she began as the keys rattled out of her grip. She shifted back to Oliver and tried to offer a smile to him. She couldn't find the strength to be pleasant but was able to tender her voice to kindness. "Oliver, please go. Please don't make a scene."

Oliver looked at her again, breaking the madness in his eyes. There was the soul struggling to be good. She could see it, but no longer believed its ability to completely overcome. He nodded reluctantly to her and let the meanness return with a nasty look at Ben as he walked away.

Lizzie bent down to pick up her keys and rose to find Ben's arms circle about her. She looked over his shoulder and watched the silver Jeep leave Jefferson Park. "Are you okay?" Ben pulled back to look at her face.

Lizzie nodded, unable to find the strength in her voice to speak. She hugged him tightly and let loose the tears her panic froze earlier. "My meeting ended early. I came to help you pack."

"He's mad," she swallowed as she released the embrace. "Because of me."

Ben wiped the tears from her cheeks. "It isn't your fault."

"I'm the only one who can fix this."

"What do you think you can do, Elizabeth? You can't reason with him. You know that."

"Lily took everything away from him. Everything. He could have had a perfectly happy life. He could have married the daughter of the blacksmith, but Lily…" the words were exiting her mouth without the cognition of the memory. "Lily went back to him to try to forget… you. Just like I did. I have to fix this Ben. I have to put right what she did to him."

"How are you going to do that? How could you possibly give him what he lost? You don't want to be with him," his jaw was very tight.

"I don't know. I just know I have to stop his sadness," she faded with a look at the blue spring sky.

"What if he kills you, Elizabeth? That won't stop anyone's sadness," he took her shoulders.

"He won't kill me."

"He's waiting to put you in a position to die or have to live like us."

"That won't happen."

"Elizabeth, I don't know what I will do if he hurts you again," he folded her into another furious embrace.

Lizzie loosed one of her arms and stroked his cheek. She kissed his lips softly. "Ben, he isn't going to hurt me. He can't hurt me any more than I've already hurt him. I have to undo that. I have to make peace with him."

"He's too mad to understand peace."

"Charlotte told him Lily would come back to him and put right what happened in the Fulton House two hundred years ago. I have to put it right, Ben. No one else can do that." She didn't know how that would happen. She knew only that as Oliver released Lily from her sorrow, Lily now had to release Oliver from his.

Chapter Thirty-Nine

Lizzie was still breathing deeply as she sat at her desk. She hadn't run more than a mile since the marathon. She was glad to make use of the cool July morning and test the path on this side of the Charles. She felt the oxygen in her veins and realized how much she missed it. She checked her emails, confirming the schedule for Saturday's anniversary party. It was the biggest event yet. Andrew sent a half dozen messages about plates and cutlery, even though they confirmed all the rentals two nights earlier. Lizzie sighed with a happy annoyance. It was still early enough that she found Andrew's attention to these details charming. It allowed her to concentrate on food and figures.

The business was a healthy distraction from the apprehension that hadn't left her since April. She settled happily into her new life with Ben. It didn't feel new, just like something that was waiting for her to come back. It didn't diminish her content and it helped her optimism.

She knew Oliver didn't leave Massachusetts. He didn't try to contact her in the two months since his appearance at Jefferson Park. Lizzie hoped he was busy settling into his new job and consumed with the details of his move. Ben was still worried. He didn't like when she went for her run before he left for the office. She indulged him and carried her phone, even though she hated the weight of it in the pocket of her shorts. Oliver was no where to be seen. He was probably writing syllabi.

She glanced to the left of her keyboard and noticed an off white envelope. She recognized the red address as that of the clinic. After so many months of mystery, the clinic underwhelmed her on her first visit the week before. It wasn't much different than the corridors of Mt. Elm, just a good deal quieter. Nevertheless, she felt her slowing heartbeat pick up speed again as she fingered the flap on the back. Ben put it there, so he already knew the outcome. She opened it and looked at a couple pages of numbers and letters she didn't understand. At the bottom of the last page, she saw in Ben's handwriting. "You passed."

She smiled broadly, forgetting the anniversary party and her other unchecked emails. She half wished Ben would indulge his overprotective habit and visit her on his lunch break. If he knew and saw her going for a run, wouldn't he want to taste the benefits? No… Ben wouldn't do this impulsively. He was probably anticipating her blood much more than she anticipated giving it to him. He wouldn't squander it on a spontaneous morning. She suspected there might be a delay for a few more weeks to coincide with her birthday and the fact she couldn't find her passport.

She left her office and was on her way to the shower when she heard the door knock. She ran through the list of possible deliveries and hoped that it was her new mixer. She still felt the elation of her run until she recognized the dark eyes of Oliver looking at her. Her water bottle slipped from her grasp as she stepped back a few strides.

"Lizzie."

"How did you get in here?" she thought of the doorman and Ben's insistence on screening all visitors to the apartment.

"I want to talk to you," he shut the door and stepped further into the apartment.

"Yes," she caught her breath and tried to collect her thoughts.

"Did you just go for a run?"

Lizzie studied his calm expression and saw no indication of hunger for her endorphins. "It was pretty pathetic," she made herself laugh. "I haven't… as you can probably tell, I've been sampling a lot of recipes lately."

"You look the same as you did… in April," he looked down. "Please, can we talk about that?"

"Yes," she bent down to pick up her water bottle. "I think we should."

She showed him the large couch and decided to sit on one of the chairs. She eyed the full rack of wine by the dining room table and wondered if she should do that just in case. It was only 9:30. That was reckless. She needed to be clearheaded and aware of everything that was going on. Wine would help Lily's memories. Lizzie didn't want them to control what she did, what she had to do.

"So you took the job at UMASS?"

"I did. I have too many reasons to stay here."

"I hope I'm not one of them," she said slowly, but with every effort of emphasis.

"Of course you are."

"Oliver…" she shut her eyes and drew in a breath. "I am happy here. I am happy with Ben. Can't you see that? If you really do love me, don't you want me to be happy?"

He looked at her. She could see his thoughts struggling behind his eyes. "I want you to be happy."

"Then, it is best if you leave us be," she saw him shift his eyes downward.

"What are you afraid of, Lizzie?" he wasn't lifting his eyes. She couldn't see if his eyes changed as his voice had. "Why do you need me to stay away? Are you afraid you will second guess your decision to go back to him?"

"No."

"What happens when you have another memory?"

"I won't," she sat stiffly in the chair. "I learned everything I need to know about Lily. But it doesn't matter, because… because she is dead, Oliver. I am a different person. I make my own decisions. I choose Ben. I chose him the first … I knew after the reunion that I wanted him more than anyone else."

"But you didn't know who you were then."

"I knew exactly who I am. I didn't understand Lily, but I always knew her," she dared herself to touch his hand. "Oliver, I'm sorry. I'm sorry that she hurt you. I am very sorry that I… I have done the same thing. It isn't fair to you… because all you ever were and ever tried to be was my friend."

"That's not all I ever was," he revealed his darker eyes. They were still human, very human. They were hurting from a heartache as old as he was.

She pulled back her hand quickly, afraid her oxygenated blood got too close to him. "Oliver, why do you want Lily back if she was so horrible to you? She used you as she had been used by Horace Fulton and Charlotte. She didn't have a heart. Why do you want to win it?"

"You have a heart, Lizzie. You are what she always wanted to be, but could never become. Don't you see that? Part of that is her unfulfilled wish to marry me."

"I don't want to get married."

"Not to Ben. But…" he took her hand back to his own. "Lizzie, you know this is what she wanted. She wanted it so badly she let herself die when she couldn't have it."

"She wanted to marry the father of her child. Not a monster," Lizzie hardened her voice as she clenched the fingers in his hand to a fist. "You became everything she hated, Oliver. You lost her – you lost your only opportunity for her when you became one of them."

"It was everything she ever wanted. She only loved monsters. She loved Horace. She loved Charlotte. And she loved Ben. She only loved the ones who used her and mistreated her. That's what she … that's what you want, Lizzie. That's why you never dated anyone else. You were waiting for us, because you knew no one else would be as exciting or thrilling. And after that you couldn't go back, could you? Even your doctor had something to do with vampires. Don't tell me this isn't what you or Lily wanted. It's all you've ever wanted."

Lizzie stared at him. Did he know about Claire Chamberlain? There was something about his stare that implied he knew everything. He knew about Eric. How? How did he know these things? Was he that clever? Or did he follow her? He knew enough to show up one day at the coffee shop when she and Andrew hadn't signed a lease. He knew her time at the marathon to be there when she finished. He knew when she would go back to her apartment from Ben's. He knew where Ben lived. He knew… he knew all about her.

"But I love Ben," she whimpered as her confidence drained from her.

"I loved Charlotte," he answered. "I was blinded by that love."

She shut her eyes and drew in a breath. She saw Ben standing over Lily's lifeless body and walking away. She saw a girl with red curly hair lying in the mud with blood crusted at her throat. She saw the unmarked grave and the lime falling over her body. She saw Ben take her gloved hand…

"Eloise wasn't Lily," Lizzie opened her eyes wide.

"You said you remembered."

"I remembered that she had red hair," Lizzie took back her hand and stood up from her chair. "I… I was there. But I wasn't her."

Oliver shook his head slowly and then quickly as if pushing the argument out of his mind. "That girl was Lily. Charlotte told me."

"She told you because she knew you were still angry at Lily. You didn't know about the baby. You still blamed her for … you still believed she was going to leave you. You wanted to punish her through that helpless child. Charlotte knew you hated Lily. She wanted to protect Lily and let her… let her go to Ben."

"Charlotte hated Lily as much as…"

"But she loved her, too. She told… she told Maria what you both were. She told her long before Ben ever knew she knew. She knew Maria was Lily and sent you after Eloise."

"No," Oliver shook his head.

"Yes," Lizzie nodded her head as the thoughts became clear in her head. "Maria didn't understand. She never fully understood, but she loved Ben."

"He's been filling your head with this."

"Ben knows nothing about this. He…" Lizzie froze as she saw Oliver's eyes. They had the anger she once saw in Ben's eyes, but not the struggle for restraint. "Oliver, please. I'm sorry. But you should know. You have to… Lily came back to him, not you."

"She loved me."

"She loved the boy. Her friend, Tom. He died. You became… you became like Charlotte when Lily died. Ben became human again. He lost the monster and you became it," Lizzie explained as she walked slowly away from him. She left her cell phone in her office. Why hadn't she kept it in her pocket?

"Why did you let him manipulate you again?" he followed her slow steps, shortening the distance between them.

"Oliver, you are the one… please go."

"Lizzie… he doesn't… he can't love you like I do."

"He doesn't."

"He isn't the one you are meant to be with."

"He loves me. Elizabeth Watson. Not the ghosts of his past."

"Lizzie…"

"He didn't leave me to die."

"No," he protested, almost desperate.

"I don't want you here," she rushed towards the staircase. She flew up the stairs to her office. She couldn't find the phone on her desk. Where was it? She raced down the hallway to the bedroom. She went to the dresser and looked through her purse.

"Lizzie, you can't mean that," he entered the bedroom.

She trembled as she took her next breath. There wasn't anything in that room with which she could defend herself. "Please," she lost the force of her voice. He came closer towards her, backing her against the furniture. "She didn't want you, Oliver," Lizzie snarled. "She wanted you to kill her."

"She wanted the baby to die," Oliver shook his head. "She came back to me."

"No," Lizzie looked up and glared. "She did not."

"Lizzie," he reached out to grasp the back of her head. "You want this. I know you feel obligated to Ben… but you gave yourself freely and willingly to me. How can you tell me now that this isn't what you want?"

"Because you left me to die. Because you don't care about hurting me."

He dropped his hand. "Don't you understand, Lizzie? I… I want you to be like me. I want you to be with me forever. Not as Lily. As you are now… as Lizzie."

"I don't want to go on forever," Lizzie felt the pressure of the wood against her back as she heard the door open and shut from downstairs. "I want to be human."

"You would be human. I am human."

"No, Oliver. YOU are not human."

Oliver grasped her shoulders and forced a kiss on her lips. He pulled back and looked at her helplessly. "Doesn't that make you feel human?"

Lizzie felt her eyes fill with tears, wondering where Ben went if he really entered. "It terrifies me."

"Of course it terrifies you," Oliver slid his hands down along her arms, grasping her fingers. "The things that frighten us are the most worthwhile."

"Not this time," Lizzie raised her hands to push him away.

He pushed her back, holding her in place against the dresser. She felt the speed of her heart increase as he pressed against her. "Lizzie," he caressed her neck and bent down to kiss it.

Lizzie looked over his shoulder, hoping a shadow would appear in the doorway. Where was Ben? Maybe she imagined the door. She was still alone. By herself. He could overpower her and force her down and take her clean healthy blood. She moved her chin and forced his kiss away from her neck to her lips. He relaxed his pressure, allowing her to reach behind and grab her purse. She swung it at his head and pulled herself away. "Leave!" she shouted so Ben would hear her.

"No," Oliver grabbed her again. He raised his arm almost too quickly for her to see it. She felt the pain strike across her face and force her to the ground. She hit the floor hard and thought she should get up and run, run from the room, run from the apartment… but a sudden movement startled her from that thought. Ben pushed Oliver to the ground beside her.

"Elizabeth, go," Ben urged as Oliver shoved him back to the other side of the room.

Lizzie stood as though she were made of clay. She couldn't go or run as she planned. She saw Ben grab a chair and force it against Oliver. Oliver pushed it back. He was stronger than Ben. He was going to hurt Ben. He could kill Ben. But Ben was quick. He moved away from the chair as it shattered the mirror in the room. He went to Lizzie and pushed her into the hallway, guiding her quickly back down the staircase.

"Take my car and go. Go somewhere he can't find you. Go now!"

"No," Lizzie shook her head as Oliver grabbed Ben from behind. Ben shoved his elbow into Oliver's gut and tripped him as he lost momentum. Oliver recovered and got up quickly, slamming a fist down on his head. Lizzie froze, suddenly aware of their strength and their anger, unleashed after years of restraint. One of them was going to die. She knew that was the only way it was going to end.

The impulse filled her before the thought registered completely. She went back upstairs to the closet in her office. She found a box of things from Jefferson Park. She knew it was in there. She heard another crash from downstairs, causing her hand to shake as she moved the contents of the box around again. Her fingers still rattled when she found the small gift bag. She pulled out the antiquated compact and rushed into the bathroom. She didn't know if it would work… what it would do to her. Another crash forced any more hesitation out of her mind. She dumped the ancient powder into a glass and mixed it with water. She swallowed the chalky substance and felt an immediate need to purge her body of it. She held her jaw tight and summoned the strength to leave the bathroom and walk back down the stairs.

She came back to the living room, where Ben was fighting to hold off Oliver. His head was bleeding. Had she ever seen the blood come out of one of them before? Did that mean anything? Did it mean that Ben was… She lowered her eyes and saw Oliver had something in his hands, a broken leg from one of the stools.

"Oliver," she called, letting the pretense overtake her expression. "Let him be."

"I will finish this," Oliver gnarled, flashing his sharp teeth.

"Oliver," she forced herself between them. "Please leave him be."

She didn't look at Ben, not even to check if the wound was serious. It couldn't be. She couldn't think about Ben. She had one thing to do. She took Oliver's hand and led him through the doors to the balcony. She pressed her lips to his and knew his passion was redirected. She took herself away from him and touched his temples with her palms. "This is what is supposed to happen," she leaned her neck towards him and let him bite into her. She saw Ben stand up and race to the door. She met his eyes as Oliver took more of her blood and froze Ben in place inside the apartment.

Elizabeth felt the lightness of her head. With every ounce of her strength she pushed him away. He stepped back and grinned at her for a moment with satisfaction. Then his mouth soured. "Lizzie, what did you do?" he looked at her.

"I set you free," she cried as he faltered and squinted out the light of the sun.

Ben stepped onto the balcony. "Stay away, Ben," Elizabeth said firmly.

Oliver's skin reddened and started to blister. He was in pain and looked at her as he sank lower to the ground, clutching his stomach. "Finish it," Oliver muttered.

Elizabeth took the broken stick from his hands and stabbed it through his chest. She closed her eyes, fearing an explosion of blood or something grisly. She opened her eyes slowly. There was no blood. No burnt up corpse. Just him staring lifeless at the sky.

Elizabeth felt the weight of her body collapse her knees. She sat on the floor of the balcony, prompting Ben to come near. “Ben, stay away. I’m poison,” she swallowed, slowing her breath. She felt the heat of the July sun on her cheeks. She leaned her head against the edge of the balcony and then it all went cold.

The room was dark when Elizabeth woke up. She was in the guest room. She sat up slowly and saw Eric sitting by the dresser. “What… what are you doing here?” she asked groggily.

“Kate called me,” he smiled and moved to the bed. “She’s downstairs with Ben and the others.”

“The others?” Elizabeth could hear voices echo outside the door.

“Two of their lawyer friends,” Eric took her blood pressure and listened to her heart. He flashed a small light in her eyes.

“How long have I been out?” she felt the shock of darkness after he removed the light.

“It’s 9:30,” Eric looked at her. “Do you remember me bringing you up here?”

“No,” Elizabeth closed her eyes, seeing a dream of someone standing over her … and a sharp pain in her arm. She looked above her left elbow and saw a small bandage.

“That was the chelation agent. It should be working the lead out of your system.”

“And then I went back to sleep?”

“I imagine you are in shock.”

“Did he take too much blood?”

“No… I mean emotional shock,” Eric looked at her and offered a smile. “Physically, you’re fine.”

“Am I going to get sick?”

“No,” Ben said from the doorway. “He gave you a treatment I developed at the clinic. It will get the lead out of your bloodstream within a few weeks. There should be no lasting effects.”

Elizabeth couldn't meet his eyes. All the details of what happened before she blacked out replayed vividly in her mind, especially the green eyes watching what she did. "Good."

"Even so, we have to monitor your health until then," Eric eyed Ben cautiously. "Just to make sure you aren't suffering any symptoms. It will be best if you keep a healthy distance from Ben during that time."

Elizabeth looked at him, wondering what Kate Chiang told him about her and Ben. Did any of it matter now? Ben might not want her to stay knowing what she was capable of.

"It's just a precaution," Eric smiled at her silence and looked towards Ben in the doorway. "Not a quarantine."

"You are a very brave woman, Elizabeth," Dr. Chiang came beside Ben in the doorway.

"I'm not brave," Elizabeth shook her head. She looked at her hands expecting to see traces of blood. But there was nothing.

"You're very clever. How did you know to do that?" she went to Eric's side. Elizabeth couldn't tell if it was a need to protect herself or her favorite source. She saw him slip her hand into his and knew it wasn't just about blood.

Elizabeth looked towards Ben and let her eyes water. "I didn't know," she breathed out. "I didn't know if it would actually work. I just wanted to weaken him and stop him from hurting Ben."

Ben left the door and grabbed her hand, ignoring Dr. Chiang's attempt to stop him. Elizabeth felt the warmth of his fingers and then retreated her hand, shifting away from him on the mattress. "I didn't know it hurt him so badly," she dropped her head, unable to look at any of them. "I didn't know that I would be able to do that."

"Ben explained he was already infected. You didn't make him sick, Elizabeth," Kate softened her voice. "The powder you … what you put in your blood set off more severe symptoms of what he already suffered. He wouldn't have survived the rest of the evening. You stopped his pain."

"I killed him," she sobbed, still staring at the blanket over her lap.

"It was self-defense," Ben said coldly.

"It was murder," she muttered and then looked up suddenly. "Are we going to have to call the police?"

"No," Ben answered firmly.

"But Eric said you have lawyers here."

"Yes, and they will take care of this," Ben pulled back a second urge to reach for her.

"Take care of this? What do you mean? He has a life, friends, students… a new job. People will wonder why he isn't there. He can't just disappear," Elizabeth protested.

"He died in a horrible accident," Kate said without any emotion. "That's all they need ever know."

"What about his wife?" Elizabeth looked at Ben suddenly.

"I spoke to Alison," Ben looked down. "She knows what happened. They are still married, so there are legalities that must be settled. But… she doesn't, we needn't fear she will interfere with anything."

"What about the… body?"

"Eric and I have taken care of that," Kate squeezed her partner's hand.

"But I… killed a man. I have to … pay some consequence."

"Haven't you already?" Ben looked at her helplessly.

Elizabeth eased her head against the wall. It was still all too vivid in her mind… and yet distant as a dream. "I…" she looked down at her hands.

"Ben," Kate let go of Eric's hand and rested a hand on Ben's shoulder. "I will go downstairs and finish up with Scott and Barbara. We can let ourselves out."

"Thanks, Kate," Ben flashed a quick grin of appreciation at his colleague but kept his focus on Elizabeth.

"I still want you to go to the clinic tomorrow morning. Just to ease my conscience. I want to make sure you haven't been exposed."

"Yes, Dr. Chiang," Ben agreed quietly.

"Elizabeth, if you feel anything - especially muscle pain - please call me," Eric turned to collect his things from beside the bed.

"Mm hmm," Elizabeth responded and looked back down to her hands as Ben closed the door behind him.

"It will be all right, Elizabeth," he sat on the foot of the bed, keeping a safe distance from her.

"Are you…" she let herself look up for the bruise on his head. There was nothing there. Not even a tiny scratch. "Ben, I'm sorry."

"You don't apologize, Elizabeth," he set his jaw. "Not for this."

"I… did something terrible," she blurred the attention of her gaze.

"He would have killed you," Ben breathed out. "You had no choice."

"He wanted to change me into what he was. And he did that. He made me a killer."

"Elizabeth," Ben reached a hand across the bed. She went to take it but shook her head. "I can only get infected if I touch your blood. Is your hand bleeding?"

"No," she looked at her palm once more just in case and then let him take her hand. "Does it ever leave you?"

"What?"

"The guilt of taking a life?"

"No, Elizabeth," he sighed slowly. "It will never leave you."

"I don't know what I feel right now. I still… I still don't believe it happened. That I really…" she touched her neck with her free hand, knowing she couldn't feel the marks to confirm they were there. "Do you forgive me?"

"For what?"

"For letting him in. For not listening to you. For… letting this happen."

"You knew it was going to happen," Ben tightened his hold of her hand. "You knew you had to do this."

"To take away his life?"

"Think of how many lives he's taken, including yours."

"But… that's," Elizabeth heard Charlotte's words without hearing Charlotte's voice.

"He would have killed you again," Ben clenched his jaw. "You stopped him from doing it a third time."

"No," she stopped the blurring of her eyes with a direct look at his. "Ben, I wasn't Eloise."

His eyes narrowed and revealed his impatience. "You knew what she looked like."

"I knew what she looked like because I helped to bury the body."

Ben swallowed weakly, the realization shaping the new expression of his eyes. "Maria?"

Elizabeth nodded, allowing a little elation to come through the heavy sorrow. "I don't remember much at all. I just…" she shut her eyes. "I don't think she wants me to remember. She was so sad. But she needed Oliver to know. I needed to tell him that I've always come back to…"

Ben let go of Elizabeth's hand and paced to the other side of the room. "Maria left me," he said weakly. "If you are her… and she was Lily…"

"Ben, I know it's too much. It isn't worth understanding. I don't want to understand it any more. I want to go on with my own life now. My life as Elizabeth… whatever it might be after this. After today."

"It will be whatever you want it to be."

"Are there really no repercussions for this? Legally?"

"It was self defense, Elizabeth," he looked at her eyes. "And even if there was no legitimate … it would be much more complicated to involve any authority in this matter."

"Why were the lawyers here?"

"Because Oliver has a lot of unfinished business. He has an estate that must be settled. We have to explain his death in a way that won't reveal what he was."

"What about those who knew he was a vampire? Won't they be curious how he died?"

"We shall deal with that if it happens. Alison knows… she wasn't surprised," Ben bit his lip. "She knew what he was capable of. I think a part of her is relieved."

"But it was still…" she shut her eyes as she started to feel the tears that weren't there minutes before. "What did they do to his body?"

"He will be cremated this evening."

"He's outlived his family too long to be buried with them."

"The consequence of choosing our life, Elizabeth," Ben looked at her sadly. "Maybe we can bring the ashes back to California. He always liked the forests there. I think that is where he was most at peace, where he felt the most human."

"Can we do that? Is that right for me to do?"

"Why wouldn't it be?"

"Because I took him out of this world," she started crying again.

"No, Elizabeth. You said it. You set him free."

She curved her mouth up, but didn't feel the elation of a grin. She wanted to reach for his embrace, but knew she would have to wait weeks, perhaps months before she could trust herself to be that close to him. "Ben, I don't want to live here anymore."

"I don't either," he paused, showing Elizabeth the restraint in his urge to satisfy her wish for his arms. "I will go wherever you want to go. I'll leave Boston if that's what you want to do."

"No, I don't want to run away. I just don't want to stay in this apartment."

"We'll go to a hotel tomorrow and then start looking for a new home," he took her hand again and cautiously kissed the back of her fist.

She smiled at him and breathed out in relief. "Thank you."

*****

The morning sun still hid behind the clouds, stubbornly refusing to turn the sky blue. It kept the moisture in the air as much as it kept it on the blades of the grass, soaking her slippers as she ran across the field. They were already standing outside the shop. Annie was there and saw her approach when she pulled away from her nephew. He followed Annie's eyes to her as he went to his mother. The brown eyes lightened and allowed a smile to soften his somber expression.

He turned back to his father and offered a few brief words before taking her elbow towards the other side of his saddled horse. The poor old mare was burdened with his musket and sack. She wondered if the animal would make it to camp without collapsing.

She saw the restraint and allowed herself to forsake her own to kiss him. He might not return. He might not survive the British muskets or the cold at camp. That was the reason she left Harriet alone at breakfast. She didn't want him to leave her thinking she never cared for him, that she didn't want him to do everything he could to come back alive.

She saw the appreciation of his happy expression when he stepped back, no longer concerned with the watchful eyes of the wheelwright and his wife. She muttered the apology she rehearsed all the night before and as she watched Harriet hem and haw over her porridge. She was sorry for rejecting him, for not going to the church and becoming his wife. It didn't matter what his family wanted. She saw what he wanted in the love of those brown eyes. Love that no other person ever gave her. She told him when he came back, things would be different.

He accepted her words and walked away with a smile… with enough hope, she prayed, to give him reason to come home. He embraced his mother once again before mounting his horse. He gave her one last glance before leaving. Before going to an uncertain fate. Before leaving and possibly never returning.

Lily turned away and walked back through the dewy morning.

Elizabeth opened her eyes. There was a small amount of light seeping through the blinds of the hotel room. She could make out the shadows of furniture in front of her as her senses warmed to the sensation of Ben lying beside her. She turned over to face him. He was awake and moved his eyes slightly to meet her own. The freckles under the green eyes were evident, even in the dim light. He needed to get more blood soon.

"You aren't keeping your distance," she whispered to him, as if someone was watching their room and would report him for not sleeping in a separate bed.

"You are worth the risk," he smiled and touched her cheek. "You were dreaming. I could tell by the smile on your face."

"I don't … I don't remember," Elizabeth said weakly. She knew Oliver was in her sleeping mind. She knew it was goodbye, but the details were losing shape.

"It doesn't matter," he kissed her lightly on the forehead. She smiled before turning back to her left, spooning herself into his side. She shut her eyes, feeling the sensation of dew on her feet and fell back asleep under the watchful stare of the green eyes.

Chapter Forty

Elizabeth took the opportunity of quiet and wiped off her hands. She smiled at her volunteer staff, a handful of boys and girls from the honor society. She saw herself amongst the quartet laughing and serving barbeque to the endless line. She gave them another nod of approval and excused herself to find Ben.

"Miss Watson."

"Mr. Benson," she repeated the smile she offered to the high school kids. "It's a great turnout."

"It's the best one we've had in six years," he beamed proudly. "I can't thank you enough for all you've done."

"It's been my pleasure," she looked towards the stage, happy to see that Jack's band wasn't playing yet.

"Here," Mr. Benson held up an envelope. "I wanted to give you something. We've had so much more…"

"No, no, no," she took his hand gently. "I told you, the food is my donation."

"At least let me pay for your travel."

"Don't worry, Mr. Benson. My boyfriend is underwriting whatever costs we can't cover," she found the green eyes in the crowd, trying to look interested in the conversation at his table.

"He's already been very generous."

"Yes," she nodded. "We want to do this for Melissa. In honor of Oliver."

"Your family has been very good to ours. Between you and your cousin, this has been a terrific evening."

"Thanks."

"I'll be sure to spread the word. Your food is excellent. I know a few people who are looking for a caterer."

"Give them my name," she smiled and made her way to the table, satisfied with the gratitude from Melissa's father.

Elizabeth came behind him, seeing Sara talking to another woman she hadn't seen since the reunion. She rested her hands on his shoulders and listened to the discussion that probably bored Ben to tears. She was surprised none of the other men at the table broke away from the discussion of potty training.

"Sara," Elizabeth greeted when there was a pause in the conversation.

"Lizzie," Sara exhibited her extra effort towards friendliness. In their brief emails about the event, Elizabeth didn't tell Sara she and Ben were together again. She imagined the increased push to her smile had something to do with that.

"Did you enjoy your dinner?" she squeezed Ben's shoulders as he looked at her softly.

"I can't believe you did this all by yourself," Heidi's smile was more genuine.

"My partner is floating around here somewhere," Lizzie shifted her glance, certain Andrew found the table with Davis, Meg, Nora, and Mark. They didn't have any obligation to Springs loyalties. "He does a lot of work. He's the genius behind all the sauces."

"That's so exciting," Heidi continued. "Ben says you're doing well."

"It's okay. Not as steady as I hope. But it gave me time to do this for the Bensons."

"And time to buy a house," Sara added, apparently bitter about another fact Elizabeth left out of the emails.

"We found a nice house in Cambridge. I have a great kitchen and an office. And there's room to grow."

Sara lifted an eyebrow towards Heidi and a glance at Elizabeth's naked left hand. She decided to leave Sara to her speculations and took Ben's arm. "I hope you'll excuse us. I have friends who came to see Jack's band."

Ben waited until they were out of hearing before he started laughing. "How on earth did I pretend to like that woman?"

"She was different at Springs."

"You were always there," he pulled her against him.

"She's a good soul. Her heart is in the right place. She just thinks you are odd. Probably because she realized at some point you didn't really like her all that much."

"And I'm living in sin with you," he kissed her cheek.

Lizzie laughed as they arrived at the table of her friends. "The band is on in a few minutes. I should probably go find the guys," Jack offered his chair.

"Thanks, Jack."

"How's the food?" Andrew twisted out of Davis' arm to glance at the buffet.

"Things are quieting down. I told the kids they can put out the apple cobbler when Jack starts playing," Elizabeth explained as Ben presented a beer. She didn't enjoy alcohol as much since Kate told her she had to wait six months until their next blood share. It seemed more like medicine every night. But the damp bottle was perfect at the end of her long day.

"It's a success," Davis lifted up his bottle to clink hers. "I know this is a charity gig, guys, but it's one of the best spreads you've put out yet."

"It's the biggest spread," Andrew moaned in exhaustion. "Although, those firefighter friends of Mr. Benson were a big help with the grills."

"Yeah, I'm sure you both liked their company," Meg laughed over her beer.

"I'm sure both Mr. and Mrs. Benson appreciate everyone's help today," Nora lifted Rose to her shoulder and beamed at Elizabeth. "This is a really impressive crowd."

"All of Lizzie's groupies," Meg grinned.

"We came to support Jack, too," Nora nudged her husband to nod in agreement.

"Did they do anything like this for Oliver's memorial fund?" Jen asked Ben.

"There wasn't a barbeque like this," Ben pulled a chair beside Elizabeth. "But there has been an overwhelming response to his memory."

"It really is impressive how many people rallied to his cause," Jen interjected. "I read in the paper how some of his students started a recycle center - and how another group is lobbying in Congress. The memorial fund is for scholarships, too, right?"

"At his college in California," Ben nodded, squeezing Elizabeth's hand. "His widow set that up and got many alumni who took his classes to contribute. He inspired a lot of his students. "

"Another Coldbrook boy who made good," Jen smiled at Ben.

Elizabeth looked at the rest of her friends, who only knew Oliver as the brother for whom she left Ben so abruptly less than a year ago. They didn't know the hero of the debate team, or the boy who gave Melissa Benson rides home from softball practice, or the madman who came to her apartment two months ago. None of them knew what he really was. None of them knew the vampire. None of them knew Thomas.

"That's an amazing legacy," Nora breathed out. "There are people who live for eighty years who couldn't accomplish that much. It's really impressive what he was able to do in his short lifetime."

"Yes," Elizabeth's voice faltered. She saw the quick glances of all her friends and smiled. "So I hope in his honor, we will all recycle our bottles tonight."

Mark was the first to laugh. "Sure thing, Lizzie," his humor revealed a note of encouragement. "So what's the next job for you two? Is it another party we can crash?"

"Nothing until they get back from their romantic getaway," Andrew chuffed.

"Oh that's right!" Meg exclaimed. "London?"

"A week in London. Then France. Then Italy," Ben explained proudly.

"Hey what about the Fulton House?" Meg took a sip of her beer. "Do you think you'll ever go back there?"

"I haven't been there for almost a year," Lizzie glanced at Andrew.

"But you loved that place," Nora patted Rose's back.

"We need our Saturdays," Andrew shrugged.

"Did you leave, too?"

"I'm going to finish out the summer until Paula can find someone new."

"You don't think you'll go back again?"

"Maybe I'll find a new museum," Elizabeth lifted her beer.

"Yeah, the Fultons are boring," Meg shook her head. "You need something more dramatic."

Elizabeth laughed quietly. "The Fultons aren't boring. Not all of them."

"Eh," Meg shrugged her shoulders. "I think you'll be okay without them."

"Yeah," Elizabeth nodded. "I think I will." Ben wrapped his arm around her. Elizabeth rested her head on his shoulder and smiled at her friends as the band began to play.

ABOUT THE AUTHOR

Jessie Olson lives in Worcester, Massachusetts. She has worked at various museums and historic sites, giving tours and exploring the neglected corners of the past. She enjoys theater, running, and themed dinner parties. *An Ever Fixéd Mark* is her first novel.

Made in the USA
Charleston, SC
08 February 2012